A book that turned out to be a page-turner. *The Y Factor*, which is written by a man I call the Tom Clancy of Christian authors. If you love a story with intrigue and adventure, it is a must-read.

—*Spotlight* Magazine, Winter 2008

The Y Factor has the potential to be a breakout novel in the Christian action-suspense-thriller genre that *The Hunt for Red October* was for Tom Clancy! A compelling story line, riveting action, and masterful intrigue that blurs the lines of fiction and current world affairs. Liam Roberts has a unique way of incorporating science, military tactics, computer technology, and politics to create a real-world environment without bogging the reader down with too much detail. Top-notch from beginning to end!

—Eric Reinhold
Author, The Annals of Aeliana Series

THE
Y
FACTOR

LIAM ROBERTS

REALMS

SCOTT—
MAY YOU ENJOY THIS!
BLESSINGS
Jim Robt
PSALMS 45:1

Most STRANG COMMUNICATIONS BOOK GROUP products are available at special quantity discounts for bulk purchase for sales promotions, premiums, fund-raising, and educational needs. For details, write Strang Communications Book Group, 600 Rinehart Road, Lake Mary, Florida 32746, or telephone (407) 333-0600.

THE Y FACTOR by Liam Roberts
Published by Realms
A Strang Company
600 Rinehart Road
Lake Mary, Florida 32746
www.strangbookgroup.com

The characters portrayed in this book are fictitious. Any resemblance to actual people, whether living or dead, is coincidental.

Design Director: Bill Johnson
Cover design by Amanda Potter

Library of Congress Cataloging-in-Publication Data:
Roberts, Liam, 1952-
  The Y factor / by Liam Roberts.
    p. cm.
  ISBN 978-1-59979-623-9
  1. Geneticists--Fiction. 2. Muslim scientists--Fiction. 3. Terrorists--Fiction. 4. Karachi (Pakistan)--Fiction. I. Title.
  PS3618.O31585Y3 2009
  813'.6--dc22
                                                    2009011168

09 10 11 12 13 — 9 8 7 6 5 4 3 2 1
Printed in Canada

ACKNOWLEDGMENTS

I ECHO AN ACKNOWLEDGMENT BY RAVI ZACHARIAS THAT began: "This book comes to publication trailing clouds of kindness of others." Among all others, my wife, Marsha, is first. Her gentle encouragement in the early stages made all the difference.

I am thankful for my children—Brad, Lindsay, and John—who provided rich family experiences for this manuscript. Brad and John: thank you for the critique of all things military; and Lindsay: for all things culinary.

Appreciation is extended to my wife's "Bible Buddies"—Kitte, Connie, Carolyn, Sue, Joy, Patsy, Diane, Pam, Jacqui, and Lynn—who were prayer warriors through the process and provided great editorial support.

JT and LeDonna: thank you for gainful employment while I pursue this avocation.

Thanks to my brother, Dean, who is a living testimony to the power of prayer. Your critique was helpful.

Much gratitude is extended to Kathy, who asked me to write something for her homeschooled grandchildren. We never dreamed this book would be the outcome of that simple request.

I want to acknowledge the prayer and encouragement from Sam and Bob. Thank you for taking the time to read my early work and prodding me forward.

Finally, I am extremely grateful for the wise counsel of my editor, Susan, and for Debbie, who expertly nurtured this project to fruition.

PROLOGUE

Friday, May 13, 2005
22 Rabī' al-Ākhir, 1426 AH
Cairo, Egypt

Hamdi Tantawi crested a rise and gazed over the rooftops of the Cairo slums at the majestic minarets silhouetted against the sanguine glow of the setting sun. The broad dome of the *masjid* loomed over the geometrically perfect compound, now teeming with scores of worshipers, like so many ants swarming to the refuge of their nest.

Hamdi frowned, critically surveying the outskirts of the crowd. He would be vulnerable once he passed beneath the ornate arbor and entered the walled courtyard. He struggled to free his mind from the pervasive dread that preoccupied him of late. *The* masjid *is a house of worship.* Surely his safety would be assured here, of all places. *Allāhu is most wise, most merciful*, he thought to himself.

But if not... His mind drifted back to the e-mail he'd sent to Eric. Hamdi could think of no one else to trust. No one but his former roommate would care if anything happened to him.

The threats directed at him had recently increased in intensity. Although they might not be acted upon, bitter sorrow was often visited upon those who dismissed the resolve of the Muslim Brotherhood.

Sending the e-mail comforted Hamdi, much like the rope his father used to tie to his waist when they fished. "In rough seas, it is easy to be thrown from the boat. This lifeline will be my only hope of retrieving you," his father would caution.

Hamdi knew he could count on Eric to follow the lifeline—should anything happen to him.

As he entered the compound, he pulled his *taqiyah* from his pocket and affixed it to the back of his head. He glanced left and right, assuring himself that these were indeed fellow worshipers whose only interest was their shared faith. Petty issues of doctrine and politics could be left outside.

Hamdi tugged a stubborn sandal strap from his heel and stepped into the cleansing basin to comply with *ghusl*, the ceremonial washing that is recommended during *salat al-isha*, the evening prayers.

When he'd washed the soil from his feet, he dried them and padded across the *masjid* to the prayer room. He glanced through the doorway that separated females from the *musalla*, the main sanctuary. He noticed someone enter the women's alcove from their separate entrance. She walked past an elderly woman addressing a small cluster of children with great intensity. The old woman waved her hand in emphasis and dislodged the veil of the passerby, revealing a lovely face beneath.

Hamdi was taken with her beauty and smiled as the young woman reacted to the impropriety. She exuded shame and humiliation as her eyes scanned the crowd in horror. She caught his eye for a moment, then just as quickly bowed her head and reattached the veil in a demure gesture he found enticing.

He chuckled, warmed by the incident and the brief respite it offered from his brooding anxiety.

Hamdi took a position in the sixth rank of the shoulder-to-shoulder mass of worshipers. He sank to his knees as he prepared his heart in reverence and bent forward, lightly touching his forehead to the floor. On cue from the imam, he pushed himself upright and dutifully repeated the chanted prayers.

Hamdi turned his head to the right to utter the customary greeting. "*As-salāmu 'alayka.*" He mechanically rotated his head to the left to repeat the greeting. His eyes were half-closed in concentration on the ritual precision, which differed from what was practiced in American *masjids*.

Hostile eyes stared back at him, jarring him from his quiescent intro-spection. He searched the face of the stranger, unaware of what sacramental solecism he might be guilty of.

Suddenly unsure of himself, Hamdi was relieved that the next step of the prescribed ritual was to face the imam. From his peripheral vision, however, he sensed a lingering animosity.

With heightened sensitivity, he noticed movement two rows in front of him. Another worshiper glanced over his shoulder and directed an angry stare right at him.

Soon, Hamdi seemed surrounded by nonverbal enmity, subtle manner-isms that conveyed an unsettling contempt. He tried to convince himself that his increasing concern was unfounded. This was a place of worship. Surely his unfamiliarity with the vagaries of Egyptian ritual could be overlooked. Perhaps he should explain himself as soon as the *salat* was concluded. He shook off the sensation of dread and focused on his prayers.

Salat ended with the imam pronouncing "*As-salāmu 'alaykum*" upon the gathering of worshipers.

Hamdi rose to his feet and turned to the man on his left. "Greetings, brother. I—" he stammered.

The man had turned his back abruptly, evidently not hearing the greeting.

Hamdi reached out and touched the man's elbow to get his attention. "Excuse me."

The man whirled around and loomed over Hamdi. "Do not touch me, you filthy Amrikan!" Spittle shot from lips shrouded beneath a black mustache and beard.

Hamdi retreated a half step. "But I am not an American! I am Egyptian but have only studied abroad—"

The man shuddered in rage. "Do not address me in a *masjid* of worship!" he shouted. Veins pulsed in his temples, his face ruddy from rage.

Other worshipers edged closer as Hamdi was enveloped in a ubiquitous hostility. One of the others muttered, "He is a local bird with a foreign walk."

Murmurs from the crowd intensified.

A voice sounded from beyond the hostile inner circle. "Thank you for your faithful prayers, my brothers." The crowd parted for the imam, a short, rotund figure in flowing robes. "Ah, you must be the one from Amrika!" he said, resting his hand on Hamdi's shoulder. "It has been suggested that I educate you about proper worship." His cherubic smile defused any offense that Hamdi might have felt.

Although the imam seemed oblivious to the undercurrent in the crowd, Hamdi wondered if this was his tried-and-true method of interceding in hostile situations. Regardless, it seemed to be working, and Hamdi noticed the crowd dissipate slowly. "My apologies, Imam. I will try to do better in the future. I have been away for many years and have forgotten many things."

"Perhaps we could discuss these matters over a cup of tea," he offered.

"Another time, Imam. I must be leaving." Hamdi pulled away nervously, anxious to get away from this place. He headed for an exit on the opposite side from where most of the crowd had wandered.

As he exited the courtyard into the darkened city, he heard a rustle from the shadows. His arms were pinned to his sides as a foul-smelling cloth dropped over his head.

"Help!" he shouted. His voice was muffled pathetically. "Please, some—" An agonizing pain erupted behind his ear. His last sensation was of warm fluid trickling down his neck and across his back.

ONE

Tuesday, June 14, 2005
7 Jumādā 'l-Ūlā, 1426 AH
Atlanta, Georgia

E RIC COLBURN STARED AT THE SUBJECT LINE IN DISBELIEF: *"IF ANYTHING HAPPENS TO ME…" How did this e-mail from Hamdi get in the junk folder?* As he double-clicked the entry, he noticed the date. He couldn't believe he'd overlooked it for a month, and he chided himself for not checking his junk folder more regularly.

> From: Hamdi Tantawi
> Sent: Tue 5/13/2005 1:02 PM
> To: Eric Colburn
> Cc:
> Subject: IF ANYTHING HAPPENS TO ME…
> Eric:
> I mailed you a DVD yesterday. It is important that you watch it…

Eric remembered receiving a DVD from Hamdi, but he had set it aside. *Where did I put it?* He rummaged through his desk drawers but came up empty. It wasn't in his CD rack or in his desktop in-basket. Then he remembered laying it on his entertainment center so he could watch it with Alana. He ran to the living room and rifled through the DVDs. No luck. Craning his head forward, he saw the edge of a DVD case in the dim shadows between the stereo equipment and the wall. He leaned forward, stretching his arm and probing with his fingertips until he pinched the case between two fingers. As he gently guided it upward, it caught in the wiring and dropped further into the recess.

Ignoring the precaution of unplugging something, he slid the stack of equipment forward, extracted the case, and held it up to the light. "Mapping Human Genetics." No wonder he'd forgotten about it. He'd assumed Hamdi was still trying to convince him that macroevolution was a superior theory to intelligent design.

Eric slipped the DVD into the player. A lecturer began a presentation with a superimposed title bar, identifying the speaker as Steve Olson. "The

THE Y FACTOR

DNA codebook for our species consists of literally billions of nucleotide bonds—these are the rungs on the ladder discussed in the last tutorial—and the whole thing is made up of only four different molecules. The elegance is in its simplicity! Here's an analogy that will put the design into perspective."

Eric sighed. He wanted to understand all this, especially since Alana loved it so much, but it could be so boring.

The lecture continued. "Imagine that you place a one-inch black cube in an empty field. Suddenly the cube begins to make copies of itself. Two, four, eight, sixteen. The proliferating cubes begin to form structures—enclosures, arches, walls, tubes. Some of the tubes turn into wires, pipes, structural steel, wooden studs. Sheets of cubes become wallboard and wood paneling, carpet and plate-glass windows. The wires begin to differentiate, connecting themselves into parallel but independent networks of immense complexity. Cranes are erected that are not part of the structure but are necessary to deliver the flow of materials throughout the complex entity. These cranes are then disassembled when their task is completed. Eventually, a one-hundred-story skyscraper stands in the field. It is unique from all others that have ever been assembled."

Why did Hamdi make a big deal out of this? And what did he mean by "If anything happens to me"?

"That's basically the process a fertilized cell undergoes, beginning with the moment of conception. How did that cube know how to make a skyscraper? How does a cell know how to make a human? Biologists used to think that the cellular proteins carried the instructions. But now proteins look more like pieces of brick and stone—useless without a building plan and mason. The instructions for how to build an organism must be written in a cell's DNA, but no one has figured out exactly how to read the complex message."

What is the point of all this? Eric lifted the remote but restrained himself.

"Each one of you started as a single cell. Billions of nucleotides were stored in the DNA that identifies you as unique from all humans who have ever lived. In one nucleus. In one cell. At the moment of conception. I call it the bar code of life."

Eric's patience finally wore thin. He pressed the fast-forward button, hoping something would look obvious. If not, he'd have to rewind and suffer through the lecture in order to figure out what Hamdi meant. Ten minutes into the lecture, the screen distorted into a series of horizontal bands, then rolled vertically. Eric hit the play button as the image slowly morphed into Hamdi sitting in front of a bare concrete wall in a dimly lit room.

Hamdi's appearance was alarming. He sat with slumped shoulders, his sunken cheeks lean and hungry. The poor lighting accentuated the haunted look of his eyes, clouding them in deep shadow, a stark contrast to the gleaming beads of sweat on his forehead.

Eric rewound the segment to be sure he didn't miss anything important.

Hamdi cleared his throat and reached forward, his hand disappearing at the edge of the screen. The image jerked, coming to rest at a slight angle with Hamdi's head and shoulders in the lower-right portion of the screen. Hamdi began whispering, his voice too low to be heard.

Eric adjusted the volume and leaned forward, huddling with the monitor as if it were a coconspirator.

"Sorry for the intrigue, Eric. I had to anticipate this might be intercepted. I inserted the lecture so it would be dismissed as merely an educational DVD. But I know you well enough that I'm sure you will find this.

"Things have not gone well here, Eric. Cairo is not the same as when I left twelve years ago. I do not hear laughter any longer. Children no longer play outdoors with the same abandon." Hamdi shook his head slowly, and then his stare intensified. "At first, I enjoyed my work in the Genographic Project, but soon I began to feel out of place there too. My co-workers are very devout, but they express extreme views. Most of them despise America and have been suspicious of me because of the time I spent there. I now realize that I will never earn their trust.

"Eric, bizarre things are happening in the lab, and there is no one to confide in. I brought my concerns to the lab director, but he rebuked me for being an informer. Then my co-workers began to utter threats. I tried to ignore them, but they have recently become more strident. I believe I have been followed and am starting to fear for my safety.

"I do not want to be melodramatic, but I wanted you to know what is happening in case anything happens to me. I have recorded my observations in my lab book and will read them to you in another DVD, when I am able to be alone in the lab—hopefully tomorrow. Perhaps you can help me get the information to our headquarters in Atlanta.

"Please give my regards to Alana—" Hamdi paused as his voice betrayed him. Eric detected a glimmer in the shadows and looked closer. Hamdi was crying.

"I wish I had not graduated early. I would give anything to be there and graduating with the two of—" A loud noise startled Hamdi and drowned out his comment. A look of fear swept over his features as he once again reached for the camera. "I must go now! Watch for the next DVD, and promise me you will get it to my headquarters!" The image faded to black.

Eric sat in stunned silence. He pressed the stop button and dropped the remote. "I promise, Hamdi," he whispered to the darkened screen. Eric returned to his computer, where a quick check confirmed there had been no further messages from Hamdi. He typed out a quick reply and apologized for not having written sooner. He ended the e-mail by assuring Hamdi he would personally intercede with Hamdi's employer but was concerned that he hadn't yet received the second DVD Hamdi had promised.

Before shutting down his laptop, Eric needed to find the employer's address. A Google search responded to his query before he could lift his finger from the enter key:

Your Genetic Journey – The Genographic Project – The National Geographic Society

A 5-year study by the National Geographic Society, IBM, geneticist Dr. Miles Larson, and the Saud Family Foundation to compile a genetic atlas. Project...

www.nationalgeographic.com/genographic - 34k - Cached – Similar pages

Participate   Globe of Human History
Your Genetic Journey   Public Participation Kit
Atlas of Human Journey   Genetics Overview

Eric had known the National Geographic Society was behind the project but was interested that IBM was also involved, since it was one of the firms he was pursuing. The Saud Foundation was meaningless, but Miles Larson was a name Eric recognized from somewhere. He sat back in his chair and clicked the various links below the introductory description. In a few minutes, he learned quite a bit about the firm Hamdi worked for. The headquarters of the Genographic Project were on the outskirts of Atlanta, not far from where he lived.

Another e-mail arrived. The subject noted "Delivery Failure." With a sinking feeling, Eric opened the e-mail.

Your message has encountered delivery problems to the following recipient(s):
hamditantawi@gmail.com
Delivery failed

Error Code: 550; hamditantawi@gmail.com; User account is unknown
No recipients were successfully delivered to.

Y

Eric stood in front of the massive Genographic Project headquarters, steeling himself for the expected confrontation. To bolster his courage, he flipped his cell open and called Alana at her summer job.

"This is Alana McKinsey."

"We need to meet," Eric blurted.

"Hi to you too!"

"I'm sorry. I have a lot on my mind. Have you had lunch yet?" Eric asked.

"No. Being the new girl means I get the worst time slot for lunch. I can't go for another hour and a half."

"That's perfect. I have something I need to talk to you about," Eric said.

"Sounds ominous. How about the sub shop down the street?"

"I'll be there."

Y

Eric couldn't get Hamdi off his mind. There's no way Hamdi would cancel his e-mail account without sending out a new one to his friends. The ominous tone of the DVD had been alarming, and Eric had resolved what he needed to do. He had to tell Alana about this but wasn't sure how it would be received.

If only Hamdi had not rushed to graduate early. He'd doubled up for a couple of semesters and got his degree from Georgia Tech a semester ahead of Eric and Alana. Then the job with the Genographic Project gave him the chance to return to his home country. When Hamdi left during the Christmas break, Eric was still fumbling for direction. He hadn't had a clue what he would do after graduation, except he hoped it would involve Alana. As things stood right now, Alana was scheduled to begin the graduate program at Harvard in a couple of months. As unappealing as the idea of moving to Boston was, it seemed to be his only choice to be near her.

Suddenly, he'd decided to change direction and struggled with the best way to tell her.

He was certain she wouldn't alter her plans without the assurance provided by a ring, but he wasn't ready to produce such assurance. *We're just starting our careers,* he told himself. *There's plenty of time to figure out our future.*

THE Y FACTOR

Eric strode down the street to the sandwich shop and scanned the small seating area. Alana was in a booth by the window and glanced up as he approached. She beamed, her opaline green eyes flashing recognition. His breath caught, and he savored the moment. He was distracted by an alluring silhouette accentuated by the light that backlit her sheer blouse. His eyes dropped for the briefest flicker, and then he composed himself.

"Hi," he said as he bent to kiss her. "You know, you take my breath away." Alana blushed, her complexion infused in a warm roselike glow. Characteristically, she deftly turned the subject from herself.

"So, what did you want to tell me?" she asked. "I have to be back in forty-five minutes."

"Sorry I'm late. Things took an unexpected turn." Eric paused. "Alana, I have bad news."

Alana looked at him warily. "OK..."

"I think Hamdi's disappeared." Eric quickly told Alana about Hamdi's cryptic message, the DVD he'd overlooked, and the rejected e-mail to Hamdi.

Tears filled Alana's eyes. "Oh, Eric! I can't believe this. What could have happened to him? Who can we report this to?"

"I don't know what could have happened, but I'm going to find out."

"How?"

"I took a job with Hamdi's company."

Alana stared at him with a dumbfounded expression. "You lost me. What do you mean you took a job?"

"My first impulse was to go to the police, but that wouldn't work. Hamdi's out of the country. The State Department can't help because he isn't a U.S. citizen. So I drove to the company headquarters, thinking I would barge in and raise the red flag. But then I realized—I don't have any evidence that anything has happened to Hamdi. And I started wondering how seriously they would take his unemployed former roommate.

"When I approached the guard desk at the headquarters, they asked me what I wanted. For a minute, I was speechless, trying to conjure up a believable story. I glanced down at the desk and noticed a brochure announcing job openings. The first one listed was in the IT department. Then the idea came to me. If I could get a job with the company, I might be able to get to the bottom of it."

"Eric—that's pretty impulsive," Alana said.

"I know it seems that way, but there were so many coincidences that it seemed like the right thing to do."

"What do you mean?"

"First, they were looking for someone with an IT degree, and my specialty fit their requirements exactly. Then, I just happened to have my résumé folder in my backpack with my transcript and letters of recommendation. It's like a path was laid out in front of me. The next thing I knew, I was sailing through the interview, and they offered me the job—pending a background check."

"What do you hope to accomplish by that?"

"I don't know, but I figured they would blow me off if I rushed in there to tell them my friend is missing. Besides, something happened right before the interview that convinced me this is the right approach to take."

"What?"

"A lady in the HR department was making sure I'd filled everything out correctly before my interview. She noticed that I'd made an entry in the spot where they ask if you know anyone currently employed by the NGS. She looked up and told me I should erase Hamdi's name. I asked her why, and she said that he'd been a big disappointment—that he'd abandoned his job a month ago."

"So, how did that convince you to go to work for them?"

"Don't you see? If they thought Hamdi quit his job, they couldn't care less whether something happened to him. And I'd sound like a conspiracy nut if I pressed the issue. This way, I might have a chance to figure out what happened and maybe even clear his name."

"Well, that's all well and good, but what about Boston? I thought you wanted to be near me."

"I do!" he said. "I can't tell you how much I want that. But I had another idea." Eric passed a brochure to her. "Here's the job listing sheet I picked up. The job right below the IT listing is for a research assistant to the director of the whole project—a job that's a perfect fit for you."

"I don't think so, Eric," Alana said, shaking her head for emphasis.

"Alana, don't dismiss the idea until you hear me out." He reached out and clasped her hands in his. "Alana, you're the best thing that's ever happened to me. I want the chance to take us to the next level, and working together will let us see what that means."

"You don't know what you're asking of me, Eric."

"You're right; I don't know. But what I do know is that you are the most intelligent and talented woman I've ever known." He squeezed her hands tighter. "And you are the loveliest woman I've ever known." He held up a finger to silence the anticipated protest. "It's no secret that I've played the field, but I don't want that anymore, Alana. I want you."

They sat holding hands for quite a few minutes. He couldn't tear himself away from her penetrating stare, nor did he want to.

"Are you really willing to do that for me, Eric?"

"Yes." He desperately hoped his sincerity was convincing. He couldn't bear the thought of being separated from her.

"You don't know how much I've wanted to hear that. It changes so much."

His hopes buoyed. "Alana, all I'm asking is that you at least interview for the job. I recommended you to the HR department, and they were impressed with your credentials. I remember how excited you were for Hamdi when he got his job, and I think you were just a little envious of his chance to pursue genetic research, weren't you?"

Alana shrugged her shoulders. "Just a little."

"Well, this is a chance to get in on the ground floor of an exciting research project. And they don't come any more prestigious than the National Geographic Society. Besides, with that caliber of real-world training, you could always go to Harvard later. They'd still jump at the chance to have you."

Alana hung her head, and her long golden hair swept forward, partially obscuring her face. She gently pulled her hand from his grasp and with a graceful motion tucked her hair behind her ear. It was a simple gesture but one of his favorites. He loved the tilt of her wrist, the long slender fingers.

Eric sat in the car and eyed the front door of the Genographic Project headquarters nervously. He glanced at his watch. The music on the radio began to grate on his nerves, so he reached out and stabbed the power button. *What's taking her so long?*

This had been the most incredible day in his life. He woke up unemployed, received a devastating e-mail from his best friend, landed an awesome job, and had just about convinced his girlfriend to abandon her academic dream in favor of a relationship with him. A day for the record books.

Alana had agreed to the employment interview, and now she'd been inside for over two hours. He didn't know if it was a good sign or not.

The front door opened, and Eric sat up in anticipation. False alarm. A couple of young women exited and walked toward the parking lot, deep in conversation.

He reclined his seat and thought again about Hamdi. If only he could find his friend. Hamdi had left some of his things at the apartment, but there was no clue that would help Eric find Hamdi's family. How difficult would it be to locate the right Tantawi family? How would he get past the language barrier? He had no idea where to start, but somehow he knew this job with the Genographic Project was key.

The passenger door opened abruptly, startling him. Alana dropped into the passenger seat. "Sorry to scare you, big guy."

"I wasn't scared, just startled to see such a beautiful woman trying to pick me up." He leaned over and kissed her. "So, how did it go?"

"You didn't tell me that Dr. Larson would be my boss."

"I confess I couldn't quite remember where I'd heard the name," he said.

"Are you kidding me? Hamdi used to talk about him. He's one of the chief scientists in the Human Genome Project."

"Sounds impressive."

"Impressive? They completely mapped the human DNA in ten years and finished years before they were expected to!"

"What d'ya know about that?" Eric tried to conjure up enthusiasm, but he wasn't sure what she was talking about. "So did they offer you the job?"

"Of course they did," she said with mock arrogance.

He searched her face anxiously but could not read her expression. "And what did you say?"

Alana shook her head slowly. "I told him I need a few days to think about it."

TWO

Wednesday, June 22, 2005
15 Jumādā 'l-Ūlā, 1426 AH
Atlanta, Georgia

D R. LARSON, WOULD YOU PLEASE SIGN THIS REQUISITION
for the gene sequencer for Kolkata's lab?" Vivian Knowles handed
Dr. Larson a stack of papers.

Vivian was an efficient director of research operations. She secured the
leases for all research labs and had a perfect record of bringing them online,
on schedule, and often below budget. She fastidiously managed the overhead.
Dr. Larson needn't concern himself with the price of the sequencer. If Vivian
recommended it, it couldn't be found at a better price. "I've also included a
new server and three workstations in that file folder. Please review them as
well. With your approval, I'll have them shipped directly to the lab."

"Thank you, Vivian," Dr. Larson replied. "Have the lab technicians at
the site accepted your offers?"

"I extended offers to the top four candidates. If we're lucky, we should
be able to secure three of them." She hesitated before continuing. "Dr.
Larson, one of the candidates is overqualified for the position. She's had
supervisory experience, and I was wondering—"

"We've gone over this before, Vivian. The funding stipulations imposed
by the foundation are quite clear. IBM and the society have both signed off
on them. Their money is very influential, and my hands are tied."

Vivian frowned. "But do you think the foundation would be willing to
interview my candidate?"

"I doubt it. She's a woman, and you know the Saudis would not tolerate
a woman supervising males—even hourly paid ones."

"I wish we hadn't agreed to those terms," Vivian said. "The supervisors
they select are so autocratic. It creates a turnover nightmare at many of
the locations. I wish I could just set up a lab and move on to the next one
without having to circle back for new hires. The director in Cairo is the
worst. We haven't kept an assistant more than a few weeks."

Dr. Larson replied with irritation, "I know. That's why I had such high hopes for Mr. Tantawi. He had so much potential. I just can't understand what happened." He picked up his calendar and abruptly changed the topic. "Are we on schedule to have the next two labs running by the first of August?"

"Yes. Is there a reason you ask?"

The fact that Vivian was miffed did not escape Larson's attention. No doubt she had hoped to press her point further, but he saw no point.

"Yes, there is. Ms. McKinsey will be finished with her orientation at the end of that week, and I want to plan her first field collection safari in mid-August."

"I wish you would come up with a better term than *safari*, Dr. Larson. That isn't exactly politically correct. It sounds so…colonial."

Dr. Larson merely shrugged as he scanned the lab schedule. He obviously wasn't in the mood to entertain criticism.

"Anyway, our lab sites in both Kolkata and Tokyo will be fully operational as scheduled. This is a good segue to a pressing problem." Vivian had gotten his attention, and she seemed prepared to make the most of it. "There is concern that the data streams coming from these new labs will overload the existing network architecture. We simply don't have the bandwidth to absorb the vast amount of data coming through the pipeline. When can we expect some relief in this area?" she asked.

"All in good time. Have you seen Eric Colburn's file?"

"No. I know he's starting this week, but I haven't had a chance to review it yet."

"I'm sorry I won't be here to welcome him aboard. I wanted to personally introduce him to our team, but you will have to do so in my absence. I think he will do well in the role of assistant director of network engineering. He is young, but he's brilliant. He gives me confidence that he can solve the transmission bottlenecks we've been experiencing. That will be less expensive than buying more bandwidth. Eric also has a solution for utilizing our servers more efficiently, which will forestall hardware upgrades in the near term," he said.

"Do you anticipate any problems with Justin Preedy's decision to delay his retirement?" she asked.

"I don't think so. I did tell Eric that I see him as a candidate to eventually assume Justin's role. Eric will have his hands full with the assistant director's position and enough of a challenge with our transmission problems without the distractions of managing a department."

The intercom beeped. "Dr. Larson, there's a call for you on line three," the receptionist announced. "It's Dr. Alomari from Cairo."

"Thank you, Stephanie," Dr. Larson said as he picked up the receiver. "Hello, Ahmed. How are things in Cairo?" He knew the egotistical doctor would resent the familiarity of his given name, but Alomari needed constant reminders of who was in charge.

Larson heard a slight intake of breath from the other end. Dr. Alomari responded with his characteristic thick accent, "We are ahead of schedule here." Without pause, he announced, "I am in receipt of communication from the foundation. They wish me to take directorship of the Karāchi facility. Our staff can be trusted to carry on without supervision until my replacement can be secured."

Dr. Larson glared at the phone. "Ahmed, you are ahead of the *revised* schedule. Need I remind you that the revision was necessitated by your running off highly talented assistants? In actuality, your lab is a month *behind*." He paused to emphasize the reprimand. "Hamdi Tantawi would have been able to manage the lab with your departure, but you managed to run him off as well," he said in a tone thick with sarcasm.

Alomari scoffed. "You should stop sending me these indolent Amrikan workers. They are a waste of my time. The Tantawi fool abandoned his job six weeks ago. Why do you persist in bringing him up?"

Dr. Larson sat forward in his chair. "I beg to differ. Hamdi was an excellent employee. I supervised his training myself."

"He had an insolent attitude and was slothful in his work."

"You are wrong, Alomari. Did you check with his family as I asked? Something must be wrong."

"It is not my concern. I am too busy to coddle a *Kafir* like him."

"What did you call him?" Larson pressed.

"It is nothing. Never mind." Alomari's sigh carried clearly across the phone line. "I will proceed with the transition plan as dictated by the foundation. If you object further, you can take it up with them. Perhaps you would like to resume this discussion with Prince Khalid himself?"

Dr. Larson shifted uncomfortably in his chair. The conversation had gotten out of control, and he was once again stymied by the mystery of why Hamdi quit without notice. His professional pride could not accept it, and Alomari knew exactly where to prod. "That won't be necessary, Ahmed. I will approve your transfer to the new facility," he said in a feeble attempt to retain some dignity.

Dr. Alomari wasn't going to let him off that easily. "Your approval is not needed. I didn't call for your endorsement, only to extend professional courtesy. Further, I am modifying the schedule for your so-called safari collection effort to the end of August. My replacement will require adequate time to assure the highest standards are adhered to."

"You don't have that authority!" shouted Dr. Larson. His hand choked the handset, and he blurted, "We must not deviate from the sched—" The line suddenly went dead. He glared at the phone's console as if willing it to reconnect. Frustrated, he slammed the phone down. "I will not be trifled with."

Y

Cairo, Egypt

Dr. Alomari sat at a computer console and entered the command to transmit the latest batch of data. He scratched his neck and wiped the sweat from his fingers on his robe. The dry desert winds made Cairo an uncomfortable habitat for one accustomed to traditional Muslim trappings, including long robes, turbans, and full beards. He longed for his imminent return to his beloved Pakistan, where the climate was more to his liking, both environmentally and spiritually.

The Prophet would be displeased with the enfeebled state of Islam in the modern world. So many were Muslim in name only. They had been seduced by the godless West and had renounced Allāhu and his call to jihad. Alomari smiled with smug satisfaction that their inevitable demise would be no different than the hated *Kafirs*—unless they could be roused from their slumber to take up the scimitar against the accursed Zionist Crusaders. *Allāhu akbar!* His research may prove to be the inspiration that would awaken them! His goal was now within reach. And his professional genius would be vindicated at long last.

The arrogant scientific community had dismissed his research and humiliated him. They would soon be forced to acknowledge that he needed no peer review to validate his claims. After all, who could possibly qualify as a peer?

Y

Atlanta, Georgia

Eric glanced at the incoming call on his cell phone. "Hi, Alana. What's up?"

"I thought you might like to know that the Genographic Project has a brand-new employee."

"Oh yeah? Should I worry about policies against dating co-workers?"

"It depends on who you want to date."

Eric smiled. "There's only one I can think of. So, you took the job?"

"Yes."

"That's great!" Eric could hardly contain his excitement. "What was it that clinched the deal?"

"Dr. Larson called me and told me he needed a decision. If I turned him down, he had another candidate lined up and was ready to extend an offer. You'll never guess who he was talking about."

"Who?"

"Liz Smith."

Eric hesitated. "Our valedictorian?"

"Thanks for the reminder. Yes, *that* Liz Smith."

Eric cringed. He knew losing the valedictorian race was a fresh wound and regretted having mentioned it. "Well, I think the job is a perfect fit, and Dr. Larson has the best research assistant he could possibly find."

THREE

Wednesday, July 20, 2005
14 Jumādā 'l-Ākhira, 1426 AH
Atlanta, Georgia

ERIC CONSIDERED THE FRUITS OF HIS FIRST MONTH OF FULL-TIME employment. His first two weeks had been spent under the tutelage of his quirky boss, Justin Preedy, but then he was given more analytical freedom.

The genographic computers were networked in a worldwide WAN (wide area network) that collected the data at the central server in Atlanta. Due to the enormous amount of data being transmitted, Eric's continual challenge had been to resolve bandwidth chokepoints.

He understood the system pretty well and felt confident that his potential solutions would work. Eric felt less sure about Preedy, who had delayed his retirement for reasons no one fully understood. For now, Eric tried not to upset the apple cart. He reluctantly admitted to himself that he now wanted this job to work out as much as he wanted to solve the mystery of Hamdi's disappearance.

Alana's work would soon take her on collection safaris, separating them for long stretches. Eric was troubled with Alana's itinerary that would take her to countries with so much religious and political unrest. It was an uncomfortable reminder that his best friend had been sent to a similar situation and was now missing.

His work was consuming and challenging, but so far it had taken Eric no closer to understanding what happened to Hamdi. His messages to Hamdi continued to bounce back.

Eric's thoughts drifted back to the farewell dinner for Hamdi. He smiled at the memory of his frustration in finding the restaurant.

Sunday, December 12, 2004
29 Shawwāl, 1445 AH
Atlanta, Georgia

"You must have gotten the directions wrong," Alana muttered.

Eric fought the urge to vent his irritation toward her. "The restaurant is supposed to be right here in Buckhead, just off of I-75!" He set his jaw in determination and waited for a break in traffic before executing a tight U-turn. "It must be on the other side of the road," he reasoned. "Pano and Paul's is a pretty fancy restaurant, so it should be easy to spot."

Alana motioned to a retail strip. "Why don't you pull into this shopping center and ask?"

"I don't need directions," he snapped, even as he pulled into the deceleration lane. "I'm just going to see if it's over on the other side of the plaza." He was irritated for feeling the need to explain. "I doubt anyone in the West Paces Ferry Shopping Center would know where to find a fine-dining restaurant," he smirked.

As Eric rounded the end of the strip center, he stared in silence.

Alana voiced the obvious, "There it is."

Did he detect gloating in her voice?

The exclusive Pano and Paul's sat squarely in the middle of a strip center, flanked by a Laundromat and a dollar store. "That sure looks out of place," Eric said, as if that would vindicate his navigational shortcomings.

He cast a sideways glance at Alana, hoping that she would drop the issue.

Alana seemed preoccupied with the visor. She flipped it down, opened the mirror, and adjusted the intensity of the lights, which illuminated her delicate features. She tipped her head back and forth, frowning slightly at perceived imperfections. She affirmed her suspicions, evidenced by a wrinkle of her nose as she flipped the mirror closed with a dismissive swat.

Eric marveled at her beauty and was incredulous that she found fault. "What's wrong?" Eric asked. "How could you possibly find anything wrong in that mirror?" He reached out and stroked her cheek. "Absolutely breathtaking," he whispered.

Alana cast him a disapproving look. Time to change the subject. She released the shoulder strap and smoothed the diagonal creases it had pressed into her blouse. "Let's go. We're late, Magellan."

Eric winced. He'd hoped she'd be more forgiving.

They entered the restaurant and approached the maître d' podium. A hand rose from the main dining room and waved at them, catching their attention.

"There's Hamdi!" Alana said. She pointed at the booth he occupied and spoke to the approaching maître d'. "Our friend already has a table."

"I will escort you," he replied.

Hamdi rose from the table as they approached. A handsome grin lit up his swarthy complexion. He opened his arms wide and embraced Alana with enthusiasm, and then he slapped Eric on the back. "How are you two?" he asked.

"We're fine," Alana answered as she slid into the booth. Eric and Hamdi took their seats as well.

Two attendants descended, one filling the water glasses, the other placing crisp linen napkins in their laps.

Eric took in the surroundings. A massive crystal chandelier dominated the center of the room, framed by satin ceiling drapery that elegantly swept from a peak above the chandelier to the corners of the room.

Alana ran her hand across the red satin seat back and said, "This is the nicest place we've been to. Can we afford it?"

"Now that I'm gainfully employed, yes!" Hamdi replied.

Eric added, "It seems a fitting place to celebrate Hamdi's departure." He lifted his water glass. "Since Hamdi does not imbibe, we'll toast his new adventure with water."

"Thank you," Hamdi said as the glasses clinked softly. "Although the Quran forbids me to drink alcohol, I do not have a problem if you want to order some wine."

Eric glanced at Alana and shook his head. "No, that's OK. We're fine with water. Besides, this place will be expensive enough."

"This project is going to rewrite history, and I am excited to be part of it," Hamdi said. Alana's eyes glimmered in vicarious excitement.

"Dr. Larson believes he will be able to determine when—and most likely where—each branch of the human family tree first separated," Hamdi explained for Eric's benefit. Eric sighed. He had hoped the conversation would be a little more generic, not genetic, but he should have known better. When these two biology majors got together, talk inevitably turned to science.

"I still don't understand how that's possible," Eric said. "I thought you couldn't determine direct lineage unless you had DNA samples from multiple generations."

"Dr. Larson's research is an amazing breakthrough, actually," Hamdi offered. "There are two kinds of DNA we study. The first is the Y chromosome because it does not recombine with its X counterpart. It's the only one that remains intact from generation to generation."

Alana chimed in. "For example, if a man has no sons or they don't survive, then his Y lineage ends with his death and—"

Eric interrupted. "Why does it matter if Y chromosomes are identical?"

"Because there are periodic spelling errors in DNA replication. When this happens, the error is passed down to all the descendants of the man who carried them."

"That's right," Hamdi said. "So our job is to collect samples from different population groups and then figure out where the populations intersect." Hamdi smiled at Alana. "It sounds like you're getting interested in our research."

She shrugged her shoulders.

"What about women?" Eric asked. "Can you analyze the X chromosome in the same way?"

"Unfortunately, no," Alana answered. "It's impossible to segregate maternal or paternal lineage with any accuracy."

Hamdi interjected, "There is another option, however. The Genographic Project is comparing mitochondrial DNA."

Eric frowned in confusion.

"It is an entirely different kind of DNA that has also mutated over countless generations. We are mapping the variations to points of convergence in the female side of the family tree. Dr. Larson told me that we have amassed enough data to determine when the first man and woman lived."

Alana asked, "You mean Adam and Eve?"

Hamdi laughed nervously. "Well, every religion has a creation myth, of course. But I'm inclined to think Adam was a symbol of mankind rather than a biological individual."

Eric cringed as he saw the fire light up Alana's eyes. He slid back in the booth. "Careful, Hamdi. You're about to unleash the green fire! When she gets worked up, her green eyes shoot flames."

Alana maintained her composure and asked, "Why do you think it's a myth?"

"Come on, Alana," Hamdi said. "We've been down this path before. We're talking about science here."

"And as I've said before, there isn't anything incompatible between the two. Is there anything in the genographic research that would indicate otherwise?"

Hamdi smiled, and Eric wondered if he'd intentionally set Alana up.

"As a matter of fact, we have proven the number of years back to the earliest human female is tens of thousands earlier than to the earliest male. We know this because the amount of variation in mitochondrial DNA is much greater than in Y DNA. That means the point of convergence is much further back in time on the female side of the family. Thousands of years after the first man and woman, disease and warfare must have eliminated all but a narrow variation of the Y chromosome. By chance, there was one man who sired male children in an unbroken lineage down until today."

"So you think you've got it figured out," Alana said. "It all comes down to chance."

Hamdi shrugged. "Of course; that is the underlying concept in macroevolution."

Eric cut in again. "But how can you calculate the time frames accurately?"

"Dr. Larson uses this analogy: if his secretary typed out a manuscript, he could tell you how long it took her to type it."

"How?"

"It is simple. He knows how many errors she makes per minute. Just count the typos in the manuscript and do the math. The same is true with the mutations in DNA. We know the rate of mutation, so the math is pretty straightforward."

"That makes sense," Eric said.

Alana sat forward in her seat. "I have another theory. If you've found more variation in women than in men, it could be due to a single event." She paused for effect. "There's one event that explains how all but one strain of the Y chromosome disappeared."

"And what event could that have been?" Hamdi asked.

Alana smiled. "The biblical flood."

"Another myth. You Christians believe this flood was universal, but the Quran teaches it was merely a local flood. Even if it really happened, it would not have wiped out humanity."

"Hear me out," Alana persisted, as Eric knew she would. "A biblical flood may fit the data better than your hypothesis. The Bible tells us that only eight people survived the Flood. In addition to Noah and his wife, his three sons and their wives were saved from the Flood. All other humans perished. Now, regardless of whether you believe this is literal history, there are interesting possibilities."

Eric stifled a grin. He loved it when Alana challenged Hamdi's worldview. Her tenacity seemed to heighten her beauty.

"Here's a hypothesis," Alana said. "Since Noah and his sons carried the only surviving Y chromosomes, that would mean the convergence of the male side of the family would be Noah himself, right? All males alive today would be descended from one of his three sons. However, the female point of convergence would be different. We can assume that the wives were from different families—and consequently would have a certain amount of variation in their DNA. Even with a slight amount of variation, it pushes the point of convergence much further back into the past. The female side of the human race would then appear to be much older than the male side, wouldn't it?" She smiled confidently. "That woman would be the biblical Eve."

Eric grinned. "Gotcha, Hamdi." Then he reached out and took Alana's hand, and she squeezed back.

Y

Eric still remembered that squeeze. At the time, they didn't dream they would end up working together—and ironically for the same firm as Hamdi. Alana had been ready to leave for Harvard, and Eric hadn't thought anything would stop her from going.

But something had stopped her, and he knew it was more than any concern for Hamdi. *Is Alana the one?* Eric found himself asking this question on an almost daily basis. *With college behind me, am I ready to make a lifelong commitment?*

The phone on his desk rang and roused him from his reverie. One of the servers had gone down.

FOUR

Thursday, August 4, 2005
29 Jumādā 'l-Ākhira, 1426
Atlanta, Georgia

Eric lifted the lid and peered into the pizza box and smiled. "You want the last piece?"

"I can't eat another bite or I'll explode," Alana said. "Be my guest." She slumped into the corner of the couch in her apartment and watched Eric at the other end as he devoured the last of the pizza.

A warm contentment enveloped Alana. Eric was like her brother in so many ways. He was funny, smart, and Brad Pitt handsome. And for a computer geek, he was very athletic. She loved watching him launch his lanky frame with reckless abandon at a racquetball on the courts. Competition brought forth a fearlessness she found sexy.

Between bites, Eric said, "I can't believe how much I've learned about genetics at NGS. If you'd told me a year ago I'd be interested in anything about genetics, I'd have said you were crazy.

"At first, the vocabulary was pretty intimidating. Hydrogen bonds, adenine, cytosine, guanine, thymine, nucleotide bonds, and all that. Some of this is pretty dry. But now that I have the big picture, I admit that I find it interesting," he marveled. "Which reminds me—I was reading an article in *Discovery* magazine and wanted to see what you think." Eric pulled a magazine from his backpack and handed it to her. It was folded back to a picture of an upheld hand and the title "The 2 Percent Difference." "It's about the genetic similarities between chimpanzees and humans."

Alana looked surprised. "This is pretty current. The chimpanzee genome was just published in *Nature* last September."

"This author is pretty convincing. He indicates that chimps and humans have genomes that are 98 percent identical; therefore, we must be genetically related to a common ancestor. You have to admit, Alana, it sounds pretty convincing."

"Yes, it does. But the research is so fresh, and we still don't understand the interaction between multigene traits. I think we should avoid a rush to judgment." Alana shook her head slowly. "And it irritates me that they're so quick to debunk the idea of an intelligent designer while unwittingly mimicking the Creator's very techniques."

"What are you talking about?"

"Intelligent designers in their labs use transgenetic manipulation to create new crops that thrive in harsh climates. They took specific DNA segments from unrelated species and introduced them into another species. In other words, it took *intelligence* to identify useful genetic code and *design* it into an unrelated species."

"That's a great point."

"What's more, the similar patterns of DNA across unrelated species is an argument *against* evolution," Alana said.

"How's that?"

"The atheist Richard Dawkins stipulates that evolution is based upon blind chance—even though the idea violates a foundational tenet of science. Reactions are due to *actions*, not statistical probabilities. Most evolutionists are guilty of sleight of hand when attributing causality to pure *chance*.

"So if we were able to rewind history multiple times, Dawkins asserts that life would evolve in radically different ways every time due to chance reactions to unique conditions. The fact that identical DNA sequences are present across species invalidates that principle.

"In addition, the food chain requires the protein basis between species to be somewhat aligned or else higher life forms could not be nourished by the lower ones."

"Another good point," Eric affirmed. "The argument seems to boil down to microevolution versus macroevolution."

Alana laughed. "It would seem you've been paying attention after all."

"Believe me, I hang on your every word!"

"But you're right. Microevolution is merely environmental adaptation of species. What creationists and evolutionists disagree upon is macroevolution—the idea that adaptation can be expanded to the creation of new species. But the stark evidence is, no mutant has been discovered with a new, fully functional organ that might signal an evolutionary offshoot. Functionality is the death knell for macroevolution. Mutants are normally so malformed that survival of the fittest assures their destruction. They are usually sterile, and those that aren't die before they can reproduce."

Realizing she had once again lapsed into her habit of lecturing, Alana paused to be sure Eric was keeping up. "The despair among evolutionists is typified by James Watson, the Nobel Prize laureate. He became so frustrated with the pre-Cambrian explosion of fully formed species—and the links that are *still* missing—that he proposed an outrageous theory. He says the seeds of life on Earth must have been sent across the cosmos from some distant planet by intelligent beings."

"You're kidding!" Eric said.

"Evolutionists talk about science being constrained to the natural realm, yet Watson sees nothing 'supernatural' about his crazy idea."

Eric brightened. "This job is going to be perfect for you. You understand it, and you're not afraid to say what you think."

Alana nodded as she nestled into the cushions and closed her eyes.

Eric chuckled. "Don't tell me you're getting bored with this stuff."

"Never!" Alana opened her eyes halfway. "But I'm so tired. I don't know if I can stay awake any longer." Her yawn added emphasis.

"Well, give me a kiss, and I'll head back to my apartment. I need to get a couple of hours of study in so I can ace the final," Eric said. He scooted closer to her.

Alana leaned into him as her lips sought his. They were motionless for a long while. Eric reluctantly pulled back. "I guess I'd better get moving," he said without conviction. "Unless you'd like me to sleep on your couch for protection?" he asked hopefully.

"Protection from what?" Alana asked, anticipating his answer even before she saw the smirk on his face.

"Oh, I don't know; an evolution terrorist maybe."

She laughed at their running joke.

"I don't think so, Romeo. If I let you sleep here, my reputation might be tarnished. Besides, I don't think you'd sleep too soundly—if at all. You'd torture yourself with the thought of me lying in bed on the other side of that door."

"Of course I would. And that's not all I'd be thinking about." His fingers toyed with the edge of her shirt.

Alana pulled back. "Eric—you know how much I care for you. Everything in me wants to…you know, but…"

"I know. We've talked about this before. You don't want to disappoint Mommy and Daddy."

"That's not fair," Alana protested. "You know it's not as simple as that."

"Sorry," he muttered. "That was a half-baked attempt to show you I understand. I guess I made a mess of it." He got to his feet and grabbed his bike helmet from the table. He turned toward the door, struggling to suppress the insistent sensations that had become a distraction in the past few moments.

Eric pulled the door open and gazed back at her as he turned into the opening. The reading light cast a diagonal beam across her profile. Her face was partially hidden in shadow, but he detected a tear stubbornly perched in the corner of her eye. It broke free, drifted across the softness of her cheek, and was lost in the shadows.

For an instant, his body twitched, as if to turn back, wrap her in his arms, and reassure her. He seemed to keep hurting her over this same issue. Now if he said anything else, he'd only make matters worse. *Why are relationships so difficult?* he wondered.

Resolved to honor Alana's wishes, he closed the door softly behind him. As he did so, he thought he heard a stifled sob from within.

FIVE

Tuesday, August 9, 2005
4 Rajab, 1426 AH
Atlanta, Georgia

Eric's desk phone rang, startling him out of his focus on bandwidth issues.

"Eric Colburn," he said.

"Dr. Larson would like to meet with you," said the voice of Dr. Larson's assistant. "He's ready for you now."

"Be right there." Eric pursed his lips and blew out in irritation, hoping Dr. Larson wanted to talk about bandwidth, not genetics. Despite passing the final on his online course, Eric found technology much more interesting.

Dr. Larson was on the phone, but he waved Eric to one of the visitors' chairs across from his desk.

"I need to have the new lab director in place as soon as possible," Dr. Larson noted with an edge to his voice. "I know...yes. Please do. Good-bye." He came around his desk and enthusiastically shook Eric's outstretched hand. "Good to have you aboard. I'm sorry I wasn't here when you started."

"Thank you, sir. I'm happy to be here," Eric replied.

Larson lowered his voice and put a hand on Eric's shoulder. "I hope you have not experienced too much resistance to our decision to hire someone so young for this position while passing over the existing staff."

"I haven't detected any, sir. I think I've earned the team's confidence with my work."

"Very good." Dr. Larson opened a leather portfolio and consulted his notes. "Eric, we're about to throw you into the thick of things. We're having Stephanie book you a flight to Cairo on Monday."

"Cairo, sir?" Eric asked, suppressing the thrill of going to the very city where Hamdi disappeared. It almost seemed too coincidental.

"Yes. The director transferred to a new lab weeks ago. You are probably aware that since then, the data stream from Cairo has been problematic?"

"Yes, sir. I've been working on it."

"Then you know the lab technicians are not adequately trained to deal with the problem. Mr. Preedy and I feel this situation will better acquaint you with the weaknesses in our network architecture so you can begin to implement a solution."

"Thank you for your confidence, Dr. Larson."

Dr. Larson frowned. "Eric—there's another reason I'm sending you to Cairo."

"What is that?"

"We had an employee abandon his job in Cairo a couple of months ago. Just between us, I had a vested interest in the young man, and I would like to have you try to contact him."

"You would be referring to Hamdi Tantawi, sir?"

Dr. Larson looked at Eric curiously. "As a matter of fact, yes. How do you know about him?"

"We were roommates in college, Dr. Larson."

"Well, then, I suppose I picked the right man for the job of contacting him. I must tell you, I never understood why Mr. Tantawi abandoned his job. He was motivated and enthusiastic about the Genographic Project."

"Yes, sir, he was." Eric realized that he had begun speaking of Hamdi in the past tense. "And he isn't the kind of guy who just walks away from his responsibilities."

"I didn't think so either, Eric. At first, I wanted to believe there was a good reason for him missing a few days of work. But he's never come forward with an explanation for his behavior."

Eric had long wanted to speak with someone about Hamdi's e-mail. But could he trust Dr. Larson? He made up his mind. "Sir, there's something you need to know." With that, Eric proceeded to tell Dr. Larson about the message from Hamdi and the discontinued e-mail account.

Dr. Larson brooded over Eric's story for quite a while. Then he seemed to come to a decision. "Eric—I agree this information is troubling. However, unless we have something more substantial to go on, I am not able to do anything. If you find evidence of wrongdoing in Cairo, bring it back with you, and I will respond accordingly. Otherwise, I have to assume that any troubles Mr. Tantawi had with co-workers in Egypt were based upon religious differences.

"Let me be clear. Your primary goal is to resolve the IT issues in the Cairo lab. I did not hire you to play amateur detective. That being said, I would like you to look into the matter of Mr. Tantawi's disappearance."

"You got it, sir!"

"Very well, then." Dr. Larson hit the intercom button on his phone.

"Yes, Dr. Larson?" came the prompt response.

"Would you arrange for Eric's travel to Cairo, please?"

Y

Alana stepped off the elevator on the eighth floor and approached the receptionist. "Hi, Stephanie. I understand Dr. Larson is expecting me?"

"Yes, you can go right in."

Stephanie had called ahead by the time Alana walked the length of the hallway. Dr. Larson opened the door as she approached and greeted her warmly. "Good morning, Alana! Please come in and have a seat."

"Thank you. What did you want to see me about?"

"I hope your passport is current, Ms. McKinsey."

Her eyes widened. "Yes, sir, it is."

"Good. I've decided to include you in our trip to Kolkata next Monday afternoon. We're going on what I refer to as a collection safari." He handed a bound booklet across the desk to her. "Here's a procedure manual that you need to become acquainted with. It explains the protocol we follow when collecting blood samples in the field. Be sure to read the section on sharps and biohazards. Many of the locations we will be visiting have a high incidence of HIV and other blood-borne diseases, so we adhere to the highest safety standards. By the way, you can find a PDF of this document on the server. I recommend you download a copy to your laptop. You'll appreciate having three pounds less baggage."

"Thank you. I'll do that."

Dr. Larson rolled to his desk's side arm. "Our goal is to obtain as many blood samples as possible during the first week. We want to begin processing samples at the new facility very quickly. They are in a training mode now, and we don't want to experience a lull in their processing. Full production volumes will reinforce the training."

"I've never drawn blood before," Alana said.

"We'll train you in the field. It isn't difficult. The important thing is to develop the knack for minimizing pain to the subject. The experiences of the first subjects can have great influence over how many others will come forward to submit samples. Some of the indigenous groups we work with are very superstitious and associate pain with bad karma or evil spirits. Having happy subjects practically guarantees a large sampling, and that, in turn, is critical to obtaining statistical reliability."

Alana was confident she would learn quickly. "Yes, sir, I understand."

"This week will be busy, so you may not have much of an opportunity to prepare for our safari. However, we'll take advantage of the long flight to Kolkata. I'll fill you in on our objectives for the safari and how we establish parameters for interpreting the data."

SIX

Friday, August 12, 2005
7 Rajab, 1426 AH
Cairo, Egypt

It was well past midnight in Cairo. A lone, shadowy figure sat in the silent, brooding lab. Red and green LEDs in the server room pulsed rhythmically, casting dim shadows into the gloom. An occasional flicker erupted on various components as test packets were routed through the internal network.

Suddenly, the inbound LED on the firewall flickered in a rapid burst then slowed to a steady pulse. The server's RAID array, normally dormant at this hour, was roused from slumber. A flurry of activity ensued as the hard drives were spun up. Blinking LEDs accelerated to a continuous burn as a massive amount of data was accessed. The outbound LED on the firewall flickered in earnest as it struggled to accommodate the demand. Data was streaming—flooding—through the ether to an unauthorized location.

Satam smiled in satisfaction.

Atlanta, Georgia

"Let me carry your tray for you," Eric volunteered.

"Thanks. I'll get the drinks." Alana grabbed the two cups and filled them from the soft-drink machine.

Eric selected the table with the least amount of trash and cleared it by the time Alana joined him. "I'm glad you called me or I probably wouldn't have broken away for lunch. Then I'd have a headache by the end of the day," Eric said.

"I wasn't sure if I should interrupt you. I had hoped we might cross paths earlier in the week. When we didn't, I wondered if you might be avoiding me." She noticed a shadow pass over his features.

"No, not at all," he said hastily, his eyes darting away from hers.

She salvaged his pride by not pressing the point. "Are you worried about Hamdi? Have you heard from him?"

Eric shook his head. "All the e-mails I've sent have been undeliverable. Someone shut down his Gmail account, which makes me very suspicious."

"How do you think you're going to find him?"

"I just came across an old letter in the apartment. I think the return address might be his parents'. I'll start there."

"Eric, what if—"

He shook his head. "No. I'm not going to believe that. Not yet." He forced a smile. "Let's just enjoy our lunch."

Alana nodded and sipped from her drink. "With both of us leaving on our trips, it seemed like a good idea to see each other."

"I agree," Eric said. "Is everything ready for your assignment?"

"The new lab came online two weeks ago. A collection team is being assembled now. Dr. Larson and I will be training them. Then we're scheduled for a collection safari to initiate a steady supply of lab samples." Alana decided to keep the conversation on business a little longer. "Everything is happening pretty fast. There's so much to absorb."

Eric groaned. "I know what you mean. Justin Preedy has had me working on the network. I can't help but feel that he resents the relationship I have with Dr. Larson. I think he has mixed emotions about retiring next year and views me as some sort of threat. The rest of the staff is friendly, though. There's a guy named Joey Hampton who's really good. Overall, I'm impressed with our computer network. They've spared no expense with the hardware. I doubt any of my classmates will have a chance to administer a network this sophisticated."

"That has to be pretty satisfying. This is what you worked hard for," she replied.

Eric paused. "Well, yes, in the professional sense, but no in the personal." He reached out and covered her hand. They sat silently for a moment. He gave her hand a squeeze. "I was a jerk last week, and I want to say I'm sorry."

Alana could see the sincerity in his eyes. "Thank you for taking the initiative. I've been so anxious to talk to you about it, but I didn't think I should make the first move. It means a lot to me that you apologized. I've had relationships where guys acted as if nothing ever happened while they're secretly pouting."

She noticed his face soften.

"I have a confession to make." He hesitated. "I was pouting. And I wasn't truthful earlier; I was avoiding you. I'm sorry for that too. Look—I want you to know that I'm willing to change. I'm still getting used to the idea that this relationship could… well, it's more serious than anything I've had before. Just be a little patient with me, OK?"

Soothing warmth swept over her as she savored the significance of his comments. "I'm not an expert either when it comes to relationships. I've made my share of mistakes. But I know you're different. And we're different than anything I've known before."

They sat there for a few minutes in silence.

Finally, Alana spoke again. "Hey—I have an idea. When we get back from our trips, why don't we commute together? It's about an hour's drive, which has to be less time for you than taking the MARTA. It would give us a couple of hours a day to stay caught up. Now that we're making big bucks, we can even afford a nice dinner a couple of times a week. And I can't think of anyone I'd rather—"

Eric interrupted her by gently placing his index finger on her lips. "You had me at 'hey.'" The allusion to one of their favorite movies communicated that she needn't try so hard to convince him. "I would love to spend the time with you too."

SEVEN

Monday, August 15, 2005
10 Rajab, 1426 AH
Over the Mediterranean Sea

LADIES AND GENTLEMEN, THE CAPTAIN HAS TURNED THE SEAT BELT sign back on. Please return to your seats and fasten your seat belts securely around your waists. We're expecting some turbulence and ask that you remain seated until further notice." The flight attendant's voice was strained with fatigue. She'd been much livelier at the beginning of the flight. Eric couldn't fault her, though. The passengers up in first class had been demanding; he'd seen the attendants scurrying to keep them happy.

Eric looked down on the inky void of the Mediterranean. He craned his neck and could just make out a hazy transition to gray at the horizon. He figured he should see the shoreline in a few minutes. More accurately, he expected to see a line of bright dots illuminating the coastal highway. He was anxious to stretch his legs after the brutal flight from the States. He wasn't claustrophobic, but after many hours of flight, the cabin was pressing in on him.

After having his fill of the view, Eric slept briefly. In his dream, he took a step that wasn't there. He was jolted awake and fought the disorienting panic. The rough landing signified their arrival. The coastal view had escaped him after all. Eric sat up and was surprised that he'd dozed off. He leaned forward and groped under the seat in front of him for his backpack. It was unzipped and was collapsed nearly flat.

The laptop was missing.

Eric stretched his arm farther but was restrained. He fumbled for the seat belt release and disengaged the buckle. With a grunt, he bent to the right, and lowered his head across the empty seat next to him. The laptop was nowhere in the darkness below the seats. He bent further and looked beneath his own seat. Nothing. When was the last time he'd seen it? It was right before they had passed above Gibraltar. That was over an hour ago.

"Are you looking for this?"

Eric sat up and peered between the seat backs in the direction of the voice. His laptop was being pushed through the void. "Yes! I've been looking all over for it." He grasped the protruding end as it was handed off. He couldn't yet see who his mysterious benefactor was.

As the laptop cleared the gap, he observed a lovely eye staring back at him, eyeliner and mascara framing an iris that was dark, almost black. As the benefactor sat upright, he could see her soft olive complexion, petite nose, and jet-black hair.

Eric lifted his chin and shifted forward in his seat, inching toward a better view over the seat back. "Thank you so much," he said. "Where did you find it?" She came into full view. In the early morning tranquility of an overnight flight, dim cabin lighting enhances natural beauty, and Eric's benefactor was no exception. She was lovely.

She laughed easily and said, "It gave me quite a start. When the plane hit some turbulence, I felt something bump my foot. I reached down and caught your computer as it slid forward. It is so thin that it slid easily beneath the restraining bar. But you were asleep, and it seemed a shame to wake you."

"Well, thanks again. I just started my new job, and I'd hate to lose the company's laptop on my first assignment. My name is Eric," he said, extending his hand. Her hand was small in his and surprisingly soft.

"I am Shoshana Barak. It is a pleasure to make your acquaintance. You are American, yes?"

"Yes, I am. But please don't hold that against me!" he said with a self-conscious shrug. "Not all of us are arrogant and insensitive."

"I would never assume such a thing," she responded.

"Your name sounds Israeli. Am I right?" he asked. The plane had slowed considerably as it lumbered toward the gate.

"Yes, but I live in the United States. I work for the Israeli Cultural Exchange in Atlanta."

"Egypt seems to be an unusual destination for an Israeli, doesn't it?"

"Under normal circumstances, yes. My original flight was canceled, and the only remaining option was to make a connection through Cairo. I am actually heading to Rome, so this is very much out of my way."

The cabin lights reluctantly flickered to life. The flight attendant's voice came across the intercom. "On behalf of the captain and crew, I would like to be the first to welcome you to Tel Aviv."

There was a collective gasp and rustle of clothing as many of the passengers glanced out of the windows in alarm, and in some cases, panic. The flight attendant smiled and continued. "But since this is Cairo, I guess I can't do that!" Sighs of relief swept through the cabin, followed by nervous laughter.

Shoshana explained to Eric, "The last place many of these passengers would want to find themselves would be Israel in the middle of the Palestinian uprising. As you can appreciate, they are not very comfortable with my people."

"Yes, I can certainly appreciate that," he nodded. "How much of a layover do you have until your connection?"

"Two and a half hours. I think I will find a café. If I do not consume some coffee, I am afraid I will fall asleep and miss my flight."

Eric had thought of little but Hamdi during the long flight, but he knew it was too early in the day to try to track down his friend's family. "It is pretty early in the morning here, and my biological clock is all mixed up," he said. "I'll tell you what—I could use some coffee too. I would be honored to buy a coffee for you. It's the least I can do after you rescued my computer."

Shoshana smiled sweetly. "That would be very nice. Thank you."

Y

Cairo, Egypt

Eric sipped his latte carefully. He'd burned his tongue on more than one occasion, usually when he was distracted. After a couple of sips, the caffeine energized him. He would need the boost to fortify him for the work ahead.

Shoshana gingerly sipped her espresso. She was ebullient and talkative in spite of the wear and tear of the long flight. "Tell me, Eric, what is your job with the National Geographic Society?"

"My job is information technology. I'm overhauling the society's wide area network in order to transmit to our servers in Atlanta. We're risking data corruption if we can't regulate the transmission."

"That sounds impressive." Shoshana responded. "What is the nature of all this data that is being sent?"

Eric was much more alert now and was equally talkative. "It's a relatively new project for the society. They coined a term for it, the Genographic Project. The idea is we're using the data to map the descent and migration of the human family. It's a worldwide project that will include hundreds of thousands of blood and saliva samples."

"I don't think anyone has designed a computer that can transmit saliva and blood." She smiled.

"That's true. It would sure make my job easier if they did. There's a whole lot that happens before the data hits my computer network. I could bore you with an explanation of how it works, but you'd learn more by checking out our Web site. Just go to the National Geographic site and search on the key word *Genographic*."

"Tell me more about the project's goal."

He paused to assess the sincerity of her interest. "OK. You know that DNA is the basic building block of genetics, right?"

She nodded.

"Well, we look at only a small part of the DNA from each of the samples. It's a special part from which we can determine your maternal or paternal lineage. We're interested in certain segments—called markers—that contain random mutations. It's been determined that various mutations have occurred over many, many generations. These are located in sections of our DNA that don't seem to affect physical traits. Once a marker has occurred in someone's DNA, every generation that follows will carry that identical marker. We're analyzing the data to find matching markers across various population groups. When two groups share the same marker, that means they descended from the same individual in the distant past. Does that make sense, or have I confused you?"

Shoshana smiled. "No, I think I understand. I will certainly check the Web site. It sounds like a fascinating process."

"It is," Eric replied. "And it takes very sophisticated lab equipment to process the DNA samples. Each of our lab sites is processing thousands of samples at any one time."

"That is interesting. May I ask one question? My people are very interested in genealogy. Can you tell me if many Jewish people have been involved in the project?"

"That's a good question. I don't know the answer, but I'll be happy to find out if you'd like me to."

"Yes, please. Here is my card." Shoshana pulled a card from her briefcase and handed it to him. "Would you contact me when you return to Atlanta? I am curious because the Torah has much to say about genealogy. Our belief is that it contains an accurate record of God's chosen people and how His favor was bestowed on certain lineages and withheld from others. Most lineages outside of His covenant became mortal enemies of my people, and that continues until today."

"My girlfriend knows a lot about the Bible, but I'm not as familiar with the history. Why would God's covenant with the Jews relate to your enemies?" Eric asked.

"The most vivid example is provided by Abram's firstborn, Ishmael. Abram did not completely trust God to give him a son in his old age, so he took matters into his own hands. His barren wife encouraged him to follow the custom of the day and sleep with her handmaiden, and that union brought forth Ishmael. God later appeared to Abram and gave him a new name—Abraham. God admonished him that he'd misunderstood the prophecy of a future son. God's plan was to provide a son through Abraham's wife, Sarah. This came to pass as God had prophesied, and they named their son Isaac.

"Some scholars believe that Isaac's lineage was favored because both of his parents came from Mesopotamia—the land between two rivers—which is in modern-day Iraq. Sarah's handmaiden, Hagar, was Egyptian, which meant Ishmael was a half-breed. God Himself prophesied that Ishmael would be a wild man and that his hand would be against everyone and everyone's hand would be against him. Most importantly, the Lord also said that he would contend with his brother, Isaac, and the same prophecy is repeated later about Ishmael's descendants. Is this not exactly the outcome we see today?"

Eric was puzzled. "I'm not sure I follow you."

Shoshana responded deliberately. "One of Ishmael's sons was named Kedar. Two thousand years later, one of Kedar's descendants was named Muhammad, who founded Islam. So the prophecy of contention between brothers lives on in the progeny of Isaac and Ishmael: the Jews and the Muslims."

Atlanta, Georgia

The airport intercom emitted a raucous burst of static and then came to life. "Now boarding all first-class passengers on Delta flight number fifty-four thirty-nine to JFK International Airport at gate one twenty-four."

Dr. Larson rose awkwardly from the waiting area seat. Alana followed suit. One of the perks of traveling with National Geographic's leader was traveling first class.

They boarded the plane and settled into the nicest airline seats Alana had ever experienced.

Dr. Larson, an experienced traveler, was asleep by the time the wheels

---

Liam Roberts   39

left the runway. Alana pulled out her laptop, needing to distract herself for a while. The opening screen was her Sudoku program. Alana had stumbled upon the numbers puzzle long before the daily newspapers caught on. Eric was just as hooked and liked to race her because that's what guys do. He usually won—not surprising for a computer geek.

EIGHT

Tuesday, August 16, 2005
11 Rajab, 1426 AH
New York City

T HE LANDING AT JFK WAS UNEVENTFUL. DR. LARSON AND ALANA
considered dinner possibilities in order to fill the three-hour layover.
The aromas in the new food court were appealing, but the choices were the
fast-food variety.

"This might satisfy us in the short term, but we would pay dearly at thirty
thousand feet," Dr. Larson observed. "Since we have to go to the international gates, we should find a suitable restaurant in the main terminal."

Alana agreed. They found a steak house that was part of a national
chain. The food was adequate for airport fare, and they had sufficient time
to enjoy their meal before heading to the terminal.

They lifted off on a northwest bearing, which took them over Manhattan.
Alana leaned into the turn as the pilot banked the plane. She gazed down as
the heart of the city came into view. It was well past midnight, but the city
was ablaze with breathtaking activity. Alana could make out the island of
Manhattan with its myriad lights framed by the black void of the Hudson
and Harlem rivers. The Empire State Building was an easy landmark to
hone in on, as was the Chrysler Building. It was mesmerizing to watch the
clusters of light that outlined each skyscraper as the plane accelerated. The
lights pirouetted gracefully in the shifting perspective. Alana found herself
captivated by the view. Two brilliant beams of light rose defiantly from the
city and stabbed through the cloud cover—the site of the twin towers.

She hugged herself as a melancholy shiver coursed through her. "Lord,
rest their souls," she whispered in prayer for the brave Americans of
9/11. She continued to stare at the beams until the plane banked left and
the beams retreated into the wake. The plane swept over the ocean and
smoothly ascended to cruising altitude. There was nothing left to see but
the abyss of the Atlantic. At the first opportunity, Dr. Larson stretched
out his seat and dozed again.

Alana reached for her laptop again, beginning to see a pattern in traveling with Dr. Larson. She closed the Sudoku program, intending to read up on genographic protocols a little further. She scanned her desktop for the icon and noticed a flashing e-mail icon. Her broadband connection obviously wasn't working up here, so her e-mail must have updated while she was in the airport. The message was from Eric. She eagerly read it:

From: Eric Colburn
Sent: Tue 8/16/2005 11:02 AM
To: Alana McKinsey
Cc:
Subject: It's 11:00. Do you know where your boyfriend is?

Hi, sweetie! I miss you already.

I've arrived in Cairo and I'm sooo tired! I imagine you'll be in even worse shape by the time you get to India. I think I can wrap things up here within a few days. I may need to visit another of our labs, but I won't know for sure until I've run some diagnostics on the systems here.

I think someone broke into my laptop while I was asleep on the plane. When I fired it up this morning, a couple of icons were in the wrong place. I ran a spyware and virus scan on it, but it came up clean. I'm not sure how concerned I should be, but I'm going to be more careful.

Hey—I learned some cool stuff about Cairo that you'd be interested in. The limo driver was a great tour guide. We drove past a massive garbage dump as we came into Cairo. He told me they call it Garbage City because people actually live in the dump. Believe it or not, they're mostly Christians. They're outcasts here, and the dump is a sanctuary where they aren't persecuted by Muslims. They make a living by salvaging stuff from the dump and selling it in the market. They worship in Cave Church, which is a huge cave they carved out of the side of a mountain. Pretty amazing.

Well, I'm practically falling asleep writing this. I'm going directly to the lab to start some diagnostics. If I go to the hotel first, I might lie down, and I don't know if I could get back up.

Love ya!

E

Alana sat back in her seat and read the last line again. This was the first time Eric had used the L word. Admittedly, it was couched in casual slang, so it may not have any significance. On the other hand, it could be a subtle way of communicating that Eric's fear of losing his freedom was being slowly overpowered by his desire for a relationship with her. She smiled dreamily and rested her head on the seat back.

Dr. Larson stirred and rolled over in his sleep. She glanced across the aisle and noticed his eyes were open. He was gazing at her, which made her slightly uncomfortable.

"You are a lovely sight to awaken to," he commented, then changed the subject. "What are you working on?"

Alana ignored the first comment and responded, "I just checked my e-mail and was about to read the sharps procedures and the biohazard protocols."

"I admire your energy, but they will surely put you to sleep," he replied. "I'm confident you will have many questions. The flight attendants will be serving breakfast in about five hours. If you come up with any questions, I'll be happy to answer them over a cup of coffee. In the meantime, I think I'll get some more sleep."

"OK," she said.

Dr. Larson closed his eyes.

Alana wrote a quick response to Eric:

> From: Alana McKinsey
> Sent: Thu 8/16/2005 8:12 AM
> To: Eric Colburn
> Cc:
> Subject: RE: It's 11:00. Do you know where your boyfriend is?
>
> Hi, sweetie, to you too!
> We took off from JFK a little while ago, and I just read your e-mail. I think I'm going to become too familiar with jet lag. I just noticed that my e-mail is date stamped three hours before you sent yours, cuz I'm responding to you from an earlier time zone. That's just a little confusing! That church in Cairo sounds very interesting. I'd love to visit it sometime. For now, I wanted to let you know I was thinking of you and miss you very much.
>
> Love,
> Alana

"Well, that was a little more direct than his sign-off. Let's see how he responds," she muttered under her breath.

Dr. Larson was snoring loudly in his seat bed.

Alana flipped back to the procedure manual and read a couple of sections. Fatigue began to envelop her as the soothing drone of the engines vibrated into her seat and diffused through her body. Alana leaned back and rested her head for a moment. She softly closed her computer, then her eyes.

Karāchi, Pakistan

Dr. Alomari had nodded off at his desk and was startled awake by the chime of the gene sequencer. He struggled to his feet and tore off the printed results. Nodding in satisfaction, he loaded the next set of samples, which would take the remainder of the night to process.

His telephone beckoned from his office. He typed in the last sequencing command and scurried to silence the ring. Fearing that the call may have already cycled to voice mail, he snatched the phone from the cradle as it started the fifth ring. "*As-salāmu 'alaykum,*" he shouted breathlessly.

"Peace be to you as well, Excellency. And may Allāhu be merciful.

"What do you have to report, Satam?" Alomari asked.

"The body of the Amrikan will not be discovered."

"Very well. Let us hope that is the end of it." There was a pause on the line.

"Is there more?"

"Yes, Your Excellency. Another Amrikan is due to arrive today. What would you like me to do?"

"Watch him carefully. If he suspects anything, I expect you to show some initiative for a change."

"Yes, Your Excellency."

Alomari slammed the phone into its cradle and sat heavily in his chair. *These meddling Amrikans must be stopped,* he thought. His goal was within reach, but it depended on an uninterrupted stream of vital data. He would not tolerate further setbacks.

His genius was soon to be acknowledged by the many filthy *Kafirs* who had humiliated him. Their Islamphobia was palpable after the destruction of the twin towers, but they were too cowardly to admit it. They propped up the scathing peer review of his work as justification for denying him the recognition he was due. But he knew the real reason. The infidel Crusaders had held his people down for centuries.

Soon, they would pay dearly. Allāhu had ordained it.

THE Y FACTOR

NINE

Tuesday, August 16, 2005
11 Rajab, 1426 AH
Cairo, Egypt

ERIC ARRIVED AT THE LAB AND IMMEDIATELY NOTICED IT WAS empty of any personnel. That was curious. The lab should be open on a weekday, and he was unaware of any local holiday. His arrival should have been expected. He pulled out his ID and waved it at the magnetic lock. The door clicked and he entered.

The facility was dimly lit. He found the light switch and flipped it. The lobby lights flickered twice, then settled into a dull greenish glow. Eric could see into the lab through windows on the interior wall, but the door was secure. His ID didn't trigger this magnetic lock. He pulled out his PDA, which he'd programmed to override an inconvenience like this, but then thought better of it. He had no particular interest in entering the empty lab, and it'd be awkward if someone discovered he'd overridden the security system.

Eric found the server room and performed a quick inventory of the equipment. He then connected his laptop to a spare Ethernet port on the network switch and booted it up. The log-in screen appeared after a few minutes:

Genographic Project: Cairo Lab
User Name: _____
Password: _____
Domain: NGSCairo

Eric supplied his credentials and was granted access. He first checked to see if Alana had responded to his e-mail. Not yet. He assumed that he wouldn't receive a response until she connected through the Delhi airport, assuming she'd find an available hot spot.

He had quite a few diagnostic utilities to run. Eric decided to launch them while waiting for the staff, since some of the procedures would take a bit of time to complete. He established a connection to each of the server drives and checked their utilization stats. Surprisingly, the drives had only 26 percent available space.

"That's crazy," he muttered. "This lab hasn't been open long enough to consume that much space." He launched a utility to scan the server array for the largest files and their creation dates.

While that query was running, he launched a virus scan and Trojan virus removal utility. His initial concern was that a Trojan file might have granted access to hackers.

Next, Eric checked the user log-in permissions. He needed to confirm that access to server drives was limited to IT staff. It was relatively simple to block lab techs from browsing secure areas. Everything looked in order. He noticed that the former lab director, Dr. Ahmed Alomari, was still listed as an active user. Since that was no longer needed, Eric deleted his log-in permissions and closed the administrator utility.

A piercing, warbling horn interrupted his concentration. It seemed to emanate from a distant source, so Eric assumed it wasn't the building's fire alarm. The horn stopped abruptly and was replaced by a muffled voice broadcast from a loudspeaker. A man's voice chanted rhythmically in a foreign dialect. At first, Eric did his best to ignore it. Then it dawned on him that this would be the Muslim call to prayer, which men all over the city would answer. Although Hamdi had never been very observant of the Muslim prayer requirements, Eric knew Hamdi's father and uncles were fastidious about them. At least now he knew where the staff was in the middle of the workday. Morning prayers. Five times a day Muslim men stopped their activities and bowed to the east in prayer.

The first computer query finally completed. Eric scanned and sorted the log that had been generated and noticed quite a few large files. They had a similar name structure beginning with NGSCE followed by a series of six numbers. They all ended with a file extension GIG. Eric furrowed his brow. He was not familiar with GIG files. He checked a reference Web site and could not find any known program that utilized that extension. Next, he opened the SQL console and scanned the data transmission section. This was the procedure that automatically connected to the Atlanta servers and uploaded the genetic sample data. This occurred every night at a predetermined time, and Eric wanted to see if there was a reference to GIG files being created in preparation for transmission. He found no reference to them, which heightened his curiosity.

Eric scanned the listing, and another pattern emerged. The file creation dates and times were consistent. A new file was created every seven days around 1:00 a.m. local time. He checked the calendar, confirming the most recent one had been created on Saturday.

Eric rolled the office chair to the cabinet housing the server equipment. The firewall was manufactured by Cisco, so he should be able to obtain the software he needed from their Web site. Before he shut the cabinet door, he checked the LEDs on the face of the firewall. Both the internal LAN and external WAN were functioning properly.

He rolled back to the console and logged into Cisco's Web site. He selected the "Support: Downloads" option and entered "Activity Log" as the key word search term. The screen provided a listing of matches in descending order of applicability. He scrolled through the synopses and selected the most promising one:

> This utility will log both outbound and inbound data transfer requests. On outbound activities, the destination IP address will be logged. On inbound requests, the utility will capture all originating IP addresses and log-in responses. Duration of connection is captured on all transmissions.

Eric created a hidden directory, set exclusive access, and secured it with an encrypted password. He then downloaded and installed the activity log utility, determined to solve the mystery of the GIG files. Unfortunately, he'd have to wait several days for the next file to be created and transmitted. He pulled a sticky note from his wallet and read the name scrawled on it: Satam Suqami. The senior lab technician would show him around in the absence of a director. Maybe he would ask Satam.

Returning to the main lobby, Eric glanced through the windows. The lab was still empty. Abruptly, the rear lab door opened, and a group of Arabs purposefully strode into the lab, pulling scull caps off their heads. They fanned out through the lab, taking up positions at various workstations.

Eric pressed a buzzer located beside the door. One of the technicians appeared startled by the sound. He walked to the security door and pressed the intercom button. He said something in a language Eric could not understand.

"Do you speak English?" Eric asked in loud a voice. He checked himself. Yelling would not enhance the translation. "My name is Colburn, and I'm here to see Mr. Suqami."

The technician nodded and pressed something below the window. A buzzer sounded, and the lab door swung open. He stuck his head into the

---

Liam Roberts   47

opening. "Yes, we expect you. Mr. Suqami in office," he said while pointing to a small office near the back. As the technician opened the door enough for him to enter, Eric was carried back to his high school biology lab. The chemical odors wafted into the lobby and singed his sinus passages. The sensation was very much like a tingling burst of nasal spray.

Eric blinked back tears and approached the office. He knocked, stuck his head through the opening, and said, "Mr. Suqami? My name is Eric Colburn."

"Ah yes, I have been expecting you. I noticed someone in the server room and assumed it must be you. I had many time-critical tasks, so I could not be distracted enough to introduce myself."

"That's no problem. I did some routine checks." He paused before changing the subject. "I've been anxious to find out about Hamdi Tantawi. Has anyone been in contact with him since he left the job?"

Satam's face grew taut. "He abandoned his job. We have no interest in quitters."

Eric bristled. "Hamdi is a friend of mine and is no quitter. This isn't like him, and I'm sure there is a good explanation."

"It is no concern of mine. I have a job to do and refuse to coddle soft Amrikans."

Eric felt his face flush in anger. He wanted to grab this guy by the throat, but his sense of diplomacy kept him from overreacting. He clenched his fists and said a quick prayer to calm himself. "I would like to see if his family's phone number is in his personnel file." He pulled a tattered envelope from his pocket. "I also want to confirm the address on this envelope."

"That is not possible. I burned it."

"What? The NGS would not approve of that. There are policies you're supposed to follow."

"I told you. It is none of my concern."

This was going nowhere fast. "I'll deal with that later. In the meantime, I would like to see how your lab is laid out."

Satam abruptly stood and motioned to one of the lab technicians. The tech came to his office door and asked a question.

Eric did not understand the question, or Satam's clipped response, but the tech reverted to English and addressed Eric. "I will be happy to escort you."

Eric followed him from the office without further comment to Satam, who seemed uninterested in their departure. To the technician, Eric said,

"I would like a quick tour of the lab. I haven't seen one in action and am very interested in how the processing works."

"As you wish," the young man replied. He led Eric to the back of the lab and pointed to a roll-up door. "This is the receiving dock. We receive daily shipments of blood samples from the collection teams. Twice each month we receive replacement lab equipment, chemicals, and other supplies.

"Over here is where the blood samples are unpacked. You can see the Styrofoam containers with a recessed space for a pouch of dry ice. All blood samples are in test tubes with a captive plug that seals them from contamination. The bar code on the side of each tube is applied at the site of the sampling. A matching bar code is affixed to the questionnaire filled out by the subject. The bar code also includes the GPS coordinates of where the sample was collected."

Eric knew about that part and offered, "That information is captured in our database and is used to create distribution maps where we plot genotype percentages found in each region."

"Exactly." The man turned to the next section and pointed to a group of technicians. "They are moving the test tubes from the shipping container into special racks that they mount in the centrifuge. Buffers are added, which suspend the blood cells in the solution. The samples are then purified and washed while spinning the cells at high speed in the centrifuges.

"At this point, we have a concentrated cluster of cells. Next, the cell membranes are destroyed, which releases the chromosomes. This is done at the last machine in this aisle." They turned the corner and went down the next aisle.

Eric pointed to a series of machines that looked like oversized fax machines. They took up the whole aisle. "What do these devices do?" he asked.

"These are PCR machines that amplify particular DNA segments."

Eric asked, "What does that stand for?

"Polymerase chain reaction. It's a complex process that actually amplifies the genetic markers. Millions of copies can be made in a matter of hours."

They moved on to the last aisle. "These machines are the gene sequencers. The amplified DNA is drawn up in very small capillaries. Different types of DNA migrate at specific rates and will separate into bands. These bands are detected by lasers, which collect information about the marker types and their respective values." They moved farther down the aisle to a cluster of computer workstations. "This is where the data from the gene sequencers is loaded into our computers for analysis. Each subject's DNA is matched against a well-defined list of haplotypes."

"I know what those are," Eric said. "They're the various genetic subgroups of the human family that have been identified. Since we are testing for only twelve markers, our groupings are fairly broad."

"Correct."

"Since we're testing for so few markers, it seems like we have a huge quantity of PCR machines. This equipment must be expensive."

The tech did not respond. After a slight pause, he announced, "I am needed for a problem on one of the centrifuges. If you will excuse me?"

"Certainly," replied Eric. "Don't let me hold you up. Oh—before you go, can you tell me where I can get some coffee? I'm really tired from the long flight. If I don't get some coffee in me, I'll pass out."

The tech frowned as if he didn't understand all of Eric's comments. He evidently deduced enough of them and motioned toward the front door. "There is a small café across from the mosque."

Y

Satam returned to his desk. He was organizing his files when his phone rang. "*As-salāmu 'alaykum.*"

"Satam, this is Dr. Alomari. Can you speak?"

"Just a moment." Satam rose from his desk and shut his office door. Returning to his desk, he picked up the phone. "Yes?"

"I have just received an alert that files in your lab have been scanned. I attempted to log in remotely but was denied access. What is going on there?" Alomari demanded.

Satam twisted the receiver cord. Alomari had been ruthless when he worked here, and Satam barely escaped his many purges. The man still intimidated him, even being so far away.

"I do not know," he stammered. "Just a moment." He parted the slats on his office window and glanced toward the door. He lowered his voice. "The Amrikan is here from headquarters. He has been working in the server room."

The silence on the other end of the line was unnerving. After a long pause, Alomari barked, "Tell me more."

Satam described the visitor and added, "He asked about Hamdi."

"What did you tell him?"

"Nothing. But he told me that Hamdi is a friend, and he is going to try to contact him."

"Where is he now?"

"He left the lab and is at the café. He will be returning any minute," Satam replied.

"Contact the others. I do not want this Amrikan out of your sight."

Y

Eric wiped the sweat from his brow and began to question whether coffee was the right choice. He was sure the café wouldn't offer iced coffee; this wasn't Starbucks, after all. And the employees worked at a far different pace. They seemed in no hurry to serve the many patrons queued up in the hot sun. Eric couldn't understand why he was the only one bothered by the inefficiency.

He finally placed his order, accepted a steaming cup, and found a small stand where he intended to add his usual condiments. He lifted various lids and curled his lip, debating the health risks. It then occurred to him that the coffee was hot enough to kill any bacteria.

His arm was bumped, nearly upending his drink. He turned angrily toward the source as hot fluid burned his fingers. An imposing man in a turban and robes stared intently at him. "You are Amrikan with society?" the man asked in broken English.

In spite of the thick accent, Eric was pretty sure he understood. "Yes, why?"

"I was worker in lab. Alomari hate me. I work no longer at lab." He paused. "No one is knowing what Alomari doing at lab."

Eric was taken aback by the intensity. "Dr. Alomari no longer works here," he told the man.

"That not matter. He still in control," the man exclaimed. "They afraid. I was not, so I work no longer. I am knowing things about Alomari. You need also to know."

This was getting uncomfortable. The afternoon heat accentuated his discomfort as rivulets of sweat trickled down Eric's back. "I don't know what I can do for you. I have nothing to do with the staffing at the lab. If you'll excuse me—"

The man looked panicked. "No!" he shouted. "You need to be knowing!" He glanced nervously over his shoulder. He whipped his head back around and leaned close.

Eric suppressed a gag from the odor that enveloped him.

"I have documents," the man whispered. "You will soon be knowing too."

"Documents? You mean, like, evidence or something?" This was going from bad to worse. "I'm not sure I should get involved in a labor dispute. That's not my—"

"No more talk!" he exclaimed. "You listen. Too public here. Dangerous. Meet at sunrise. Small dining place beside Hilton."

A thought occurred to Eric. "Do you know Hamdi Tantawi?"

Remorse washed across the man's features. "He was friend." With that, the man turned and scurried away. He ducked into an alley.

"Wait! What do you mean *was*?" Eric shouted. The man disappeared just as Eric noticed a sudden movement out of the corner of his eye. He turned toward the mosque and saw a huddle of Arabs. Their attention seemed to be split between glancing furtively at him and the alley. Two of them broke away from the others. As Eric watched in alarm, they crossed the street and rapidly followed the stranger into the alley.

No longer needing the coffee, Eric set it on the counter. As he turned away, a frail young man greedily snatched it up and cast him an appreciative glance.

Eric debated whether to return to the lab. Would the remaining Arabs follow him? He looked for a taxi but realized this street was probably not busy enough to find a taxi. He headed for a cross street that looked more promising.

Just as he approached a busy intersection, two taxis rumbled through, heading east. He picked up his pace, hoping to catch one heading west toward the hotel district. He looked to his right as he crossed the street and noticed something out of the corner of his eye. He turned and saw a few of the Arabs from the mosque moving toward him through the crowded intersection. They *were* following him! He wasn't about to stick around and find out why.

A taxi approached and slowed as the driver acknowledged Eric's frantic gestures. He trotted alongside the vehicle and jerked the door open before it came to a stop. Jumping in, he yelled, "Take me to the Marriott hotel. Quickly!"

The driver responded to the urgency and punched the gas. Simultaneously, the door locks clicked into the locked position. The taxi lurched, throwing Eric off balance. He fell back into the seat as the taxi stalled. A face set in a wicked grimace appeared at the driver's window, accompanied by fists beating on the roof of the cab. "Get moving—now!" Eric shouted.

The driver hunched over the steering wheel, pumping the gas and firing the ignition. More angry faces appeared as the reluctant engine fired to life. The taxi lurched again, but the driver had improved his skill with the clutch.

They accelerated away from the intersection, a blue haze swirling in their wake. Eric looked out the rear window to affirm they weren't being followed.

The driver careened through the traffic, narrowly missing a few pedestrians. "You can slow down," Eric said. "No one's coming after us."

The driver looked at him in the rearview mirror but barely slowed.

"Do you speak English?" Eric asked.

"Not good," was the reply.

Eric pulled an envelope out of his pocket and handed it to the driver. "Can you read the address on this?"

The driver glanced at the address. Eric could see fear reflected in the mirror. The driver shook his head vigorously. "No! Marriott is where I go."

Eric didn't have the energy to argue. He was exhausted and decided he needed sleep more than he needed to solve the mystery. Maybe he'd try again tomorrow.

TEN

Wednesday, August 17, 2005
12 Rajab, 1426 AH
Over Afghanistan

Dr. Larson woke up and stretched. He noticed Alana staring at her computer screen, deep in thought. "You are working very hard," he commented.

She returned his glance. "I'm just rereading a section to make sure I understand everything. You told me you'd be ready for questions over coffee. I have a few ready for you."

"Absolutely," he replied. "Before that, I need to use the facilities." He reached into the overhead bin and pulled his toiletry kit from his carry-on luggage. Then he headed to the restroom.

By the time he returned, the flight attendants were serving coffee and juice. He ordered one of each. The breakfast that followed was simple and tasted surprisingly good.

"So, what questions did you have in mind?" Larson asked.

"The first one is regarding the sampling techniques," Alana said. I noticed on the Web site that people can order cheek swab kits if they want to participate in the study. Yet we go around the world collecting blood samples. Wouldn't it be much easier to use the cheek swab kits in the field as well? It seems we'd get a higher level of acceptance from the people groups that are skittish about giving blood samples."

"Excellent question," Larson remarked. "The answer is quite simple. You are aware that we have many partners in this project?" She nodded. "One of the significant partners is the Saud Foundation. Have you heard of it?" This time, she shook her head. "It is controlled by a family of the same name, a very powerful family. Some would say they are one of the most powerful in the world. In fact, they are the only family with a country named after them." Dr. Larson left the thought dangling, drawing her into a guessing game.

Alana was quick to engage. With barely a pause, her face lit up. "You mean Saudi Arabia?"

He smiled proudly, as a professor delighted by a favored student. "Yes, they are the ones bankrolling our project. One of their princes is very interested in our project and visits our facilities from time to time. One of their funding stipulations is that the field collections be blood samples, not saliva. I am not sure why they should be concerned with such a minor detail, but I will gladly comply with their requirements.

"I will mention an anecdotal incident, however. We were in the final negotiations with the Saud family. It was right before a lunch break, and our CFO was frustrated with the high costs of blood sampling. He forcefully expressed his opinion, and the Saudis abruptly demanded a break for lunch. We agreed. It's better to reconvene with clear minds and full stomachs. Negotiations are more agreeable following a delightful lunch.

"Anyway, during the lunch break I excused myself. I was in a private stall when a couple of men entered the restroom. One of them said, 'The life is in the blood! I will not compromise on this point.'

"It was obvious they were members of the Saudi negotiating team. They finished their business and left the room. I rejoined the luncheon without their realizing I had overheard them. After lunch, I pulled my team aside and told them we would acquiesce to the Saudi demands. The expense wasn't that significant, especially since they would be the major funding source. We secured their sponsorship within the hour."

"That is fascinating," remarked Alana.

"Why?"

"Well, he quoted something directly from the Bible," she replied.

"The Bible? What does that have to do with anything?" He sniffed.

"Actually, quite a bit. But I don't want to offend you. Do you want me to continue?"

"I'm waiting with bated breath," he remarked.

"OK. You know about the Old Testament, right?"

He shrugged with a noncommitted expression.

"It's basically a Jewish book that recounts how God called the Jews out from among the nations and established a covenant with them. In the process, God laid down a number of rules for them, many of which regarded blood."

"Really?"

"Yes, in fact, blood plays a central role in both the Old and New Testaments." Alana caught herself. "Am I boring you?"

"Not at all. I consider myself a student of history, but I have had questions about this. Continue."

"OK. Blood plays a role in the first two sins recorded in the Bible. When

Adam and Eve had sinned, they hid their nakedness from God with fig leaves. God replaced the leaves and covered them with animal skins. Now, this may seem a bit of a stretch, but the use of animal skins implies that the animals were slain; therefore, their blood was shed."

Dr. Larson raised his eyebrows skeptically.

Alana shrugged. "I know—it may seem thin. But many biblical scholars believe this foreshadows the role Christ would later play when He 'covered' our sins by shedding His blood. When you look at this passage in the context of the full Scriptures, it makes sense. When Cain murdered his brother, the Lord said, 'Your brother's blood is crying out from the ground.' One more example, and then I'll stop. Have you heard about the plagues that God brought down on Egypt?"

Dr. Larson nodded again.

"Well, the Bible tells us that Pharaoh would not let the Jewish slaves go, so God brought the plagues as a sign and a warning. The last plague was the most horrible. The firstborn from every household would die—even in Jewish households. However, there was a way of escape that seems archaic by today's standards. They were to sacrifice a spotless and unblemished lamb, then paint their doorposts with its blood. If they did this, then the angel of death would pass over the household. This is the Passover tradition and also prefigures the work of Christ. He was spotless and pure, yet He became a sacrifice for all of us. As with the Passover, if we trust in the blood of the sacrifice, we pass from a death sentence to life. Isn't that cool? There are countless examples like these in the Bible."

"So how did we get on this topic?" Dr. Larson asked.

"Because of what you heard in the restroom that day. I'm sure the Saudi didn't realize that he was quoting a verse from the Torah, where the Lord prohibited eating meat with blood in it. The reason given for the prohibition was, 'The life is in the blood.'"

Dr. Larson was puzzled. "But Muslims do not engage in animal sacrifices like the Jews."

"Actually, they do," she replied. "Hamdi once told us they slay a lamb when a baby is dedicated. It is hauntingly similar to the Passover symbolism."

Dr. Larson sat quietly for a few moments. "After listening to you, I'm more confused about the significance of the blood sampling. It makes me suspicious of their motivation in funding our work—and of what it may cost us."

Y

Cairo, Egypt

The server alarm wouldn't stop. Eric quickly diagnosed the problem and corrected it. Then the firewall began chirping. Before he could attend to it, the battery backup sounded its alert. This was his worst nightmare. All the systems were breaking down simultaneously. The cacophony worsened as each alarm warbled in unison.

Y

He awoke with a start. His bedside phone was ringing insistently. Eric snatched the phone from its cradle. "Yes?"

"This is your five o'clock wake-up call," replied a soothing feminine voice.

"Thanks." He felt stupid when the phone clicked without a response. He had thanked a computer.

He stumbled to the shower and rotated the faucet to high. He relaxed under the hot jets and allowed the pulsating spray to massage his weary shoulders. Why was he getting up this early? What could be gained from meeting with a crazy man? Eric had resigned himself to the meeting, so the second-guessing was not going to change his decision. He dressed and left his suitcase hanging open. He wouldn't be gone long and would straighten things up when he returned.

Eric exited the hotel and waved off a taxi. He only had to walk a couple of blocks. In the moonless predawn hours, the foggy darkness engulfed him. The Hilton logo burned through the mist, surrounding itself in a glowing halo. The small diner was nearby. Quite a few patrons were already seated at courtyard tables. Eric preferred the warm interior and asked for a table near the front window. He ordered coffee.

A voice boomed behind Eric. "I pleased you choose to come."

Eric jumped nervously at the man's sudden appearance. "I'm not sure this is a good idea. I saw two men follow you from the marketplace yesterday afternoon."

"Yes, I was knowing that. They were not difficulty. I go to Garbage City. Muslims not follow there."

So that's what the odor is, Eric thought. "Hey—I know all about that. My limo driver told—"

"I bring this." The man paused and peered warily around the diner before sitting and handing over an envelope and a logbook that looked similar to

---

those Eric had seen at the lab. "Take log to America. You will be knowing what to do."

"Can you tell me what this is all about?" Eric asked.

"I not know English good. It hard to tell." The man swiped perspiration from his forehead with his sleeve, which pulled back to reveal a small tattoo in the web between his index finger and thumb.

"That's an unusual place for a tattoo," Eric commented, diverting the conversation away from the cloak-and-dagger intrigue.

"It mean I Christian. This is Muslim country. Tattoo required. Dangerous for to be Christian."

Eric had delayed the most pressing question, fearing the answer. "What happened to Hamdi?" he asked.

"I work with Hamdi. He see things too. We talk together." He pointed at the logbook. "Hamdi made English writing. You understand, yes?"

Eric glanced down at the logbook. "These are Hamdi's notes?"

"He disappear that night. I think he dead so I take papers."

A pang of sorrow spread through Eric's chest. It didn't seem possible. Hamdi was so young, so energetic. He fanned the pages and recognized the handwriting.

The stranger glanced out the front windows, past the courtyard tables. Eric followed his stare and saw men lurking in the shadows across the street. A flicker of recognition flashed across the Christian's face. "There is danger—I go now."

"But I need to know—" The man was on his feet instantly and loomed over Eric. He thrust his hand forward, causing Eric to flinch involuntarily.

The Christian stuffed a small scrap of paper in Eric's shirt pocket. "This have name is friend. He Christian—you trust. Find he in Garbage City." With that, he hurried toward the exit.

The Christian wound his way through the patio tables when a turbaned man cut him off. The Christian froze as the man shouted at him venomously. He screamed, "*Allāhu akbar!*" and did something completely unexpected. He hugged the Christian.

Surrealistically, the two men seemed to levitate into the air before Eric's eyes. Time slowed as their bodies seemed to expand, then dissolve in the mighty blast. Reflexively, Eric turned his head as the windows imploded. He was lifted and thrown across the diner and roughly deposited beneath a pair of tables, one of which tipped over him and sheltered him from the debris. He lay there in a semiconscious state, gazing aimlessly at the yellow ceiling. Bits of cloth and paper floated through the smoke and dust like snowflakes.

A face appeared above him. The mouth was moving in earnest, but Eric heard nothing. The merciful silence enveloped him. Then the dawning sun set prematurely in Cairo.

ELEVEN

Wednesday, August 17, 2005
12 Rajab, 1426 AH
Delhi, India

ALANA NEEDED TO STRETCH. THE HOURS IN WAITING AREAS and planes were taking their toll. The Delhi airport was their last stop before Kolkata, and the connecting flight was scheduled to arrive shortly. This would be the last chance to limber up her muscles, so she strolled through the concourse.

An overhead television caught her eye. A scene of carnage was broadcast with images dominated by pulsing lights and flashes of maimed and bloody bodies. Although she couldn't understand the language, the crawler was in English. The words revealed that a bomber blew himself up and killed a number of others in a café. Finally, the dateline announced the location as Cairo, Egypt.

Alana felt light-headed, stumbled backward, and caught herself on a row of seats. She eagerly sought more details, but the rolling script taunted her. Details were endlessly repeated, and precious new information was sparingly doled out. Eric couldn't have been anywhere near the blast. It had occurred at dawn in a popular diner. When the camera panned toward the sunrise, she could see the illuminated Hilton logo flickering through the smoke. Eric was staying at the Marriott. Alana finally inhaled. She convinced herself that he was safe. Besides, with his jet lag, the only place he would be at dawn was in bed.

The script was relentless. The Muslim Brotherhood, an offshoot of al Qaeda, claimed responsibility. Alana reached up and pressed the channel selector until she found FOX News, gratefully in English. Predictably, they were reporting the same incident. The iterations marched across the screen: thirteen fatalities and twenty-four serious injuries. Conflicting reports noted one, possibly two, bombers were involved. The scene was horrible, with body parts everywhere.

She'd had enough. Alana returned to the waiting area and sat next to the dozing Dr. Larson. She whispered, "Dr. Larson?"

He stirred and sleepily asked, "Huh? What?"

"I'm sorry to wake you, but I need to tell you about something. There's been a bombing in Cairo."

"Cairo, Egypt?"

"Yes. It happened near the Hilton hotel. You know the city—is that anywhere near the Marriott, where Eric is staying?"

Dr. Larson hesitated. Alana could tell he was mentally reconstructing the area. "I think it's a couple of blocks away."

"Do you suppose we could call the lab in a little while? Just to be sure Eric is safe?"

"Absolutely. I will be happy to do so. They won't be open until after we're in flight, so I'll have our home office make the contact for me."

"Thank you, Dr. Larson." Alana would be so relieved to get a definitive answer. She could see the monitor in the distance. The story continued to dominate the broadcast. "What is wrong with those people?" she asked rhetorically. "I just don't understand the Muslim mentality. They'll blow up their own people, women, children. It doesn't matter. Anything can be sacrificed for their warped agenda."

"I think I can understand their plight," Dr. Larson said. "After years of refugee camps, poverty, oppression, and religious persecution, the despair becomes too much for them."

Alana's burgeoning emotions had reached their limit. "With all due respect, Doctor, that's a bunch of psychobabble," she fumed.

Dr. Larson raised his eyebrows but said nothing.

"This incident occurred in Cairo. If there are any refugees there, it's the Christians. Next door in Sudan, Christian women and their children are sold into slavery after their husband's skin is filleted while they're forced to watch. There are hundreds of thousands of orphaned Christian children in slavery."

"Surely that is an extreme situation," Dr. Larson said, "not the responsibility of every Muslim."

Alana continued, "I sat in the audience and heard Dr. Ravi Zacharias recount a personal conversation he had with the head Islamic imam at the University of Bethlehem, who was bemoaning the bad rap his religion receives due to a 'few' misguided terrorists. Ravi asked him a direct question. 'Sir,' he said, 'if your daughter converted to Christianity, what would be your response?' Without hesitation, the imam replied, 'I would kill her.'

"Ravi responded, 'That is why Islam is a violent religion at its very core.

You cannot enforce compulsive religion to this degree and then expect the civilized world to accept a peaceful façade.'"

Dr. Larson sat silently for a moment.

"I'm not making this up," Alana said softly.

"You know, I hadn't really given it much thought," Dr. Larson said, "but I've been unsettled by this whole issue. Something hasn't been ringing true, but I didn't have the time or inclination to think it through. I admit that my viewpoint has been influenced by the media spin on the subject."

Alana sighed and looked a little chagrined. "Well, I'll get off my soapbox now. I'm sorry to get so worked up, but it hits close to home with my brother on active duty in Iraq, and now Eric being in Cairo when this incident erupts."

"I didn't know you had a brother in the military. What does he do?"

"He's a lieutenant commander with the SEALs," she replied. She tried to downplay it, but she always swelled with pride when telling people about her big brother.

Larson excused himself, and Alana opened her laptop to check her e-mail. She noticed her message to Eric had uploaded when they first landed in Delhi two hours ago. That should have given Eric more than enough time to reply. She checked her in-box, but it was empty. She slumped in disappointment, anxious to see if he picked up on her use of the L word. Now she second-guessed herself. *Maybe I scared him off and he doesn't know how to respond. I shouldn't have been so forward.*

She felt her face flush, momentarily fearful that she had expressed love only to have it unrequited. If there is a reasonable explanation for Eric's silence, she could not come up with one. Maybe she should send a follow-up e-mail and be more casual. No—she didn't want to smother him. She vacillated between options that would balance her embarrassment and dignity but found no apparent resolution. Unless...her eyes lifted to the carnage on the television screen once again.

Cairo, Egypt

The emergency room was in pandemonium. Medical staff shouted urgent commands throughout the facility. Tempers flared at the least provocation. Unimaginable pain elicited piercing screams from victims. The anguished cries of loved ones punctuated the din.

Bloody stretchers crowded into every available space. Nurses cycled between them as best they could, checking the condition of all patients—and to confirm whether they still were patients. If not, their heads were solemnly covered with sheets. In spite of valiant triage efforts, the number of covered heads steadily increased in a Dantesque scene.

Eric lay mercifully unconscious outside one of the viewing rooms, awaiting his rotation to the surgical suite. The IV bag supplied vital fluid to his body but seemed to be losing the race with the blood that saturated his bedding. Towels had been wedged beneath his arms as a dike against the flow.

An orderly with a clipboard in hand approached Eric's gurney. He consulted his notes one last time, placed his pencil between his teeth, and laid his clipboard at Eric's feet. He hunched his shoulders and leaned into the gurney, guiding his load through the maze of stretchers. The double doors clapped loudly behind him.

Y

Delhi, India

Although the flight to Kolkata would be mercifully short, cabin fever threatened to overwhelm Alana. She needed a distraction and decided to probe Dr. Larson. "I was fascinated by the recent updates on the Genographic Project Web site, particularly the information about the patterns that are emerging from our data."

"It is indeed fascinating," he agreed. "We're rewriting anthropology through our efforts."

Hamdi said the same thing, Alana thought.

Dr. Larson continued, "It starts with the earliest DNA markers. Africa appears to be ground zero, so to speak, since there are a number of unique markers found only in Africa. Then something interesting happened. A migration of worldwide proportions began from one man whose offspring left Africa for unknown reasons. Maybe they were obsessed with wanderlust. Or they may have been following scarce game. Regardless of the reason, virtually all non-African men in the world trace their lineage back to this individual.

"The first migration out of Africa seems to have occurred about fifty thousand years ago and surprisingly left isolated DNA markers in Australia. The big mystery is how the earliest wanderers made it to such an isolated place without leaving a swath of DNA markers across the region."

"Ocean travel?" Alana offered.

"There is no archaeological evidence to suggest boat-making skills had developed at this time, so how would this hunting and gathering band cross the hundreds of miles of ocean to populate Australia? In contrast, if the migration was land based, the challenges of the terrain would seem to stretch the pace of travel over many centuries. If that were the case, we would expect to see large populations of descendants across the region—which we don't. It has been a conundrum.

"This is where our research project is unique. We combine many scientific disciplines to arrive at plausible theories. Here's what we have concluded: the earliest archaeological data in Australia allows us to establish an approximate date of the first arrivals.

"From paleontology we know this was during an ice age when the sea levels would have been low, as much as one hundred meters lower. We have reliable undersea data that our parent corporation has mapped—one of their specialties, as you know—that illustrate the terrain of that era. You may have noticed this map on our Web site. It reveals interesting possibilities. First, the terrain—to say nothing of the shortened distance—is less formidable. The continental shelf around Africa, Saudi Arabia, India, Indonesia, and Australia was exposed during that era. And the region of open ocean through Indonesia would have been a narrow strait of less than thirty miles. The migration was most likely along the shoreline that was later submerged when the water levels rose again. This would explain why archaeology has never found evidence of this migration."

He continued enthusiastically. "The next logical step was to search for any of the Australian aborigine DNA markers that might have been left behind by their ancestors along the assumed route of migration. If we could succeed in finding evidence, it would strengthen the theory. And we accomplished just that!" He waved his arms with the flourish of a magician. "We found one individual in India who carries a marker that is otherwise found only in Aborigines. That is the reason for our new lab in Kolkata and this collection safari. We want to collect many more samples in India to see if we can find a statistically significant sampling that will support the theory."

"*Mmm,*" Alana murmured. "Isn't it possible that the individual with that marker is a descendant of a person who traveled back to India centuries after the migration to Australia?"

Dr. Larson nodded. "If that's the case, then we probably won't find many more of this particular marker. However, if we find quite a few of the markers spread across the region, it might show a pattern consistent with a migratory band that occasionally left descendants behind."

"I can see how easy it would be to misinterpret the data," Alana interjected. "There could be many reasons for the appearance of a marker that is otherwise only found in a different geographic region. It may not imply a migratory pattern at all. A lone individual could theoretically leave random markers in a region far from home, and that would be seen as an anomaly."

"Precisely. There are many variables, so we look at distribution maps that are compiled from our sampling to see if there is a significant percentage of a particular haplotype in any given region. If the percentage falls below a particular threshold, we assume it is due to a random event and not representative of a migratory pattern.

"A common anomaly in the data is attributed to our warlike nature. Invading armies historically have considered rape one of the spoils of war. There have certainly been many markers left behind due to this unseemly side of human nature. Although it is distasteful to think about, as scientists, we have to acknowledge this."

"It sounds like we have a challenge to make sense out of the data," Alana commented.

"Indeed, it is daunting. I am thankful for IBM's participation in our project. Their computers ease the burden of data analysis."

"Can I ask another question?" Alana asked. "You said earlier that the earliest man came from Africa. Is it possible that the earliest man came from the Middle East, and some of his descendants migrated into Africa?"

Dr. Larson thought about this for a moment. "Theoretically, yes. Why do you ask?"

"I'm curious. Can you tell me what you are basing your African origin theory on?"

"As I said earlier, we incorporate many scientific disciplines in formulating our theories. In this case, the evidence comes from anthropological and paleontological research," he replied. "Drs. Louis and Mary Leaky spent their careers searching for hominid fossils in the Olduvai Gorge in Tanzania, eastern Africa. They found a number of convincing early hominids that were certainly the ancestors of Homo sapiens. Therefore, we assume the earliest man evolved in this region. I suppose you're going to take issue with that conclusion?"

Alana's smile was disarming. "Well, I promise to not get preachy. All I ask is that we keep an open mind. If that is the only reason you place the origin of man in Africa, there may be another way of looking at the data. What if the Leakys' fossils were merely genetic dead ends and not related to the later appearance of humans? After all, it was only a couple of years ago that evolution charts listed Neanderthals as our ancestors, right?"

"Your point is well taken," Dr. Larson replied. "You are alluding to the recent extraction of DNA from Neanderthals?"

"Yes," Alana responded. "At last count, I believe we're up to eleven Neanderthals who have yielded viable DNA. The research articles are conclusive: there is absolutely no genetic link between the two species. Humans are a species distinctively unique from Neanderthal."

"I read a couple of those reports," Dr. Larson replied. "By the way, our genographic research has validated that conclusion. We have taken countless DNA samples from Western Europe all the way to China—the region once populated by Neanderthals. We have never found a sample that carries evidence of Neanderthal DNA. So we can draw two conclusions: the species did not descend from a common ancestor, and they did not interbreed either."

Alana grimaced. "I'm sure the evolutionists will offer their pat answer."

"And that is?"

"When they don't like the data, they just push the date of convergence further back in time. It's a typical evolutionary *post hoc, ergo propter hoc* conclusion."

Dr. Larson mused. "The tendency to confuse coincidence with causality."

"Yes. All hominids look similar, ergo they must share a common ancestor. My point is that their deductive logic may be fallacious." He had given her an opening, and she took it. "For years I sat in classrooms and heard authoritative pronouncements of one evolutionary 'fact' after another, facts that later were proven to be fraudulent, misclassifications of fossils, or errors in dating techniques. The conclusions were driven more by wishful thinking than scientific inquiry. The minions in the news and entertainment media were only too anxious to propagate each new fanciful idea—especially if it poked a finger in the eye of creationism."

"That sounds a bit conspiratorial," Dr. Larson cautioned.

"There are too many examples to recount, but here's a glaring one," she offered. "I was flipping channels the other night and paused on the opening scene of *X2: X-Men United*, a very popular movie. In the opening scene, Halle Berry's character led a tour of middle schoolers past a museum display of Neanderthals. She taught her students that Neanderthals mated with Cro-Magnons and produced Homo sapiens. Very persuasive in a culture war in which our celebrity-crazed society salivates over pronouncements from best actresses—and is too lazy or distracted to pursue truth.

"Anyway, back to my earlier point. If the Neanderthals were a genetic dead end, then maybe the other hominids were as well. Unless we can extract DNA from the older hominid fossils, the data is up for a variety of interpretations, isn't it?"

"I suppose," he replied. "You know, that idea is more realistic than we would have thought just a few years ago. The progress with the Neanderthal DNA was considered impossible a decade ago. Even more astounding is what a paleontologist at North Carolina State recently accomplished. She found organic matter in the femur of a T. rex."

Alana was stunned. "Dinosaurs died out fifty million years ago. How could organic matter survive fossilization?"

"It's an extraordinary story. The T. rex fossil was at a very remote site inaccessible by land vehicle. Although the fossil was intact *in situ*, it was so large they had to break the femur in order to lift it out by helicopter. Normally it would have been scandalous to intentionally break a fossilized bone. No one expected to find anything of interest inside fossilized bones, so no one even looked. In this case, the thickness of the bone shielded the interior from mineralization, and the organic matter in the marrow was still viable. I'm sure we will be reading a lot about it in the years ahead. Maybe *Jurassic Park* will prove to be prophetic—just like your Bible." Dr. Larson winked.

Alana laughed. "Very funny." She considered the ramifications. "If organic material can be pulled from a T. rex, wouldn't it be incredible if the same could eventually be done with those early hominids? I'll make a prediction. If that ever comes to pass, I bet the evidence will come down on the side of the Creation model, not evolution's. After all, whenever there's been a seeming debate between science and the Bible, new evidence eventually exonerates the Bible. It's just a matter of time."

"Well, if that were the case"—he paused—"we'd turn evolution on its ear because the one variable evolutionists count on is time."

"Exactly."

TWELVE

Thursday, August 18, 2005
13 Rajab, 1426 AH
Cairo, Egypt

THE NURSE BLOTTED ERIC'S FACE AND FOREHEAD WITH A COOL, damp sponge. His fever had broken, and he was showing the first signs of rousing since coming from surgery eighteen hours ago.

As she placed the call button in his right hand in case he awakened, she wondered about this young man. His clothing appeared to be American. His wallet contained a picture ID that identified him as Eric Colburn, but the company name merely showed NGS surrounded by a yellow rectangle, and hospital authorities had not been able to determine what that meant. There had been no other identification. They had notified the American embassy with all the information available, assuming he really was American. Hopefully the mystery would be solved soon so they could notify his family. The nurse checked his IV and catheter bags once more before returning to her station.

Had she looked back one last time, she might have noticed his leg twitch. Then his eyelids fluttered.

Kolkata, India

"Dr. Larson speaking." He held his cell phone tightly to his ear because the signal was weak. He turned back and forth in the elevator to see if he could improve the signal strength.

"…is…qami callin…rom…iro la…offic…uld call you…cause Mr.… unavail…"

"I'm sorry; you're breaking up. Hold on—I need to exit the elevator. OK, can you hear me now?" It was a hackneyed phrase, but still the most effective.

"I said, this is Satam Suqami calling from the Cairo lab. Your office said I should call you directly."

"OK, go ahead, Satam. What can I do for you?"

"I was told you wanted a report on Mr. Colburn. I regret to inform you that he did not come into the lab yesterday or today. I knew he had not left for the States because his laptop computer is still set up in the server room. He left it running a diagnostics routine on Tuesday."

An uneasy alarm gripped Dr. Larson. "Eric was staying at the Marriott. Have you called them to check his room?"

"Yes, sir," he replied. "They said that his bed had been slept in, but he must have left the hotel early. No one remembers seeing him. His suitcase and personal items are still open in the room, so he couldn't have intended to check out."

Dr. Larson shifted into crisis management mode, issuing staccato commands. "Satam, here's what I want you to do: Call the local hospitals and find out which ones are treating the victims of this morning's bombing attack. Describe Eric to them, and see if you can find out any details. Be prepared to go to the morgue and identify his body. Call me as soon as you know anything. Do it now!"

"Yes, sir," Satam curtly replied.

In spite of the grueling flight, Alana was too distraught to rest. She had checked into her hotel room, plugged in her laptop, and checked her e-mail before unpacking. Still no reply from Eric. Her bedside phone rang. "Hello?"

"Alana, this is Dr. Larson. Are you presentable?"

"Yes, Dr. Larson. Why?"

"I need to come down and see you about a couple of matters, but I'm waiting for a return phone call. I just wanted to alert you to expect me. I'll be down in a few minutes."

"That will be fine."

Twenty minutes later, Alana heard a soft knock at the door. Checking the peephole, she saw an egg-shaped Dr. Larson. She opened the door, beckoned him in, and sat on the side of her bed. He planted himself directly in front of her.

"Alana, there's…no easy way to…to…to say this," he stammered. "Eric is missing."

Alana's hand flew to her mouth. "What are you talking about?" she asked tearfully.

Dr. Larson was too slow to respond. She noticed his eyes cutting over her shoulder to the television in her room. The bombing was still the headline story. His eyes locked on hers, and he remained silent a moment too long.

Alana turned her head and stared at the offending telecast. She cried out in anguish as her worst fears were realized.

"Alana—wait. Don't jump to any conclusions. I would have come earlier, but I was waiting for a return call. We should have some news shortly."

Suddenly Alana slid off the bed to her knees. She looked up at him, tears streaming. "Would you pray with me?"

He nodded and awkwardly got to his knees. She remembered his arthritic hip once it was too late and wished she'd encouraged him to remain standing. His pained expression changed to one of expectation. She suspected he wasn't acquainted with the protocol beyond bowing his head.

Alana prayed softly. "Heavenly Father, You know my heart is heavy. I beseech You, Lord: keep my love safe. Send Your angels to protect him. Lord, I trust Your wisdom and will draw upon Your strength no matter the outcome. Give me peace of heart and the strength to endure this." In order to allay any pressure for Dr. Larson, she concluded with "Amen."

She was surprised to see Dr. Larson surreptitiously wipe moisture from his eyes. Alana acted as if she had not noticed while he struggled to his feet. When his cell rang, he answered before the first ring ended. "Satam?" he yelled. He grimaced, nodded, and said, "OK. Get to the hospital *now*. Call me as soon as you confirm anything."

He pressed the end button and looked at Alana. "That was Satam, one of our technicians in Cairo. He called me earlier to tell me that Eric was missing. I had him call the hospitals that received victims of this morning's bombing, just in case. Only one of them has any survivors, so he's heading there now. He's confirmed that as of this afternoon—their time—there were three surviving foreigners, two of whom are men. We should hear something shortly." Dr. Larson paused. "I think I should leave you alone. I'll call you as soon as I hear anything."

Alana merely nodded her assent.

The door latched loudly as he departed.

Cairo, Egypt

The nurse looked up from her paperwork and glanced at the patient board. The call light from room 312 was brightly lit. She hadn't expected that signal for quite some time yet. Maybe the patient rolled on top of the call button. She decided to finish her paperwork before checking.

The elevator doors opened, and a gurney with swinging IV bags bumped over the threshold. An orderly pushed it to the nurses' station, and she glanced down at the heavily bandaged little girl who seemed lost in the bed sheets and medical paraphernalia. She smiled at the one eye that emerged from the gauze. "Hi, honey," she said soothingly. "We have your room all ready for you." With that, she helped the orderly guide the gurney down the hall. She completely forgot about the call from room 312.

Y

Eric could not get oriented. He had awakened a number of times and tried to focus, but his surroundings seemed surreal. Before he could put any cogent thoughts together, the sedatives and painkillers would overtake him, and he would slip away again. Disjointed images flashed through his fitful slumber. He dozed erratically for quite a while.

During a brief moment of lucidity, he realized he was in a hospital bed. A round object in his hand must be for the drawstring on the window shade. He was asleep again before he could raise the shade. He woke up awhile later and corrected himself. He now thought it was some sort of remote control.

When he roused again, he couldn't remember if he'd depressed the button or not, so he pressed it as firmly as he could. A sliver of pain pierced his arm and shoulder. He cried out pitifully and drifted off again.

Images continued to flash through his mind. He couldn't differentiate between those dredged from his subconscious and those from his flickering eyelids. A boat on the seashore. His mom tucking him into bed. Alana backlit by the sun. A full moon breaking through clouds. Satam standing beside his bed. His graduation certificate being handed to him. The staccato images marched on.

Y

Kolkata, India

Time seemed to slow down for Alana. She flipped channels in a daze, looking for updates on the news channels. In the distance, she heard a muffled cell phone ringing. The sound seemed to emanate from the hallway.

A short while later, there was another knock on the door. She opened it to see Dr. Larson with a broad smile on his face! He was just flipping his cell phone closed. She stepped back, not daring to breathe.

"He's alive!" Dr. Larson thrust his fist in a victory gesture, which seemed slightly out of character. "Eric was in the diner when the bomb exploded. He's in recovery in one of the hospitals." Dr. Larson's voice caught as an emotional shudder swept over him. "My lab assistant went to his room to confirm. He tells me that everything is intact, but he's lost a lot of blood. The nurse told him that Eric's injuries were limited to his back and buttocks. He evidently had his back to a window as the bomb ignited, and shards of glass flew into him. They've all been removed, and he's had a few stitches, but otherwise, he will be OK. He may have difficulty sitting down for a while though."

Alana laughed with the wave of relief that rippled through her. She was light-headed and closed her eyes to regain her equilibrium. "Thank You, Lord!" she whispered. Then she opened her eyes and smiled brightly. "That is such a blessing! Thank you so much for finding out so quickly. I wouldn't have been able to sleep." She paused, reflecting on the familiar ring tone of the cell phone she'd heard outside her door. "Was that your cell phone ringing in the hall?"

"Yes, it was. I didn't want to be too far away when we received the news."

"But you didn't have to wait out in the hallway. That was so considerate of you. Thank you."

"It was nothing," he said. "You needed time to be alone. Now you can get a good night's sleep. I'll call you in the morning, and we'll have breakfast in the hotel before heading to the collection site. There are some supplies we need to purchase, especially bottled water. You don't want to drink the water in the places we'll be visiting." He grimaced. "Good night."

"Good night, and thank you again, Doctor." As he left, Alana collapsed on the bed. She tucked a pillow to her stomach and wrapped herself around it. She lay in a fetal position and was in the midst of a prayer of thanksgiving and praise when she drifted off to sleep. Her spirit was willing, but her flesh was weak.

THIRTEEN

Friday, August 19, 2005
14 Rajab, 1426 AH
Cairo, Egypt

A SLIGHT CREASE IN A SLAT INTERRUPTED THE PERFECT SYMMETRY of the miniblinds. The morning sun was low in the sky and a ray of sunlight found its way through the gap. It steadily crept across the room as the minutes advanced. Ascending the side of the hospital bed, it traced a path across the mattress and eventually found its way to Eric's face. In his dream, the world was suddenly bathed in a brilliant red glow. He opened his eyes and recoiled from the intensity of the assaulting beam.

Eric was fully awake now and tried to sit up in an unfamiliar bed. Bad idea. Needles of pain stabbed across his back and butt. He moved gingerly and propped himself up with pillows.

He sat motionless for a few moments, puzzling over his predicament. Recent events were jumbled and wouldn't fit into a coherent picture; clarity was elusive. Eric frowned at the device lying in the disheveled bedding. When recognition dawned on him, he grasped it and depressed the button, which evoked a painful pulling sensation in his shoulder.

A number of minutes passed. Finally, a nurse briskly entered the room. "Hi, sleepyhead!" she said in a cheerful but thick British accent. She approached the bed and disengaged a bed rail. She flicked the drip chamber of an IV bag and leaned forward to note the urine level on the catheter bag. "Did you have a nice nap?" she asked.

"I don't think so," Eric stammered. "Where am I?"

"Abo al-Reesh Student Hospital in Cairo," she replied. "You were brought here after the explosion."

"Explosion?" Eric exclaimed. "Is that what happened?"

"You don't remember?"

"Not really. Details are missing, but some are starting to come back to me."

"There was a terrorist bombing in a local café. You were found in the rubble and brought here. You're one of the lucky ones." She picked up his chart that hung from the footboard. "You only had an ID badge on you. All we know is that you are Eric Colburn. You are American, yes?" She flipped pages on the clipboard.

"That's right. I work for the National Geographic Society."

"Ah—that is the meaning of the yellow rectangle. We notified your embassy, but they hadn't discovered anything yet. I will confirm with them that you are American and let them know that you're awake now."

"Thanks." Eric closed his eyes and attempted to reconstruct the events. So many conflicting images collided in his head, some real and some he hoped were not. "I remember sitting at a table in a diner."

"Is that all you remember?" she asked.

"I dreamed that two men rose into the air. I'm starting to think it wasn't a dream after all. Was anyone killed in the bombing?"

"A dozen or so died at the scene, and another ten have died of their wounds in the hospital. Some will be better off if they don't live. You were very fortunate. You had glass fragments in your back and bum. We got them out, and you're healing nicely. We'll remove the IV after the doctor's seen you. And now that you're conscious, we'll take the catheter out as well. You should be out of here by this time tomorrow."

"That's good. It seems like I have someplace I need to be, but I can't remember where." Eric yawned mightily.

The nurse fluffed his pillows. "Why don't you try to get some rest? Your body is healing and needs more rest than normal. And it looks like you're a little loopy from the painkillers."

"Can we stop the meds?" he asked. "I need to clear my head, and I think I can handle the pain."

"I'll check the chart." She turned to leave. "I forgot to mention it—your personal effects are in the cabinet beneath the window. Your clothes were cut off in surgery, but anything salvageable was put in a plastic bag. Your tennis shoes are about the only thing you can still use. I'll be back to check on you later. Do you want the lights on or off?"

"Off, please. I think I'll rest until the doctor comes in."

"Oh—one more thing. The police want to take your statement about the bombing. They've taken statements from all the other surviving victims, and you're the last. We were supposed to notify them when you woke up. I'll try to put them off as long as I can so you can nap. If you'd like, I'll ask the embassy to send a staff member to assist you during the interview. The bobbies here are a bit rough around the edges. More like an inquisition, if you take my meaning."

"That would be nice. Thanks." Eric rested his head on the pillows and tried to sleep. His mind raced as new memories emerged from the mist. Many details were still disjointed, but he was confident that he'd sort everything out as soon as the drugs wore off.

Kolkata, India

Alana awakened and rolled on her back, staring vacantly at the ceiling. She reminisced about everything that had happened over the past couple of days, and the relief warmed her. She had been so afraid yesterday. It was difficult to comprehend how close she had come to losing Eric. Forever. She had never lost anyone close to her and wasn't prepared to deal with it.

"Thank You, Lord, for sparing me—and more importantly—for protecting Eric." She got up and realized she had slept in her clothes. With the travel time and a night of sleep, she'd been in the same clothes for over two days. A shower would be wonderful. The bedside phone rang. What now? "Hello?"

"Dr. Larson here. Good morning, Alana. I trust you rested well?"

"Yes! As soon as I shower, I'll be anxious to get started."

"Excellent. Dress light. It will be a hot and humid day. I'll meet you in the dining room in an hour."

"I'll be there."

Alana savored her first sip of coffee. It was rich and carried a hint of chicory. "I needed this!" she exclaimed. They were seated in the shade of a beautiful tree that took up a large part of the courtyard behind the main dining room. A pleasant breeze carried a floral scent. Alana gazed up at the intricate lattice of limbs and root runners. "This tree is amazing. What kind is it?"

"It is a banyan, a type of fig tree. You see the formations that support the outstretched limbs? As the tree grows, it drops new root structures from the limbs. They thicken and provide support for the growing limbs. The largest banyan in the world is in Pune, India, about seven hundred kilometers southwest of here. The tree measures eight hundred meters around its perimeter. I saw it last year when I was on a safari."

"That's amazing." She took another sip. "Where are we going today?"

"We're in the West Bengal province for the next few days. Then we'll be going east into Bangladesh for the remainder of our safari. The coastline turns southward from that point and is the gateway to Indonesia. If our theory is right, the early Aborigines would have traveled that route on their way to Australia." He raised an eyebrow. "I hope you're remembering to take your antimalaria meds."

"Absolutely," Alana assured him.

"While I'm thinking about it, I need to go over a couple of ground rules. Do not stray from our camp, and be aware of your surroundings at all times. We will have armed guards as part of our team. Be sure one is always within sight. There are wild beasts you don't want to encounter, and some may be of the human variety."

Alana's stomach clenched involuntarily.

FOURTEEN

Friday, August 19, 2005
14 Rajab, 1426 AH
Cairo, Egypt

ERIC'S VARIOUS TUBES HAD BEEN REMOVED, AND HE WAS BEGINNING to feel normal again. He rose from the bed and gingerly edged to the window. The sun had set over Cairo hours ago, and the night lights illumined the city. A throat cleared conspicuously, and he turned self-consciously, groping with one hand to confirm his hospital smock was securely tied.

A young woman leaned against the door frame, grinning mischievously. "That's OK. I didn't see anything—except the bandages on your butt." She walked toward him with her hand extended.

Her brown eyes met his, and he instantly felt safer. Soft auburn hair framed her face, trimmed neatly at the chin. An olive green belted dress gave her an all-business look.

"I should introduce myself," she said. "I'm Melanie Wagner. I'm with the State Department and am here for support. The police are down at the nurses' station and would like to ask you some questions. I want to emphasize that you are not a suspect. It has been difficult to obtain accurate details from the other survivors, so they are anxious to speak with you. Before they come in, is there anything you would like to tell me?"

"Yes," Eric replied. "Can you get in touch with my company and let them know where I am? I wish I could talk to my girlfriend to let her know I'm OK. I think she's somewhere in India or Bangladesh."

"We've already been in touch with National Geographic. They evidently discovered where you were and officially requested the State Department look after you. They also wired funds for you." She handed him a folder and a paper bag. "The bag has a change of clothes donated by one of the embassy staff. They should be a reasonable fit. The money is in the folder along with a plane ticket home. The reservation is for Monday night, if you're up for it. If not, it can be changed." She waited while Eric examined the contents. "Is there anything else before the police question you?"

"Yes, but I don't know where to begin." Eric gingerly sat on the edge of his bed and motioned for Melanie to sit in the guest chair.

"I can't shake the feeling that I might have been one of the targets for the bombing," he said.

Eric detected a flicker of disbelief in Melanie's eyes. "Mr. Colburn, this city is full of intrigue, and our citizens often claim they've been followed or have stumbled on something suspicious. It usually amounts to nothing."

"Let me explain," Eric said. "There's something not right at our computer lab here in Cairo. Unauthorized files are being created and consuming our resources. I had a creepy feeling about some of the staff, like they were hiding something. Then when I went out for some coffee—and I know this sounds paranoid—I *was* being followed. The most alarming thing is, I was meeting a former lab employee at the scene of the explosion. He gave me evidence that had been collected by another worker who disappeared months ago. His name was Hamdi Tantawi, an old friend of mine. He wrote me right before he disappeared and mentioned that his co-workers had threatened him. His disappearance has to be connected with the evidence he collected."

"Where is this evidence?" she asked.

"It isn't with my things. It must have been lost in the explosion."

"Or it was stolen from the scene," Melanie offered.

"I guess that's possible. You know, I saw the bomber. He actually hugged the guy I had met with. He embraced him just as the bomb went off. So if he was a target, maybe I was too."

Melanie frowned. "You could be right. The media represent these bombings as random events, but we know they often have specific targets in mind. Nothing these terrorists do is random. In my official capacity, I can't recommend this, but off the record, I wouldn't tell police about having met with the primary target. They may detain you, and based upon what you've told me, it may not be safe for you to remain in Cairo."

"OK. Let's get this over with."

Melanie went to the nurses' station and returned with the police. She made the introductions, and Eric proceeded to tell them a slightly incomplete version of his story. The police probed, sometimes asking him the same questions a second or third time. Finally, the interrogation was winding down. The primary inquisitor closed his notebook and asked Eric if he was going to be staying in Cairo in the event they needed to ask him any more questions.

"Well, I have a ticket back to the States in four days. I fly out on Monday night."

The officer looked at him curiously. "My English not very well, but that is not four day; it is three."

Now it was Eric's turn to look confused. "Today is Thursday, isn't it?"

"No, it is *yom al-jama'a, fourteen Rajab, fourteen twenty-six AH,* which are nineteen of August in your calendar." He glanced at his watch and corrected himself. "Correction, it past midnight, so already *yom as-sabt.*"

"That means Saturday," Melanie interjected.

"But the bombing was this morning," Eric protested.

"No, Thursday morning," the officer said. "You unconscious for more than a day. We have wait two day to speak to you."

Eric cut his eyes to Melanie, who nodded her affirmation.

"You rest now," the officer said. "Here my card if you think of anything more. *Ma'a salama.*" With that, he and his partner got up and left Eric's room.

They had just turned toward the elevator when Eric sat forward abruptly and called out to them. "Officers! I just remembered something else."

They turned back and reentered the room. "Yes, Mr. Colburn?"

"I just remembered that the bomber shouted something right before he ignited the bomb. It sounded like '*Allah akar.*' I've heard that phrase twice since I've been here. What does it mean?"

The officer opened his notebook and jotted an entry. The scratching of his pencil accentuated the anticipation of his response. The point of focus seemed to be the stub of the eraser that bobbed erratically. He finished scribbling and snapped the notebook shut for emphasis. His eyes bore into Eric's as if he were unworthy to hear the translation.

"*Allāhu akbar* means 'God is greater,' Mr. Colburn. God is greater than the false gods." He turned and left the room.

Eric was stunned. He absently fingered the bandage that secured the IV port to his wrist and asked Melanie, "What time is it exactly?"

"About twelve-fifteen. Why? Do you have a hot date?"

"No. Remember I told you that something's not right at our lab? Well, I left my laptop with a monitoring utility in place. I think someone hacks into our server at about one o'clock every Saturday morning, and I planned to be there to monitor it. I thought I had another day." I need to be there in the next half hour. His eyes darted around the room. "Can I ask you a favor?"

"Certainly," she replied.

"I don't suppose I could get you to take me to the lab, could I?" he asked.

"But you haven't been released by the doctor yet, have you?" She protested.

"No, but I can't wait for that. I have to go now. I'm off antibiotics, and I can heal on the move as well as here in a hospital bed."

"There's no one on duty staff this late for me to ask permission. I may catch flack from my boss tomorrow."

"But you'll do it?"

She hesitated a beat before saying yes.

Eric rummaged through the bag Melanie had given him and pulled out the clothes. Melanie discreetly turned her back as he peeled off the hospital smock and groaned in pain. He pulled the loaned shirt over his head, then stood up and stepped into the pants. "You can turn around now," he said as he finished dressing.

"I don't want any flack from the nurses," Eric continued. "You go ahead of me and ring for the elevator. I'll watch from here. When the elevator comes, press the hold button until you see me approaching, then release it. If we time it right, I'll slip in just as the doors are closing."

As planned, Eric slipped through the elevator doors without drawing attention to himself. He reached up and unscrewed the ceiling light. It flickered and died. "I want to check out the lobby without being on display," he explained. The elevator thudded to a stop, a muted chime signaling their arrival on the ground floor. Light intruded across the threshold as the doors slid open, but the elevator remained in shadow.

Eric scanned the area and saw something that made him pause. He abruptly backed into the shadows, bumping into Melanie, who was following closely. "What's wrong?" she asked.

"We have a problem." Eric gestured toward the entrance. "See the two men over there?"

"Yes," Melanie whispered.

"They were watching me from the mosque the other day. This isn't a coincidence. There's no way I can get through the main entrance without them seeing me." Eric thought for a moment. "Can you drive your car around to the back of the hospital? There has to be a loading dock for receiving supplies. If you park near it, I'll find you. Just act casual—they have no reason to be suspicious of you."

"OK. I'll be waiting." As Melanie exited the elevator, the doors began to close, so Eric pressed the "door open" button. The doors retracted, accompanied by a warning buzzer. Melanie initially turned toward the sound, then hesitantly continued toward the exit.

One of the Arabs rose from his seat and gazed toward the elevator with a puzzled expression. He shifted his gaze to Melanie, who made momentary eye contact. He strode past her and approached the elevator bank.

Eric quickly pressed the second-floor button. As the doors slithered together, his last sight was of the Arab abruptly stopping midstride, glancing curiously over his shoulder at Melanie. Then he turned around. Eric frantically stabbed the "door open" button. The elevator lurched in stubborn refusal and began its upward journey. There was nothing he could do to warn Melanie.

Y

Melanie pressed her key fob when she was two paces from her car. She scrambled into the car and started the engine before risking a look over her shoulder. The Arab she'd seen in the lobby was sprinting toward her. She put the car in gear, automatically activating the door locks just as her pursuer yanked the latch. It held. She jerked the wheel to the right, pulled out of the parking slot, and stole a glance at the mirror. The Arab was shouting into a cell phone and gesturing emphatically.

Y

The doors slid open on the second floor. Eric rapidly pressed the buttons for the fourth and fifth floors, then the close button. He slipped through as the doors reversed themselves. He hoped the main display in the lobby would not betray his location. The empty elevator proceeded toward the destinations he'd programmed.

Eric skirted the nurses' station and scurried through a maze of hallways until he found a vantage point with a window. He looked down on a parking area and emergency room entrance but saw no loading dock. He continued down a number of passageways and found another window. This time, he saw several dock doors on a small wing protruding from the hospital. He searched for a fire escape. There was none. Mentally he triangulated where the loading wing would intersect the main building and searched for an accessible window above it. A door sandwiched between two patient rooms boasted a placard with unintelligible Arabic symbols. The Coke icon beneath them didn't need translation, however. Eric opened the door to what appeared to be a staff lounge. A weary intern was curled up on a couch along the side-wall, snoring softly. The window Eric had been looking for was set in the far wall, above a sink and grimy countertop.

Eric rushed to the sink and rose on the balls of his feet. He could make out the gravel roof over the receiving wing directly below the window. He quickly hoisted himself up on the countertop and flipped the window latch. The snoring faltered, then went silent. Eric froze. The snoring resumed. Eric pulled up on the lower pane, but it wouldn't budge; it was painted shut. Eric rummaged through a drying rack beside the sink and found a knife. He scored the paint around the window, then used the knife for leverage to loosen the warped sill. The pane shuddered open with a loud protest, then stubbornly wedged to a stop halfway up the warped frame.

"'eyh da? Shismak?"

Eric faced the rumpled intern. "Sorry, guy. No speaka da Arabica."

The intern frowned and shouted again. *"Shismak?"* With no response from Eric, he lumbered to his feet and stormed from the room.

Time to go. Eric was thankful his injuries were limited to his backside. He'd have to exit the window feet first, on his belly. He turned awkwardly and pushed his feet through the opening. As he backed out, the window frame scraped against his shoulders. Eric paused for the pain to subside, then kicked his legs and wiggled his way through the opening, letting his elbows absorb the weight of his body as he passed the point of equilibrium.

Eric scrabbled against the wall with the tips of his sneakers and fully extended his arms. It looked to be a drop of about five feet. He plummeted to the gravel but was unable to absorb the shock with his knees without planting his face in the wall. The burning impact vibrated through his feet and ankles. He backpedaled and barely avoided falling on his recent injuries.

At the roof's edge he scanned the area for Melanie. No sign of her. He found a maintenance ladder near an air-conditioning compressor and descended.

A vehicle approached. He recognized Melanie as her car crawled into the delivery bay and stepped from the shadows. The high beams flashed in recognition, and the door locks clicked a welcome. "Get in quick," she shouted.

He settled gingerly into the seat. The car abruptly accelerated, causing the door to swing shut.

"We may have company," she said. "I was followed out of the lobby but got away as one of your buddies called for reinforcements."

Eric glanced behind them as Melanie made a quick turn down an alley. He maintained the vigil as she navigated additional turns. "I don't see anyone," he said at last. He turned around in the seat. "Do you know how to get to the lab?"

"Near the Bab Zuwayla mosque?" she asked.

"Yes."

"No problem. There's no traffic at this hour. We'll be there in ten."

They parked in a wide section of the street a short distance from the lab and crept through the shadows.

Eric's ID appeared to be intact, but as he held it up to the entrance console, he wondered if it had been damaged in the explosion. The LED blinked from red to green and a soft click broke the silence. They entered the darkened building, and Eric guided Melanie through the lobby to the server room. "Keep watch for any visitors while I check my laptop," he said huskily.

Eric pressed the escape key a couple of times to clear the screen. He entered his password at the log-in and pressed enter. The system clock displayed 00:58. "We're just in time," he whispered. Then he hunched forward and peered at the display in disbelief. "Oh no! My program was aborted!"

His fingers flew over the keyboard as he tried to invoke the software before the critical moment. The processor seemed to resist his intrusion, and he muttered vehemently as he faced another log-in prompt. He frantically responded and pressed enter. He jerked his hand back a moment too late as he remembered that he should have hit tab instead of enter. He clenched his fist, awaiting the inevitable log-in failure. "Why do we make stupid mistakes at the worst times?" he muttered.

He logged in again, this time hitting tab to advance to the password prompt. With exaggerated caution, he entered the password and clicked enter.

The main menu appeared as the clock advanced to 01:01. He could see the newest GIG file had been created minutes before. He'd missed it. No telling what else they'd done to his computer. Why had he ever thought it was safe to leave it there? Eric slammed his fist on the desktop.

Melanie jumped and motioned for him to be quiet. "I hear noise from the street," she whispered.

Eric opened the firewall log and saved a copy to his local drive. He hibernated the laptop and unplugged the Ethernet cable, then hurried to the door, stuffing the computer into his backpack. He peered through a crack in the door. Something was happening in front of the lab. He motioned Melanie to the side and pushed through the door. "Quickly—follow me!" he whispered.

They scurried through the lobby and faced the lab door. Eric knew his ID was useless at this door—their only pathway to safety. No longer concerned about security, he pulled his PDA from his backpack, careful to cup his hand over the display as he turned it on. He aimed it at the security sensor and pressed a series of icons. The magnetic latch clicked. They entered the lab and quietly slid the door into the jamb just as the latch at the front door clicked. Eric held up his PDA and pressed a few more icons as he ducked below the windowsill to the lobby. The red LED on the security console blinked rapidly three times, then burned solid.

"I turned off access to the lab and engaged the magnetic lock override on the main entrance door. Once the door shuts behind them, they won't be able to open it again. They'll be trapped in the lobby, which buys us a few minutes." He crouched low and scurried into the darkened lab. "Stay low and follow me."

They inched between the gene sequencers in the second aisle. Above the humming of the lab equipment, they heard insistent sounds at the lab door behind them. Loud exclamations in Arabic punctuated the banging on the windows. The safety glass spiderwebbed but was held in place by the embedded wires.

Eric brushed past the lab coats and opened the exterior door. Melanie followed him into the night.

Melanie's car was out of the question. They would be seen entering the main street. Instead, they made their way to the nearby alley.

At the far end of the alley, a breeze carried an awful stench. Eric turned purposefully into the wind.

Melanie suppressed a gag and covered her nose in revulsion. "Where are you taking me?"

"To the only place we'll be safe. Garbage City."

FIFTEEN

Saturday, August 20, 2005
15 Rajab, 1426 AH
Kolkata, India

Alana was disgusted by the squalor. This was the most densely populated section of Kolkata and the living conditions were horrid. Some of the dwelling units wouldn't be adequate to coop the chickens that pecked furiously amid the debris littering the bare soil. A naked child splashed through a puddle of suspicious content, ignoring rats that drank greedily along the edge. Goats and sheep roamed aimlessly between the shacks and rooted through piles of rubble, indifferent to the mass of humanity.

"How could Mother Teresa minister here so many years and not be overcome with despair?" she asked Para.

Parminder Chadha had been recruited from Kolkata University to act as a translator for the safari. She was intelligent and exuded a captivating serenity. Her almond-shaped eyes were striking. Their jet-black irises seemed to float on alabaster surfaces, lending a mildly surprised expression to her dusky features. Her frequent smiles were engaging, self-consciously revealing glimpses of pearl-white teeth.

Para's English was excellent and carried the characteristic lilting of the Bengali accent so pleasant to the American ear. "Mother Teresa was a determined woman," Parminder said. "She had a faith like no one else."

"Did you know her?" Alana asked.

"Not personally. When I was a girl, she came to my school often. I was very impressed by her devotion." Para turned to address a young man who was next in the queue. She motioned for him to come forward and be seated at the table while explaining the purpose of the consent document.

He nodded and made a mark that would suffice for his signature.

Parminder interrupted her conversation with the man to inform Alana, "You may proceed. He has given consent." She turned back to the man and began questioning him about his family, noting his responses on her clipboard.

Alana passed her a bar code sticker to identify the form and affixed a twin label to a test tube. She swabbed the man's forearm with alcohol and deftly inserted the needle. When the test tube was inserted into the base, it filled quickly with a turbulent flow of blood. Parminder was impressed. "You are very gentle." She smiled. "He did not even flinch."

"My first victims would disagree, but after the first hundred, I learned a few things." Alana glanced at the line of villagers. "It looks like we have about fifty more to go. Then we can return to the hotel and a nice warm bath."

Y

Cairo, Egypt

Melanie extracted a handkerchief from her handbag and spritzed it with perfume. She pressed this firmly to her nose to mask the odors. Tucking her bag securely under her arm, she hurried to catch up to Eric. Each step was carefully planted to avoid the offal that stained her shoes and pant legs. "I've heard of this place but never ventured near it. How can people actually live here?" she asked.

"The fundamental drive to be safe is a powerful force," Eric observed. He slowed his pace as they approached the glow of a campfire flickering between the huddled silhouettes of decrepit Christian believers.

Suddenly, a pack of rotund creatures converged on them from the shadowy mounds of trash. Melanie shrieked as one pressed its moist snout into the back of her knee. The unexpected pressure caused her knee to buckle, and she almost pitched headlong into the refuse that surrounded her.

Eric caught her by the arm. "Are you OK?" More of the animals converged on them, squealing in delight. He recognized their characteristic grunting. "They're pigs!" he exclaimed. "I can't believe it. I've never seen so many in one place."

"They are a necessary inconvenience." A mellifluous voice emanated from the darkness. "The swine keep the followers of the crescent away." Whoever was speaking was fluent in English.

Eric shielded his eyes from the glow of the flames. "I can hear you, but I can't see you."

"I am a servant of the Messiah, Jesus. You are Americans?"

"Yes."

"What brings you to this place?"

"Actually, I'm looking for someone." Eric tentatively approached the fire. "A friend gave me his name. Anwar."

The man materialized from the darkness, wrapped in a soiled blanket clutched together by gnarled, scarred hands. "Ah." His smile revealed recognition. "You seek Anwar. I will take you to him. May I ask why you seek him?"

"The friend who gave me his name was killed," Eric explained. "He was assassinated in the café bombing a few days ago."

The smile faded, and the man blanched. "Come. We will go to Anwar. My name is Gamal. I am at your disposal."

They trudged through the unseemly moraine of civilization that defined Garbage City. The footing was made treacherous by the shifting shadows cast from mounds of debris that seemed to flicker in the firelight.

Eric was intrigued and asked of his host, "Do the Muslims really stay away from here?"

"Pigs have been declared *haraam*—that means forbidden—in the Quran, which is taken very seriously here. The followers of the crescent detest swine and believe that to even touch one would bar them from paradise."

Eric thought of Hamdi, who had never struck Eric as overly religious but nevertheless passed on the bacon. Islam was inseparable from the culture.

As if reading his thoughts, Gamal said, "Our country has become more fundamental over the last twenty years. Many of our people go to work in Saudi Arabia, where they are exposed to the Wahhabi sect, then return with a more fervent view of Islam. They are eager to silence detractors, especially Christians. But here we are safe."

Eric and Melanie retreated to a somber silence as they concentrated on keeping to the narrow path through the garbage. They eventually arrived at a dilapidated hut set between hills of trash.

Gamal called out a greeting, and a man appeared in the entrance. They carried on a conversation in Arabic. The man abruptly dropped to his knees in the dirt and rocked silently, tears glistening in the reflection of a distant fire. He muttered a reply to Gamal, who explained to Eric and Melanie, "This is Anwar. He says you are welcome in his home and asks that you forgive his emotion. He had not seen his friend for a number of days and had feared that he had been abducted or killed for his faith. Such a fate is common among us."

"Please tell him how sorry I am about his friend," Eric said. "I was with him when he died and was injured myself. He gave his life trying to warn me about something going on where he used to work. Does Anwar know anything about this?"

Gamal translated. They carried on a long conversation while Anwar lethargically prepared a campfire. Eventually Gamal turned back to Eric. "He claims that his friend—Farouk—was a martyr. Farouk was convicted by his faith and tried to expose a man named Ahmed and his Muslim conspirators. They accused Farouk of treachery and expelled him from the laboratory."

"The man you are speaking of is Ahmed Alomari," Eric clarified. "Would you ask Anwar if he knows what Farouk planned to expose?"

While Gamal and Anwar conferred at length, Eric dropped to his haunches and poked a stick into the fire, launching a flurry of embers that flitted upward through the smoke like butterflies sprung from a cocoon.

Finally, Gamal turned to Eric and said, "He is not certain, but Farouk had—according to Anwar—a diary that detailed what Alomari was stealing."

"I think he means a lab journal. Farouk gave it to me, but it was lost in the explosion. Would you ask him if Alomari was stealing equipment or supplies? I can't believe he could get away with that."

Another conference ensued. Anwar was very animated as he mimicked writing on one hand with the index finger of his other. Gamal replied, "Farouk told Anwar that they were not stealing machinery. I am having a difficult time translating. He said something about blood. Does that mean anything?"

Eric couldn't figure that out. "Our lab processes blood samples, but I don't think Alomari would be stealing them. Ask him if that's what he means."

Another conversation. Anwar shook his head and repeated his writing motions. Gamal turned to Eric and Melanie. "They were not stealing the blood, but information *about* the blood. I think that is the meaning, but Anwar is not certain."

Eric immediately saw the connection to the mysterious transmissions. Alomari was stealing sampling data. Eric was more confused than ever.

Eric glanced at Melanie expectantly. She shivered involuntarily and grasped her elbows in front of her, edging closer to the fire. She returned Eric's stare. The reflections from the crackling embers danced across her features. Her eyes were deep in shadow, which made her pronouncement seem more ominous. "In your hospital room I told you that nothing these terrorists do is random. We may not be able to figure out their objective, but whatever it is, it can't be good. I can assure you of this though: the closer you get to discovering it, the more dangerous you are to them."

How close did Hamdi come? Eric wondered.

SIXTEEN

Sunday, August 21, 2005
16 Rajab, 1426 AH
Kolkata, India

ALANA DRESSED FOR HER THIRD DAY ON THE SAFARI AND packed up her belongings. They were scheduled to check out of the hotel this morning. The safari would take them too far to return before sunset, and the roads were too dangerous at night.

The plan called for making camp at the distant collection site for a number of days. Alana had never been enamored with camping. No matter what the weather was like, she would awake with clammy garments and sticky tendrils of hair. To her, roughing it meant a modern hotel, hot and cold running water, room service, and a pool.

She entered the banyan-covered courtyard and saw Parminder wave enthusiastically. "Good morning," Para greeted her. "I hope you slept well, because you may find it more difficult the next few nights."

"Good morning, Para." She grimaced. "I can hardly wait. I'm really going to miss Kolkata and the creature comforts of a hotel." She lifted her head across the courtyard. "There's Dr. Larson. I think he's looking for us." Alana waved her hand to get his attention.

Dr. Larson spotted the women as he stood in the archway to the courtyard. He made his way to their table. He sat heavily in an empty chair, looking at Alana wearily as he labored for breath and blotted his brow. Alana noticed his grim expression and prepared herself.

"There is more bad news from Cairo. Eric is missing—again. He disappeared from his hospital room shortly past midnight and never returned."

Alana inhaled sharply as he held up his hand. "That is not all. A man and woman were seen leaving the Cairo lab less than an hour later. The man was carrying a backpack and fit Eric's description. A fire had been started in the lab, and it burned to the ground. The police are seeking Eric for questioning."

Y

Cairo, Egypt

Eric and Melanie had made their way from Garbage City to the embassy shortly after dawn. She was so covered in grime that the marine guard failed to recognize her as they stumbled to the gate.

After showering, Eric was thoroughly examined by the embassy medical staff who repaired his torn stitches and redressed his wounds. He was given antibiotics with the assurance that they were manufactured in America, not Egypt.

Eric and Melanie reunited in the dining room for a satisfying breakfast and a hot coffee. After breakfast, Melanie escorted Eric to an office with an auspicious nameplate framed on a mahogany door: "Deputy Ambassador Morgan Campbell."

They stepped into the spacious office and approached a cluttered desk with an oversized LCD panel partially obscuring the occupant. Melanie leaned around the monitor to make eye contact with the diminutive official. "Mr. Campbell, this is Eric Colburn, the National Geographic employee I debriefed you about."

Mr. Campbell tipped his head and peered over the rim of his bifocals. He glanced at Melanie first, then stared at Eric for a long moment. Without comment, he motioned for them to take seats. He pushed against his desk, retreating in his chair just far enough to cross his legs. He expelled a long sigh as he crossed his arms and settled back and rocked slowly against the backrest. "Well, Mr. Colburn, you certainly have been keeping our staff busy these past few days."

Eric was uncertain as to how he should respond. "Yes, sir; thank you, sir. I appreciate it."

Mr. Campbell ignored Eric's comment as he consulted a legal pad in front of him. "I just got off the phone with the Egyptian Ministry of the Interior. It seems you are being sought for questioning in an arson investigation."

Eric was caught completely off guard. "Arson? I stuck a stick in a camp-fire early this morning, but—" He glanced at Melanie for confirmation.

Her astonished look mirrored his own. "Sir, I was with Eric from the time he left the hospital until we showed up at the gate. I can assure you that he was not involved in anything of that sort."

The deputy adjusted his bifocals and frowned at his pad. "According to the ministry, a man and a woman who fit your descriptions were seen fleeing from the scene of the arson at about one thirty this morning."

"But we were being chased from my company's lab at that time." Eric protested.

Mr. Campbell was clearly exasperated. "I'd be careful how you express that to the ministry. The laws here are quite different from those back home. A statement like that would be construed as self-incrimination and would land you in solitary confinement, or worse. Egyptians do not observe technicalities like *habeas corpus*, and they don't like young Americans. They assume all of them are here looking for drugs."

Eric and Melanie sat in silent confusion.

"The *lab*, Mr. Colburn. You might want to avoid confessing that you were running from the very lab that burned to the ground this morning."

Eric was astonished. "*Our* lab? The National Geographic lab? I can't believe it." He looked at Melanie for reassurance.

She sat forward. "Sir, it's true we were being pursued. I had to leave my car because they had cut us off. I can assure you that the lab was intact when we left it. Eric is innocent of any arson charge."

Mr. Campbell opened his drawer and pulled out a large antacid container. He unscrewed the top and shook out three round tablets. He chewed noisily between words. "Ms. Wagner, I will report your alibi to the ministry. Your reputation with them may make the difference in clearing Eric. The two of you should wait in the library while we try to get this mess cleaned up." He turned back to his computer monitor and began typing.

Eric and Melanie were in the library reading the official arson report when the phone rang. Melanie answered it and listened silently to the caller. She smiled at Eric and thanked the caller. As she replaced the handset she announced, "Good news! The ministry is willing to accept my testimony, and you've been cleared of all charges. However, there is one caveat. They want you to leave Egypt immediately. You will be permanently placed on the visa blacklist as *persona non grata*."

"But my business here is not finished." Eric hated the thought of leaving without knowing what happened to Hamdi—and why.

"I'm afraid it's not up for discussion. An embassy staffer has already been dispatched to collect your things from the hotel. We'll leave for the airport within the hour," she responded.

They sat in the crowded waiting area for the Egyptian Air flight to the States. Eric appreciated Melanie's company. She was the only friend he'd made in this hostile country. Two marines from the embassy stood a discreet distance away and maintained an alert readiness.

Melanie turned to him and said, "Eric—I hesitate to alarm you, but I think you should be very careful if you intend to further investigate the events of this past week."

"What do you mean?" he asked.

"While you were with the medical staff, I met with the head of our security detail. As you can appreciate, embassies are targets, especially when we're in countries that harbor terrorists. In Egypt's case, they turn a blind eye to the hostile anti-American rhetoric and blatant recruiting that goes on here. We're taught to be vigilant and report any suspicious behavior and to carefully observe faces around us whenever we're out of the compound.

"When I crossed the hospital lobby, I got a good look at a few of the men loitering in the waiting area, especially the one who chased me to my car. Our security chief had me look through our threat database, and I identified two of the men from the hospital. They are Muslims with known connections to the Muslim Brotherhood, which is affiliated with al Qaeda."

Eric was stunned. "Maybe they weren't after me. Maybe you were the target. You are a well-known embassy staff member after all."

Melanie shook her head. "That's a possibility, but look at the facts. First, you found something suspicious on your computer network, and a day later you were almost killed in a terrorist bombing. Admittedly, Farouk was the primary target, but they knew you were meeting with him. Eric—they may have killed Farouk because of what he knew. If they did, then it stands to reason that you need to be eliminated too. With your connections, you're more dangerous to them than Farouk. I believe they may have come to the hospital to finish the job.

"The clincher is that they came to the lab. If I were the objective, they would have set up a cordon near the embassy. Instead, they headed straight to the lab. Had they arrived first, we would have walked into a fatal ambush. Once it was obvious that you escaped with your laptop, I think they torched the lab to hide any incriminating evidence. As a *coup de grâce*, they implicated you in the crime, counting on you being detained in Egypt, where it'd be easier to finish you off. Now you're about to slip from their grasp, which is why we have two marine guards and agents stationed in the airport for backup."

"I just came here to figure out the problems with our network," Eric said. "How did I end up in the middle of murder and mayhem?"

"You asked too many questions," Melanie said. "Just like your friend Hamdi. My purpose in rehashing all this is to make you aware of the danger you're in. Be cautious when you return home. These people have sleeper cells in the States, and they won't hesitate to come after you. Be wary, and don't assume the attack will come from someone who looks Mideastern. Many misguided Americans have been duped by these fanatics."

Melanie pulled a card from her wallet. "Take my card. It has a Washington DC phone number that will automatically connect to my cell phone in any U.S. embassy or consulate. Call me if you see anything suspicious."

"Thank you, Melanie." As Eric tucked the card in his wallet, he noticed another card, which he withdrew. "Hey—something suspicious happened to me when I flew into Cairo last week." He held up the card for Melanie. "This woman got hold of my computer, and I think she broke into it. I didn't become suspicious until later."

"Who was she?" Melanie asked.

"She said she was Israeli, but to tell you the truth, I don't know if I could tell the difference between an Israeli and an Arab. Can you check her out?"

"You bet I can. I'll have an answer before you land in the States." She glanced at the card. "It says here that she's with the Israeli Cultural Exchange. I have a hunch about something, but I'll withhold comment."

His flight was called, and Eric got up and awkwardly faced Melanie. Eric held out his hand, then changed his mind. He embraced her tightly and whispered in her ear, "Thank you for everything. I couldn't have gotten through this past day without you."

As he pulled back, she smiled at him. "It was all in a day's work. After all, we're here to serve our citizens. I have to tell you though—you're the most interesting citizen I've met since I've been here."

Eric grabbed his backpack and grimaced as he hoisted it over his shoulder. He changed his mind and shrugged the strap to the crook of his elbow. "I always thought the 'remain in your seats with your seat belts firmly secured' thing was a pain in the butt. This trip is going to take it to a whole new level," he said as he walked to his gate. He turned and waved one last time.

Eric settled into his seat as carefully as he could. He checked his laptop and saw that he had medium signal strength from the airport's wireless network. He sent a quick e-mail to Alana before he was forced to shut down. There wasn't time to convey what had been happening to him, so he told Alana he'd give her the details later. He signed off "Love ya" and clicked send.

SEVENTEEN

Wednesday, August 24, 2005
19 Rajab, 1426 AH
Atlanta, Georgia

Eric's return to headquarters was delayed because Dr. Larson insisted he take a couple of days to recuperate, which had worked wonders.

Now he was back. He set his Starbucks cup on his desk and pulled his laptop from his backpack. He docked it and logged into the network.

He glanced at his phone and noticed nineteen voice-mail messages, which reminded him to check his e-mail. The screen showed messages still downloading from the server. Thirty-four and still scrolling.

He leaned back in his chair and sipped his coffee. The door flew open as Justin Preedy stormed into the office, catching Eric midsip. Reflexively he sat up, causing the chair to lurch into the upright position. Steaming coffee sloshed over the rim. Eric winced and looked at his boss expectantly while he brushed liquid from his shirt.

Mr. Preedy glared at him with hostility. "What in the world happened in Cairo?" he bellowed at Eric, balling his fists. "I spent the weekend handling calls from the State Department and the Egyptian consulate. Now we have a destroyed lab and lost data that will set us back months. Explain that to me, why don't you?"

"Hey!" Eric shouted as he rose to his feet. "Take a chill pill. I was cleared of all charges. Don't try to pin any of that on me."

Preedy rested his fists on Eric's desk and leaned forward, shifting his weight to his knuckles. "You'd better watch your attitude, cowboy. We have a number of hard questions that you'd better have the right answers for. Meet me in Ms. Knowles's office at ten o'clock sharp for a debriefing. And if you continue with that attitude, you might as well clean out your office now."

"You're the one who came in here with an attitude. My response was reasonable compared to your verbal abuse."

Preedy looked ready to launch into another assault but seemed to think better of it. He pressed his lips together, turned, and left the office.

"Give me a break," Eric muttered to himself. His knees were twitching from the adrenaline rush. He sat down. *That was so uncalled for. Whatever happened to being presumed innocent?* He hoped Preedy hadn't bad-mouthed him around the office already.

Eric needed to get his mind off of the confrontation and started through his voice mail. Most were mundane data processing issues or sales calls. The most interesting was from Shoshana. Eric ignored the remaining messages and dialed the number she had left. The phone rang three times, then clicked to a voice prompt. Her message indicated she'd be out of the office for the remainder of the week. The message droned on with numbing options.

Why did people make it so difficult to leave messages? They insisted on covering every eventuality. It was an agonizing waste of time. *Just give me the beep already.* Eventually, he was allowed to leave his message.

Eric remembered that Melanie would have run a check on Shoshana by now. He called the number on her card and was frustrated to hear another recorded message. At the tone, he said, "Melanie, this is Eric Colburn. I got back to the States OK. I'm following up on our conversation about Shoshana Barak. Were you able to find out anything about her? Give me a call back when you have a chance."

It was time to wade through the e-mail messages. One of the oldest was from Alana, dated last Thursday morning. He should have checked earlier.

He'd been thinking about her frequently, and reading her message accentuated his loneliness. How long would it be until she returned? He finished her letter, and his eyes locked on the sign-off. *Love.*

Eric appreciated Alana's transparency; she held nothing back. Why did he struggle with offering the same honesty to her? He reluctantly acknowledged that her sensitivity was having an impact on him.

He'd always controlled his emotions. Others were kept at a careful distance, but Alana had insinuated herself through his defenses. In intimate settings he found his attraction to her to be intoxicating, and his resolve to remain detached would weaken. It had never been this way with anyone else.

He hit the reply button and began a complete account of his Egyptian adventures, ending with the confrontation with Preedy. Eric signed off with "Love ya" again. He sat and stared at it for a minute and stretched his finger toward the DEL key. He pressed it four times and replaced the comma. Then he typed his name and contemplated the change. It now read "Love, Eric." Why did this make him uneasy? He was gripped by uncertainty and fought the impulse to retype the sign-off. He clicked send before he talked himself out of it.

His phone rang, and he glanced at the console. It displayed "EXT 222: J HAMPTON." That would be Joey Hampton, the youngest member of the IT team. Joey hadn't gone to college, but he was brilliant—one of those self-taught geniuses who hated the structure of a classroom. Eric decided to answer the call. "Hey, Joey. What's happenin'?"

"Hey, dude. I know you're wiped out from your trip, but I wanted to see if you need me to follow up on anything from the Cairo lab."

"Yes, as a matter of fact, I do. Hold on a minute while I open a document." Eric clicked on the icon and launched the file he had saved in the lab. An error message flashed on the screen: "FILE CORRUPT OR NOT A VALID DOCUMENT." He couldn't believe it. He selected the repair option. No luck. As a last resort, he launched a utility to scan the file's machine code.

Eric was scanning through the code when Joey interrupted him. "Are you still there?"

"Oh—yeah. I'm sorry. I was distracted. My file was corrupted, and the underlying code indicates it was last accessed earlier this morning, which is bogus. Hold on a minute." He pressed a few more keys. "OK, I found part of what I was looking for. I don't have time to go into it right now, but I think someone was hacking into the Cairo network and stealing data. I was able to get a screen capture of the firewall log, but now that file is corrupted. I've recovered a partial IP address. Would you check the Internet registry and see if you can find where the IP address comes from?"

"Sure. I can get you into the neighborhood for sure."

"OK—the address starts with…" Eric rattled off several numbers. "I can't make out the last digits in the address, but you'll at least be able to determine which country—maybe even the city—the address is from. I'll get back to you after my meeting with Ms. Knowles and Preedy."

"I'll have your information by then. Hey—watch your back with Preedy. He's loaded for bear, and you're looking a lot like Boo Boo right now."

"Thanks for the warning, Yogi. Listen—I have one more question. Have you ever heard of a GIG file type?"

"G-I-G? No. Want me to check it out?"

"Yes. And would you query our servers in all the labs to see if you find any files with that extension? And be sure to check in any hidden directories in the process."

"No problem. What are you looking for?"

Eric hesitated to answer. He was unsure if he should get into the details right now. "I don't really know, but I suspect it may be a type of compressed file. Whoever is tapping into our system may be covering their tracks by encrypting the compressed files before transmission. I think they're minimizing the bandwidth in the hopes of going unnoticed by having a smaller footprint. Failing that, they're making sure we can't read the files and discover what they're up to."

"Wow—sounds sinister."

Eric checked the time. "Thanks again, Joey. I'll call you later. Bye." Eric had just enough time to follow up on a hunch. The online course he'd just completed at Georgia Tech included access to the campus research library, so he assumed he could still connect. He accessed the log-in portal and entered his credentials.

No problem. He searched the registry for articles on data compression algorithms. The listing was quite lengthy, so he added "genetics" as an additional filter. The screen updated with a reference to a two-year-old article:

Comasi, D., al-Calafali, F., Mateus, E., Alomari, A., & al-Bertrani, L. (2003) Human Genetics 112, 443–449.

Eric scanned the précis, which noted the challenge of data storage and transmission in genome mapping research. This confirmed his suspicion that geneticists were concerned about data compression.

Then he spotted something he'd almost overlooked. One of the authors in the study was named Alomari. That was a strange coincidence. Prior to his visit to Cairo, that name would have been meaningless. He didn't have time now, but he made a note to look up the article and check the author's first name. There couldn't be too many Alomaris in genetic research. Eric secured his laptop and headed to the elevator.

When he exited on the eighth floor, he headed to Stephanie's desk. She was just finishing a phone call and smiled at him. "Hi, Eric. You don't look any worse for the wear. It's nice to have you back."

"Thanks, Stephanie. It's been a rough first month. Hopefully things will be a little less exciting in the future."

"I hope so too. Ms. Knowles is expecting you. I should warn you that

Mr. Preedy has already arrived as well." Her nonverbal message was clear: Eric was walking into a major confrontation. "You can go on in."

"Thanks again, Stephanie." It was reassuring that she seemed to know who the good guy was.

Eric took a deep breath and entered.

Ms. Knowles stood and walked toward him. "Welcome back, Mr. Colburn. Come in and have a seat."

"Thank you, ma'am," Eric replied. He took a seat and muttered to himself, "Let the inquisition begin."

Ms. Knowles established the agenda quickly. "Eric, Mr. Preedy kept me apprised of the events in Cairo as they unfolded last week. I'd like to hear your frontline observations." She showed remarkable restraint, given the disastrous outcome at the lab.

"Certainly," he replied. "As you know, I arrived in Cairo last Tuesday morning. My objective was to determine to what extent the Cairo lab was contributing to our network bandwidth problems. If I could solve that, the solution could possibly apply elsewhere. I also wanted to get in touch with a former employee, Hamdi Tantawi."

Preedy smirked. "Another disappointing recruit from Georgia Tech."

Ms. Knowles cast a disapproving glance at Preedy but said nothing.

Eric continued. "I think I discovered the reason for the transmission problems—and something worse. I think our security has been breached and someone is stealing our data. And I think I know who."

Preedy fidgeted and glanced nervously at Ms. Knowles. He interrupted as if to assert his authority. "You didn't report that to me this morning, Colburn," he interjected with another glance at Ms. Knowles.

"Well, to be honest, you didn't really give me a chance." He directed his attention to Ms. Knowles, who represented the best refuge for a fair hearing. "When I arrived at the lab, I found our server drives had less than twenty percent available space and evidence that unauthorized files were being created. I suspect they have been transmitted to an unknown location on a regular schedule."

"What kind of files, and who is responsible?" Preedy demanded.

"I'm not sure," Eric responded carefully. "I'm still researching it. I have a hunch, but I'd rather wait until I can get confirmation."

Preedy was agitated. "Nonsense. Ms. Knowles and I demand to hear what your suspicions are. Speak your mind."

Eric hated to be put on the spot, but he didn't seem to have a choice.

"Well, there's a lot of circumstantial evidence, but the first thing that's suspicious is a series of files consuming a massive amount of space. The file type is GIG, which is odd because there are no software applications anywhere that create or can read GIG files. So they are either being renamed to disguise their real purpose, or someone has implanted their own application deep in the BIOS of our servers."

Eric hesitated again as he mentally debated whether he should withhold his conclusion. He decided to lay out his case. "I think I may know the significance of the GIG extension. I think it's an English acronym for an Arabic phrase: *Allāhu akbar*. I heard the same phrase twice in contexts that made me suspicious. I later found out that it's a common Muslim praise that translates 'God is greater.' I think that's what GIG stands for."

Preedy smirked. "That's a convoluted stretch of logic."

"There's more. You know I was a victim in a bombing. What you don't know is that I was meeting one of our former lab techs, a man named Farouk. He gave me evidence collected by Hamdi that implicated Dr. Alomari in th—"

Preedy's expression turned dark. He sputtered, "Dr. Alomari! How dare you even repeat what an embittered former lab tech said about our most senior lab director. Let's see this evidence."

"I don't have it anymore." Eric was crestfallen. "It was lost in the explosion."

"That's convenient," Preedy said triumphantly. He looked a little too pleased with the direction this was going.

Eric desperately struggled for a repartee; he could only fume in the indicting silence. "Whatever. Besides that, Dr. Alomari and all the lab techs in Cairo are Muslim, and the suicide bomber—"

Preedy interrupted again, effectively keeping Eric on the defensive. "Are you a Christian, Colburn?"

"How does that relate to my report?"

"Just answer the question," Preedy sputtered.

"Well, I'm not as faithful as I should be, but yes, I am." Eric surprised himself with his candid response. He wondered what Alana would think.

"I thought so. You know, I'm sick and tired of you Christians seeing Muslim terrorists behind every rock. You preach family values, but I'm here to tell you that hate is not a family value. I've heard enough of your speculations about Alomari and Islam in general. Do you have anything substantive to add?"

"Yes. I think they are the ones who burned the lab—in order to divert attention from whatever they've been up to—and to pin it on me."

"There you go again!" Preedy spat in exasperation. "Well, the investigators did ascertain that the fire began in the server room. By your own admission, you were the last one in there. Under the circumstances, I can see why you would conjure up a terrorist threat. The last I heard, terrorists are more interested in kidnapping and beheadings. Come to think of it, I can't recall ever seeing a Aljazeera broadcast of an al Qaeda's database theft." Preedy smugly glanced at Ms. Knowles, who had remained silent up to this point but was suppressing a smile.

She returned his glance and then turned to Eric. "Mr. Colburn, your evidence is very thin. I understand you have an unimpeachable alibi from a young lady on the embassy staff. *My* question to you is—why would you take an unauthorized person into one of our secure server rooms at one o'clock in the morning?"

Eric looked helplessly at Ms. Knowles. Everything had seemed so clear to him in Cairo, but he had to admit the case he had built looked pretty shaky now. He wished he had not blurted out his suspicions before he had hard facts to back them up. Preedy goaded him into this premature debriefing, then pushed the right buttons to put Eric on the defensive, which is an impotent position in any debate. "Look—I know this sounds weak, but I'm still researching some leads. Just give me a little—"

"No!" Ms. Knowles's face was set sternly. "You will not waste any further society resources on this matter. You have a job to do, and we expect you to do it. Let me remind you that you are still on probation. Any discipline on our part will await Dr. Larson's return from India. We need to consult with him prior to meting out our official response."

Eric couldn't believe how rigid Ms. Knowles had become. He thought they had a good relationship. Preedy was more influential than he realized. If only he had come to her directly.

Ms. Knowles stood, signifying the termination of the interview. Eric got to his feet, nodded at her, then left the office. He closed the door behind him and skirted Stephanie's work area. He wanted to slink back to his office and be alone for a while.

Eric had never been more humiliated in his life. Now he began to doubt his decision to take this job. As he reflected upon it, he couldn't think of anything good that had happened yet.

The elevator arrived and he entered, turned, and pressed the button for the seventh floor. As the doors slid silently closed, he noticed Stephanie watching him surreptitiously. "Great," he said to himself. "I suppose everyone knows about this."

EIGHTEEN

Friday, August 26, 2005
21 Rajab, 1426 AH
Dhaka, Bangladesh

T HE SAFARI HUMVEES FINALLY FOUND PURCHASE ON RUDIMEN-
tary pavement. For days they had alternated between wet lowlands with
mud being slung from the tires and arid zones where the vehicles kicked up
asphyxiating clouds of dust. Alana's muscles were sore from the lurching. It
was like an intense workout after a prolonged absence from the gym.

They were on the outskirts of Old Dhaka. When they crested the last
hill she saw skyscrapers on the horizon. Civilization was near, and she
longed for this day to end. Old Dhaka was mostly populated by Kuttis,
who have their own dialects and culture. Their tribal roots were ancient, so
Dr. Larson was counting on them being a tight genetic pool with minimal
influence from later immigration.

On the other hand, New Dhaka was a melting pot that would yield little
benefit for their research. Whatever it lacked as a genographic resource,
however, it would more than make up for in its amenities. The thought of
a bubble bath was intoxicating.

The Humvees came to a halt in the center of the village square. Curious
village residents crowded the caravan as naked children begged for handouts. Alana had become somewhat jaded by this. She'd given generously at
the first few stops in India, but eventually was overwhelmed by the sheer
magnitude of the poverty. As bad as India had been, Bangladesh was far
worse. There were over one hundred forty million people crammed into
the country. With one thousand people per square kilometer, it was three
times denser than India, making the poverty virtually inescapable.

Alana looked at Para and could see that the safari had taken a lot out
of her as well. She had been such a great help, and they had become close.
Alana was going to miss her greatly when she returned home—which she
hoped would be soon.

They worked quickly in getting their equipment organized. Para had
become proficient and was now assisting with drawing blood. Alana and

Para each had an assistant who took the demographic information from the patients. Dr. Larson had recruited a local translator and was learning as much as possible about the tribal history.

By late afternoon they had finished and were packing up their equipment when they heard the rumble of vehicles coming toward the center of the village. Shouts of alarm sounded at the burst of an automatic weapon. All heads turned as three military vehicles rushed the courtyard in a billowing cloud of dust and rapidly took up positions blocking any egress. Dr. Larson motioned for his translator to come with him as he limped toward the obvious officer in charge.

Alana was worried by what she knew of this country. She had learned that corruption was rampant and extortion was a way of life. In its thirty-some years of existence, it had had thirteen different heads of state and four military coups.

She surveyed the weaponry and recalled much of what her brother had taught her about munitions. Two of the vehicles were jeeps painted in the camouflage of a distant war but equipped with fairly new fifty-caliber machine guns. The enormous brass cartridges glistened in their ammunition belts, which were lengthy enough to engage a small army. Each fifty-caliber was manned by two soldiers. One stood behind the weapon firmly gripping the dual handles while the other stood at the side and assured the cartridge belt fed smoothly into the firing chamber. Three of the infantrymen hoisted RPGs on their shoulders, fingers poised on the triggers. The remainder of the dozen men fanned out with their automatic rifles pointed at the safari staff in an efficient—and deadly—military deployment. The telltale banana-shaped clip on their weapons identified them as Kalashnikov AK-47s and made clear this was not a military exercise. These men were ruthless and would not be trifled with.

Dr. Larson appealed to the officer. "My name is Dr. Larson, and these are my papers issued by your government authorizing us to be here. We are with the National Geographic Society and are on our way to Dhaka."

The translator began interpreting to the officer, who continued to glare at Dr. Larson. He slapped the papers to the dirt and ground them beneath the heel of his boot. His other hand rested casually on his sidearm as the translator emphatically punctuated his translation with gestures.

Para turned to Alana in alarm. "He is not translating properly! He is saying something different!"

"What is he saying?" Alana demanded.

Liam Roberts

105

"Wait a moment—oh no. They are in collusion! He is telling the officer where Dr. Larson keeps his funds."

The officer began yelling at the interpreter, and Dr. Larson looked puzzled as heated comments were exchanged.

Para whispered, "He told the officer that we do not carry any narcotics. The officer is enraged. He doesn't believe the interpreter. Now the officer is accusing him of keeping the narcotics for himself. He is calling him a betrayer."

The officer drew his sidearm, and his troops rotated their guns in unison. The interpreter realized he had only moments to live as he faced a deadly serious firing squad. He fell to his knees, clasping his hands in front of him, babbling loudly.

Para breathlessly continued to interpret. "He is begging for his life. He has a wife and chi—"

The courtyard erupted in a tremendous volley of gunfire. The pungent cordite cloud was nauseating. Smoke obscured their view with the brooding silence of early-morning fog. Even the insects in the nearby jungle became deathly still. As the vapors dissipated, they could see Dr. Larson slowly retreating. The officer and his men turned their attention to him. The officer's face was red with rage as he bore down on a new victim. Dr. Larson backpedaled until a root blocked his progress. He tripped and fell backward.

The officer straddled him with his arm thrust directly at Dr. Larson's face. His weapon seemed an extension of his flesh as it quivered ominously in time with the violent shuddering of the officer's body.

Dr. Larson lay there, looking down the barrel of the officer's gun. He was completely helpless, not understanding a word being shouted at him.

Suddenly, Para jumped from the Humvee and sprinted to Dr. Larson's side. Numerous weapons pivoted to this new threat as she began shouting responses to their accusations in Bengali. She fell to her knees and leaned over Dr. Larson's prone figure, sidling between him and the instruments of death. Her fingers splayed, as if to expand her zone of protection, and pressed against Dr. Larson's chest. Tears streamed down her face as she pleaded earnestly with the assassin.

Time drifted in slow motion for Alana. This was the most surreal experience of her life. She was helpless and completely beyond her resources. She closed her eyes and prayed earnestly, "Lord! Please confuse our enemies. Put a hedge of protection around these innocent people. Do not let evil have its way. Lord Jesus, hear my prayer!"

The officer began shouting questions at Para. She evidently understood them because she responded. The officer's rage subsided, and many of the weapons were lowered. Para was obviously not a threat. The officer shouted another comment, and she nodded her head, then bowed in submission as relief spread across her features. She turned and whispered to Dr. Larson, then helped him to his feet.

The officer holstered his weapon and shouted commands at his men. Two of them pulled from the pack and confronted two of the safari's Humvee drivers. They pointed their rifles at them, then swept them to the side while jerking their heads in the same direction. Their language was unintelligible yet very clear and easily understood. "Get out of the vehicles...*now!*"

The two drivers and their passengers jumped from their vehicles and moved hastily backward, putting distance between themselves and the murderous weapons.

Dr. Larson asked Para something, and she in turn relayed the question to the officer. He shrugged and seemed to give his assent. Para and Dr. Larson quickly made their way to the safari team. Dr. Larson was in charge once again. "They are confiscating two of our Humvees. We're being allowed to remove our equipment before they drive away. Quickly, everyone. We need to remove everything and stow it on the remaining vehicle." Alana shuddered, and a sob caught in her throat. She couldn't comprehend that she'd almost witnessed her mentor being shot in cold blood.

The military caravan was maneuvering from the courtyard when the men threw their weapons in the air and courageously fired a series of bursts in celebration of their victory. Once again, the plaza was overwhelmed with dust and smoke as the last of the vehicles departed.

Para walked toward Alana in a daze. Her face was still wet, and dust darkened the tracks of her tears. Alana rushed to her and embraced her with an enthusiastic hug while Para's arms hung limp at her sides. They stood motionless for a long time. Alana leaned back and grasped Para's shoulders, gazing into her eyes. "That was the most gallant, selfless act of heroism I have ever seen!" she exclaimed. "You thought nothing of your own life. We owe you our very lives! I am so honored to call you my friend." She couldn't think of anything else to say. Words seemed so insufficient to express her gratitude.

Dr. Larson limped feebly toward them, and Alana backed away, making room for him. It was his turn to hug Para. He gently enveloped her small frame in his embrace and nestled his head on top of hers as he wept shame-lessly. "Thank you, my child. I owe you a debt that can never be repaid. I will live to see my grandchildren because of your bravery." His hand cradled her head as he stroked her silky black hair.

Para eventually pulled free of his embrace and self-consciously looked from one to the other. "I have come to love you and appreciate the work you have entrusted to me. You are like family and I could do nothing less. At first I was petrified and could not move. I looked at the body of the interpreter and realized he could have been me. I must confess that I felt very afraid. Then, for some reason, a story Mother Teresa had told at my school came into my mind. She spoke of a woman in your Bible who was asked to risk her life for her people. Her cousin came to her and pleaded with her, saying, 'Perhaps your whole life has been preparation for a time such as this.'

"That is what came into my mind, Dr. Larson, as you were about to be murdered. I realized that I was the only hope you had and it was my duty to respond. I knew in my heart that my whole life and all of my training was for a moment such as this."

Atlanta, Georgia

Eric sat on the MARTA and rested his head against the window. The steady rhythm of the tracks punctuated the engine vibrations and soothed his headache. In spite of working a short week, he was exhausted. His emotions were still raw from the confrontation with management, and he'd immersed himself in his work as a distraction. He seemed to think more often of Alana and wondered if she had received his latest e-mail. He was anxious for her to return to the States so he could share his concerns with her and receive the encouragement that only she could offer.

He was suddenly aware of a new vibration and scrambled to extract his cell phone from his jeans before the call tripped to voice mail. By the time he flipped the lid and said, "Hello!" it was too late. The call was certainly not from Alana, but he checked anyway. The number was unfamiliar, and he decided to check the message later.

Eric glanced out the windows and noticed the next stop was his old campus. He didn't have anything better to do, so this would be a good time to check out the library. This was his own time, and he was free to investigate the Cairo conspiracy if he wanted to. Eric exited the train and hopped on the

Tech Trolley, a shuttle service that ferried students around campus. During the short ride, he flipped his cell phone open and checked his messages.

"Hey, Eric! This is Joey. Listen—I didn't forget to follow up on the things you asked me to check the other day. But the word went out from Preedy that he had you working on a project and you weren't to be disturbed. We figured there was something else going on, but I didn't want to get on his bad side. Now it's the weekend and we can do what we want, right? So give me a call and I'll tell you what I found out. I think you'll be very interested. Later, dude!"

Eric smiled. Joey was such a character. He hit redial, and the phone was answered on the first ring. "Took you long enough!" Joey laughed.

"Hey, Joey. You were right about Preedy. I didn't want to get you caught in the middle."

"I don't trust the phones at work," Joey said, "so now you have my cell. What's up with Preedy lately? He's pretty uptight."

"Well, the Cairo lab disaster set the project back months. It will take some time to get a new lab set up and replace all the equipment. Fortunately, we didn't lose much data, only the most recent batches." Eric changed the subject. "So what did you find out?"

"Remember the IP address you gave me?"

"Yes. Where is it located?"

"This will sound strange, but I double-checked. Would you believe Pakistan?"

"Really?"

"Yes. Karāchi, Pakistan."

"Where's that?"

"It's on the Arabian Sea in the southeast corner of the country. It's been a significant port of trade for centuries. The city is enormous with fifteen million people packed into a small geographic area."

Eric laughed. "Have you ever tried out for Jeopardy? You have a knack for trivia."

"Well, Wikipedia is just a click away."

"Joey, I just had another thought. Do you remember that the last two digits of the IP address had been corrupted?"

"Yes."

"Well, there are only ninety-nine possibilities if we want to figure out who is accessing our data, right?"

"I see where you're going. You want me to ping all ninety-nine and see which ones are valid, then check the Internet registry to see if we can narrow the field. Maybe our sinister culprits will have a name that'll give them away, like Data Thieves 'R' Us. Am I getting warm?"

"You're hot, Joey!"

"Nice of you to say so, but I have a girlfriend."

"Funny. Hey—did you have any luck finding any GIG files?"

"That was a challenge. I submitted a system-wide query and came up empty. Not a single one."

"Darn. I was hoping for some vindication."

"I wasn't finished," Joey said. "I pulled the backup tapes from the Atlanta lab, and you'll never guess what I found." He paused for effect. "Every one I checked was full of GIG files."

"Really? I wouldn't have thought of checking that."

"Hey—that's why they pay me big bucks. The curious thing is that only the older backup tapes have GIG files. Want to know when they stopped getting backed up?"

"I don't have a clue."

"August sixteenth, the day you showed up in Cairo. I think you put someone on the alert and they did some housecleaning."

"Wow. This means someone at the headquarters might be involved. I want to hack into those GIG files and see what's in them."

"I already tried. They're heavily encrypted. I've got a utility running to crack the code, but it hasn't been successful yet. I hope I have something soon."

"Thanks for all your help, Joey. You've done a lot, but I need to ask you to check on one more thing."

"Sure. This is the most fun I've had all year."

"You may have heard of Dr. Alomari? Well, he recently transferred out of the Cairo lab. Could you see which lab he transferred to?"

"Sure. I'll connect into my office PC and check the personnel records. I'll send you an e-mail."

"Thanks."

"Wait a minute—the nightly backup just started, so I'm locked out of the system until morning."

"No problem. Let me know when you find something."

Y

Dhaka, Bangladesh

The remnant of the safari limped into Dhaka and arrived at the hotel by 11:00 p.m. They checked in and dispersed to their rooms. Alana was too exhausted for the bath she had looked forward to, but a hot shower was a close second.

She put on a bathrobe and was toweling her hair when she thought about her laptop. She plugged it in and connected to the hotel's wireless. She clicked her e-mail icon and returned to the bathroom while the files downloaded.

Alana finished up in the bathroom and turned off the light. She flopped on her bed, pulling her laptop across the sheets. She lay on her stomach and tilted the monitor to accommodate her viewing angle. An e-mail from Eric had arrived! She quickly read it and was amazed at how much he had gone through in Egypt.

There was one bit of information missing, however. Alana trusted Eric but couldn't dismiss something Dr. Larson had told her about the Cairo lab incident. Official reports said Eric was seen leaving the lab with a woman. Who was the mystery woman, and what was Eric doing with her in the middle of the night? And why had he conspicuously not mentioned her in his e-mail? All these questions swirled in her mind, but she quickly dismissed them when she noticed the difference in his sign-off. He had dropped the "ya" after "Love."

Alana leaned back on the headboard and closed her eyes, thinking about what this meant. If he was saying he loved her, then who was the woman in Cairo? She just wanted this trip to be over so she and Eric could stand on the same continent and talk things out.

The air conditioning felt wonderful, and the bed was so soft. Alana reached out and flicked off the bedside lamp, then slid between the cool sheets and drifted off to sleep.

NINETEEN

Saturday, August 27, 2005
22 Rajab, 1426 AH
Atlanta, Georgia

JOEY LAUNCHED HIS REMOTE ACCESS SOFTWARE AND LOGGED onto his office PC. The software made it seem like he was sitting in front of his office PC instead of his own apartment. He switched to the utility working on the GIG file but was disappointed that it had not made any progress, and he began to doubt he would succeed.

Joey browsed to the company personnel directory and searched the listing for "Alomari." He found the entry and expanded the volume. There were various tabs, including résumé, hiring information, and job postings. He selected the postings tab and read through the information, his eyes widening at the last entry. He grabbed his cell phone and pressed redial.

Y

Eric entered the library as soon as the guard unlocked the front door. By the time he'd gotten across campus the previous evening, the library had closed. Frustrated at having to make a second trip, he wanted to finish this up as quickly as possible.

The librarian directed him to the stacks on the east end of the third floor. He found the previous editions of *Human Genetics* and pulled the 2003 volume. At the research table, he found the issue that had been cited in his earlier research and flipped to the article, which turned out to be a sidebar to a longer one that expanded on some findings from the European Human Genome Project—a competing organization that lost the race to the American project.

The article dealt with the problem of data storage and the need to compress the vast amounts of data while assuring data integrity. The authors had tried a number of compression techniques and had experienced unsatisfactory results. The sidebar noted that they were in the process of developing a custom compression algorithm.

Eric's phone buzzed. He thought of ignoring it until he glanced at the display. "Hey, Joey. Did you find anything?" He kept his voice at a library whisper.

"Yes, I did! Two guesses where the esteemed doctor is now located."

"From your tone, I would guess Karāchi."

"Then you would be right."

"Hold on a minute. I was just reading something here." Eric skimmed the information in front of him. He stared at the page for a long moment with the phone cradled uncomfortably against his shoulder. He still felt a pulling sensation from his wounds. "I thought so. I just found some more information on him. He's listed as a coauthor of a two thousand three research article I'm looking at. The article talks about their efforts to develop a proprietary file-compression algorithm. My hunch is this is describing the early development of our GIG files."

"It sounds like a good hunch."

"But something still bothers me."

"What's that?"

"Alomari must be the one behind these GIG files, but what's his objective? I understand the need to compress the data before transmission. Smaller files make it less likely he would be discovered. Keep in mind, the NGS noticed bandwidth problems long before I was hired, but no one figured out the real reason. It was a fluke I put the puzzle pieces together in Cairo. But something doesn't make sense. I understand his interest in the data because he's a geneticist. But how do Islamic terrorists fit into this? As much as I hate to admit it, Preedy may be right. What would terrorists want with genetic data?"

"Well, since you're still formulating your conspiracy theory, you might want to add Preedy to the cast of characters. He's always seemed secretive to me, and I think I know why he's gotten more intense since the Cairo disaster."

"Why's that?"

"I'd rather not talk about it on the cell. Have you eaten lunch yet?"

"No. Do you want to grab a sandwich?"

"Sure. You're on Tech's campus, right? Why don't we meet at the Commons? I can be there in fifteen minutes. Go ahead and order me a Philly cheese sub."

Eric reached to close the journal he'd been studying and thought of checking one more thing. He ran his finger down the page at the end of the article to the section that included the curriculum vitae on each of the coauthors. He found the section on Alomari. "That explains a few things," he said to himself. He headed for the photocopier.

Y

Eric picked up the order just as he saw Joey come through the door. He raised his head and nodded toward an available booth. They navigated the tables and arrived at the same time.

Eric handed Joey the page he'd copied at the library. "Check this out."

Joey applied a generous slather of ketchup to his sub and read the document.

Eric explained. "That's Alomari's curriculum vitae. Notice the various articles he's published?"

"Yeah."

"Well, the last article he published received horrible reviews. If you can believe it, he tried to make the case that Muslims are genetically superior. His research methods were trashed in the peer-review process, and he was professionally humiliated. From that point on, no science magazine would agree to publish him. He's finished as a researcher."

"I guess that's why he came to work at the NGS."

"I think so," Eric said. "So what did you want to tell me about Preedy?"

"Did you know Preedy has his own server in his office?"

"What? That can't be. I've mapped the whole network, and every server's accounted for."

"Believe me. I've seen it. You know the row of bookcases behind his desk? There are cabinets along the base. I was dropping a printout on his desk one evening just as he was leaving. He ushered me out of his office, and I turned back to say something to him as he flicked the light switch off. In the darkened office, I noticed some LEDs blinking behind his desk. One of the cabinet doors was ajar, and from my angle I could see the outline of the server illuminated in the LED glow."

"Have you scanned the network for it?" Eric asked.

"Of course I have. I went through all the internal IP addresses on our network, and all of them are accounted for. I even pinged all the unused addresses just to make sure nothing was hiding out there. Nothing came up."

"That's strange."

"But wait—there's more! What do you figure a small server would cost?"

"I'd guess three grand."

"That's about what I figured. Well, I checked with that cute blonde in accounting, Wendy Bennett. You know her?"

Eric grinned. "Oh yeah. She's a hottie. I didn't think accountants were that hot."

"That one is! And she's pretty smart too. She's got the whole package." Joey grinned knowingly. "You know, I think we should have Larson examine her DNA and see if we could clone her. The world would be a better place."

"Focus, Joey, focus."

"You're right. So, I asked Wendy if she would check our computer assets and confirm everything was accounted for. She didn't find any extra servers. I asked her if she was certain, and she told me anything over five hundred dollars has to be capitalized on the inventory list."

Eric only nodded, his mouth full of sandwich. He took a sip of his drink. "That sounds right," he said finally.

"So, how could Preedy get a personal server and not have it accounted for?"

"It beats me. But I'm dying to know what's on it. If we can't detect it on the network, we can't hack into it. I guess I'll have to get into his office." Eric smiled.

Joey asked, "How do we pull that off?"

"Not we—me. I have an idea, but I don't think I should get you involved in this. I'm about to cross a line, and it isn't fair to drag you with me."

"Forget that. If you don't trust me, that's one thing, but I think I've earned the right to see this through."

"I trust you, Joey, but I would feel awful if you got fired because of me."

"Hey, I'm young, good-looking, and brilliant! I'll land on my feet."

"OK. Well, here's how we can get into Preedy's office." Eric pulled his PDA out of his backpack.

"That's just a pocket PC. How's that going to pick a lock?"

Eric smiled. "You know how our security system works?"

"You mean our ID badges? Sure. They have an embedded radio frequency identification device in the badge. It's the same RFID technology that'll eventually replace bar codes. I read that Wal-Mart has ordered all their vendors to include RFID on all products by a deadline or they won't carry their products."

"That would be a big account to lose." Eric took another sip. "Do you know how RFIDs actually work?"

"No. I haven't read the details about the technology, but I'm curious.

It seems the need to transmit data would require a power source, but that wouldn't be practical."

"Well, the chips don't have the ability to transmit; they're passive emitters. And you're right; a power source isn't practical—or cheap either. This is the cool part. The chip includes an antenna. When it gets within range of an RFID transmitter, it receives the radio beam and converts the energy into an electrical impulse, which powers the chip. The chip then transmits its data back through the radio beam. So the need to wave a bar code in front of a laser is eliminated."

"That is too cool." Joey nodded.

"Yes, but there's a security breach."

"Really?"

"Most chips aren't encrypted, and they contain writeable ROM."

"They can be overwritten?"

Eric grinned knowingly. "You know what that means?"

"I sure do. If you could figure out how to transmit info to the ROM chip, then the whole system's vulnerable. Why don't they have better security?"

"It's just like the early Internet. Technology geeks tend to be optimistic and trusting, so they didn't build in any security into the Internet. I guess they believed people are inherently good and wonderful technology would bring the good out in them. Well, they aren't, and it didn't. Now we're paying a huge price with viruses, worms, and hacking.

"In the case of RFIDs, it's too expensive to include security. A chip that can be overwritten costs about a dime, but an encrypted chip is about five dollars. If Wal-Mart demands RFIDs on every package, they couldn't afford to sell a pack of gum with an encrypted chip. They'd need to sell bulk packs of fifty because of labeling costs. Here's the crazy thing: there is a way to lock down the writable area of the cheap chips, but most companies don't want to. They think they might need to reuse the chips and are afraid of the cost of scrapping used chips."

"So, they'd rather take the security risk. I guess convenience has its price."

"Exactly." Eric pulled a slim device from his bag. "I bought this RFID reader-writer for my PDA." Eric inserted the device into the slot of his PDA. "Check this out." He turned the screen so Joey could read it.

Joey stared at the screen. "Hey, that's my personal information." He was looking at his photo from the NGS personnel file, a picture of his driver's license, Social Security card, and a screen full of personal data. "Where did you get all that?"

Eric laughed. "I just picked your pocket—electronically. You must have your company ID in one of your pockets. Once you got within five feet of me, I snagged all your data."

"That's scary."

"What's even scarier is that I can take someone else's data and write it to your ID badge because our RFIDs aren't locked or encrypted. For example…" Eric used his stylus to scroll through a number of RFID files and stopped when Preedy's picture displayed at the top of the screen. He smiled raffishly. "How'd you like to be Preedy for a day?"

TWENTY

Sunday, August 28, 2005
23 Rajab, 1426 AH
Atlanta, Georgia

ERIC BLEW A RIPPLE ACROSS THE SURFACE OF HIS COFFEE. JOEY had picked him up an hour earlier, and they stopped at McDonald's for breakfast and a final strategy session.

Eric pulled his PDA from his backpack and pointed at an icon on the screen. "This is the program I created that'll replace the ID on my badge. I got the idea from a *Wired* magazine article about an RFID trial in a European store. All the items in the store are tagged with RFID chips, and the customers are checked out electronically without having to remove anything from their carts.

"A hacker created a program that could read *and* write RFID chips. He went in the store and pulled the data from a cheap bottle of wine, then used that to overwrite the chip on a very expensive bottle. The store's computer recorded the sale of a bottle of wine and didn't know the difference. The staff had so much confidence in their security that they didn't look closer. They were satisfied with a glance that the receipt matched the products in the cart."

Joey laughed. "I guess the same thing could be done with bar codes. You could print up a label ahead of time and take it with you. In the store, you could stick it on top of the legitimate label."

"I suppose so, but the major difference is the clerk usually handles bar code product and may notice it. The motivation behind RFIDs is to reduce the transaction costs, and employees are expensive. If a company doesn't need staff to unload and reload grocery carts, they can save money." Eric gathered all the trash and moved it to one side. "We need to review our plan for this morning. I've been thinking about it, and I don't want you going in Preedy's office with me." Joey started to protest, but Eric cut him off. "Hear me out. If I'm caught, that's one thing, but there's no sense in both of us going down. Besides, you'd still be free to figure out what's going on while I sit in a cell somewhere."

Eric spread out some notes. "We have to be careful. There's a security log that captures all the data from the various sensors. I need you to hack in to the log and monitor it. I'll have to check in at the guard desk and pass the elevator sensor as myself. Then I'll swap my ID to Preedy's in order to get into his office.

"As soon as you see the activity record for the entry to Preedy's office, you have to delete it within ten seconds. If you miss that window, the ID record will be compared with all personnel in the building. The system will howl if it spots the mismatch. Then, when I exit his office there will be a second entry. This happens anytime anyone opens a secure door from the inside. If we don't delete the second entry within ten seconds, the system will detect an exit that isn't matched by an earlier entrance and will also send an alert. If either of these things happen, security will be on me before I can get to the elevator."

Joey gave a low whistle. "Wow, that's pretty sophisticated. If it didn't compare scans with the on-site personnel, we wouldn't have to worry about the log at all," Joey observed.

Eric nodded. "That's right. But the logs may be reviewed at a later date, and I don't want to chance it. We can't risk having Preedy more paranoid than he already is. He'd make life intolerable if he suspected someone was snooping in his office."

"I thought of something else," Joey cautioned. "You'll need to take the stairs up to Preedy's office. We don't want to leave behind a record of the elevator moving back and forth between our floor and Preedy's, right?"

"Exactly. There aren't any sensor locations on the stairwell exits or on my office either. Just the main entrance, elevators, and the offices in the executive suite."

"Well, I'm ready when you are."

"Let's roll."

Y

The Genographic Project parking lot was nearly empty when Eric and Joey arrived. They checked in at the guard desk and took the elevator to the seventh floor. As they exited, Eric whispered, "There was a reason I wanted to go over everything before we got here. Let's be careful what we say—just in case."

Joey nodded. "I'm cool with that."

They entered Eric's office, and he pulled his laptop from his backpack.

He set it up and launched a search utility. "I think the security software is on the NGS zero four server. It's segregated from the rest of the servers, but I can map to the right drive. Let me take a look." He clicked a few keys. "Here it is."

Eric scrolled through the subdirectories and found the LOG directory. "OK, Joey, here's the file you want to watch." He double-clicked the icon and opened the log. "See here?" This is where we checked in with the guards." He pointed to the last entries on the screen:

28 08 05 09:06:51	Colburn, Eric	HQLobby
28 08 05 09:07:19	Hampton, Wilbert	HQLobby
28 08 05 09:07:56	Hampton, Wilbert	Elevator 1
28 08 05 09:07:59	Colburn, Eric	Elevator 1

"Wilbert?" Eric laughed. "What's up with Wilbert?"

Joey flushed with irritation. "I hate my first name. I go by my middle name, Joseph."

"That's too funny. OK, Wilbert. When I enter Preedy's office, you'll see a new line appear right here below the last entry. Right-click it, and a pop-up option box will appear. One of the options is delete. Remember—it's important that it's deleted within ten seconds."

"I can handle it. No problem," Joey replied.

"OK, then. I'll swap the ID on my card and get going." He tapped a series of options on the PDA, aimed it at his ID, and pressed a command icon. It chirped once, signifying the swap was successful. Eric headed out of the office and called back over his shoulder, "See you soon."

Eric bounded up the steps to the next floor and opened the fire door. He didn't expect anyone to be on the floor, but his pounding heart urged caution. He crept silently to Preedy's office, and the door sensor blinked red twice, then solid green, signifying authorization. A soft click invited him to enter. The door opened without resistance.

On the floor below, Joey saw the entry appear on the computer screen:

28 08 05 09:29:21	Preedy, Justin	Office 804—Entry

He double-clicked the line of text, and nothing happened. In a surge of adrenaline, he remembered he was supposed to right-click the entry. He did so, and a dialog window popped up. He quickly selected delete. The entry disappeared. Now all he had to wait for was Eric's exit from the office.

Eric moved quickly to Preedy's desk and sat in the high-back executive chair. He swiveled around to face the bookshelf and opened the lower cabinet door. There was the mystery server, right where Joey had described it. There was no monitor for the server; nor was there a mouse or keyboard. Eric was confused. He then noticed a small device perched in the shadows above the server. Leaning forward, he reached into the dark recess and found a remote control with a button labeled "Monitor" and four numbered LEDs on the face. He pressed the button a few times, but nothing seemed to happen other than a faint chirp with each press.

Eric pressed again and noticed something flicker in the glass door of the bookcase. He focused on the reflection and saw the computer monitor on the desk behind him. Something had changed on the screen. He rotated in the chair, pointed the remote over his shoulder at the server, and pressed. The screen blinked in sync with chirps from the cabinet. The remote toggled between Preedy's desktop computer and the server. He rolled to the desk and checked the "My Computer" properties to confirm he was on the server console.

Eric pulled out his PDA and clicked the icon for the infrared scanner functions. He selected the learn mode and pointed Preedy's remote control at it. Both devices emitted their respective chirps, which signified that his PDA had captured the remote's infrared command. He could now use his PDA to perform the same functions. He smiled; his PDA had a stronger broadcast signal than the remote. It'd be funny to walk past Preedy's office and transmit the command to switch screens on him.

Eric cautioned himself that this was no time to be distracted with practical jokes. Why did humor rise to the surface at the most stressful times? He needed to focus and get out of Preedy's office quickly.

He returned the remote to its proper place and closed the cabinet. He then pressed the infrared icon on his PDA to test it. He confirmed that he was able to switch computers and power down the monitor from the PDA.

Joey struggled with boredom. He launched a Minesweeper game and selected the expert option, then moved the game window to the left side of the screen and the security log to the right. That would allow him to watch both simultaneously. He played against the game clock while keeping an eye on the log. He was a couple of minutes into the game and noticed a change out of the corner of his eye. He glanced at the log and saw a new entry:

28 08 05 09:46:43   Preedy, Justin   HQLobby

He reflexively right-clicked the entry and was about to click delete when a jolt of adrenaline shivered through him. Realization turned to horror in the next heartbeat. The entry was from the lobby! That didn't make any sense. Eric wouldn't have used Preedy's ID in the lobby. He was still in Preedy's office. Something was horribly wrong. Joey was paralyzed by indecision. He jumped up from the chair and ran to the window. "Oh no!" he gasped. Preedy's Porsche was parked next to his own car in front of the building.

He returned to the desk, where a new entry had appeared on the screen.

28 08 05 09:47:49   Preedy, Justin   Elevator 2

Y

Eric scanned all the server directories and made a couple of notes. Everything looked fairly routine. He noticed a directory for labs and expanded it. Each of the society labs was listed. He expanded the Cairo lab and saw a series of directories with obscure names. Each directory's date stamp was displayed, and Eric was sure there was a pattern, but it wasn't immediately obvious. He didn't take the time to figure it out. He clicked in one of the directories and saw what he had hoped to find: a huge GIG file. He clicked another directory and found the same thing.

He returned to the root directory and noticed a folder titled NRUBLOC. That was an odd name, which raised his curiosity. He clicked the contents, and a long list of text files scrolled on the screen. The newest file carried an e-mail icon. It was his last e-mail to Alana. He sat back and shook his head in anger. He quickly confirmed a number of files were his e-mails to and from Alana and Joey.

Eric returned to the root directory and noticed an executable icon. He double-clicked it and immediately saw a Minesweeper screen. The game was in progress. As he watched, the timer sequenced past 354, then 355. Then he noticed something next to the Minesweeper screen. There was a security log window partially obscured by the game board. Something was familiar about the background image behind the two windows. Eric suddenly realized he was looking at an image of his own computer screen. This was a spyware program that snooped on Eric's laptop in real time! It was as if he were looking over Joey's shoulder.

Eric enlarged the screen to get a better look at the security log. His eyes fell on the same entry that had alarmed Joey, and it took him about the same amount of time to arrive at the identical conclusion.

Then he heard a muffled but distinctive chime from the elevator bank.

Eric panicked. Preedy was on the floor and most likely headed to his office. Eric was trapped with no place to hide.

Eric quickly swiveled in the chair to confirm that he had closed the cabinet door in front of the server. He swiveled back to the desk and realized he had only one option. He slid forward off the chair onto his knees. He doubled over and scooted under Preedy's desk. The modesty shield would conceal him from the front side of the desk.

He heard a magnetic click at the door. He patted his pocket and froze in terror. Where was his PDA? He'd left it on the edge of the desk. He leaned forward and hooked his wrist up and over the edge. His fingers grasped nothing but air. Then his thumb brushed the edge of the PDA. He shifted his grip and snatched it from the surface. He mentally calculated the line of sight from the doorway and was confident the computer monitor would have shielded the movement as Preedy entered.

Eric desperately hoped Preedy would not sit in his chair. He knew the lingering body heat in the leather would betray his presence. As he hunched in the shadows, the seat of the chair was at eye level. The foam padding had been compressed from Eric's weight and was still expanding to its normal state. Eric cringed, knowing this too could give him away.

He heard footsteps muffled in the carpet. Preedy's shadow fell across the carpet between the desk and cabinet. As the cabinet door opened, Eric realized he'd left the monitor on with the spyware software displaying his own laptop screen.

In one motion, he inserted the earpiece jack, which would suppress the PDA speaker, and pressed the number one, then five. He could only pray that the screen above him went blank before Preedy turned back toward his desk. If Preedy turned his monitor back on, the game would be up.

The cabinet door closed, and Eric saw a shoe appear near the chair. The shoe pivoted toward the windows and then disappeared. He heard muffled footsteps, then another magnetic click. The door closed, and Eric strained to detect any further sounds. When he was sure Preedy had left, he crawled out from under the desk. He pressed five on his PDA and waited for the monitor to light up. The screen came alive, and he pressed one to toggle to Preedy's computer, which was still displaying his laptop downstairs. He could see the security log's latest entries:

28 08 05 09:48:15   Preedy, Justin   Office 804—Entry
28 08 05 09:51:40   Preedy, Justin   Office 804—Exit

Eric worried that Joey might delete Preedy's exit from the office instead of the one when Eric would exit. If so, Preedy might be able to reconstruct the timeline. If he hurried, it wouldn't matter. He quickly shut down the spyware program and then turned the monitor off. Everything was now as he'd found it. He exited Preedy's office and sprinted to the stairwell. He silently opened the door and stepped through. As he carefully closed it behind him, he heard the door on the floor below shut quietly. Preedy had taken the stairwell. He was on the IT floor, only a few paces from Eric's office.

Joey would be expecting to see an elevator notation for Preedy on the security log.

Y

Joey was panic-stricken. He'd been watching the entries on the screen and followed Preedy's progress as he entered then exited his office. He worried that Eric had been discovered and wondered if the guards had been called. Joey waited for Preedy to enter an elevator and was poised to delete Eric's exit as soon as it displayed.

Where was Preedy? Where was Eric? The tension was killing him. He realized he'd better have a good cover story. He opened an Excel file that contained data transmission and bandwidth calculations that he and Eric had been working on. Then he toggled back to the log screen. He heard footsteps outside the door. He glanced at the screen. The entry he'd been waiting for appeared:

28 08 05 09:52:27   Preedy, Justin   Office 804—Exit

That was Eric's exit from Preedy's office! He positioned his cursor and prepared to delete the entry when Preedy suddenly loomed in the doorway and rapidly approached the desk. "What the blazes are you doing in here?" he demanded.

Joey's heart jumped, and his face undoubtedly betrayed guilt. His hands were unsteady, and he panicked that he would fumble the critical deletion.

Preedy was seconds away from rounding the desk. In desperation, Joey had to make a snap decision: either delete the critical entry and be incriminated when Preedy caught sight of the security log, or expand the Excel screen to have a plausible cover story in place. There was no time for both. He opted for Excel. He double-clicked the Excel banner, which expanded the window to full screen, hiding the log window beneath it. "I'm…" Joey stammered. The cursor vibrated nervously on the screen.

"He's helping me," Eric announced from the doorway. He stood there wiping his hands with a paper towel he'd grabbed from the bathroom. "Is there a problem with that?" Eric asked. He hoped to distract Preedy and give Joey time to clear any incriminating evidence.

Preedy scowled as he looked back and forth between them. "What's so important that you both are here on a Sunday?" he growled suspiciously.

"We have a backlog of work and wanted to get through some of it before the workweek starts. I didn't think we'd get a lot of flack for putting in unpaid overtime."

Preedy didn't seem satisfied. He was about to make another comment when an alarm sounded in the hallway. Preedy leaned across Joey and hit the intercom button on Eric's phone. He buzzed the guard's desk. The guard answered, and before he could identify himself, Preedy barked at him, "This is Mr. Preedy. What is that alarm?"

The guard replied, "Just a moment, sir. I haven't had the opportunity to pull up the code yet." His deference had an edge to it, bespeaking contempt. Before Preedy could offend him further, he abruptly blurted, "Please hold." In a classic passive-aggressive maneuver, music erupted from the speaker. The music was a bouncy Carpenters' song from the seventies and mocked Preedy's frustration.

Eric and Joey smiled conspiratorially.

Preedy's irritation at being treated so casually was escalating. The music finally stopped, and the guard casually commented, "It's only a sensor alarm, sir. Let me check here. It's coming from office eight hundred four. That's your office, isn't it, sir?"

Preedy's face reddened. "Who are you, Barney Fife?" he sputtered. The intended insult was probably lost on the young guard and made him look foolish for the effort. "Of course it's my office. Call the police and get to my office immediately. I'll join you there. And turn off that alarm!"

"Yes, sir. As you wish, sir!"

Preedy rushed out of Eric's office and yelled over his shoulder, "Come with me, you two," as he stormed to the stairwell.

Eric stole a glance at Joey, who shrugged his shoulders helplessly. "I couldn't delete it," he whispered. "By the time your entry displayed, he was storming in here, and I couldn't delete it without him seeing me. The damage is done, so I'd better exit the log." He leaned over the computer and closed the Excel window, then the security log.

Eric and Joey entered the stairwell as Eric pulled out his PDA. "Hold up a minute. I need to get rid of Preedy's ID and replace mine before we get too close to his office." They exited the stairwell on the eighth floor as the guard arrived in the elevator. He made eye contact with them and winked. They all entered Preedy's office together. He was seated at his desk and was typing furiously on his computer. They came around his desk and saw that he was viewing the security log.

It was fortuitous that Joey had exited the log or Preedy would have received a warning that the log was already in use.

Preedy had isolated the two entries that were responsible for the alarm:

```
28 08 05 09:51:40   Preedy, Justin    Office 804—Exit
28 08 05 09:52:27   Preedy, Justin    Office 804—Exit
```

"Look at this," Preedy imperiously addressed the guard as he rotated the LCD. "What is the meaning of this?"

"Oh, that isn't a problem. We have that happen from time to time." The guard goaded Preedy with indifference. "Someone opens a secure office door from the inside, then remembers something left on their desk and they double back before the door closes. When they open the door a second time, it creates a double entry, just like this. The system doesn't normally sound an alarm since this happens a lot during the workweek. But after hours, we have a heightened concern for security and set the sensitivity threshold much, much higher. I also carry my bullet in my shirt pocket here—" He grinned mischievously, patting his breast pocket—"just in case we have a real emergency." Barney played the part perfectly.

Preedy flushed. "But I didn't open my door twice. And these entries are thirty seconds apart."

"Well, maybe you opened the door wide and it took too long to close, or it caught on the jamb and it took awhile to engage the latch. Either one might explain it."

Preedy was agitated and was in an uncomfortable position. Nothing was missing from the office, so he was bordering on paranoia by pressing the issue any further. "All right. I'll take this up with your supervisor tomorrow. You may all leave now. I am going to finish up here and go home." He looked at Eric and Joey. "I want you two out of the building before I leave. In the future, I want to know in advance if you enter the premises after hours."

Eric had had enough of the arrogant posturing. "Look, Preedy," he said, "there's no reason for your haughty attitude. You may have Ms. Knowles buffaloed, but I'm going to Dr. Larson as soon as he returns. You're a short-timer here, and it's time for the transition. You may have built the system here, but it's time for a new guard."

Eric saw Joey smiling in his peripheral vision and wondered if he'd gone too far. Well, something had to be said. Preedy had been intimidating employees for years. It was about time someone stood up to him.

Preedy flushed again. He ordered them out of his office and slammed the door behind them.

Eric felt an exhilarating sense of relief. The battle lines were now clearly drawn. It was better than the awkward truce that had characterized their relationship.

They headed for the stairwell, where they could talk without being over-heard. As the door shut behind them, Joey turned to Eric and exhaled loudly. "That was way too close," Joey exclaimed. "I'm sorry about the log entry. I just didn't have any time."

They hovered in the stairwell for a few moments to finish the conversation. Eric leaned his head toward the door to listen for any sounds. "That's OK. I'm just happy the guard wasn't suspicious. Even if he was, he was more interested in goading Preedy than launching an investigation. It's obvious there's a history between them. I think Preedy is worked up because he has something to hide."

"So, what happened in there?" Joey asked.

"I found his server right where you described it. You can imagine what I found on it—a bunch of GIG files. And there seemed to be a pattern to them, but I didn't have time to figure it out."

"Well, that sure ties him into whatever is going on, doesn't it?"

"Yes, especially since someone went through the trouble of getting rid of all other evidence. My vote is for that someone being Preedy. It galls me when I think about how he mocked me when I mentioned the GIG files to Ms. Knowles. Oh—and guess what else he has on his secret server? He has a spyware program that snoops my computer. I launched it and saw you playing Minesweeper."

Joey hastily explained, "That didn't keep me from watching the log. I was just trying to calm my nerves."

"Don't worry about it. I also found a bunch of our e-mails in an NRUBLOC directory—whatever that means."

Joey thought about it for a minute. "That's an easy one to figure out."

"What do you mean?"

"It's your name, dude. NRUBLOC is Colburn spelled backwards."

TWENTY-ONE

Tuesday, August 30, 2005
25 Rajab, 1426 AH
Dhaka, Bangladesh

ALANA MISSED ERIC TERRIBLY. SHE HAD BEEN APART FROM HIM for over two weeks, and now it would be at least that long before she'd see him again. She had gotten her hopes up that she'd be heading back to the States with Dr. Larson, but the plans abruptly changed. He was going back alone, after a stop in London, and was sending her to Tokyo to help with a new lab that had just come online. She reluctantly admitted she had learned quickly and knew she should be flattered that he trusted her enough to handle the assignment on her own. Still, she knew Eric was back in Atlanta, and she wished she were there.

The collection team had finished packing everything for shipment, and now they faced the inevitable good-byes. This was almost as hard as not being able to reunite with Eric. Alana was especially disappointed at saying good-bye to Para. They had grown close over these past weeks, anticipating each other's thoughts and working in smooth tandem.

The thought of Tokyo intimidated her. She would have to meet a whole new set of people to work with, this time without the familiar presence of Dr. Larson, who had already departed, and without Para, who had become a good friend.

Alana finished packing her last bag and rolled it over to the door. The bellhop would gather all her things for her. She checked her watch and headed down to her last breakfast with Para. They wouldn't have much time together. Para was waiting at a table, as usual. Alana joined her and saw that a fresh cup of coffee was waiting for her, steam roiling above the surface. "Good morning, and thanks for the coffee!" She smiled.

Para was subdued, evidently gripped by the same melancholy that Alana was experiencing. She made an attempt at a smile. "You are welcome."

Alana reached over and grasped her hand. "Are you OK?"

Tears welled up in Para's eyes. "I was until you asked me. I am going to miss you. You are like the older sister I never had."

"Para, you're like a sister to me too, and I wish you could come with me. If only you spoke Japanese, you could go with me on my next assignment."

Para laughed through the tears. "I know many languages, but not that one. I do have a request, though. I have had a dream for a long time. When I am finished with my studies, my dream is to come to the United States. Until I met you, I didn't think it would ever come true. Now, however, I have you as a friend, and it seems possible."

Alana was excited at the possibilities. "Para, I think Dr. Larson would help after what you did for him. Maybe he could find a job for you at National Geographic."

"That certainly gives me something to look forward to." Para smiled. "But for now, I guess it is good-bye."

"Not good-bye," Alana corrected with a teary smile. "See you later."

Atlanta, Georgia

Eric had put in a couple of hard days and was exhausted. Time passed quickly when he focused on his work. It made him less anxious for Dr. Larson's return, which should be in a couple of days. He planned to share his suspicions with Dr. Larson personally. He wasn't sure if he could trust Ms. Knowles and didn't want to risk having Preedy probe her for details.

As he left the headquarters, ominous storm clouds were gathering. He walked briskly toward the bus stop and arrived just as the first raindrops began to fall. A gust rattled the limbs in the nearby trees. His cell phone rang, and he pulled it from his pocket. He didn't recognize the number. "Hello?"

"Hello, Eric." The soft feminine voice was familiar, but he couldn't place it. "This is Shoshana. I am back in Atlanta."

"Hello, Shoshana. How are you? Did you get my message?"

"I am fine, thank you. And yes, I received your message. Thank you for returning my call. As I indicated, I have some information you may be interested in."

"That sounds intriguing, Shoshana. When would you be available?"

"Are you doing anything this evening? If I am not being too forward, I thought perhaps we could have dinner together."

Eric hesitated. He still suspected that Shoshana wasn't who she claimed to be. But she knew so much about the Muslim worldview that he was anxious to question her further. And he was very curious about what she wanted to tell him. "I don't have any plans, so yes, I think we should get together. Where should I meet you?"

"Look to your left, Eric."

"Huh?"

"Do you see the black car with the flashing lights?"

Eric whipped his head to the left. A dark car sat parked at the curb across the intersection. The windshield wipers beat a slow cadence, and the emergency flashers pulsated in time with the beat. "Shoshana, what is going on here?"

"I am in the backseat, and the door is unlocked. We'll pull up in front of the bus stop so you don't have to run through the rain."

The emergency lights flicked off, and the headlights came on. The car slid effortlessly to a stop in front of him, and the door opened. Just like in a movie. He could see Shoshana in the shadows. She was alone, except for the driver.

Eric hesitated. No one knew about this meeting. Alana's face flashed through his mind even as he looked into Shoshana's dark eyes.

Shoshana seemed to read his mind. "Eric, I appreciate your hesitation. Please wait a moment while I make a phone call that will reassure you." She pulled a cell phone from her purse and pressed a series of buttons.

Eric stood at the edge of the bus stop, pelted by gusts of wind and rain. His shoes were soaked, and his pant legs turned dark as the moisture wicked its way upward. He could hear Shoshana speaking in low tones on the far seat of the limo. She leaned forward and stretched her hand out toward him. "There is someone who wishes to speak to you, Eric." She waved the phone impatiently to emphasize the importance of the call.

Eric hesitated to comply. He tentatively took the phone from her grasp and stepped back under the shelter. "Hello?"

"Eric? Is this Eric Colburn?" Another familiar voice.

"Yes. Who is this?" he asked.

"It's Melanie Wagner."

Eric shook his head as he tried to align these events in some semblance of order. Things were moving too fast. He needed to gain control. The situation was so unnerving that he could only manage a simple question. "Melanie?"

"Yes, Eric, it's me. I know this must be surreal for you. I checked out Ms. Barak but was barred from calling you until I received clearance from the deputy ambassador. You've seen Mr. Campbell at work, and you know he does things his own way. I had hoped to call you soon, but Ms. Barak interceded. She knows Ambassador Pembroke personally and contacted him a few minutes ago. He summoned me to his office and handed the phone to me. I've been instructed to assure you that you can trust Ms. Barak implicitly."

"Wow." Eric felt like he was putting a puzzle together blindfolded. "But how did she know that we knew—?"

Melanie cut him off and with a note of urgency said, "I'm sure it will all make sense when you hear her out. Ms. Barak will tell you everything you need to know. All I can say is that she is someone you want on your side. You've seen how nasty these terrorists can be, and you need someone with her resources."

"OK, Melanie. That means a lot coming from you."

"Eric, keep in mind all the things I said at the airport. Be careful, OK?"

"I will. Thank you for all your help."

"You're welcome, Eric. Good-bye."

"Bye." He stepped forward and stooped for a better view of the car's interior as he handed the phone to Shoshana. "Here's your phone."

"Would you like to come in out of the rain, Eric?"

"Sure." Eric awkwardly stooped, stepped into the limo, and shut the door. The street sounds were muted in the luxuriant interior of the limo as it slid silently from the curb.

A block away, in a darkened office on the eighth floor of the society headquarters, Preedy lowered his high-powered binoculars and stared silently as the black vehicle disappeared into traffic.

Y

It was a short ride through traffic. Eric was still sorting through his confusion when the limo pulled up to a nondescript Italian restaurant. As they exited the limo, Eric glanced at the driver for the first time. He could only see a three-quarter profile but was certain he'd seen him before. "Hey—I know him!"

Shoshana sharply interrupted him. "Please do not speak further. It is not wise out here in the open. We will continue our conversation inside. A table is waiting for us."

They entered the restaurant and were escorted to a booth in the back. Eric was impatient to voice many questions. "OK, Shoshana. What's with all the cloak-and-dagger stuff? How long have you been following me? And exactly who are you people?"

"Eric, we are free to speak in here, but I must caution you to be careful elsewhere. This location is owned by people favorable to our cause."

"This is an Italian restaurant." Eric stated the obvious.

"Yes, it is; Italians who happen to be Jewish. Our people are all over the world, but we are united in our passion for our homeland. I will partially answer your question and hope that you will be satisfied. I must choose my words carefully. We represent an organization that has Israel's security interests at heart."

"Are you with Israeli intelligence?" Eric asked.

"Mossad? Not exactly. I am not at liberty to reveal any more at this time. My superiors are not yet confident that you can be fully trusted. Will you be satisfied with that explanation for the time being?"

"I guess I'll have to be."

"I understand a lot has happened since we talked in the Cairo airport."

"That's for sure. You wouldn't believe what's happened to me."

"I assure you, Eric, I will not be surprised at anything you tell me."

"Actually, I'm not sure I'm ready to get into all that. Melanie Wagner told me I could trust you, but there's something that I have to deal with first."

Shoshana leaned back and waited serenely. Shadows flickered across her face from twin candles that struggled against a draft. The dim light softened her features, giving Eric a new appreciation for her beauty.

"I don't know how to ask this any other way than to be direct." He set his face. "Did you hack my laptop on the plane to Cairo?"

Shoshana responded without a blink or pause. "Yes, I did. I need to be forthright with you. Our meeting on the plane was not accidental. We have been following the Genographic Project for quite some time and have suspected it was compromised by Muslim extremists. We were aware of your hiring and that of Ms. McKinsey. We thought it curious that the National Geographic would hire inexperienced college sweethearts. We were determined to find out how the two of you fit into the organization. I followed you to Cairo because you work for Justin Preedy. I suspected that you were a courier delivering sensitive information to the terrorist cell located there. In retrospect, it appears Ms. McKinsey and you are what you seem to be."

"But why would you be concerned with Preedy? He's not a Muslim," Eric asked.

"No, he's not. However, his wife is, and he is sympathetic to their cause due to her influence over him."

Eric was stunned. "Preedy has a Muslim wife? You can't be serious!"

He sat back and thought through the implications. "This is what Americans call an *aha* moment. It explains so much. I couldn't figure out why he became so vicious when I mentioned a Muslim connection. I thought he protested too vehemently."

Shoshana nodded. "By the time we had arrived in Cairo, I had gone through your laptop thoroughly and was convinced you were not carrying sensitive material."

"I knew there was something different when I turned the computer back on."

"My apologies for the intrigue, but this is a serious situation, and Israel's security is at stake."

"I don't understand. Why would the Muslims be interested in the Genographic Project? And how could that present a security risk to Israel?" Eric was hopeful he would finally get answers to the questions he had been voicing for weeks.

"We're not quite sure, but we think we're close to the truth. Whatever it is, we know how it will fit in to their timetable."

"What do you mean?" Eric asked.

"To understand the connection, you must gain an appreciation for the Muslim mind and culture," Shoshana replied. "It is an entirely different way of thinking than you are accustomed to." She paused while a basket of bread and dinner salads were arranged on the table. "The historic weakness of the Islamic quest for world domination has been the hatred between their various tribes. For example, the Sunnis and Shiites have been assassinating each other since the eighth century over the rightful heir to Muhammad's empire.

"When the majority of Muslims united under their caliphate form of government, they enjoyed military success. As Roman influence declined, Islam swept across Africa, Asia Minor, and all of Spain. Sharia law was imposed, and conquered peoples were given three choices: be executed, convert to Islam, or pay extortion for the opportunity to live as a second-class citizen—an intolerable existence called *dhimmitude*. The Crusades were a defensive response to ruthless Islamic conquest, the impetus being the indiscriminate slaughter of Christian pilgrims to the Holy Land."

Eric was shocked. "I thought they were drunken warmongers who destroyed Jewish settlements across Europe."

"There was a dark side to the Crusades, to be sure. My people suffered horribly under rogue bands of Crusaders. However, once a civil government was established, my people—as well as Muslims—preferred to live under that government than in neighboring Islamic regions."

"But wasn't this the beginning of European colonialism?" Eric asked.

"Not exactly. Most surviving Crusaders returned home to their families and farms. There is no basis for the charge that they were motivated by land grants that would come by way of conquest. The important fact is, the Crusades held the Islamic advance in check for a few hundred years. Muslims eventually wrested back control of the Holy Land and resumed their assault on Europe.

"The golden age for Islam ended when their last charismatic leader, Suleiman the Magnificent, died in the mid fifteen hundreds. After that, the eventual breakup of the Ottoman Empire was a matter of time. As the empire descended into chaos, the Mideast was colonialized by the British until World War II ended. Then the Exodus began. My people were weary from generations of persecution in virtually every country we had migrated to after the Diaspora—"

Eric interrupted, "The what?"

"It comes from the same Greek word as *disperse*. My people had been scattered from our land for nearly twenty centuries. No matter where we went, we were despised as no other people have been. In spite of systematic persecution throughout our history, we somehow survived and have maintained our cultural integrity. We believe it was God's hand that kept us from being extinguished from the earth."

"Isn't that a bit ethnocentric?" Eric asked.

Shoshana's smile was disarming. "I don't think so. Think about the ancient people of the Middle East: the Chaldeans, Babylonians, Persians, Moabites, Philistines, and others. Where are their descendants today? They have been assimilated into various other peoples. Yet the Jews persist—in spite of concerted efforts to annihilate us."

"You have a point," Eric conceded. "So how does this relate to the Middle East today?"

"There were two jihads in which the Muslim nations rallied in overwhelming numbers against Israel and swore to drive us into the sea. The first was in 1948. We had scarcely proclaimed our national sovereignty before being immediately attacked from all sides by Muslim forces. It was a bitter time for my people because the British had allowed Muslims, but not Jews, to own guns. All hope was lost as we were hopelessly outmanned and outgunned. Then a miracle happened. Just like in the Torah, God confused our enemies. For reasons that are still debated today, they agreed to a cease-fire. Had they pressed on, I would not be alive today, because my parents were in the last stronghold that was about to be overrun by the Muslim hordes.

"During the cease-fire, your country did the unthinkable. Against unanimous world opinion—and protest—the United States formally acknowledged the state of Israel. This one act was the guarantee of our survival. For the first time, our leaders were able to purchase armaments on the world arms markets. During the ten-day cease-fire, we were able to ship arms to our country and finally had the means to defend ourselves. When fighting resumed, we beat back the invaders and secured our borders.

"Just as miraculously, in nineteen sixty-seven, during one of our holiest feast days—Yom Kippur—the Islamic nations united once again and vowed to drive us into the sea. They attacked on all fronts in a treacherous assault while we were humbling ourselves in prayer and fasting."

Eric interjected, "They seem to have little respect for religious observance of other faiths."

"That is stating the case mildly. Muslims have a long tradition in this regard, even against rival Muslim tribes. A favorite tactic has been to assassinate opponents when they are most defenseless—while in prayer in their mosques."

"I admit this is a lot more complicated than I realized," Eric said.

"I apologize for being so verbose," Shoshana answered, "but it's important that you understand the context behind the terrorism we face today. If you will indulge me just a little more, my history lecture is almost complete."

"Please, go ahead."

"In the Yom Kippur War, we were outnumbered ten to one, yet we once again won the day. This time we drove the Egyptians back across the Sinai and expanded our holdings in the north into Lebanon and east into Syria. Most significantly, for the first time in nearly two millennia, Jerusalem was once again under the flag of a free nation called Israel.

"The Arabs have been seething ever since. Ominously, there is recent evidence that they finally recognize a key element in the stagnation of Islam: the absence of a unified Islamic leadership that can inspire the faithful. They know the time for petty jealousies is past if they hope to vanquish us. We are too strong for them otherwise.

"Now this is the point I want you to understand. Muslims are very sensitive to symbols. The key to enflaming Islamic passion is to rally them around a symbolic cause or event. You saw the violent, worldwide rioting that took place in response to a few humorous cartoons published in Denmark? That was an orchestrated response by the Muslim fundamentalists, a test to determine the effectiveness of coordinated efforts by their extremist factions.

"Now the Muslims believe they have an appropriate symbol around which they can rally their hordes. In two years, we will celebrate the fortieth anniversary of Jerusalem's restoration to Israel. You may not be aware of it, but forty-year time frames are significant, both in the Torah and the Quran. On that symbolic date, the Muslims intend to reveal something significant they have gleaned from the genographic data they have stolen. We are not yet certain what it will be, but we expect it will energize the Islamic faithful and enflame a jihad to wrest Jerusalem from our control."

"I can't imagine anything in our data that could excite anybody but a genealogy nut," Eric offered.

"Do not underestimate the Muslims, Eric. My people believe this is the most serious threat to our security in forty years. We are concerned about the latent, pent-up rage that is waiting to be unleashed in the Muslim world. The ruling families in the moderate Islamic nations have grown fat, lazy, and corrupt. They have worshiped at the golden calf of American commerce, and their people bitterly resent them. The riches have flowed to a select few while the majority of the people are languishing in squalor. Up until recently, their rulers have been able to deflect their rage with anti-American sentiment. But a new day is dawning.

"The preparations are being made right now, and the unrest of the Muslim masses is at a peak. The recent worldwide increase in suicide bombings is only one indication of this. The extremists are poised to launch the most devastating jihad in history and will be calling all Islamic faithful to join a mighty, unified Islamic nation in their holy cause. The world has never seen the likes of what is about to be unleashed."

Eric sat back in his chair, mentally sifting the implications of Shoshana's account. What could Muslim extremists possibly want with genographic data? Eric wished he could talk to Alana, knowing she might have some insight into how science and religion converged—she usually did. But Alana was still on the other side of the world.

TWENTY-TWO

Sunday, September 4, 2005
25 Rajab, 1426 AH
Tokyo, Japan

ALANA ARRIVED AT TOKYO INTERNATIONAL AIRPORT, CLEARED customs, and retrieved her baggage. She was prepared to hail a taxi when she noticed a young woman holding a National Geographic sign with her name handwritten on it. The woman, obviously Japanese, was petite, nicely dressed, and observantly scanning the crowd. Her eyes landed on Alana, and a look of recognition lit up her face. She approached Alana and bowed slightly. "Greetings, Ms. McKinsey. I am Si Matsuura. I will be your driver and interpreter during your visit with us. Let me help you with your bags."

"Thank you, Si."

Alana stepped through the automatic doors to a beautiful day. The sun was past its zenith, and the sky was clear. A gentle breeze wafted from the east. "I appreciate the low humidity after the jungles of Asia," Alana commented.

"It isn't always this way, but today is exceptional," Si responded in perfect English. They loaded the baggage into the trunk of Si's car and headed out of the airport.

Si looked at Alana in the rearview mirror. "Will you want to go directly to your hotel?"

"Yes, please. I am tired from the long trip. I think I'll get a good night's sleep and start fresh tomorrow."

"That will be fine. The collection team isn't expecting you until then. We are excited to get started on the research."

A few minutes later, Si glanced at Alana once again and pointed to a building in the next block. "That is your hotel. I'll signal for a valet if you would like to check in."

"Thanks." Alana got out of the car, then stuck her head through the open passenger window. "Do you have any dinner plans?"

"No, I do not."

"Would you join me for dinner? I hate to eat alone in unfamiliar places. Besides, it will give us a chance to get to know one another."

"That would be very nice. Did you want to go to your room first to rest?"

"No, I'll just freshen up."

"Very well. I will have the valet park the car. When you are finished checking in, you will find the restaurant opposite the bell stand."

"OK. I'll see you in a few minutes."

Alana was smiling as she joined Si in the booth. "I'm so excited to be here. Your country is so beautiful."

"Yes, it is. But it is fairly small. It is about the size of your state of California. But there is much land that is not appropriate for settlement, so the cities are very crowded."

"What is wrong with those other areas?" Alana asked.

"Volcanoes," Si replied.

"Are you serious?" Alana was surprised. "I saw Mount Fuji as we came in from the airport. Are there more?"

"Yes. Japan has one hundred ninety-two volcanoes, of which fifty-eight are still active."

"Wow. I never realized there were that many."

"In addition, there are over three thousand islands that make up my country. Many of them are too small to support agriculture or domestic animals." Si ordered a platter of sushi for the two of them. While they waited, Si shared a number of additional items of interest about Japan.

The food arrived, and Si gave Alana a brief explanation of the various delicacies. "The chef at this restaurant is well known. He has other sushi restaurants in Tokyo and personally trains all of his chefs."

"I like to dip my sushi in a soy sauce with wasabi," Alana commented. "My boyfriend says I make it too hot—it makes him break out in a sweat."

Si laughed. "That sounds just right for me."

"How long have you been employed with the Genographic Project?" Alana asked.

"Only two weeks. I just graduated from college with a degree in biology. I am very anxious to be involved in this project."

"I just graduated a few months ago myself. Will this be your first collection safari?" Alana asked.

"Yes. Is this the first time there have been samples taken in Japan?"

"No. My understanding is that some initial samplings were taken, but now we've been directed to launch collection efforts throughout Japan,

Korea, Indonesia, and the Philippines. The new lab here will be the processing center for this whole region."

"We are pleased that Tokyo was selected for the lab site," Si replied.

"It's a logical location," Alana informed her. "Tokyo is the most central. Korea would be too far north, and Indonesia is too volatile. We're having enough trouble with the labs located in other Muslim countries to risk that."

"I've been through orientation," Si said, "but I'm not sure I fully understand our research objectives."

"You'll be fascinated," Alana responded. "We're combining many scientific disciplines as we uncover the ancient migratory patterns of our ancestors. For example, anthropologists have always theorized that rice cultivation sprang up independently throughout Southeast Asia and the Pacific Rim. We believe that history will be rewritten because of our discovery that all these population groups share a particular DNA marker. Our hypothesis is that this region was part of the Great Migration. It appears that a relatively small group sprang from a common ancestor and gradually spread from one location to the next, with each new offshoot bringing their rice-cultivation expertise with them."

"Can anyone really prove that?" Si asked.

"DNA changes everything," Alana said. "If you examine a topographical map, you can see why they fanned out along the coastal areas. There's an imposing mountain range that blocks access to the interior, so they followed the path of least resistance. This isolated gene pool has unique markers that set them apart from other population groups that swept north, then east around the mountains into the colder climates."

"That's interesting. So, we're going to identify how closely related these groups are to each other and which group spawned the others?" Si asked.

"Yes. I'm sure you will be interested in the origin of your ancestors. There's been some debate, as you know, about the first people to populate Japan and whether there were successive waves of immigrants that interbred. We should finally determine the answers to these questions. I can't wait to get started." Alana said as she signaled the server for the check.

Atlanta, Georgia

Eric took a sip of his drink and kept an eye on his IM buddy list. Joey's screen name popped up when he came online. Eric put his cup down and launched a message to Joey.

BizTekGuy: Yo, Joe! RUN?

The screen quickly updated with the response:

WallCrawler: Hey, EC! I 4get... What does RUN mean?
BizTekGuy: aRe yoU iN? C'mon, Joey, you have to get with the program!
WallCrawler: OK, OK. I'm working on it.
BizTekGuy: I have some interesting things to tell u. Can u come 2 our last meet loc?
WallCrawler: b there in 15.

Eric smiled as he imagined Joey rushing to the Commons in anticipation of the newest wrinkle in their research. He was about to shut down his IM session when he noticed that Alana was online. He quickly typed a message before she logged off:

BizTekGuy: Alana! How r u? I miss you so much...
GirlGenes: Eric! I miss you too. Other than that, I am OK. I'm glad to be out of India. I wish you were here with me. This country is beautiful.
BizTekGuy: I wish I could be there! I'm busy here, which takes my mind off of how lonely I am without you. How much longer will you be away?
GirlGenes: I'm hoping it won't be more than a month. We'll see.
BizTekGuy: I'll write you an e-mail later. There's a lot I need to fill you in on. Look for an e-mail from my Gmail account. I don't want to send it through the company e-mail. I have to sign off cuz I'm meeting Joey in a few.
GirlGenes: Bye for now. I love you, Eric.

Eric hesitated as he watched the pulsing cursor on his screen. If he signed off quickly, Alana might think he had left before her message displayed. And she might be hurt if he didn't respond.

He fought the inner turmoil. His familiar reluctance was being replaced by a poignant realization: had he died in Egypt, Alana would never have known how he felt about her. His mind drifted to an imagined scene in which Alana was grief-stricken over the grave of her unrequited love. Life was too fragile. There might not be another chance to express himself to the woman he had come to love so deeply. How could he *not* tell her? How could he prolong her uncertainty?

He would do everything in his power to protect her from the anguish he had conjured up in his mind. The cursor beckoned in pulsing patience. His fingers raced across the keys as he mentally acknowledged an emotional point of no return.

> BizTekGuy: Alana, I love you too. Whatever happens, I want you to know that. I pray for the chance to love you the way you deserve to be loved. I'm not sure what all that means yet, but I am no longer afraid to explore it with you. I have to go now but will write to you soon.

Eric smiled in contentment. He was light-headed from the adrenaline that coursed through him. He leaned back in his chair and laced his fingers behind his head. This was a nice feeling. He could definitely get used to it.

Joey! Eric abruptly realized that Joey was probably waiting for him. He jumped up from his chair and grabbed his new jacket. The nights could be chilly this time of year, especially on a bike.

Tokyo, Japan

Alana stared at the screen through welling tears. She brushed them away and cupped her hands to her face. She parted her fingers and peered through them with another glance at the screen. The message had not changed. She smiled and imagined a future that suddenly had so many possibilities. She threw herself back on her bed and thrust her fists into the air. "YES!"

She lay there for a long time with a serene smile on her face. An observer might have assumed she had drifted off to sleep, but that would be incorrect.

"Amen," she eventually murmured.

Atlanta, Georgia

Eric locked his bike and sprinted into the Commons. It wasn't hard to find Joey. He was sitting on the edge of a table with his feet perched on one of the seats. He waved so Eric wouldn't miss him. "Hey, dude, what took you so long?" Joey asked, meaningfully glancing at his watch.

"I'm sorry. After I finished chatting with you, I noticed that Alana was online. We chatted longer than I intended."

"Been there, done that." Joey nodded. "So what's so exciting that you dragged me out of bed?"

"You were asleep? I'm sorry I woke you up." He shrugged off his jacket.

"I didn't say I was asleep. I had my TV on and was watching some highlights of our win over Auburn yesterday. Not bad, knocking off a top-twenty team, huh?" Joey pumped his fist emphatically.

"You got that right!" Eric replied. "The Ramblin' Wreck looks pretty tough this season. So how did you see my chat if you were watching TV?"

"I was checking the Internet during commercials, so I heard the *ding* when your chat posted to my screen. You sounded pretty urgent, so I jumped up and ran out half dressed."

Eric had not noticed Joey's clothes. He was wearing jeans, tennis shoes with no socks, and a sleeveless T-shirt. As if on cue, Joey shivered. "It's cold in here," he complained. "They don't need the AC in this weather."

"Here—you can borrow my jacket," Eric offered. "I worked up a sweat biking, so I'm actually pretty warm." Joey had purchased two drinks, and Eric grabbed one of them. "And I'm thirsty too. Thanks for the Diet Coke."

"Sure. So what's up?"

"I don't think I told you about this, but I met an Israeli woman on my flight to Cairo."

Joey responded with a puzzled look, confirming that this was new information. "What does Alana think about that?"

"I didn't mean I'm interested in her. The Israeli woman works with the Cultural Exchange here in Atlanta. At least that's what her business card says. Well, I had dinner with her the other night, and she had some interesting information. She confirmed that there's a Muslim faction that's pilfering data from our Genographic Project. She's not certain what they're after, but she's convinced that it fits into an Islamic plot to start another holy war with Israel."

"Wow. Why did she tell you all that?"

"Her people have been interested in our project since they stumbled on the Muslim connection. They've been watching us and checking up on our staff."

"So they discovered the Muslim connection too?" Joey asked.

"Yes. It sounds like we've been right on target. This is the part you're going to love. Guess who has a Muslim wife?"

Joey shrugged.

"Would you believe Preedy?"

"No way!"

"Yes way! Not only that, but she might be tied to extremists, which makes Preedy sympathetic to their cause. We have to be more cautious than ever. We know he's monitoring my laptop and should assume our work area is bugged. That's why I wanted to meet you here."

"Aren't you being a little paranoid?" Joey asked.

"Maybe, but just because I'm paranoid doesn't mean the world *isn't* out to get me." Eric smiled.

"Funny," Joey replied. "So, what's the next step?"

"I haven't thought that out yet. The first thing I want to do is check out Preedy's Muslim connection. Doesn't his wife work part-time at the society?"

"I think so. Why?"

"If I can get into the personnel records, I should be able to find her employment documents. Maybe there's something in there that will be useful."

"Oh no," Joey complained. "Don't tell me we're doing the RFID shuffle again."

"No. Preedy will be watching us too carefully. He's probably alerted the guards to notify him if we show up after hours again. I wouldn't be surprised if he has surveillance cameras in his office by now. I think I can find the information I need the old-fashioned way. I'll just hack into the personnel server."

"Well, let me know if I can help. In the meantime, I need to get some sleep. It's going to be a long day tomorrow. If you find something, let me know."

"Sure. Do you have a Gmail account? We have to communicate off the grid from here on out."

"No, but I have a secure MySpace blog. We can write notes to each other there, and I have a pretty secure password." Joey pulled out a business card and began writing on the back. "Here's the log-in and password. Just select 'Blog' at the top of the screen and then 'Post a Message.'"

"Cool. I like it. I'll access it from my PDA. I don't want Preedy snooping in on our conversation with his spyware. He may even have a keyboard-capture utility set up to lift the password as we type."

"Good point. I'm going to head home."

Joey headed out while Eric sipped on his drink. A minute later Eric remembered Joey had his jacket and abandoned his drink, hoping to catch Joey.

As the automatic doors parted, the deep grumble of a high-performance engine caught his attention. He turned toward the sound as a black sedan shot into the roadway from the dimly lit parking area. The pedestrian in the crosswalk didn't have a chance. The sedan accelerated as the body rolled across the hood and bounced once on the windshield. The car veered to the left and sped away as the poor guy rolled off the roof onto the macadam.

Eric broke into a sprint as he yanked his cell phone open and stabbed out 9-1-1. He breathlessly shouted to the operator, "Hit-and-run accident! Georgia Tech Commons! Pedestrian down! Send medics now!" He flipped his phone closed as he approached the victim, who was facedown on the pavement. Nausea gripped him as he hovered over the torn flesh and broken limbs. He managed to avert his head just in time as he violently vomited on the asphalt, barely avoiding his new jacket.

TWENTY-THREE

Tuesday, September 6, 2005
2 Sha'bān, 1426 AH
Tokyo, Japan

Alana finished packing the last of the samples in the car as Si hopped in the driver seat. "Do you know how to get to the lab from here?" Alana asked.

"Yes," Si replied. "It's only a couple of kilometers."

"Good. We should get there before they shut down for the day. I haven't been to the lab yet, and I'm interested in seeing how it's laid out."

"I'm sorry. I thought you got a tour on your first day. If I had known, I would have taken you there myself."

"That's OK. We've been pretty busy. This is a perfect opportunity since we're so close. It doesn't make sense to call for a courier when we can drop the samples off ourselves."

Si hummed along with the music on the radio as they weaved their way through the traffic. She pulled up to a white four-story building in a commercial district. There was no sign advertising the lab's presence, and Alana was sure she would have missed it had she been driving.

They unloaded the samples and carried them around the corner to the front entrance. The magnetic lock clicked as they approached, allowing them to push through without slowing their pace. The main lobby was tastefully decorated but lacked a reception area or guest chairs. Si headed directly toward a door opposite the front entrance and pressed a button next to it. They heard a buzz from the other side.

Si explained, "Our badges don't have security clearance to the lab, so we have to wait for one of the technicians."

The door opened, and a handsome young man tentatively stuck his head through the opening. He smiled. "Hello, Si. How have you been?" He glanced at Alana with a puzzled expression.

"Hello, Muhammed. I'm fine, thank you." She smiled warmly and nodded toward Alana. "This is Alana McKinsey. She was sent from headquarters to organize our collection teams. We thought we'd bring the samples in ourselves since we were so close."

"A most excellent idea," Muhammed replied. "It is nice to make your acquaintance, Alana. Please, let me take those for you." He reached out and took the samples from Si. He turned toward Alana and motioned for her to stack her samples on top. He shouldered the door and pivoted through the opening, holding the door with his heel. "Please come in. Would you like a refreshment?"

Both of the young ladies affirmed that a bottle of water would be appreciated.

"Follow me," Muhammed replied.

Si wrinkled her nose as the lab odors wafted through the opening. Alana smiled. "The smell reminds me of my labs at the university. Believe it or not, I kind of miss it."

They followed Muhammed down the aisle along the side of the lab. Alana was curious about this aspect of the project. "Muhammed, would you have time to give me a quick tour of the facility?"

"Absolutely. This isn't a performance review in disguise, is it?"

Alana laughed. "No! Absolutely not. I can honestly say that I'm from headquarters, and I'm here to help!"

"OK then," he replied, looking relieved. "We just received an e-mail from Dr. Alomari that was critical of our production rate, and the timing of your visit seemed a bit coincidental."

"No, let me assure you that I have nothing to do with Dr. Alomari. I've never even met him and only know him by reputation. Why would he have any say in your production? He doesn't have any oversight of this facility."

"Maybe not directly, but he was responsible for hiring most of the technicians here. He seems to have a long reach, especially to those within his inner circle."

"I take it you're not one of them?" Alana asked.

"No. In spite of my name, I am not a devout Muslim. That seems to be the qualification for the inner circle."

"I see. Well, your secret is safe with me. Now, how about that tour?"

Atlanta, Georgia

Eric awoke with a start in the ICU waiting room of the Grady Health System. He glanced at the clock and realized he'd been there for thirty-five hours. He sat upright and dropped his head in his hands with his elbows perched on his knees. He said a quick prayer for Joey, then stood and stretched. He needed some caffeine and wandered out of the waiting room on a quest. Approaching the nursing station, he saw a nurse he recognized from yesterday's shift looking up from her computer terminal.

"Good morning," she said. "Would you like an update on your friend?"

"Yes, I'm worried about him."

"Well, he's still in ICU. He's in a coma, and we're concerned about brain swelling. His broken arm and leg have been set, and he has internal injuries, including a ruptured spleen. So far, there've been no iatrogenic complications, and the doctors are guardedly optimistic."

Eric wasn't sure whether or not to be encouraged. Doctor speak could be so ambiguous.

"There's nothing you can do for him right now. Why don't you go home and get some rest?"

"I need to go to work. Joey and I work together. With both of us out yesterday, the work is probably backing up. Can I give you my cell phone number? I'd appreciate a call if there's any change in his condition."

"Certainly. I'll call you myself. If there's been no change by the end of my shift, I'll call you anyway."

"Thanks a lot." Eric grabbed a cup of coffee from the cafeteria and headed for the parking lot. He pulled Joey's keys from his pocket and looked for the car. The medics hadn't let him ride in the ambulance, so he had driven Joey's car from the Commons, knowing Joey wouldn't mind. His bike barely fit behind the front seats. He had to turn the front wheel sideways and wedge it between the backseat and the door. The armrest bent a couple of spokes, but he could fix those later.

It was a new experience, driving the interstate to work. He just might have to break down and buy one of these carbon factories and contribute a little more pollution.

Y

When Eric exited the elevator on the seventh floor, he almost collided with Preedy, who was briskly walking past the elevator bank on his way into the IT department.

Preedy backed away from Eric slightly with a shocked expression. Then his surprise morphed to a scowl. "Colburn! Where have you been? We didn't hear anything out of you all day yesterday, and here you are wandering in at lunchtime, looking like a homeless bum. And we haven't heard anything out of Hampton either. What is it with this department? Maybe I need to clean house and get some legitimate programmers in here."

Eric was too exhausted to put up with Preedy's ranting. "What is it with you, Preedy? You have such a need to control the orbit of everyone in your gravitational field. I know it won't matter to you, but Joey is near death in the hospital right now. He was mowed down in a hit-and-run the other night, and I'm the only eyewitness. I had a ton of police reports to fill out, and I've been in the ICU at the trauma center, praying that Joey pulls through." With exaggerated politeness, Eric continued, "I'm sorry if my business attire is a bit shabby; I've slept in the hospital for the past two nights and haven't been home yet."

"That's no excuse for not calling in." Preedy's face was flushed in anger— and something else. "I'm putting this incident in your personnel file. When Dr. Larson gets back next week, you can expect a summons to his office for a 'come to Jesus' talk."

"That's rich coming from you." Eric couldn't contain himself. "I resent you using my Lord's name in vain. Maybe I should report you to personnel for religious harassment." Eric knew he should just walk away before he said something he'd regret, but he couldn't restrain himself. "By the way, you might be interested that the police have classified Joey's accident as attempted murder. Even though it was dark, it wasn't hard to notice the turban worn by the driver. It seems my suspicions about the Muslim connection are justified." Eric knew he had gone too far, but it felt so good to needle the jerk.

The veins in Preedy's forehead throbbed as he clenched his fists in rage. Eric expected another tirade, but instead, Preedy turned and stiffly walked away.

TWENTY-FOUR

Tuesday, September 13, 2005
9 Sha'bān, 1426 AH
Tokyo, Japan

SI DROPPED ALANA AT HER HOTEL AND PROMISED TO PICK HER up in the morning for another day of collections. Alana walked through the lobby and decided to catch up on some reading over a pot of tea in the restaurant. She settled in and was halfway through an article when she heard a couple talking in hushed tones as they approached her booth. They stopped abruptly as they passed.

"Alana! Is that you?"

She looked up in surprise. "Oh my gosh! Kyle—I can't believe it's you! What are you doing here?" She scooted out of the booth and threw herself into his arms. They pulled back, smiling warmly.

He turned to his companion and awkwardly said, "Honey, I'm sorry— this is Alana McKinsey. Her brother, Anthony, was my roommate at the academy. Alana, this is my new bride, Susan."

"It is so nice to meet you, Susan! And congratulations on your wedding. Tony has told me so much about you, I feel like I already know you. By the way, Tony was devastated that he couldn't attend your wedding. He's on deployment in Iraq—"

"I know," Kyle interrupted. "You don't have to make excuses for him. He'd have been there if he had any say in the matter, but the job comes first. In my heart, he was still my best man."

"Can you sit with me?" Alana asked. "I'm just winding down from a long day at work, but I'd love to catch up with you."

Kyle deferred to his wife, who nodded enthusiastically. They slid into the booth and signaled the server for refreshments.

"So, what brings you to Tokyo?" Alana asked. "Are you here on your honeymoon?"

"No. We had a great honeymoon, but now I'm back on the job," Kyle replied. "I'm stationed here with the USS *Ronald Reagan* carrier group. My fighter squadron deploys for a six-month tour of the Pacific Rim next week. Susan will stay in our new apartment while I'm deployed."

"That's great. Tony told me you're flying the Super Hornet. I understand that only the best of the best get that opportunity. I'm so proud of you!"

Kyle blushed. "Well, I've had a few good breaks," he replied with modesty.

"Don't let him fool you," Susan interjected. "He works hard at what he does, and he's busted his chops for this opportunity."

"That's just what a proud wife should say!" Alana smiled. "You have good reason to be proud of him."

"OK, let's stop talking about me," Kyle said. "I can't believe the coincidence of running into you. I thought you'd be in Boston by now. Weren't you going to Harvard?"

She shrugged. "Well, you remember correctly. I was all set to go to grad school. Then out of the blue, I received a great job offer from National Geographic, and I'm here on business." She gave them a brief outline of the Genographic Project and her role as a research assistant.

"Your job sounds so interesting, and you get to see the world," Kyle said. "You can always go back for more schooling." Kyle paused, then continued. "I'd like to hear about your brother, Alana. How is he doing? Can you tell us anything, or is it classified?"

"I don't think Tony would tell me anything that's classified, but I'll be careful. It's funny, he's told me things that I later heard on FOX News. Sometimes I think the news networks know more than our military officers."

"You're not alone in that observation," Kyle agreed.

"Well, where do I start? You know he and Julie have a little boy, right? Ethan is so smart. I happen to have some pictures with me." She drew out her wallet and proudly displayed the pictures. "Julie is taking care of the home front while Tony's gone."

"Are the rumors about commendation true?" Kyle asked.

Alana laughed. "He's gotten a number of commendations and is well liked by his men. He's the OIC of a platoon, something he's looked forward to for a long time."

"That stands for officer in charge." Kyle interpreted for his wife's benefit. To Alana, he said, "Susan hasn't gotten used to military acronyms, but she's learning fast. The SEAL community has a different command structure than I'm familiar with. Hasn't Tony been on a number of different platoons?" he asked.

"That's right." Alana nodded. "They have a two-year rotation with each platoon. They go through eighteen months of training, then deploy for six months. Tony started out as the third officer in charge in his first platoon, then advanced to second OIC. Now he has his dream opportunity: leading his own platoon."

"That's great. I'm happy for him." Kyle replied. "I can't wait to get back to the States and spend time with him again. Do you know when his deployment will be up?"

"No," Alana said. "Julie says there's always a chance it could be extended. Things are pretty fluid in Iraq right now. It's become a magnet for all the terrorists in the world. I've e-mailed him a few times but haven't had a response. I guess he's too busy."

"Actually, he probably hasn't gotten them yet," Kyle said. "He's on a sensitive deployment, and I don't think he's allowed to check his personal e-mail. Have you tried his military e-mail?"

"No, I thought it was for special forces communications only."

"I could relay a message to him for you," Kyle offered. "I'm sure that would get through. Just be careful what you say."

"That would be so nice. Thank you."

"When you send it, I'll translate it into our secret code language just in case it's intercepted."

Susan looked puzzled, but Alana laughed. "I almost forgot about that." She explained to Susan, "Tony and Kyle developed their own code language for their fellow plebes in their first year at the naval academy. They were able to keep secrets from the upperclassmen who harassed them about *everything*. Tony taught me the language, and we used it in our e-mails to each other." She smiled at Kyle. "I'll save you the trouble of translating. I still remember the code. This will be great. Let's trade addresses so we can stay in touch." Alana pulled out a card and wrote her address, and Kyle did the same. "Would you add your phone number as well?" Alana asked and turned to Susan. "If Kyle is going to be gone on deployment, why don't we get together and hang out some? I think I'm going to be here for a few weeks."

"I'd love that!" Susan replied hopefully. "I haven't met anyone here, and I was worried about being lonely when Kyle leaves."

"I understand. I've been lonely myself. I've wanted to do the tourist thing since I've been here, but it's no fun doing it alone. What do you think?"

"It sounds like a lot of fun. Give me a call!"

Y

Eric parked Joey's car and entered the hospital. The receptionist waved in recognition. He was spending so much time here that he knew many of the staff by name.

"Hi, Rhonda. Pulling the late shift again?" he asked.

She wrinkled her nose in disgust and nodded her answer as she picked up an incoming call on the switchboard.

Eric found the correct elevator bank and pressed the button. On Joey's floor, he got off the elevator and looked toward the nurses' station. The duty nurse recognized him and sadly shook her head in response to his unasked question. There had been no change. Joey had been moved to a room that allowed visitors, so Eric camped out there most evenings. Sometimes he ran into Joey's parents holding vigil as well. Joey was in a coma and was fed intravenously. It was against regulations, but the nurses would let Eric have Joey's dinner tray. He was getting pretty used to hospital food, which wasn't much worse than his mom's cooking.

Eric stayed by Joey's side for a few hours but decided to go back to his apartment to sleep. As always, he wrote a note of encouragement to Joey, just in case he woke up in Eric's absence. He tucked it into Joey's hand and whispered, "Surf's up!" in his ear. He figured if anything would jolt Joey from the coma, that would do it.

TWENTY-FIVE

ALANA, KYLE, AND SUSAN DESCENDED THE LONG GANGPLANK TO the dock and glanced back at the enormous aircraft carrier they had just toured.

"That was amazing," Alana remarked. "It's like a floating city."

"I'm constantly impressed with how much responsibility is delegated to young men and women," Susan said. "Kyle was flying fifty-million-dollar jets when he was twenty-three."

Alana said, "Kyle, I want to thank you for including me in the tour. I feel like I've imposed on your last day together."

"Don't worry about it," Kyle reassured her. "We still have our last evening to enjoy. Before you go, let me show you one more thing." Kyle gestured toward a building set back from the dock area. They walked from the bright sunlight through the front entrance into a wood-paneled room featuring a sitting area with plush chairs and sofas. "After you, ladies." Kyle lightly brushed his wife's back with his hand as he directed them through a wide archway. "Three," he commented to a hostess, then turned to the two women. "This is our officers' club. I thought you ladies might be thirsty after the tour."

They ordered drinks and appetizers.

"The air conditioning feels wonderful. It was hot on the ship," Susan commented.

"Yes, it can get hot and stuffy at times. It's easy to get overheated, especially with all the stairs you have to climb."

"Those aren't stairs; they're ladders," Susan retorted. "And they're everywhere. Then there are the hatchways between all the rooms that you have to step over. No wonder sailors are so fit."

Kyle nodded. "It does separate the men from the boys."

They talked for quite a while, sampling the appetizers. Alana marveled at the changes in Kyle. He was obviously in love with his wife and was a different man than she remembered. She felt the familiar twinge of loneliness as her thoughts turned to Eric.

"Who are you thinking of?" Susan asked.

"Does it show?" Alana blushed, realizing how transparent she was. "I have a boyfriend back in Atlanta. I miss him. Seeing the love between the two of you is a reminder of what I have to look forward to."

"That's nice of you to say, but I hope we haven't made you uncomfortable," Susan commented.

"No, not at all. It's refreshing, and I hope you always show your love for each other the way you do." Alana scooted her chair back from the table. "Well, I'm going to head back to the hotel. I have some preparation to do for the week. Thanks again for including me." Alana rose from the table. "Kyle, be safe. Susan, I'll call you in a couple of days. Maybe we can go shopping next weekend."

"I'd love it! *Sayonara!*"

Alana smiled. "*Konbanwa!*" she replied.

Atlanta, Georgia

"Eric! Joey's awake!"

Eric winced. He hadn't anticipated the loud exclamation or he'd have kept the phone at arm's length. Nevertheless, the news overshadowed his irritation. "When?" he shouted back at the phone.

"Thirty minutes ago. We noticed his brain-wave activity was spiking. Then he woke up. Come as soon as you can! He's asking for you."

"I'm on my way!" As he pressed the end button, Eric realized he didn't know whom he was thanking. It could have been any one of a number of nurses. They'd all taken a liking to Eric and were sympathetic with his loyalty to Joey. The unmarried nurses seemed to compete with each other for the opportunity to keep him informed. It was probably one of them.

Eric threw on a sweatshirt and grabbed Joey's keys. He took the stairs two at a time and sprinted to the car.

He pulled onto one of Atlanta's numerous Peachtree streets and accelerated as the light at the next intersection turned, scooting through while it was still yellow. "Yes!" he exclaimed. The lights on this stretch were synchronized, so he'd have to increase his pace or risk running a red light at one of the upcoming intersections. A slowpoke in front of him threatened to thwart his navigational skills. Eric shot a glance over his left shoulder and eased into an opening in the next lane. Accelerating even more, he overtook the lumbering vehicle on the right and was able to merge in front of it as the slowpoke braked for the yellow. Eric raced through the intersection, again beating the red light. He smiled into his rearview mirror at the loser who puttered to a stop.

He gained on the synchronized lights and passed through the next two intersections on green. He could ease off on the accelerator now. Eric moved to the far right lane as he anticipated a turn in the next block. He pressed the brake, which gave no resistance. He effortlessly jammed it to the floorboard with no result.

Eric looked up in terror. The back of a MARTA bus was expanding rapidly. It sat on the far side of the intersection, lights blinking as it dropped passengers. There was no opening to his left. He grabbed the stick and downshifted, then yanked the emergency brake as hard as he could.

The engine whined in protest, and the tires squealed as Eric threw the wheel to the right. He slammed the heel of his hand into the horn, warning the pedestrians who were stepping off the curb. The car fishtailed. He couldn't risk overcorrecting or he'd slam into the bus—or the pedestrians.

Eric's only option was to yank the wheel farther to the right, which threw the car into a spin. He thanked the Lord that it was a one-way street, as the spinning car skidded diagonally across the side street.

His head was thrown back against the headrest from the centrifugal force. As the car rotated through a complete circle, Eric saw his opportunity to turn into the spin. The diagonal slide continued, however, and he slammed broadside into a parked car. His head now pulled to the left, and he heard glass shattering as the air bag deployed. It slammed his head back against the window frame. He felt something warm trickle down the back of his neck and fought for air as the bag pressed relentlessly against his chest. His peripheral vision turned dark as the first of the pedestrians ran to his aid.

"Can't breathe..." he wheezed, then blacked out.

Y

Eric felt pressure on his forehead and opened his eyes. A paramedic was poised above him, applying a bandage to his forehead. It took a moment to realize he was lying across the front seat of Joey's car with his head facing the passenger door.

"Welcome back," the medic said. "You're pretty lucky. It could have been much worse. Hold still while I wrap your head. You have a gash on the back, and it looks like glass fragments are embedded above your eyebrow. Don't let all the blood scare you. It isn't as bad as it looks. Head wounds tend to be bleeders."

"Was anyone else hurt?" Eric asked.

"No. A couple of bystanders are talking to the police now. They're singing your praises. They said it was pretty heroic how you avoided them." The medic turned to his partner. "Bring the gurney, and help me lift him." He turned back to Eric. "Do you have any back or neck pain?"

"No, just my head."

"OK. We're going to lift you now. Let me know if you experience any other pain." They lifted Eric easily and strapped him on the gurney.

"I think I'm OK," Eric said. "I don't want to go to the hospital." That was stupid, he thought. He'd been on his way to a hospital.

"Why don't you relax and let us do our job?" The medic admonished him. "It's better to err on the side of caution. Your adrenaline is running pretty high right now and could be masking injuries you won't feel for a while."

Eric noticed a wrecker in front of the car. As soon as the medics wheeled him away from the car, the mechanic hoisted the front end and prepared to haul it away. He walked over to Eric and handed him a card. "Here's the name of the garage we're hauling your car to. Give us a call tomorrow because we need your insurance information. We'll have a repair estimate ready for you by then." He paused for a moment. "Are you a weekend mechanic or something?" he asked Eric.

"No, why?"

"I noticed fluid dripping from the front passenger-side wheel and stuck my head underneath. The brake line nipple wasn't tightened down, and fluid was leaking."

"What does that mean?" Eric asked.

He answered the question with a question. "My guess is that you had no brakes, right?"

Eric nodded and immediately regretted it as a wave of pain warned him to be still.

"The nipple is on a hex nut that you loosen to bleed air from the brake line—which is a hydraulic system. The nut was wide open, so pressing the brake would only expel the fluid from the system."

"But I've been driving the car for several days and haven't noticed any problem. Are you sure it couldn't come loose from road vibration?"

"Not likely. The whole undercarriage has road grime all over everything.

The grime has been wiped away from the nipple, and the hex nut has fresh wrench scratches on it. It looks like the nut wasn't tightened after bleeding air out of the line."

Eric didn't have a response. He laid his head back as the medics dropped the backrest in preparation for loading. The legs collapsed as the gurney was rolled into the ambulance. One of the medics jumped in the back with him while the other turned on the siren and pulled into traffic.

"Where are you taking me?" he asked.

"To Grady. They have the only trauma center in town."

Eric smiled but kept his head still.

"What's so funny?" the medic asked.

"That's where I was heading when I crashed. My friend has been in the ICU for two weeks and just came out of a coma. I was rushing to see him." Eric fell silent as he reflected on all that he needed to tell Joey. It was going to be so good to have him back in the land of the living. He was surprised at how much he missed Joey's companionship.

The ambulance rocked him gently as it wove its way through traffic. Once in the emergency bay, paramedics wheeled him into the trauma center and took him directly to a curtained waiting area. He was transferred to the hospital gurney, and his oxygen line was transferred to a spout protruding from the wall. The medics collected their things and departed for the next crisis.

After a while, Eric was wheeled into the bowels of the hospital for X-rays, then returned to his waiting area.

After another long wait, a doctor arrived. A brief introduction was followed by an equally brief interrogation. There were more serious traumas to attend to, and Eric sensed his minor injuries were a distraction. The doctor confirmed Eric's assumption. He injected a local anesthetic into Eric's forehead and used tweezers to extract some glass fragments. They made a peculiar grinding sound that resonated through his head as the tweezers pinched, then slipped off of the bloody fragments. Eventually, the doctor pronounced that he had retrieved all the shards and stitched Eric's wounds. Finally, he wrapped his head in bandages and gave him some pain meds.

Eric was not allowed to cut through the hospital to the main entrance, so he had to exit the emergency room and walk around the block to the main entrance. Rhonda was at the front desk. Eric knew he must be a sight from her shocked expression.

"What happened to you?" she asked, eyeing his bloodstained shirt. "You look worse than most of our patients."

"Just a little car accident," he replied with a shrug. He turned away from her and headed to the elevator. He got off on Joey's floor and for a moment thought about taking a circuitous route to Joey's room. He wanted to avoid the nurses' station in his eagerness to see Joey but decided it would be rude to do so. The nurses had all been so nice to him, and they'd taken the time to call him.

When they saw him, their reaction was much like Rhonda's. They flocked around him and expressed concern for his condition. The attention was nice, but, as expected, they wanted to know all the details of his accident.

He felt claustrophobic and smothered in the tight hallway, made more so by the hovering women. He hesitated, looking from face to face. "I don't mean to be rude, ladies," he assured them, "but I'm anxious to see Joey. I have a lot to tell him. Can I give you the details later?"

The head nurse looked sympathetic and patted his shoulder reassuringly. "I understand, Eric. It's good therapy for you, and it certainly helps patients out of their comas when loved ones talk to them."

"I don't know if I can take the credit, but at least he's out of his coma now."

The nurses glanced at one another in puzzlement. One of them impulsively turned toward Joey's room to check for herself. She made eye contact with a couple of the nurses and shook her head in mute affirmation.

The head nurse again spoke for the group. "Eric, Joey's condition hasn't changed. He's still in a coma." They nodded with sideways glances that affirmed their unanimity.

Eric backed up in shock. "But you called me…someone called me. She was so excited—"

The nurses again exchanged puzzled looks. "We've been on duty since six this morning. None of us called you, Eric."

TWENTY-SIX

Wednesday, September 22, 2005
18 Sha'ban, 1426 AH
Tokyo, Japan

"H ELLO?" ALANA ANSWERED THE PHONE IN HER ROOM.
"Alana! I'm being followed!" The voice on the phone was contorted with fear, but she was sure she recognized it. "Susan? Is that you?"

"Yes! Alana, I'm so afraid. Help me!"

A shiver of fear shot through her spine. "Susan, where are you? What happened?"

"I was shopping and a Mideastern man approached me. He asked me if my husband was a pilot at the air base. Before I could think, I replied, 'Yes. Did something happen to him?' Then I realized I shouldn't have told him. I left my groceries and ran from the store!"

Alana heard a rustling sound, and Susan was no longer talking. She could hear a racing engine and squealing tires in the background.

Then Susan came back on the phone. "Alana, are you still there?" she asked breathlessly.

"Yes, Susan. What's happening?"

"I dropped the phone. They're following me. I thought I could make a couple of turns to get away, but it didn't work. Alana, they're gaining on me. Help me!" Susan was hyperventilating and difficult to understand.

"Susan—where are you? I'll call the police and—"

"I'm pulling into my apartment now. I'll run inside and lock myself in...wait." There was a long silent pause.

Alana could not hear any engine sounds and assumed that Susan had killed the ignition. She heard a chime and realized a car door had opened. She heard Susan shout, "Get away from me!" A door slammed. The engine roared to life, and tires squealed. She heard a loud thump, and the phone went dead.

Y

Atlanta, Georgia

Eric sat back from his computer in frustration. He extracted the backup tape from the external drive and threw it in the box with the others. It was the last one from their nightly backup utility. Joey had confirmed that all the tapes prior to August 16 had GIG files on them, but Eric had just checked them all and couldn't find any evidence to support what Joey had said. Someone had gotten to the tapes and erased the evidence.

He could think of only one other place where he might find a surviving GIG file—on Preedy's secret server. But he didn't have a way to get into the server, especially without Joey's help again. Besides, it was too risky with Preedy lurking about.

Eric's thoughts went to Joey again. On impulse, he called the hospital and connected with the nursing station. Still no change. How long would it be? Would Joey ever pull out of the coma? Eric needed someone to talk to. He reflected on how helpful Joey had been when they had worked together. It wasn't the same without him.

Eric suddenly remembered a detail. Joey had attempted to crack a GIG file he had obtained from a backup tape. He had never reported success, so Eric assumed the encryption was too resilient. Maybe Eric could succeed where Joey hadn't.

He returned the box of tapes to the proper shelf and exited the server room. Joey's cubicle was just down the hall. He sat at Joey's desk and logged on to the PC. A scan of the hard disk revealed no GIG files. He hadn't expected to find any. Joey wouldn't be that careless. He surveyed Joey's work area, then opened the desk drawers and rifled through the contents. He extended his hand into the pencil drawer and clawed the back with his fingertips. Nothing.

Eric was about to admit defeat as he thought of any other possible hiding places. None came to mind. Deciding to help himself to Joey's tin of cinnamon Altoids that sat next to the monitor, he opened the tin and peeled back the paper. A small rectangular plastic box sat beneath the paper. Eric smiled to himself. The backup tape was hiding in plain sight. He was glad he shared Joey's love for Altoids.

"What is that?" a voice asked from behind Eric. "Is that one of our backup tapes?"

It was Preedy.

"What are you doing with a backup tape outside of the server room?" Preedy demanded.

Eric did not have a response.

"I'll take that." Preedy thrust out his hand, palm up, and jerked his cupped fingers twice. It reminded Eric of the subtle gesture made famous by *The Matrix* movies. It was a challenge to a fight. Was Preedy signaling a challenge here?

As much as Eric would love to punch Preedy's lights out, he restrained himself. Nothing would be gained by a direct assault. He relinquished the tape and sulked back to his office, ignoring the triumphant grin on Preedy's face.

Tokyo, Japan

Alana called Susan back but was immediately connected to her voice mail. She dialed 1-1-0, the emergency number she'd see on a card in her hotel room.

"Is this the police? I only speak English," Alana shouted.

"What is the nature of your emergency?" the voice replied in English without the slightest hesitation.

"I think my friend has been kidnapped. She's an American, the wife of a navy pilot."

"Where are you now?" the voice asked.

"I'm not with her. I mean, I'm not where she was kidnapped." Alana was flustered and realized how confusing this sounded. She gave the operator Susan's address and urged her to dispatch a patrol car. "I'll meet your officers there and explain everything."

Minutes later, Alana slammed the taxi door behind her and burst into Susan's apartment complex. She found a pair of police cruisers parked at severe angles in front of Susan's apartment, with dozens of blue flashing lights. They effectively blocked any through traffic and had attracted a crowd of curious bystanders.

Alana noticed one of the policemen had a red armband, signifying he spoke English. She announced that she had called in the emergency and hastily explained everything that had happened.

At that moment, Alana's phone rang. She looked at the display. "It's Susan!" she told the policeman. "Hello!" she shouted into the phone. "Susan—are you OK?"

"Yes!" came the reply. "I'm at the naval air station. They followed me to my apartment, and one of them tried to get in my car. I pulled away, and I think I ran over his foot. I needed to find a safe place and remembered the marines at the main gate on the base. I figured that would scare them off."

"Hold on a minute, Susan. I'm at your apartment. The police are here." She turned to the officer with the armband. "Mrs. Hammond is safe! She's at the Yokosuka Naval Base."

"I need to speak with her," he said.

"OK. Just a minute." She turned back to the phone. "Susan, a police officer needs to ask you a few questions."

Alana handed the phone to the police officer, who kept Susan on the line for quite a while. Finally, he handed the phone back to Alana. "She wants to speak with you again. We are finished here and will coordinate our report with your DOD, Department of Defense. Thank you for your concern."

"You're welcome. Thank you for coming so quickly." She put the phone to her ear. "Susan?"

"Alana, thank you for being there," she gushed. "I was so scared."

"Susan, is there anything I can do for you?"

"Yes. Can you get to the base? I'm too scared to drive right now. The security team says the DOD sticker on my windshield is what drew the attention of these people, whoever they are. They want to move me onto the base here where I'll be more secure. In the meantime, all my things are at the apartment."

"I'll be happy to come get you. I wish I could get in your apartment for you. I could bring some things to you now."

"I can tell you where to find my spare key."

TWENTY-SEVEN

Saturday, September 24, 2005
20 Sha'bān, 1426 AH
Atlanta, Georgia

Eric scanned his computer screen with satisfaction. The Linux operating system was a perfect solution to Preedy's spying. At boot-up, Eric could select Windows when he didn't have anything to hide but could switch to Linux if he wanted to work off the grid. Preedy would assume he'd undocked his laptop and would be none the wiser.

One success led to another. He had finally cracked the password to NGS' personnel database. He set up a search, selecting "All files and folders" and entered "I-9" for the file/folder name. He absentmindedly wiggled the mouse and was entertained by the cursor's tail as it swept through a series of synchronized circles.

Frustrated with the delay, he was about to abort the search when the first result popped up on the screen. Then a number of matches began to fill the screen. He clicked the column header to sort by file name and paged down to the Ps. There was only one Preedy. That was confusing. Joey had confirmed that Preedy's wife worked part-time for the society. Eric was certain that an I-9 form should be filled out for all employees, regardless of whether or not they were foreign nationals.

He scrolled back to the top and immediately noticed something odd. There were two listings for Alomari: Ahmed and Basira. Eric was surprised and wondered if they were related. He opened Ahmed's I-9 form. The top of the form read "U.S. Department of Justice, Immigration and Natural-ization Service." This signified Ahmed's form as an old one. Eric knew the current form was titled "Department of Homeland Security."

Above Ahmed's signature was a boldfaced warning: "I am aware that federal law provides for imprisonment and/or fines for false statements or use of false documents." He smiled at the naïveté of bureaucrats who thought this sufficiently intimidating to scare illegal immigrants. He scrolled through the form and noticed Alomari had selected "An alien authorized to work." The expiration date was a few years old, which implied that he had left the States after the initial employment period. There wasn't any helpful information on the form.

He next opened the I-9 form for Basira. Eric had no idea whether Basira was a feminine or masculine name, so he checked the maiden-name block. Alomari was noted, so this person was an unmarried woman at the time she'd filled out the form. She was listed as a lawful permanent resident. He glanced at her address and noticed she lived in Marietta, a nearby suburb. Eric cross-checked the personnel files and determined that her last name had not been changed since filling out the form. Who was she? Was she connected to Ahmed? Something to follow up on.

It was time for a strategic call. He got up from his desk and headed to the men's room. He turned on the water faucet to provide background noise and pulled the number from his cell phone's contact list. The phone rang four times, and he expected a voice mail prompt any moment.

A woman finally answered. "Hello, Eric."

"Can we meet?"

Y

Tokyo, Japan

Susan paid for the groceries while Alana pulled her car up for loading. Susan placed the fragile items on the seat and threw the paper products on the floor. They drove across the base to the bachelor officer's quarters (BOQ), where Susan was staying until her new apartment was set up. The two women fell into a coordinated domestic routine. Susan prepared a luncheon salad while Alana stowed the groceries and toiletries. They sat in her small family room and turned on the news from habit.

"Thanks for hanging out with me again, Alana. Everything seems so disjointed. I just needed a friendly face to help me get through these past couple of days."

"I'm happy to, Susan. We finished up our collections this morning, and I decided to take the afternoon off," Alana reassured her. "This will be therapeutic for me too. It takes my mind off of how lonely I've been."

"I still shudder when I remember those men following me. When the husky one approached me in the store, I was intimidated because he got so close. You know the feeling when someone invades your personal space? He smelled bad, and his breath was atrocious. His eyes were deep set with a haunted look about them. I'm sure he hadn't bathed or shaved in a week."

"Do the police or DOD security have any leads?" Alana asked.

"They both had me look at a bunch of mug shots, but I didn't recognize any of them. It turns out that my incident is not that uncommon. Other women have been approached, so new security measures are being implemented. They're warning wives to be extremely cautious, and they're offering free self-defense classes to anyone who wants them. They think it's a form of psychological warfare. If our husbands fear for our safety, their operational readiness may be compromised."

"I know what you mean. My brother sent our family a message that we should get rid of anything that advertised our relationship to a SEAL. Word came down through the command that al Qaeda was going to target the families of our special forces in order to distract them. My parents used to fly a SEAL flag along with the American flag in front of their house, and he told them they should take it down. He's especially concerned for their safety because their address is listed in his personnel file as his permanent residential address. If the terrorists really intend to go after the families, he's not confident of the DOD's ability to safeguard the databases where the information resides."

"What an awful thing. Why do these people target civilians, especially women and children?" Susan asked.

"You can't understand them by applying the rules of logic," Alana replied. "You have to remember the contrast between their holy book and ours—the Quran and the Bible. The Bible teaches us to love our enemies and pray for them; their book instructs them to hate their enemies and slay them. It boils down to this: the world will be a better place without us, and they would rather kill us than share space with us. Period. And 'us' is extended to any Muslim of a different stripe, especially moderate, peaceful Muslims who find the violent teachings of Muhammad somewhat inconvenient."

"What do you mean? I thought Muhammad was a lot like Jesus."

"Nothing could be further from the truth. In the darkest days of Muhammad's early ministry, the movement was about to implode. He led his band of followers in attacks on caravans of peaceful merchants. Pillage and murder were the only means of funding the cause. As he later solidified his power base, he had eight hundred Jewish men from one village beheaded and thrown into a trench. Muhammad once dispatched a henchman to murder a poet who had criticized him in her writings. The man entered her residence, ripped her nursing child from her grasp, and slaughtered her. Muhammad praised his warrior for valor and had his deed recorded for posterity. There's much more, but these examples are well documented."

"That's horrible. And this is the man who founded a religion?"

"Yes. He left a terrible legacy."

"But most Muslims are much more civilized today—except for a few radicals—aren't they?"

"The media would have us believe it, but I'm not so sure. I think many of them tolerate us only when it's expedient. But all bets are off when it comes to furthering their agenda. For example, my brother e-mailed me an article written by an infantry officer he knows in Iraq. His mission had been to supervise the rebuilding of a local school. After tea, smiles, and handshakes with the Iraqi townspeople, his team departed—and they were promptly struck by a roadside bomb. You'd think the townspeople would at least wait until the school was built."

Susan interjected, "It's like the uneducated rabble that led the French Revolution. They were so intoxicated with power and jealous retribution that they beheaded the intelligentsia who could have helped rebuild their civilization. They struggled for more than a century because of their shortsightedness."

"Exactly."

Atlanta, Georgia

Eric entered the restaurant and scanned the tables. He spotted Shoshana and made his way through the tables, waving off the hostess in the process. He pulled up a chair. "Hi, Shoshana. Thank you for meeting with me on such short notice."

"I always try to make time for you, Eric."

"I want to tell you about some things that have been happening to me lately. This may sound paranoid, but I think the terrorists have tried to kill me twice, and my friend is in a coma because of them." Eric watched Shoshana's face intently, looking for signs of disbelief.

Shoshana returned his stare. "No, Eric, if you knew these fanatics like I do, you would realize that sounds very believable. Tell me what happened."

Eric launched into a detailed recounting of what had happened to Joey, as well as his car accident and the ominous phone call that precipitated it.

Shoshana nodded patiently during Eric's recounting. "I had received reports of two of those incidents, Eric, but I did not know of the third. I thought perhaps Joey was run down because of his close association with you. I did not know he was wearing your jacket, meaning that you were the likely target."

"You say that you received reports. I'm even more curious about who you work for."

"At our last meeting, I told you that my superiors were not yet decided about you and that I was restricted in what I could reveal. I am pleased to inform you that you are not under any suspicion. In fact, I am authorized to offer you protection. I will assign one of my men to shadow you and…how do you say…'watch your back.'"

"Yes, that's the expression. So you *are* with the Mossad, aren't you?" he asked.

"Will you be satisfied if I do not deny it?" she asked.

"Sure."

"Very well. Let us move to another subject. We have much to discuss."

"Before that, there's something else I need to tell you. I was looking through our personnel records and found two Alomaris, Ahmed and Basira. It turns out Basira lives here in the Atlanta area. I didn't know if you knew about her. If she's connected to Ahmed somehow, maybe she's involved with the terrorists who have infiltrated my company."

"Yes, Eric, we know about her. You are correct in your assumption about her relationship to Ahmed. She is his sister."

"I knew there had to be a connection!" Eric congratulated himself on his sleuthing abilities.

"I am surprised you did not realize who her husband is, however. Were you not aware that Muslim wives often retain their maiden names?"

"No, I wasn't. I know feminazis do that, but I assumed Muslim women would take their husband's name since they don't exactly fit the liberated model. So who is she married to?"

"Justin Preedy, of course."

Tokyo, Japan

"You may proceed, ma'am." The marine guard snapped to attention but stopped short of a salute.

"Thank you." Alana navigated Susan's car through the serpentine traffic barriers. "What is all this for?" she asked Susan.

"They're designed to impede any vehicle approaching at high speed. It's SOP following the horrible bombing in Beirut, Lebanon, that killed over two hundred marines." Susan pointed to a large rectangle embedded in the pavement. "See that? It's a solid-steel barrier that juts up from the surface in an emergency. It will stop any vehicle before it can get close to our military personnel."

"That's interesting. Well, it's nice to get off the base and away from the reminders of the scary world we live in," Alana remarked. "The mall we're going to will be a nice distraction for a few hours. You'll love the shops." She rotated the volume knob on the stereo to drown out the wind from the open sunroof. The afternoon breeze was refreshing. Papers from the backseat fluttered in a gust of wind and caught Alana's attention in the mirror. She looked over her shoulder in disbelief. "Oh my gosh. I forgot to send the paperwork." She glanced at Susan. "I need to take a quick detour. The lab isn't far out of our way. They need this paperwork to match the last batch of samples I dropped off. Do you mind?"

"Not at all. We have all afternoon and evening. A few minutes won't make any difference."

Alana wove her way through traffic like a native. She pulled up and parked in the same place as on her previous visit. "You want to wait here? I'll just be a minute."

"No problem. I'm going to recline my seat a little and soak up some sun."

"OK. I'll hurry." Alana snatched the papers from the backseat and headed around the corner.

Susan laid her head back and turned to face the sun angling through the open roof. She noticed an ethnic market diagonally across from the lab. A group of young men drew her attention. Their turbans were unusually white in the afternoon sunlight.

She elbowed herself upright and lifted a hand to her brow to divert the glare. Her eyes narrowed, but not because of the sun's rays. A gnawing sense of recognition gripped her.

One of the men had glanced her way and assessed her attributes. The look in his eyes was the impetus of a predictable reaction. Men can sense the presence of an attractive woman by a certain look in another's eyes. It is a primal response, and few are able to subdue the siren song. There is great satisfaction to be found in the appraisal of a lovely woman.

This was the case with his companions, who noticed his distracted glance. Susan anticipated the reaction. As expected, every head swiveled simultaneously and found the object of interest without the slightest misdirection. Then one of the men limped forward, tilting his head, curiously alert.

Susan gasped in mutual recognition.

"Hey—you're a married woman!" teased Alana.

Susan was startled by Alana's sudden appearance. Alana rounded the car and dropped into the driver's seat. "No, you don't underst—" Susan flinched. The man across the street was shouting urgent commands and gesticulating to his companions.

Susan grabbed Alana's arm in a vise grip. "Alana! Get us out of here *now*!"

Alana turned the key and glanced up to see a group of men purposefully crossing the intersection toward them. The narrow road would not allow a U-turn. She looked in her mirror and threw the car into reverse.

The men sprinted toward the car.

She gunned the engine and rapidly backed away from them. She whipped the wheel to the left, throwing the car's back end into an alley. While the car was still rolling, she threw the stick into drive and jammed the accelerator. The wheels spun, shrieking smoke as she whirled the wheel to the right. The back of the car slid left as both women leaned right, urging the back end to follow them. With a lurch, the car obeyed and they sped into the distance.

"What was that all about?" Alana asked.

"One of those men—he was the man who chased me from the market."

Tokyo, Japan

Satam waited as Muhammed checked the fluid levels for the gene sequencers that needed to run through the night. He watched as Muhammed turned off the banks of lights and opened the door to the lobby. Then he struck. The door slammed back against Muhammed's chest and shifted his center of gravity. He fell heavily, and his wrist gave way as he attempted to arrest his fall. He cried out in anguish and rolled to relieve the pressure on the wrist. Satam waved for the two lab techs to surround his fallen foe.

"Satam! What are you doing here?" Muhammed cried out.

"That is none of your concern, Muhammed," Satam said sharply. "However, I have questions for you. Who was the blonde woman who came into the lab a short while ago?"

"Why do you want to know?" Muhammed impotently attempted defiance.

Satam stepped forward and pressed his foot onto Muhammed's damaged wrist. "Do not try my patience. I am the one who will ask the questions." He applied pressure. "Who was that woman?"

Muhammed screamed and writhed in pain. "Please, there is no need for this. She is an employee; that is all."

Satam applied more pressure. "I expect you to be more forthcoming. I want a name."

"I remember only her first name. It is Alana. She is from America, the state of Georgia. She works at the Genographic Project headqua-aaah!" He screamed as Satam applied all of his weight. There was a loud crunch as the bones gave way. Muhammed passed out.

"Revive him!" Satam barked. "Dr. Alomari requires more information from this heretic."

TWENTY-EIGHT

Monday, September 26, 2005
22 Sha'bān, 1426 AH
Atlanta, Georgia

"Come in, Eric, come in." Dr. Larson waved Eric to a seat in front of his desk. "Can I have Stephanie bring you a cup of coffee?"

"No, thanks. I have some water." Eric fished his water bottle out of his jacket.

"We have a lot to get caught up on, Eric," Dr. Larson observed. "I'm sorry my travels have kept me away so long. You've had quite a few harrowing experiences since you've joined us. I am interested in what you make of all this."

"What exactly have you heard, Dr. Larson?" Eric feared that Preedy might have already poisoned his mind.

"Why don't you tell me everything? Assume I know nothing."

"Fair enough. I appreciate your open-mindedness." Eric repeated all the events of the past two months once again. At least now he had more facts to feather into the timeline of events that had transpired. As he relayed the details, he was struck with the sensation that he was close to a whole new understanding.

"Dr. Larson, I believe we have a serious security breach," Eric concluded. "I'm not sure why the Muslim extremists are so interested in our data, but I believe Alomari is the driving influence behind it. Whatever it is, they believe their secret is worth killing over. And I just found out that Preedy's wife is Alomari's sist—"

"Eric," Dr. Larson raised his voice menacingly. "I know about Basira's family ties. Let me urge you to exercise caution in what you say next. Some of your suppositions are based upon very questionable facts, facts that could be interpreted in a variety of ways."

"But, Dr. Larson—"

"Eric!" Dr. Larson's face flushed. "Remain quiet and listen to me! I appreciate your zeal and your commitment to this organization. However, I don't share your concern about our data being compromised. We are a scientific organization, after all. That includes the sharing of our knowledge for the betterment of all. I suspect you have gotten into the terrorist's gun sights for some other reason. Whatever it is, you have exposed other members of our staff to danger."

Eric was stung by the rebuke, a poignant reminder that he bore responsibility for Joey's condition. He hung his head in regret.

Dr. Larson softened. "Eric, I see so much potential in you. I confess I am struggling between admonishment and encouragement. I am sure it is no surprise to you that Justin Preedy has called for your termination."

Eric stared with fire in his eyes. "Dr. Larson—" he began.

Dr. Larson raised his eyebrows to stifle any protest. "I do not know how you have engendered such animosity in him, but it does not appear to be related to the work you perform. Therefore, I am unwilling to act upon his demand. Ms. Knowles agrees with me on this, and she shares my enthusiasm for the contribution you make to our team. However, I have a dilemma. I have a feud between two talented people who each bring value to our organization. A wiser man than me observed that a house divided against itself cannot stand."

Eric wondered if Dr. Larson knew that he had just quoted Jesus.

"I think our organization is strong enough to stand the test, especially if I can minimize the contact between you and Justin. I have decided that our computer operations have become quite expansive and could benefit from more specialized focus. Therefore, I am promoting you to head up the broadband operations and all aspects of network connectivity. Justin will retain his responsibility over hardware and security. Maybe that will keep the two of you from fisticuffs in the hallways."

Eric was stunned. "I don't know what to say, Dr. Larson. I really thought you were calling me in here to fire me," he stammered. "I won't let you down."

"I'm confident you won't, Eric." Dr. Larson's phone rang, and he glanced at it in irritation. "I told Stephanie we weren't to be disturbed." He snatched the phone from its cradle. "Yes?" His frown was replaced by a smile. "That is excellent...Yes, it is fine. You were correct to interrupt...Very good news indeed." He replaced the phone and smiled at Eric. "My irritation with you for endangering our staff has just diminished. It seems Joseph has awakened from his coma."

Y

Tokyo, Japan

Alana was weary. Si had called in sick this morning, which made the collection efforts more difficult. The message hadn't gotten to Alana until she had held the team up for an hour, assuming Si was running late. By the time they got to the collection site, there was a long queue, and they hadn't had a break all day. Finally, there was an opportunity to sit and enjoy some iced green tea. She'd never been fond of tea but was finally won over by the popularity of the country's favorite beverage.

She checked her phone and noticed a text message. It was from Si and noted that she would be off tomorrow as well. Alana pressed the redial button.

"Hello?"

"Si? This is Alana. How are you feeling?"

"As well as can be expected."

Alana wasn't sure what she meant but asked, "You don't think you'll be well enough to return tomorrow?" she asked.

There was a long silence on the connection. "I'm not sick, Alana. Didn't you get my voice mail from this morning?"

"No, I just noticed a text message from you. I hadn't gotten around to checking voice messages yet. What's going on?"

Alana heard a muffled sob. "Oh, Alana, it's so horrible. Muhammed is dead!"

"What? How can that be? I just saw him on Friday afternoon. What happened?"

"He was murdered." Si was struggling. "The police have no clues. It just doesn't make sense. Life is so unfair!" Si sobbed again and couldn't catch her breath.

Alana paused for an extended time as she prayed silently for Si's grief. "Si, I want to be there for you. Are you at your apartment? Can I come over?"

"Yes. I would appreciate that."

"OK. I'll be there as soon as we finish up today's paperwork."

Alana directed the team with the final details and excused herself. She arrived at Si's apartment within a half hour of the call.

When Si opened the door, Alana was shocked at her condition. Her face was swollen from crying, and her hair was matted with stray tendrils framing her face. Alana instinctively stepped forward and wrapped her arms around

Si, who was still in her nightgown. Si's thin shoulders heaved in anguish, and her face twitched on Alana's shoulder. They stood there for a long while until the grief subsided. Alana supported Si and led her to a couch. She sat beside her and gripped Si's hands. "You loved him, didn't you?"

Si looked up in surprise. "We didn't want anyone to know. We are from different cultures, and both families would disapprove. We also feared the society would require one of us to change our job assignment since our duties overlapped. We were so careful. How did you know?"

Alana's eyes brimmed with tears of compassion. "I didn't. But I can feel the enormity of your sorrow, and it is more than the grief for a friend. My heart aches for you, and I wish I could offer comfort." They hugged again, and Alana placed her hand gently on the back of Si's neck. "Tell me about him," she whispered.

Si pulled away, anxious to finally share the truth of her love. "Oh, Alana, Muhammed is—" she caught herself—"he was so wonderful. He was gentle and kind and treated me with such respect and deference. I felt like a princess. No one has ever treated me like that. I will never find anyone like him again." Her grief silenced her again.

The two women talked and cried together for hours. The shadows crept across the carpet, but neither moved from the couch to dispel them with the irreverence of artificial light. Alana noted the gaunt lines accentuated by the shadows of Si's profile. "Si, when was the last time you ate?" she asked.

"I do not remember. I heard of Muhammed's death on Friday evening and haven't eaten since."

"Let me make you something," she said, rising from the couch. Si shook her head, but Alana was determined. "No—don't object." She squeezed Si's shoulder. "I insist." Alana found soup in the pantry and prepared a couple of bowls. She brought them to the side table. "Here you are. It isn't much, but I don't think your stomach could handle more right now."

They ate the soup in silence for a few minutes.

"Si, I know you are grieving, but you should come back to work in a couple of days," Alana said. "It will help you to be distracted right now. Sitting here in the dark is not good. Muhammed would want you to go on with your life."

Si did not respond but sat with shoulders slumped in defeat. She reflected on Alana's advice and finally replied, "My mind agrees with you, but my heart has given up. I don't know what to do. I'm not sure I can go on."

"Yes, you can. It will be very hard at first. But slowly you will be reminded of how much you have to live for."

"How can I be sure?"

"Si, I don't want to take advantage of your fragile emotions right now, but there is much I would like to share with you about a source of strength that surpasses all understanding. I truly believe it is the answer to your grief. You know that I am a Christian?"

Si nodded.

"Well, my faith means a lot to me. It is what sustains me and gives me strength. I would love to share this with you when you are up to it."

"Maybe. We'll see."

"OK. Will you be all right alone tonight?"

"Yes. I am exhausted. I think I will be able to sleep for the first time since I heard about Muhammed."

"Good. I'd better get back to my hotel. Tomorrow will be a busy day without you. Go ahead and take another day. Then we'll get you back on the team on Wednesday, OK?"

Si nodded her assent.

"I'll stop by after work tomorrow. I'll bring dinner, and we'll do this again." She got up and walked to the door. As she opened it, Si called out to her. "Alana, there is one more thing. Muhammed gave me some information from the lab to hold for him. He didn't want to have it in his apartment for some reason. I don't know what to do with it now that he is gone. Can I give it to you?"

"Sure. Should I take it now or tomorrow?"

"It's right here," Si said, getting up from the couch, "so you might as well take it." Si went to her bookshelf and moved some books aside. "He placed it here and warned me to keep it hidden." She pulled a plastic zipper bag from the bookshelf and handed it to Alana. "Here."

Alana took the bag and gave Si another hug. "OK. I'll see you tomorrow afternoon."

Atlanta, Georgia

Eric exited the elevator with more enthusiasm than he'd felt in weeks. The nurses saw him coming and converged with him at the nurses' station. One of them impulsively grabbed Eric's hand and pulled him toward Joey's room. There were a number of nurses gathered at the doorway, and they parted as Eric was dragged forward. Through the gap, Eric could see Joey sitting upright, propped on a stack of pillows.

Joey craned his neck and grinned when Eric appeared in the gap. "Yo, dude! What's happening?"

"Joey, I can't tell you how awesome it is to see you again."

"Hey—I've been right here all along, buddy. And I have to tell you, dude—the surf is definitely up!"

Tokyo, Japan

Alana returned to her hotel room and threw her keys on the end table. She dropped the zipper bag on the side chair and slumped on the couch. Her laptop was sitting where she left it on the coffee table. She leaned forward and pressed the power button to log on and check her e-mail. Still nothing from Eric. She was disappointed but wrote him a quick note and told him how much she missed him. She didn't burden him with the chaos she'd experienced in the past week. He had enough troubles of his own.

Alana turned her attention to the zipper bag, curious about the contents: a number of computer printouts and two DVD-RW discs. She popped the first one in her laptop and checked its contents. There were a few meaningless directories with large files in them. She double-clicked each of them but received "unknown file type" errors. She ejected the disc and inserted the second one. More of the same. There was an additional directory titled "Notes." Alana double-clicked it and found a Word document titled "Lab Evidence."

"Well, that certainly looks interesting," she muttered. The contents weren't just interesting; they were explosive.

She reopened her e-mail and typed an urgent message to Eric. She was about to attach the Word file and thought better of it. Eric had expressed concern for the confidentiality of their in-house e-mail. So she copied the contents of her message and deleted it. She launched an Internet session, logged into her Gmail account, and pasted the comments into a message there. Finally, she attached Muhammed's Word document. By the time she had finished, her hands were shaking. She clicked send.

TWENTY-NINE

Tuesday, September 27, 2005
23 Sha'bān, 1426 AH
Atlanta, Georgia

Eric paced in the waiting room of the body shop. The finishing touches on Joey's car would take another thirty minutes. To make use of the time, he booted his computer on Linux, secured a hotspot, and accessed his Gmail. He was delighted to see two e-mails from Alana. The second one was alarming:

> From: Alana McKinsey
> Sent: Mon 9/26/2005 9:11 PM
> To: Eric Colburn
> Cc:
> Subject: Important
> Eric! There's a serious problem here.
>
> One of our lab employees, Muhammed Haznawi, was murdered on Friday night. The police have no clues, but I just stumbled on something that you need to know about. One of my collection team members was Muhammed's girlfriend. I was with her a little while ago, and she gave me some things from the lab that Muhammed had hidden in her apartment.
>
> There were some computer printouts that I don't understand and two DVDs. I've attached a Word document I found on one of them. It's Muhammed's journal of what's being done by some Muslims in the lab. According to him, the lab techs have been doing full genetic profiles from our samples—not just the 12-marker test authorized by the society. Muhammed was outraged because the full profiles were against company policy, consumed our resources, and were responsible for our productivity drain. You need to read the full document. I'm sure it will make more sense to you.
>
> Let me know if I should forward these materials to you.
>
> Love,
>
> Alana

PS: The DVDs also had a bunch of huge files on them. I tried to attach one of them, but Gmail rejected them because they were so big. I'm not sure what kind of files they are; my computer didn't recognize the type. I suppose you won't have a problem with them since they're from the lab server. I can forward the DVDs if you'd like them.

"Joey! Are you awake?" Eric had stuck his head into the darkened hospital room.

"I am now. What's up?"

"I have to talk to you. It's urgent."

"OK. Come on in."

Eric flipped the switch and a bank of fluorescent lights flickered on.

Joey squinted and shielded his eyes. "That's harsh, dude."

"I know, but I need you alert. Listen." Eric filled Joey in on the contents of Alana's discovery. "Those files have to be GIG files. This may be the last chance to get our hands on one of them."

"What about all the backup tapes?"

"They've been erased."

Joey smiled. "I have one hidden in my work area."

"Yes, you did, and it was a pretty clever hiding place. But Preedy confiscated it. I'm sure it's been erased by now."

Joey moaned. "OK. Then you're right. The ones Alana has must be the last of them. What about what Muhammed mentioned in his journal? Why would the Muslims run full sequences of the blood samples? It seems like a lot of effort. What can they gain?"

"This whole thing didn't make sense when I thought they were stealing our data. Now it's even more bizarre than I had imagined."

Joey suddenly sat upright. "Do you think Muhammed was murdered to shut him up? It's the same thing that happened to Farouk."

"And Hamdi," Eric said. "You may be right. If they suspected that Muhammed was on to them, then yes, you're probably right."

"You know what you need to do?"

"Yes. I need to get to Tokyo fast."

"I wish I could help, but the doctors want me to stay in here for another week. By then the cast can come off my arm and I'll be able to handle crutches. They want to keep the leg cast on for another couple of weeks. We'll see. If you bring me my laptop, I can keep in touch with you from here."

"I'll have it sent over," Eric said as he got up to leave. "By the way, I picked your car up from the body shop this morning. It looks as good as new. Do you mind if I keep it until you're out of here?"

"No, just don't play bumper cars with it again."

"I promise."

Tokyo, Japan

"Dr. Alomari? This is Satam. We have taken care of the problem in the lab here. He will not cause any more trouble.... Yes, I am certain of it. We have been monitoring all outgoing traffic, and he did not transmit any information to Atlanta.... No, there was nothing found there, or in his residence. We checked thoroughly."

Satam hesitated before continuing. "There is another matter that is probably of no concern, but it is confusing.... Yes, of course you are the better judge of these matters. I meant no disrespect. There is a woman here from the Atlanta headquarters. She came to the lab the same day we dealt with the heretic. She had a friend with her who was recognized by one of my men.... Yes, he is reliable. He has worked with the faction monitoring the American navy. He told us this woman is the wife of a navy pilot and can identify him. The two women stumbled on us right before we cornered Muhammed in the lab.... No, we cannot get to her. She has taken refuge on a military base here.... The Atlanta woman? We are not concerned about her. She did not get a good look at any of us.... Her name? It is Alana McKinsey."

Atlanta, Georgia

"I don't approve of your plan, Eric."

"Dr. Larson, you promoted me because you have confidence in me. I really need your approval for this trip. I believe Muhammed's discovery could be linked to our bandwidth problems. If the full genetic profiles are being done at other labs too, it explains both the productivity and bandwidth problems we've been experiencing."

"As I told you in our last meeting," Dr. Larson said, "I am not as concerned with the secrecy of our data as you are. However, if our resources are being squandered to support someone else's research, I will put a stop to it. There is something else you're not telling me, Eric," Dr. Larson observed. "What is it?"

"Frankly, sir, I'm also worried about Alana's safety."

"The police have no suspects in Muhammed's murder, and there is no reason to suspect a connection between his death and the information that is in Alana's possession—or that anyone else knows she has it."

"Sir, that may be true, but should we risk it? The information on those DVDs is potentially explosive, and I don't think we should trust a courier service. Nor can you afford to have Alana fly home now—not with their backlog of work. I still think the best option is for me to go and retrieve them myself. It will give me the opportunity to check the lab servers as well. I may be able to confirm Muhammed's suspicions, which would justify the expense."

"I have a bad feeling about this, Eric. However, I will defer to your judgment."

"Thank you, sir. You won't regret it. Would you mind if I ask Stephanie to make the arrangements for me while I go home and pack?"

"That will be fine. Be careful, young man. And come right back. Report back to me and no one else."

Y

Eric parked Joey's car in the long-term parking lot and caught the shuttle to the international terminal. He checked in and got through security and customs in less than an hour. Once he arrived at his gate, he sat heavily and pulled out his cell. No battery. He scanned the terminal and spotted a pay phone. It was probably better than making a cell call anyway.

"Hello?"

"Hello, Shoshana. This is Eric."

"I didn't recognize the number on my display, but you must be calling from the airport."

"How did you know?"

"I have one of my best men on your protection detail. He just informed me that you were processed through security safely. I understand you are going to Japan."

"Yes, I am," he replied in amazement. "Your people have incredible resources. Listen, there's something I need to tell you. The first time we met, do you remember we were puzzled by the Muslims stealing the geno-graphic data? I wondered if you discovered any more about it."

"No, it remains a mystery to us."

"Well, I have some additional information for you. It appears that they are doing much more than just stealing our data. I have read an eyewitness account from one of our employees who indicated lab techs in our Tokyo lab have been running full genetic profiles rather than just the twelve-marker test authorized by our research protocol. I suspect they may be doing the same thing at other lab locations as well. And here's an inter-esting detail—the lab techs are Muslim and are affiliated with Alomari. The tech who discovered all this was murdered this past weekend and may have given his life for this information."

"That is very tragic. I will follow up on this. We have some strategic resources I can call upon. This may be the information they need to probe further."

"I'll call you when I return from Tokyo. I hope I can find out more while I'm there."

"I look forward to your call. Be careful, Eric."

Eric hung up and found a seat at his gate. He jotted a quick e-mail to Alana:

From: Eric Colburn
Sent: Tue 9/27/2005 12:10 PM
To: Alana McKinsey
Cc:
Subject: RE: Important
Alana:
I received your e-mail and have implemented appropriate responses.
If you don't have anything better to do on Thursday, how about picking me up at New Tokyo International? I arrive on JAL #3 at 6:05 p.m. your time! It's the best connection I can get at such short notice. I'm at ATL now, getting ready to board.
I love you and can't wait to hold you in my arms!
Eric

THIRTY

Wednesday, September 28, 2005
24 Sha'bān, 1426 AH
Tokyo, Japan

T HIS IS SUSAN AND KYLE'S PLACE. LEAVE A MESSAGE AND WE'LL
get back to you."

"Hello, Susan, this is Alana. Listen, I won't be able to make it tonight. I'm sorry about the short notice. You may remember—I've spoken about my team member Si? Well, something horrible has happened. Her boyfriend was murdered over the weekend, and I need to spend some time with her this evening. If you'll give me a rain check, I'll catch up with you soon. Bye."

Alana closed her cell and looked up as Si opened the door and dropped into the passenger seat.

"Thank you for the ride, Alana," Si said. "I'm just not up to driving. You've really learned to do well driving around Tokyo."

"Thanks. It's a little nerve-racking, but I was determined," Alana replied. "When the society insisted I had to have an international driver's permit, I never expected to actually use it."

Si was a long way from recovering, but being back at work seemed to be good for her. Her complexion had regained some color, and she didn't look so frail.

"We have to stop by the lab, but I'll run the samples in," Alana said.

"All right. I don't think I can take going in yet. Do you mind if I stay in the car?"

Alana pulled up to the building. "No problem." As she got out, a feeling of dread overcame her as she relived the encounter from a few days ago. "Lock the doors behind me, Si. I'll be right back." She glanced at the market across the street and confirmed there was no pack of assailants descending upon her. Nevertheless, she felt uneasy and shuffled her load to the lab as quickly as possible. She dropped off the samples and signed the appropriate forms.

Before exiting the lab, she double-checked the market and street, then dashed to her car. She signaled Si to unlock the car as she approached, and she yanked her door open as soon as the lock clicked. She jumped into the driver's seat and immediately pressed the door lock button before strapping in.

Si was intrigued. "Alana, what's the matter? Are you afraid of something?" she asked as Alana pulled into traffic.

"I hadn't wanted to alarm you, but on Friday afternoon, I stopped here to drop off some paperwork. My friend Susan was with me. She stayed in the car, and when I came out of the lab, some Arab men were coming across the street from that market. Susan identified one of them as a man who had accosted her the week before. We drove off in a hurry, and they chased us down the street. Our military people had been concerned that the one Susan spotted might be part of a Muslim extremist group. I couldn't help but think of them just now. I'm sorry if I spooked you."

"That must have been frightening," Si remarked. "What do you think they were doing here?"

"I don't know," Alana replied. "That market sells Persian-Arabian foods, so I thought they were patrons. Or maybe they were waiting for friends to get off work. There are a lot of Muslims working in the lab after all."

"Or maybe they were waiting for the last one to leave. You know, Muhammed was always the last one out. And that was the evening he was murdered."

"What are you suggesting, Si?"

"I'm not sure yet. Alana, did I tell you Muhammed's co-workers hated him?"

"No, but I remember the afternoon you introduced him. He mentioned that he wasn't as devout as the other lab techs. He said his religious views made him unpopular with the staff."

"It was more serious than that. They called him a heretic and threatened him." Alana pulled into a parking place in front of Si's apartment and left the motor running. Si stared through the windshield and seemed reluctant to get out. "Alana, I think there could be a connection between Muhammed's murder and what happened to Susan and you. We need to go to the police."

"You may be right. If we're going to do this, we should go right now and put off dinner until later. Do you want to change?"

"Yes," she said, looking at the stains on her blouse. I should be more presentable if I'm meeting with the police." Si slipped from the passenger seat and pulled her keys from her purse. Alana turned the car off and followed Si to the apartment.

As Si slid the key into her lock, a neighbor's front door opened. "Hello,

Si!" An elderly lady in a flowered housedress leaned heavily on a walker and propped the door open with her elbow. She craned her head through the opening and smiled toothlessly.

"Hi, Mrs. Anderson. Are you feeling well today?"

"Yes, dear, thank you for asking. I wanted to ask you, did Muhammed's brothers find the right picture?"

Si flinched at the reference. She stared at Mrs. Anderson and asked, "What are you talking about?"

Mrs. Anderson looked guilty. "Oh dear—I hope I did the right thing. Muhammed's brothers told me you were at the funeral parlor and sent them to fetch that nice picture of Muhammed and you for the display at the viewing. I let them into your apartment to retrieve it."

"Mrs. Anderson, Muhammed didn't have any brothers."

"Oh my."

Y

Alana waited on the answering machine for the second time in an hour. She finally heard the beep. "Susan! This is Alana aga…" She hesitated when she heard a rattle on the other end.

"Alana, I'm here! What's up? You change your mind?"

"No, but something's come up. Remember those guys who chased us the other day?"

"What about them?"

"It's hard to explain. Si and I are going to go to the police with some information about Si's boyfriend's murder. We think there may be a connection to the guys that chased us."

"You're scaring me, Alana."

"I'm sorry; I can't help it. Why don't you come with us? We can pick you up on the way. Then maybe we can grab a bite somewhere."

"I have a better idea. Since you're coming to the base, why don't we start with DOD security and let them coordinate with the police?"

"OK, that sounds even better. Can you set that up? We'll be there in thirty minutes."

Y

Alana and Si were held up at the security gate. The guard contacted Susan and granted admission. As they pulled up in front of Susan's temporary quarters, she came out and locked the door behind her. She scurried to the car and got in the backseat.

"Hi, Susan!" Alana greeted her. "This is Si Matsuura. Si, this is Susan Hammond."

Susan put her hand on Si's shoulder. "I am so sorry for your loss," she said.

"Thank you, Susan," Si replied, her eyes misting. There was an awkward silence.

Alana finally put the car in gear. Susan informed her, "The DOD investigator is waiting for us. I'll direct you to his building."

Alana followed the directions to a single-story, nondescript building in a remote part of the base. The three women entered the building and were greeted by a young marine in a starched dress uniform accented with razor-sharp creases. His cover was tucked under his arm, leaving exposed the "high and tight" marine haircut. "Good afternoon, ladies," he said. He turned curtly to Susan. "Would you do the honors, Mrs. Hammond?"

"Of course. Ladies, this is Lieutenant Carpenter." She turned to Alana first, then Si. "This is my good friend Alana McKinsey, and this is her co-worker Si—I hope I pronounce this right—Matsuura?"

Si nodded. "Yes, perfect."

Susan continued. "They work with the National Geographic Society and are doing genetic research here in Japan."

He bent stiffly at the waist and extended his hand to each of them in turn. "Thank you for coming in."

Lieutenant Carpenter motioned toward a conference room that was very inviting. The walls were covered in teak paneling and adorned with paintings of warships from every era of naval history. The large conference table was surrounded by plush chairs with padded armrests. "Please come in, ladies. Can I offer you anything to drink? We have coffee, soft drinks, and water."

They each accepted a bottle of spring water and settled into chairs on one side of the table. The lieutenant seated himself across from them and placed a portfolio on the table. He opened it and rotated it in front of Susan.

She leaned forward and gazed down at a page of photos that were clipped inside. "What is this?" she asked.

"These are photos from surveillance cameras at the airport's international terminal. They are suspicious persons that we're trying to find more information about. There are a number of pages, each one representing inbound flights over the past two weeks. Would you take a minute and see if any faces look familiar?"

"Certainly." Susan had already finished the first page and turned to the second. She continued scanning and asked without looking up, "Wouldn't these be the same photos I reviewed the last time?"

"No. We thought we'd try a different approach. Some of these photos were taken based upon tips from our agents at originating airports, and others were extracted from video surveillance feeds by our facial recognition software." He turned to Alana and Si. "While she's scanning those, I want to mention that you young ladies have been very lucky. We originally did not see any relationship between Susan being accosted and Muhammed's murder, but the incident at your lab is causing us to reconsider. Terrorist cells have been broken up more often by intuition than hard facts. It helps when we don't dismiss seeming coincidences. For instance, we—" The lieutenant stopped himself at a sharp intake of breath from Susan. "Did you recognize someone?"

"Yes!" Susan replied. "At least, I think so." She rotated the portfolio toward him and stabbed her finger on one of the photos. "This camera angle is pretty severe. It looks like he was almost beneath it, so I can't tell for sure. Are there any other photos of him?"

Lieutenant Carpenter pulled the portfolio toward him and studied the details. "Let me see…" He picked up the conference phone and pressed a few buttons. "Sergeant Jones? We have a potential target confirmation. Air Egypt three ninety-two from Cairo, twenty September. File reference AQ seven twenty-two. Can you put all photos up on the screen in here? Roger that."

He leaned over and pressed a button on a tabletop remote. A hidden screen slid silently from the ceiling along the wall opposite the door. At the same time, blinds descended over the windows, and the conference room lights dimmed. Finally, a projector suspended from the ceiling blinked on. While they waited, an aide entered and silently handed a file to Lieutenant Carpenter. The image began to focus on the screen as the lieutenant rifled through the file.

"That's him!" Susan exclaimed. "That's the same guy who chased me."

"Are you sure, Mrs. Hammond?" Lieutenant Carpenter asked, frowning at the contents of the file.

"Absolutely." She nodded vigorously.

"Well, this guy is definitely al Qaeda. His name is Murad Nashiri. His brother is Abd Rahim Nashiri, who was sentenced to death last year for being the mastermind behind the USS *Cole* bombing. Both brothers were implicated in a plot to attack another U.S. warship, the USS *The Sullivans*, ten months earlier. That plot failed when a small boat sank under the weight of explosives crammed into it. It seems our boy has a fixation with the U.S. Navy. The interesting thing is—he and his brother are Saudis with a proven connection to OBL."

"OBL?" Susan asked.

"Osama bin Laden." Lieutenant Carpenter glanced back at the report. "Let's see…there's a hospital report here. It's flagged as an unconfirmed sighting. If this is our guy, it says he was treated for an injury on twenty-two September. Three broken toes, hyperextended tendons, and severe bruising on his right foot."

"That was me!" Susan exclaimed. "I ran over his foot when he tried to force his way into my car! The date's right, so that has to be him."

"You may be correct."

Alana glanced at Si and jumped into the conversation. "How does that link him to Muhammed's…murder?" she asked, dropping her voice to a whisper on the last word, in deference to Si.

Lieutenant Carpenter cut his eyes from the report. "It doesn't; I'm connecting the dots. The fact that he was across from the clinic the afternoon that Muhammed was killed is suspicious. In addition, we've run a background check on a several people he's been seen with. I have a photo here of one of them. We think he works at your lab, but we've not been able to identify him."

"You're kidding," Alana said as she accepted the photo.

"Lady, I don't kid about this stuff. It's deadly serious. And for that reason, I recommend that you ladies take appropriate measures for your safety. I am authorizing clearance for you to stay on the base during our investigation. We'll be finished setting up Mrs. Hammond's new apartment tomorrow. You're welcome to share her BOQ when she vacates."

"Thank you," Alana said. She stared at the photo for quite a while, shook her head, and handed it to Si, who glanced at it with the same result. They shook their heads in unison. "We don't recognize him," Alana said. May I keep this copy? I can follow up with our headquarters."

"Certainly."

"Thank you for your offer of asylum, Lieutenant Carpenter. I guess we'll sleep better if we stay here a few days. What about tonight? Is there anything available in the BOQ?" Alana asked.

"My quarters has a pull-out couch," Susan noted. "You two can share it tonight."

"OK. Thanks. I guess we're done here."

Lieutenant Carpenter stood up, signaling the end of the interview. "Ladies, let me know when you want to pick up your things, and I can arrange a security detail for you." He turned to Susan. "Mrs. Hammond, I would like to make an observation before you go. Your husband, being a warrior, will be very proud of you. By inflicting a wound on this al Qaeda operative, you struck what could be deemed a decisive blow in the war on terror."

THIRTY-ONE

Thursday, September 29, 2005
25 Sha'bān, 1426 AH
Tokyo, Japan

Aʟᴀɴᴀ ᴏᴘᴇɴᴇᴅ ᴛʜᴇ ᴛʀᴜɴᴋ ᴀɴᴅ ᴘᴜᴛ ʜᴇʀ sᴜɪᴛᴄᴀsᴇ ɴᴇxᴛ ᴛᴏ Sɪ's. She threw her favorite pillow on top and shut the lid. As she opened the car door, she waved to the marine guards standing nearby. "We're done now. Should we follow you to the base?"

"Affirmative, ma'am," the guard replied.

The entourage arrived at the base without incident. Alana and Si were issued credentials that would provide clearance and proceeded to the BOQ. Susan was waiting for them. "I've cleared out all my things, so you can move right in," she informed them. "Why don't you get settled and we'll get something to eat?"

"OK," Alana said. She finished unpacking her things and set her laptop on the small desk in the sitting area. She plugged into the electrical outlet. "I see there's an Ethernet port here. Can I plug into that?"

"Yes," Susan offered. You'll be able to get to the Internet, but you're blocked from the military network. I'm going to run back to my apartment and take care of a couple of things. I'll be back in a half hour."

"OK," Alana said. Si was busy arranging her things. "I'm going to check my e-mail before we go. So much has happened in the past few days, I've not taken the time to check."

"OK. I'm going to take a quick shower." Si took her cosmetic bag and closed the bathroom door behind her.

Alana ignored most of the messages, looking for any from Eric. She found one and clicked it. "Oh my gosh!" She jumped to her feet, tipping the chair on its back. She ran to the bathroom door and pounded furiously. The drumming of the shower stopped abruptly, followed by the screech of curtain rings. She ran to her suitcase and frantically rummaged for her favorite blouse.

"What's wrong?" Si stood in an expanding puddle, wrapped in a towel.

"I'm sorry." Alana said, kicking off her shoes. "My boyfriend is arriving in a few minutes! I'm going to be late!" She regained control. "I just got Eric's e-mail. Can I get in the bathroom for a sec? I have to fix my makeup."

"Sure. I'll hurry."

"Thanks. Can I ask a favor? After you're dressed, could you call the airline and check the time of arrival while I get ready? Use my cell so I can store the number."

"Certainly. I'm so happy for you!"

Alana was exuberant. "I know! This is incredible." They traded places and Alana closed the door. "I'll just be a minute," she yelled through the barrier. She finished just as Si got to the Japan Airlines Web site.

"His flight is delayed. It won't be in for another half hour."

"That's perfect. I may be able to get there in time." She snatched her purse and cell phone and headed for the door. "Tell Susan I'll call her later. I'm sorry to be changing plans on you."

"That's nonsense. This is more important. Taking an overnight bag?"

"No, I'll be back tonight."

"I'm sorry," Si replied. "I just assumed..."

"That's OK," she reassured Si. "I love Eric, but...I'll explain another time. But right now, I have to go!" With a smile, she bolted to her car.

As Alana neared the airport, she pressed the redial button on her cell. The flight had not yet arrived.

She pulled into short-term parking and took the people mover to the terminal. The display board showed flight three at the gate. Eric would be through customs soon.

Her phone rang as she stepped on the escalator to customs. A local number. She hesitated. "Hello?"

"Hello yourself, gorgeous."

"Eric! You're here!"

A bank of pay phones came into view. Eric was leaning against one of the phones with his back to her. His bags were stacked at his feet, his clothes disheveled. She stepped off the escalator and quietly closed the distance between them.

"Yes, I am. I can't wait to see you!"

"Well, here's looking at you, kid." She spoke loud enough for him to hear her in stereo.

She waited.

Realization finally dawned, and he turned quickly. When he gazed upon Alana, her breath caught. They stared at each other without a word as he reached for her hand. He drew her to him and held her tightly for several exquisite minutes. Then he sought her lips for a tender, lingering kiss.

"I missed you so much." He brushed his hand through her hair.

"I missed you too. It is so good to see you again. How long can you stay?"

"Let's not think about that right now. I want to enjoy each moment. Can we go somewhere quiet?"

"Yes. I imagine you're famished. I know a quiet restaurant. We can relax as long as we want."

Eric hoisted his bags and looped the straps over his shoulder. He wrapped his free arm around her waist, and they set off to find her car.

The parking attendant waved her through. As they merged into traffic, Alana noticed emergency flashers at the end of the freeway entrance. As she accelerated, she veered clear of a dark SUV stranded on the shoulder. "That's a bad place to break down," she commented as she threaded into a gap between cars. She checked the rearview mirror and noticed the SUV merging into the flow a few vehicles behind them. "I guess he fixed it," she said curiously. She flipped the turn signal, merged into the next lane, and put some distance between them. Within a kilometer, the SUV had disappeared.

Y

Eric was mesmerized by the chef's knife glistening in the glare of floodlights above the sushi bar. The crab roll was quickly segmented into thin, uniform slices with deft flicks of the wrist. A small square tray was prepared with a flower of ginger and small green mound of wasabi.

Alana prepared a saucer of soy and pushed it toward Eric. He clumsily pinched the crab roll with his chopsticks and dipped it into the soy. It began to disintegrate as he lifted it free. He pinched it more firmly, completely bisecting the roll. The halves splashed back into the tray, launching a wave of soy on Eric's shirt.

Alana shook her head while he hastily pawed at the stain. "I have some stain remover that will take that out," she said.

Eric summoned the server and was provided a fork. "This makes much more sense," he said. He scooped one of the halves from the tray and lifted the dripping morsel to his mouth, barely avoiding a fresh stain.

"Well, it's still authentic sushi, no matter how you eat it. Do you like it?" Alana asked.

"It's great!" Eric fanned himself with the cloth napkin. "You added a little more wasabi than I'm used to." He blotted his brow. "It's pretty hot."

"I'm sorry. I've gotten used to it since I've been here. You can add a little more soy if you want to."

"No, that's OK." He inhaled sharply. "It cleared my sinuses."

Alana laughed easily. "It's so nice to be able to relax and laugh with you. I've been looking over my shoulder so much lately. I feel much safer being here with you."

"I don't know about that. I've turned into a lightning rod lately. You shouldn't get too close."

"Nonsense." She slid closer to nestle into the crook of his arm. "I can't get close enough." She kissed him. "I love you."

"Alana, I've waited too long to say this. I love you too." He'd finally said it. No panic, no sweaty palms. "I love you very much." It felt pretty good.

The server interrupted them. "Can I get you anything else?"

Alana pulled away, and they sat up. Eric looked at her and asked, "Coffee?"

"Sure."

"I guess I'm going to have to find a hotel room." Eric said. "I left in such a hurry, I didn't make any reservations."

"You're welcome to stay at my place."

Eric drew back. "How am I supposed to take that?"

Alana laughed. "I'm not staying there right now. I'm staying with Si on the air base. The DOD security people thought it would be a good idea for a while. I hadn't canceled my hotel room in case I could go back, so you can stay there."

"Darn. You got my hopes up for a minute."

"Eric—"

"Just kidding." Then more seriously, "Alana, you know I will honor your convictions. I fell in love with you the way you are, and I don't want to change a thing."

Y

Murad Nashiri pulled the SUV into deep shadows a block from the restaurant. A ringing tone broke the silence. The abrupt light from the touch pad reflected his harsh features in the rearview mirror. It was a face well acquainted with hatred and rage. "Murad," he muttered.

"This is Satam. Alomari has instructed that we are to do nothing to call attention to our cause. Our true objective cannot be exposed prematurely. There is nothing the Americans can discover in Japan, so we are to lull them into complacency."

"But my plans for the carrier battle group—"

"They are to be suspended until you receive instructions directly from the Tall One." Satam paused while the enormity of the information sank in. "Until then you are to assist me until Alomari's objective is secured in a few months. America was once called a sleeping giant. Arousing her from slumber always brings disaster."

"As you wish," Murad said, suppressing his resentment. "What about the American woman?"

"Alomari has plans for her. He keeps his friends close and his enemies even closer."

Murad grunted an acknowledgment rather than revealing his confusion. He didn't understand the last comment but did not want to appear ignorant.

The mirror disappeared into the shadows as the cell blinked shut. In the dark interior of the SUV, the silence was broken by an exclamation. "Allāhu akbar!"

Y

Alana's mood seemed to change after dinner as they drove through traffic on the way to the hotel. "Is something wrong?" Eric asked.

She hesitated a moment too long. "Nothing, why?"

"Maybe I'm just tired from the jet lag, but it seems you've gotten pretty quiet. Is there something on your mind?"

She tightened her grip on the steering wheel. "Well, yes, there is. I didn't want to bring it up tonight since you're so tired. I'm sure it's nothing. We can talk tomorrow."

"There's no way I'll sleep until I know what's wrong."

Alana glanced at Eric, then back at traffic. "OK. Eric, when the lab burned in Cairo, you were seen running from the lab with a woman in the middle of the night. You never mentioned her. Why not?"

Eric hesitated before responding. Alana wasn't consumed with jealousy, as some of his previous girlfriends were. The tension in those relationships had conditioned him to be evasive about platonic friendships with other women. The path of least resistance had always seemed to be the best one. "I guess it didn't seem important. Does it bother you?"

"No, it doesn't bother me that you were with a woman. And I suppose there's a good explanation for being with her in the middle of the night. But with all the details you've shared about your adventures in Cairo, it's odd that you've gone out of your way not to mention her."

"It wasn't a big deal." Eric fought the defensiveness that welled up within him. This could have a bad ending. "She was just an embassy staffer that brought my plane ticket and clothing to the hospital. Then she gave me a ride to the lab." *Why do I have to justify myself?* he thought.

"Oh. OK. So why didn't you just say so?"

Old patterns die hard. Eric retreated to a favorite. "I came all the way to Tokyo to see you, didn't I? Look, I'm exhausted from the trip, and, frankly, I'm not up to an interrogation right now."

"Interrogation? I only asked for clarification. Why are you so defensive?"

Good grief. What happened to the great mood we had? "Can we drop this for now? We're both getting worked up. I have to go back to Atlanta the day after tomorrow. I don't want to waste time arguing about stuff that doesn't matter."

"I just asked a question," Alana said. "If you don't have anything to hide, I don't understand why you're evasive with the details."

Eric sighed. "Alana, please."

"OK. All right. I'll drop you off at the hotel. You do look wiped out. I'll come by in the morning, and we can have brunch in the hotel restaurant."

"Can you get some time off?" Eric asked. "We need to look at these DVDs and figure out what's going on."

"I'll see if Si can handle things tomorrow," Alana said.

That sounded pretty good to Eric. Things would look a lot better in the morning. "OK."

Alana pulled into the hotel complex and parked in the registration slot. Residual tension made this an awkward moment. Eric leaned toward her for a good-night kiss, and she obliged, but he felt something was missing.

She sat back. "Get some rest, OK?" She rummaged through her purse and found the room key. "Here's my key. It's room six twenty-one, near the elevators."

He opened the door and hesitated before getting out. "Good night. I'll see you tomorrow."

He stood beside the car, then ducked his head low to make eye contact. An impulse prompted him to apologize, but he second-guessed himself. He didn't want to sound superficial. Another awkward moment.

Alana looked at him hopefully. Did she expect an apology?

The valet approached. "May I help you, sir?"

The moment was lost. "No, thanks." Eric grimaced. "Can you pop the trunk?" he asked Alana.

"Sure." The release clicked as he rounded the car. He grabbed his bag and shut the trunk. Their eyes met in the rearview mirror. He smiled forlornly, then turned away. He headed through the automatic doors without looking back.

Inside the room, Eric dropped his bag by the door and collapsed on the bed—Alana's bed—replaying the events since his arrival. His love for Alana was challenging him to unlearn patterns that had become comfortable.

Why can't women leave well enough alone? Why do they always insist that everything has to be talked through and talked about again, and if they aren't completely satisfied with the outcome, once more for good measure?

Eric knew the answer. *Because they possess power—the power of physical attraction. They know how to exploit our helplessness, our need to possess them.* Eric laughed softly as a new realization dawned on him. *We don't conquer them—it's the other way around.*

THIRTY-TWO

Friday, September 30, 2005
26 Sha'bān, 1426 AH
Tokyo, Japan

I'M SORRY." ERIC WAS SEATED ACROSS FROM ALANA IN THE HOTEL café. There were few patrons at this mid-morning hour, and they could talk freely. He had done a lot of soul-searching and was contrite.

Alana reached out and clasped his hand. "I know, and I'm sorry too. I know this is hard for you."

Eric fidgeted. He owed her an explanation, but transparency came hard. He didn't have a lot of experience with this and fought the temptation to be evasive. "Alana, I'd like you to understand where I'm coming from. I've had girlfriends who were consumed with jealousy. I learned to be vague when it involved contact with other women."

"Eric, you know I'm stronger than that."

"Yes, I do, and that's one of the reasons I love you so much."

"You were a real player, weren't you?"

"Alana, you know I wouldn't risk telling you this if I still operated that way. I'm not a player anymore, not since I met you."

"I believe you, Eric."

"I'm sorry I wasn't completely honest with you."

"Eric, I'm silently thanking the Lord right now. I needed to hear more than a simple apology."

"Her name is Melanie Wagner."

"Huh? Oh—you mean the Cairo woman?"

"Yes. She's a diplomat at the American embassy in Cairo. When I was surrounded with nothing but hostility, she was the only friend I had. She helped me get out of that awful country."

"I hope I have an opportunity to thank her someday." Alana folded her napkin. To Eric, that signified a satisfactory conclusion.

"Now what about the DVDs?" Alana asked. "Do you think they really mean something?"

Eric reached for his laptop in the bag at his feet. "Let's find out. When we're done here, I need to go to the lab."

THIRTY-THREE

Sunday, October 2, 2005
28 Sha'bān, 1426 AH
Tokyo, Japan

REALITY CAUGHT UP WITH THEM ALL TOO SOON. THE NEXT day, Alana parked in the short-term lot, and Eric pulled his bags from the trunk. They linked arms and trudged to the terminal.

"Do you have the DVDs?" she asked.

"Absolutely. Dr. Larson would be ticked off if I forgot. They were the reason for my trip. I have them right here in my bag. I'm confident we're going to crack these GIG files once and for all. It should provide the first concrete evidence that our research efforts have been co-opted by Alomari."

"You found no evidence of anything at the lab?"

"Nothing. These people know how to cover their tracks. It's been frustrating. I just can't figure out why they're doing it. It just doesn't make sense to me."

"Me either." Alana pulled a folded photo from her jacket pocket and glanced at it. "I almost forgot. The DOD gave me this photo of someone who was seen with that terrorist, Murad Nashiri."

"Murad's the one who attacked Susan?" Eric asked for clarification.

"Right," Alana answered. "The DOD thought this guy might be one of our lab techs, but he must be wrong because no one at the lab recognized him." She handed the photo to him. "I thought maybe you could check with personnel in Atlanta. If he was an employee, they should be able to identify him."

"Sure," he said, and absentmindedly stuffed it in his pocket.

Inside the terminal, Eric checked in and glanced at the growing customs line. "I hope I haven't cut this too close." He faced Alana reluctantly. Her head was bowed.

"Hey, cheer up. We have so much to look forward to."

"I know. I'm so glad you came, but now I want so much more. I don't ever want to be apart from you again."

"I don't either. But what doesn't kill us makes us stronger, right?"

"As much as I despise the one you're quoting, I agree."

"What?"

"Never mind. It isn't important now. All that matters is that I love you. Please be safe. If you're tempted to put your life in jeopardy again, think of me first, OK?"

"Agreed. You be safe too. Speaking of that, why don't you stay on the base for the rest of your time here?"

"I might as well. Si and I get along pretty well. We'll see how it goes."

"When are you coming home?" he asked.

"Not soon enough," she answered. "I hope in another week or so."

Eric glanced again toward the customs area. "Well, I guess it's time. I love you."

"I love you too."

Alana waved and watched him disappear into the customs crowd. She cried as she shuffled to the parking lot.

Atlanta, Georgia

Joey woke while it was still dark outside. It took a moment to get his bearings. He would be going home today. Not to his apartment, but home in the truest sense. His mom and dad would be picking him up and taking him to their place. He still had some recovery time in front of him, and his mom intended to dote all over him. That sounded pretty good. It'd barely been a month since the hit-and-run, and only two weeks since he'd awakened from the coma. He certainly wasn't ready to be back on his feet at the office. Maybe another week.

Right now, he was looking forward to getting home. He should be able to finish up the insurance paperwork and get home before kickoff. Atlanta was favored to beat Minnesota, and Dad had offered his recliner to Joey. That was a real sacrifice. They would enjoy the game together on his dad's new HDTV. What could be better than that?

Tokyo, Japan

Eric settled in for a long and arduous flight. He hoped to catch up on some sleep during the flight but intended to work through a couple of problems first.

Ironically, he hadn't found anything wrong in the Tokyo lab. Quite the opposite; productivity and data transmissions were above the established objectives. In fact, the statistics in all labs were showing the same trend. The question that bugged Eric was, What had changed? Why had conditions improved so dramatically without intervention? More to the point, what conditions existed previously that had created bottlenecks?

Eric felt the elusive solution was within reach. The extended gene mapping documented by Muhammed was the smoking gun. When they got suspicious of Alana's presence, the lab staff hastily implemented normal procedures. There wasn't enough time to establish a façade of steadily improving productivity. But that wasn't conclusive evidence of guilt. And the accusations of a dead man weren't sufficient—they could paint him as a disgruntled, paranoid crackpot. Everything hinged on cracking the GIG files.

Υ

By the time Alana returned to the BOQ, Si was asleep. She went to her computer and found an e-mail from Stephanie Youngblood. That was curious. Dr. Larson's assistant had never written before. She quickly scanned the missive, and her somber mood darkened further. She was being dispatched to Pakistan. The collection team in Karāchi was struggling, and Dr. Larson had confidence in Alana's growing capabilities. She would have to finish her mission in Japan by the end of next week and report to Karāchi by the seventeenth. Stephanie offered to make the arrangements as soon as Alana could confirm the exact date of departure.

THIRTY-FOUR

Monday, October 3, 2005
29 Sha'bān, 1426 AH
Atlanta, Georgia

ERIC RECOVERED EVERYTHING FROM THE BAGGAGE CLAIM AND WAS processed through customs. There was nothing to declare, and he finished quickly.

He called Joey on the way to the parking garage. One ring. "Hey, dude! How was the trip?"

"It was great. I have a lot to tell you. Right now I need some sleep, but I wanted to know if I could come by later to fill you in. I'd like to hear your thoughts on a couple of things."

"Hold on a minute." He heard rustling and scratching. Muted conversation. The sounds cleared. "My mom is inviting you for dinner. She and my dad are anxious to meet you. Then we can talk after dinner."

"That sounds great. What time?"

"Be here by five thirty. Mom serves at six sharp."

"I'll be there. Hey—I've been in the air for the past day. How did the Falcons do yesterday?"

"They destroyed the Vikings! We sacked Culpepper nine times."

"That's awesome," Eric replied. "I'll see you later."

Y

"Thank you for the dinner, Mrs. Hammond. It was the best meal I've had in a month."

"That's so nice of you to say, Eric," she replied. "It was nothing, really."

"Can I help clean up?"

"No, Mr. Hammond and I will take care of everything. Why don't you and Joey take care of business before he gets too drowsy?"

"OK." Eric got behind Joey's wheelchair and pushed him into the living room. He locked the wheels and dropped into an overstuffed chair. He filled Joey in on all that had happened to Alana, and they explored the possible connections to their adventures. No additional insights occurred to them.

Eric pulled out the DVDs Alana had given him. "Here are the last surviving GIG files," he announced triumphantly. "So far I haven't gotten anywhere. Why don't I leave one with you and I'll work on the other? How about a friendly wager? The one who cracks the code first gets a pizza."

"You're on."

"Well, I'm exhausted. It was a long trip, and I didn't get much rest. If I'm going to be at work bright and early, I'd better get some sleep. Do you mind if I continue using your car?"

Joey waved his good hand at his condition. "I don't think I'll be driving for a while. Be my guest."

"Thanks. Good night. Thank your mom again for me."

Y

Eric trudged up the steps to his apartment. Inside, he threw the keys and cell phone on the dresser and emptied his pockets. He patted his jacket pockets and heard something crinkle inside one of the pockets. He thrust his hand inside and found nothing. Strange. He pressed his hand against the inside of the pocket and felt resistance. His jacket pockets had two-chambered pockets with one having a zipper. He unzipped the pocket and extracted a folded photo, the one Alana had handed him in the airport. He'd been so distracted when she gave it to him that he forgot about it. He recalled what Alana had said about no one at the lab recognizing the photo as he flipped open the last fold and gazed at it. Recognition and alarm were simultaneous. *What was* he *doing in Tokyo?*

Eric snatched his cell phone and rapidly scrolled his directory. He mashed send. A voice message. He pressed the star key and received a beep. "Shoshana, this is Eric. I'm back from Tokyo. We need to meet right away. Call me when you receive this. It's urgent. Anytime, day or night."

THIRTY-FIVE

Friday, October 14, 2005
11 Ramadān, 1426 AD
Tokyo, Japan

SI RAISED HER GLASS OF SAKE IN SALUTE. "HERE'S TO ALANA, the smartest and most diligent co-worker I have ever known. May her sincerest prayers be answered, and may she have many healthy children." She smiled warmly at the small gathering.

Alana blushed and covered her eyes, her elbow propped on the table. She peered between her fingertips and shook her head. "Well, I'll demand a ring first, that's for sure."

Susan and Si laughed at Alana's obvious discomfort. Susan said, "My only regret is we didn't get to meet him when he was here."

"I'm sorry. The time just flew, and we'd been apart for so long..."

"No apology needed," Susan replied. "I've seen the syndrome before. I'm happy for you." Susan reached out and grasped her hand. "And I'm going to miss you so much."

"I will too," Si concurred.

"I'll miss both of you so much," Alana said. "I'm not being maudlin when I say that I'll think of you often and will pray for you."

"Thank you, Alana. And thanks for introducing us," Susan said. "It will be nice to have another friend to keep me company while Kyle's away."

The women enjoyed the food and fellowship for a few hours. Soon it was time for final good-byes, and Alana didn't want to extend the melancholy. "I'm going to make it an early night. My connections to Pakistan are awful, so it's going to be brutal." After hugs all around, Alana left the farewell party.

While she walked to her car, she became anxious about the trip to Pakistan. A few days of relative calm belied the forces she knew to be at work. She would need to complete her new assignment quickly, then go home to Eric as soon as possible.

Atlanta, Georgia

Eric was tapped out. Nothing was working out the way he'd anticipated. The week had begun with such optimism, but there had been no progress cracking the GIG files. Dr. Larson had been gone all week, and Ms. Knowles had relayed his expectation of some positive results from Eric's trip. Of greatest concern was the fact that a number of the techs, including Satam, dropped off the radar after the lab in Egypt was destroyed.

Eric was beginning to doubt his ability to deliver. This was a new emotion for him. He'd always succeeded with anything he'd set his mind to. Failure was inconceivable.

He dreaded any encounter with Preedy, who seemed to be growing more confident. He'd begun fabricating excuses to wander past Eric and Joey, his smug *schadenfreude* growing more obnoxious every day. Shoshana had not yet returned his calls, which was infuriating in the circumstances. To cap all this, his heart ached every time he thought of Alana, which was happening quite a bit more than in the past. He desperately needed something encouraging to happen.

The day dragged to a conclusion. As five o'clock approached, Eric packed up his things for the weekend. Tech was playing Duke at Durham and should win handily. Joey had invited him over to watch the game, which should help take his mind off his problems. They planned to watch USC at Notre Dame too. That should be a barn burner, as usual.

Eric hoisted his backpack over his shoulder and headed for the door. His cell phone rang. He glanced at the display. "Shoshana! Where have you been?"

"Hello, Eric. I have just returned from my country. I received your messages and am anxious to meet with you. Would you like to join me at our normal meeting place?"

"You bet. How about six?"

Shoshana arrived at the same time as Eric. They embraced briefly. She air-kissed his cheeks. "I am happy to see you again, Eric."

They were seated immediately, as expected, in a booth toward the back of the restaurant. Shoshana suggested they have the day's special. When the server left them alone, she said, "I've been anxious to meet with you. There's something important you need to know."

"Certainly."

Eric told Shoshana about the incidents in Tokyo and the concerns expressed by the DOD. "This is what alarmed me." He handed over the photo Alana had given him. "This is a photo of a man the DOD connected with an al Qaeda cell. They thought he worked for our Tokyo lab, but they guessed the wrong one. I recognize him from Cairo. He used to be the head technician in our lab before it burned down. His name is Satam Suqami. I have no idea what he was doing in Tokyo, but he wasn't working for us. He disappeared after the Cairo incident and has been off our payroll ever since."

"That is very curious, Eric." Shoshana buttered a roll as she mused on his news.

"I have more information. He's evidently been connected to an al Qaeda operative. I've noted the name on the back."

Shoshana turned the paper over and glanced at the handwritten name. She blanched. "Are you sure of this information?"

"Yes, why?"

"The name you noted here is Murad Nashiri. He is one of the most reviled of our enemies. If you are correct, my concern for your safety is greater. This man is thought to be connected to Osama bin Laden himself. He has a violent history.

"I am curious about the connection between Alomari's project and Nashiri's cell," she said. "I suspect they are acting as an enforcement arm for Alomari and his scientists, who would not have the necessary resources. The only conclusion is that Alomari's project has been given the highest priority by al Qaeda's leadership."

Their salads arrived, and they paused their conversation briefly as the server also refilled their water glasses.

"It concerns me that this guy is in Tokyo," Eric said when they were alone again. "I'd be freaking out if Alana wasn't staying on our navy base."

"Yes, that is comforting. Your call from the airport a couple of weeks ago provided a critical piece of information. I took your information to Israel and conferred with Israeli geneticists about the Muslim infiltration of your Genographic Project. Do you remember our conversation in the Cairo airport? We spoke of Ishmael and Isaac and the eternal war between their descendants."

"Yes, very well," Eric replied. "You indicated the Israeli-Muslim conflict is a fulfillment of prophecy."

"That is correct. Well, our scientists have a theory. They suspect the Islamic extremists have stumbled on something that will turn the tide in their favor, and the key to their breakthrough is found in the genographic research data."

"That doesn't make sense," Eric protested. "We're studying DNA markers—and when the various branches of the human family separated."

"Yes, I remember your explanation. Allow me to amplify. Do you remember I mentioned Ishmael's mother was a slave?"

Eric nodded.

"The Torah doesn't indicate her nationality. We can assume she wasn't from Mesopotamia since she did not leave Ur with Abram's band of sojourners. Since she was not of Abram's people, Ishmael was considered a half-breed and unworthy of the covenant. This was a very important issue.

"Abram, later renamed Abraham, placed an emphasis on racial purity, and this continued through the first three generations of patriarchs. First, Abram's wife, Sarah, was a distant cousin. Later in life, he insisted that Isaac's wife be from his family as well. Finally, Isaac and Rebecca specifically instructed their son Jacob to select a wife in the same fashion, which he did.

"Ironically, Jacob's twin was so consumed with resentment over his lost birthright, he took a daughter of Ishmael as his wife. It isn't hard to read between the lines. He knew this would be the ultimate repudiation of their beliefs. These were the seeds of animosity between our peoples that have borne a bitter fruit.

"The Muslims have never gotten over Abraham's humiliating rejection of Ishmael and have attributed it to the issue of racial purity. Muhammad revised the historical account more than a thousand years later. Although Muslims have claimed his authority was a revelation from Allah, Muhammad's own testimony calls that into question. For a long time, he was convinced that his seizures and visions were proof of demon possession.

"Now Alomari believes he can vindicate Ishmael's rightful claim to the covenant blessings. If he can prove that Hagar was in fact Mesopotamian, then Ishmael would have been much more than a half-breed older brother to Isaac. He would be the firstborn—and heir.

"Through analysis of genetic data—stolen from the genographic research—Alomari is nearly ready to prove Ishmael's Mesopotamian lineage. If the data supports his claims, it would be a great symbolic victory."

"I still don't get it," Eric said. "Even though Ishmael was slighted, there's been a lot of sand through the hourglass, so to speak. It's a little late to relive history, isn't it? I mean, who cares at this point? Besides, the covenant with God was based upon much more than bloodline—the Bible says it was based upon faith and righteousness."

Eric surprised himself with the sudden insight into a biblical truth that had previously eluded him. He'd have to think about this more.

"Your points are well taken, Eric," Shoshana said, stabbing a chunk of lettuce. "I couldn't have voiced them better. But you have to realize they are not trying to change God's mind. Their passion is like an immunization. They can no longer think logically.

"Earthly blessings were withheld from Ishmael and his progeny. They believe they are the rightful heirs, so they intend to take the blessings by any means possible. Their purpose is to energize and enflame the Muslim masses to accomplish this. This is the Muslim worldview and the jihadists are very adept in manipulating it.

"Alomari's team is preparing to announce irrefutable evidence that Hagar was Mesopotamian. Since he was the eldest son of Abraham, all blessings and possessions should have passed to him, not his younger half brother."

"But that has a hollow ring to it," Eric protested. "I doubt it will interest the media, and if it doesn't run as the lead story on the evening news, the story will die a natural death. As we say around these parts, 'That dog won't hunt.'"

"Eric, these people don't need Western media to prop up their claims. Aljazeera and other extremist news outlets will do their bidding. And Muslim extremists have learned to use the Internet very effectively. They will appeal to the sense of entitlement in the Muslim hordes who have insinuated themselves into every culture worldwide.

"Do not believe for a minute that their rage is focused only on the children of Jacob. Nor is their objective the sharing of political power. Nor will they be satisfied with world domination. Eric—they will settle for nothing less than absolute annihilation of everything non-Muslim. This dream is woven into the very fabric of the Quran and has been the foundation of their teaching for thirteen hundred years.

"We are certain of their intentions. The only question is how much additional data they require before they come forward with their announcement. We must interdict the flow of data, and you are the man of the hour."

Eric shifted in his chair. "Shoshana, that sounds a bit extreme. I've seen many moderate Muslims who want to live in peace with us. And besides, the Lord admonishes us to turn the other cheek."

She pierced him with her resolute stare. "I don't doubt that there are well-meaning followers of Islam. But when it comes to Muslim jihadists, the meek will surely *not* inherit the earth. Turning the other cheek only makes it easier for them to behead you."

The entrées arrived.

Next page: Karāchi, Pakistan. Enlarged, full-color map is available at www.y-factor.net. Satellite image courtesy of GeoEye. Copyright 2009. All rights reserved. Refer to the map on page 264 for an expanded view of the peninsula.

Karāchi, Pakistan

Lyari River

Mauripur RR Station

Wazir Mansion RR Station

Baba Channel

SDV Route

West Wharf

East Wharf

Hotel District

Arabian Sea

THIRTY-SIX

Sunday, October 16, 2005
13 Ramadān, 1426 AH
Karāchi, Pakistan

ALANA UNPACKED HER THINGS AND EXAMINED THE ACCOMMO-dations. This would be home for a few weeks. It wasn't much, but she didn't intend to spend much time here. At least she had Internet access, which was unusual in this country. She connected and checked.

Nothing from Eric, but then she hadn't e-mailed him since being reassigned to Pakistan. Getting things wrapped up in Tokyo had taken all of her available time. And after seeing Eric in person, e-mail now seemed impersonal. She found it hard to conjure up the motivation. However, there may not be another opportunity for a while.

She drafted a long message and shared some observations with Eric that she'd thought about on the flight. During her absence from America, she had found it surprisingly easy to bond with women from vastly different cultures. Para and Si were the best examples and gave her optimism about who she would meet in this new assignment. She clicked send.

Alana changed into her nightclothes and washed her face. The running water partially masked a noise in the background. She turned the faucet handle, and the flow reduced to a trickle.

A knock at the door.

She grabbed a towel and glanced at the clock. She hadn't ordered anything from room service. Who could it be? She hadn't met anyone yet. "Who is it?" she asked, her ear close to the doorjamb.

"It's Para!"

Alana was puzzled for a heartbeat. She stepped back and yanked the door enthusiastically. "Para! What are you—"

Two hooded men and a woman in a burka descended upon her. They threw her on the bed and stuffed a foul-tasting rag in her mouth before she could cry out. She tried to inhale, but the odor induced waves of nausea. She struggled between the need for oxygen and the urge she knew could kill her. If she vomited, the rag would aspirate the contents into her lungs.

"Listen carefully, American bimbo." The men pinned her hands and legs on either side of the bed while the woman whispered in her ear. "You are not welcome in our country. Do your work, and ask no questions. Do not bring attention to yourself. And do not speak of your beliefs or you will suffer the wrath of Allah. If you dare to contact the authorities, we will surely learn of it."

Alana's vision began to dim. Black pinpricks grew steadily and crowded the pixels of color. Then the last few pixels faded to black.

Atlanta, Georgia

"What a game! I haven't been this tense since your brakes failed," Eric said. The sun was setting on a memorable football Saturday in the Eastern time zone. Tech salvaged their pride by crushing hapless Duke, and USC was on their way to another national championship. The last seconds of the game with the Irish marked it as one of the greatest games in history. "I needed this distraction. It's good to get my mind off of work once in a while."

"I've had the opposite problem lately," Joey said.

"Let me help you with that, Mr. Hammond." Eric stacked up the hors d'oeuvres platters and carried them to the kitchen. "Don't you worry, Joey. I'll help your dad. You just sit where you are."

Joey grinned. "If you insist. After you finish helping my dad, would you bring me another Coke?"

"Has he always been this lazy, Mr. Hammond?"

"No, we raised him better. I'll finish up, Eric. Thanks for the help."

Eric brought Joey his drink. They turned the TV off, and Eric filled him in on all that had transpired with Shoshana.

"Wow, she laid a pretty heavy burden on you," Joey acknowledged.

"I don't see how we can convince Dr. Larson to intervene with Alomari without proof. Everything hinges on our ability to crack the GIG files."

"I've tried everything I can think of. Somebody knew what they were doing when they designed the security."

"We've got to find a way. I'm going back to my apartment to work on it awhile. Good night, Joey." Eric craned his head toward the living room. "Good night, Mr. and Mrs. Hammond. Thanks for everything."

"Good night, Eric."

Y

Eric parked Joey's car in a space two blocks from his apartment. Finding a convenient spot was a daily challenge this late at night. By midnight, most normal people were in for the night. It reminded him of how much simpler life was without the hassles of a vehicle. He locked the car and began the trek to the apartment. The air was damp, and the slight breeze chilled him. He zipped his jacket.

He rounded the last corner and stepped off the curb. A large, dark car approached from his left. Eric glanced sideways. Just as it dawned on him that the headlights were out, the vehicle accelerated. Something protruded from the rear passenger window.

Alarmed, Eric sprinted toward the front steps. He looked over his shoulder as someone emerged from the shadows on his right. He noticed the glint of metal at the man's side as the silencer was raised to firing position.

He was trapped. The only protection was the concrete barrier on either side of the steps. But which side to choose? Either side would leave him exposed to one of the threats.

The man in the shadows barked, "Get down if you want to live."

Eric stupidly thought of the Terminator movies. If he weren't petrified with fear, he would have laughed. Abruptly, he sided with the Terminator. Shots exploded as Eric rolled into the shadows. Chips of concrete ricocheted off his cheek. The Terminator returned fire.

The shooter in the car slumped through the open window. His weapon clattered impotently against the macadam. He was pulled into the vehicle as it accelerated from the kill zone.

Eric whipped his head around but could no longer see the Terminator. He blinked to clear the blindness from the muzzle flashes, rolled to a crouch, and cobbled his way toward the shadows. In the dim light he saw the form of a man. He heard shallow gasps and approached warily. The harsh shadows obscured the Terminator's features. Eric leaned closer. His night blindness had receded enough to identify his benefactor.

The man's breath was raspy from the rapid accumulation of fluid in his lungs. "Call Sho..." he sputtered, then was racked with a spasm of coughing.

Eric leaned even closer. "What?" He was rewarded with a spray of blood and spittle. "I'm calling 9-1-1!" he shouted, pulling his cell phone from a pocket.

"No!" the man squawked, grabbing Eric's wrist. "Call Shosha…" His mouth went slack, and a horrible gurgle expelled as his chest deflated.

Eric was frozen in indecision. He hit end to clear the digits from his screen, then placed a call to Shoshana.

THIRTY-SEVEN

Monday, October 17, 2005
14 Ramadān, 1426 AH
Karāchi, Pakistan

ALANA WAS GROGGY AND AWAKENED IN STAGES. AS CONSCIOUS-ness cohered, a sense of dread kept her motionless. Opening her eyes just enough to make out her surroundings, she carefully scanned the room without moving her head. She was alone. She opened her eyes fully and sat up. The intruders had departed. Everything seemed intact.

She could still detect the foul odor, which triggered emotional and physiological sensations that forced Alana to rush to the bathroom and vomit violently.

A shudder of revulsion swept through her. She brushed her teeth and gargled mouthwash to eradicate the horrendous taste, then cupped a handful of cold tap water and splashed it on her face. It felt wonderful. She began to feel normal. She remembered her atomizer was in her bag and pressed the plunger, waving the mist through her room to mask the lingering odor.

Alana didn't know who to contact first. She didn't have confidence that the authorities would take her seriously, so she decided to e-mail her headquarters. She addressed it to Dr. Larson and copied Eric. After an account of the attack, she pleaded with Dr. Larson to let her come home. She clicked send.

Y

Atlanta, Georgia

"Eric, Dr. Larson just called in." Stephanie said. "He asked me to tell you he'll be here in a few minutes if you'd like to wait. Can I get you a soft drink or a cup of coffee?" she asked.

"A Diet Coke would be nice if you have it."

She rummaged through a small refrigerator behind her workstation and matched his request. She handed it to him with a small napkin. "Here you are."

"Thanks." The elevator announced Dr. Larson's arrival. Eric stood to greet him. "Hello, Dr. Larson," he said.

"Good afternoon, Eric," he said. "I'm sorry our meeting has been delayed for so long. I trust your trip to Japan went well and that you have some evidence to present?"

Eric detected a dubious tone in the question and stiffened. "No, sir, the encryption has been tough to crack, but I'm hopeful. There's a lot to tell you, but I'm concerned about Alana's e-mail. Have you read it yet?" he asked with a tone of his own.

"No, I can't say that I have. As you may know, I was summoned to a hasty meeting with the Saud Foundation in Geneva last week. My laptop was stolen from my hotel, and I have been very much out of touch since. Why don't you bring me up to date?"

"Well, I received two e-mails from her. In the first one, I found out she's in Pakistan of all places. I didn't even know she was being sent there. Whose idea was that?"

"Excuse me, young man. Are you forgetting who she works for? I'll deploy my employees anywhere they are needed, and I don't need your approval to do so."

Eric flushed. He was out of line, and he knew it. "I'm sorry, sir, but the second e-mail frightened me, and I'm a little emotional right now. Alana was assaulted as soon as she arrived in Pakistan."

"What? Was she injured?"

"No, she's OK. But she's afraid and wants to know if she can come home. Whoever attacked her only wanted to scare her. They said she'd suffer the wrath of Allah if she got out of line."

"Well, I can assure you, I am concerned for her safety. But I think our security staff in Karāchi should be able to watch out for her. I will instruct them to follow up. I doubt that she is in any immediate danger. There are only two safaris scheduled, and then she can turn the operations over to her new assistant. She could be home within two weeks. I trust that will satisfy you?"

"Yes, sir, if there are no additional incidents." Eric wasn't happy. Alana was in one of the most volatile of Muslim countries, and he couldn't stop worrying about her.

"There's a lot more, sir. I recovered the DVDs in Japan. Joe Hammond and I are working on the encryption, but we haven't been successful yet. While I was in Japan, Alana gave me the photo of one of the lab techs from Cairo. It turns out that the Department of Defense security people connected him with an al Qaeda terrorist in Tokyo."

"Al Qaeda? Are they involved in all this?"

"Yes, sir, they are. In fact, Alana and her friend saw them outside the Tokyo lab the day before our murdered lab tech was found."

"Eric, I'm having trouble connecting all these dots. This is getting convoluted."

"Believe me, I know, sir. It gets worse."

"How so?"

"I was shot at last night."

"Great Scott!" Dr. Larson's eyes roamed, scanning Eric from head to toe. "Are you all right?"

"Yes, sir. I know this sounds crazy, but I would have been assassinated, except for an Israeli agent who died saving my life."

Visibly shaken, Dr. Larson sank into his chair. "Eric, what is going on? I cannot believe all this mayhem. You've become a lightning rod, and it's dangerous to get too close to you. Did you go to the police?"

"Yes, sir. I also called a friend who has been very helpful. She has connections with Israeli intelligence. The man who was killed was an agent she had dispatched to watch over me. The man had diplomatic cover, so the FBI was called in. The special agent in charge of this district interviewed me himself. I've been up most of the night."

"Eric, I'm pleased that you were not injured, but I am concerned about these incidents. I'll need to inform our parent organization and seek their counsel on these matters. In the meantime, you must be exhausted. Why don't you take the afternoon off and get some rest."

"Thank you, sir. I may knock off early this afternoon. I appreciate your consideration." Eric shifted in his seat. "Sir, there's one more detail. The FBI pulled fingerprints from a weapon that was dropped at the scene of the shooting. They matched a known terrorist. Sir, if I could be so bold—I would ask you to reconsider your decision about Alana. I'm concerned for Alana's safety. I don't trust the Muslims, and she's in a very hostile location right now."

"That isn't an easy decision, Eric. Alana's reputation preceded her. Her assignment is based upon a personal request from our most important funding source."

"Who is that?" Eric asked.

"Prince Khalid Saud himself. He said Dr. Alomari required Alana's organizational skills and was confident that she would be the best person to train the staff in Pakistan."

"Alomari?" Eric was incredulous. "He's at the center of the storm! It's his organization that's squandering our resources and dispatching these assassins!"

"An argument could be made that it's the Saudi resources being squandered. Like it or not, Alomari is in a favored position. Unless you can give me airtight evidence of his direct involvement, I am powerless to do anything."

Eric clenched his fists in frustration. "This is impossible. Alana is in danger, and you won't do anything about it. I'll give you your evidence, but you need to get Alana out of there before it's too late."

"I empathize with your feelings, Eric, and I am willing to overlook your intensity due to the circumstances. But let me warn you. Be careful whose buttons you push. You have seen how they push back with a vengeance."

"You're not telling me anything I don't already know." Eric took the last comment as a dismissal and stormed from the room.

On the way to his office, he pulled out his cell and dialed. "Joey! There have been developments. I'll fill you in later. It's time to call in reinforcements. I had a study group at Tech that I'm going to contact. Here's my idea..."

Y

Karāchi, Pakistan

Alana was discouraged by the e-mail. Dr. Larson didn't give her the courtesy of a response. He had forwarded her e-mail to Ms. Knowles, who had sent the official reply. This was a bunch of nonsense. How would Alomari know of her reputation? She'd only had two previous assignments. No. There was more than met the eye. If Alomari wanted her in Pakistan so badly, who were the people who attacked her? And what would they do if she ignored their warning?

Alana recalled a verse from the Bible she had memorized as a child. It came back to her with renewed meaning as she fell to her knees and humbly prayed: "Lord, my enemies are vigorous and strong; and many are those who hate me wrongfully. And those who repay evil for good, they oppose me because I follow what is good. Do not forsake me, O Lord; O my God, do not be far from me! Make haste to help me, O Lord, my salvation. Amen."

Y

Atlanta, Georgia

Eric surveyed each person gathered in the room and was impressed. They had assembled three of their original study group with only six hours' notice. Two more were connected via videoconference on the laptop and two by cell phones propped on the table. "Can everyone hear me OK?"

Everyone affirmed the connection.

"I want to repeat my thanks to all of you for coming to our aid. If there's any way I can ever repay you, don't hesitate to call me."

Liz Smith, the valedictorian of Eric's class, spoke up. "Eric—I know I'm speaking for everyone present. You saved our bacon on more than one occasion. We're here for you. And for Alana too. So what's up? Your e-mail said it's a matter of life or death. That was overstating the case, right?"

"I wish it were. Before I get to that, I want to introduce you to a friend of mine who works with me, Joey Hampton. Some of you can see Joey's condition. For those who can't, I'll tell you that Joey was run down by a terrorist. I was the target, but Joey had the misfortune of being in the wrong place. There have been at least three additional attempts on my life, and just this week, an Israeli agent gave his life to save me. Now Alana is in danger, and I need your help." His voice cracked. Joey reached out and squeezed his shoulder.

"I'm OK. Before I go on, I need to emphasize an important detail. I mentioned a terrorist. You need to know that we have positive confirmation that al Qaeda terrorists are involved in this. You need to be aware of the potential danger."

"Whoa there, big fella." This came from one of the speakerphones. "If we help you, are we going to be on their radar screen? It won't change my offer to help. I just want to know if I need to renew my concealed weapon permit." A harsh chuckle followed.

"It's possible," Eric answered, "but I'll do everything I can to protect your identities. I recommend we communicate through Joey's secure MySpace blog. We'll give you the access codes in a few minutes. If anyone wants out, I'll give you a few minutes to think about it. I'll completely understand."

No one moved. A couple of throats were cleared as everyone sat through an uneasy silence.

"OK, then," Eric continued. "Here's the deal. Our job is to crack some encrypted files. They're using a two-hundred-fifty-six-bit encryption that Joey and I have been unable to crack."

"What's in 'em?"

"They consist of complete genetic profiles taken from blood samples The files are probably compressed because of the amount of data involved. We don't have enough evidence to stop these people, so everything hinges on cracking these files. They contain the proof of the Islamic hijacking of my company's project.

"I'm open to suggestions—and a solution. The files have the extension GIG, which is an unknown file type. I've posted one of the GIG files on Joey's blog for you to download. Let the group know as soon as you have any success. Post your results early; post them often. Let us know your thought processes because they may be the key that can lead to someone else's solution. As our profs used to say, show all your work and you'll get at least partial credit." He paused, then said, "Let's get to it."

Eric was upbeat. They had assembled an impressive team of computer talent. If anyone could crack the code, it was this group. "Joey, would you mind coordinating everything? I have to focus on a couple of issues at the office, and I can't afford to have Preedy watching over my shoulder."

"Yes. I have more available time than anyone right now. Go ahead and focus on work, and I'll let you know of any developments."

THIRTY-EIGHT

Saturday, October 22, 2005
19 Ramadān, 1426 AH
Karāchi, Pakistan

A RAUCOUS HORN VIBRATED AGAINST THE WINDOWS OF ALANA'S room. Exhausted from the hard week and desperately wanting to sleep in, she cringed at what would come next: the insufferable chanting from loudspeakers above the nearby mosque. Impossible.

She wrapped the soft down pillow over her eyes and tucked it snugly around her ears, hoping for just a little more rest.

Alana woke from a disjointed dream and pulled the pillow from her eyes. The mid-morning sun confirmed that she'd dozed for a few wonderful hours. She found herself planning for the upcoming week and thinking about her new assistant. Razi was as gifted as Para and Si had been. Alana would be hard-pressed to rank them and was amazed at her good fortune. Razi was a bit standoffish, but they had only been partnered a week and had not spent any time just getting to know each other. Razi's primary education had been at a madrassa Islamic school. Then she finished her secondary education in the public schools. She was now in her final year at Karāchi University and hoped to advance to medical school.

The thing Alana found most intriguing about Razi was her Muslim faith. Virtually all of the people in this country were Muslim—upward of 96 percent. She had told Alana that she was Shiite, which was a small minority. Alana was fascinated and hoped to learn more. She would have to be circumspect about sharing her own faith; Christian proselytizing was illegal in this country.

Alana called down to room service and ordered some coffee and a hard roll that the locals seemed to subsist on. It wasn't too bad—if you washed it down with coffee.

Her phone broke the silence. "Hello?"

"Greetings, Alana. This is Razi. I was thinking…have you any plans for your evening meal?"

"No, I just ordered coffee and a biscuit for breakfast but didn't have any plans for later."

"Forgive me if I am too bold, but I thought you might like to visit one of my favorite dining place with me."

"That sounds wonderful, Razi! Where is it?"

"I can come to your hotel and retrieve you. Would sundown be an appropriate time?"

"Yes. Thank you for thinking of me."

"It is my pleasure."

Atlanta, Georgia

It was nearly midnight in Atlanta. Eric and Joey were burned out. One of their team members had posted a promising utility on the blog, and it appeared he had made some progress, but it hadn't panned out.

"It didn't work, Eric," Joey confessed. "I don't think the key is hexadecimal after all. Between all of us working on this, I think we're narrowing the possibilities, though. Why don't we call it a night? I'll tweak the parameters and leave it running all night. If nothing comes up by the morning, I'll work on it all day tomorrow."

"You're only offering that because Hurricane Wilma postponed the game with Miami."

"Hey—give me some credit. I'm giving up the first game of the World Series, after all. I might just wander past the TV for a bathroom break in the last inning."

"Speaking of wandering, how's the leg? It must be nice to be on your feet again."

"It's pretty weak." Joey stretched his leg out for Eric. "Look how skinny it is. It's going to take a lot of work to build the muscle back."

"Well, thanks for working so hard on this. The only way we're going to get Alana out of Pakistan anytime soon is to present some proof to Larson. It really scares me, having Alana so close to Alomari. If it's any comfort, I'll be working on this all weekend too."

"Why don't you crash here tonight? Remember what happened the last time you went home this late?"

"Will your parents mind?"

"I *know* they won't. In fact, I guarantee we'll wake up to the smell of Mom's blueberry pancakes and bacon."

"You talked me into it."

Y

Karāchi, Pakistan

Razi stood beside a car near the entrance as Alana exited the hotel lobby. Alana returned her wave and headed toward the car. A valet converged with her and opened the rear door as Razi got in the passenger seat. Alana thanked the valet. "*Pasind karma.*"

Razi looked impressed. "That was very good!"

"I'm working on the accent but have a long way to go," Alana acknowledged. She noticed a young man behind the wheel. "Is this your chauffeur?"

Razi cast a sidelong glance at the driver. "No, it is my cousin, Asadullah. Asadullah, this is my employer, Alana. She is from the United States."

"It is nice to meet you, Asadullah."

He glanced furtively in the mirror, nodded his head, and grunted.

Alana shrugged at Razi and changed the subject. "So, where are you taking me for dinner?"

"You know this is a month of fasting for Muslims, yes?"

"No, I didn't."

"It is traditional during Ramadān. Muslims are forbidden to eat during daylight hours in observance. I am taking you to my favorite dining establishment for breaking the fast. It is named Student Biryani. They specialize in Biryani, a Muslim delicacy made with rice and savory spices. They serve many varieties, but I prefer the chicken myself."

"I really enjoy trying different foods. Your favorite sounds good to me."

The drive was pleasant, and Alana asked questions about landmarks that caught her eye. Razi was an excellent tour guide.

They arrived at the restaurant, and Asadullah found a parking slot. Alana and Razi chose a table under an umbrella on the patio.

Alana noticed that Asadullah stayed in the car and glanced frequently in their direction. "Is Asadullah going to join us?"

A grimace of resentment swept over Razi's face, then quickly disappeared. "No. He is only here to watch over me. Muslim women are forbidden to venture out on their own. They must be accompanied by a male relative. My family tolerates my working because we are so poor, but my grandmother is visiting, and she insists on sending him with me for social outings." Razi spoke to the server in Punjabi. As the server departed, Razi directed her attention back to Alana. "How has it been for you here in Pakistan?"

"I've been a little unsettled. I was assaulted in my hotel room when I first arrived," Alana replied.

Razi was startled. "What? Were you ravaged? Did you call the authorities?"

Alana was uncomfortable reliving the event. "No, I wasn't raped. They just roughed me up. I was afraid to call the police. They implied that they had informers and I would suffer the wrath of Allah."

"The attackers were Muslim?"

"Yes, I assume so."

"Most surely they were Sunni. They outnumber us five to one in my country and are very powerful. They enjoy this type of intimidation."

"Well, they scared me, but they didn't intimidate me."

"That is an unusual statement. How can you separate the two?"

"Well, they scared me because of the fear of pain and the impulse to avoid it. But I am not so afraid that I would be intimidated about my faith."

"What do you mean?"

"They warned me not to speak about my beliefs." Alana shook her head, as if to erase the memory of the whole incident.

"Tell me something," she asked. "It seems that many Muslims live under fear and compulsion. What is so threatening about the claims of Christianity?"

Razi scanned the patio nervously. She seemed satisfied enough to reply. "I remember the constant warnings about Christians when I was in primary school. They used to tell us horrible stories of the things Christians did to scare us. But I have seen evil in all types of people, regardless of their beliefs."

"That is very perceptive of you," Alana affirmed. She purposely kept her voice low. "Have you ever been curious about Christian teachings?"

"No! I have been shunned by the few Christians I have known. They disliked me even though they did not know me."

Alana was consumed with vicarious shame. "Razi, please do not think that all Christians are like that. What you describe is a human weakness, not a fault of our religion."

"And not all Muslims would assault you in your hotel room," Razi countered.

"I know that." Alana did not intend to be argumentative, but Razi seemed defensive. "If you ever want to know more—"

Razi cut her off. "We must not speak of these things. It is illegal. You are a kind person, Alana, which makes your faith more appealing than what I have seen in other Christians. But embracing Christianity is out of the question—it would be at the risk of my life."

"You mean from the government?"

"No, not the government. My father and my brothers would have a holy obligation to kill me. If they didn't, I am certain that Asadullah would relish the opportunity."

"That is practiced here in Pakistan?" Alana asked. "Of course. The Prophet commanded it."

Come to Me, all who are weary and heavy laden, and I will give you rest. Take My yoke upon you and learn from Me, for I am gentle and humble in heart, and you will find rest for your souls. For My yoke is easy, and My burden is light. Alana wanted to say the words aloud to her new friend. But spoken aloud, they would cause so much sorrow.

THIRTY-NINE

Monday, October 24, 2005
21 Ramadān, 1426 AH
Atlanta, Georgia

THE HOUSE WAS SILENT IN THE EARLY-MORNING HOURS. During his convalescence, Joey preferred to work at this hour. There were fewer distractions. But the work could be just as frustrating, and he was stumped. Maybe a shower would clear his head.

He limped to the bathroom and rotated the showerhead to massage, then opened the faucets as much as possible. The pelting felt wonderful. Self-imposed barriers to his solution seemed to wash away as he reflected on the team's progress.

A fresh insight occurred to him.

Joey jumped out of the shower and wrapped himself in a towel, puddles trailing after him to his computer. The fragile thread of logic might break if he wasted any time. If that happened, the ends would fray and elude any attempt to reconnect them.

Joey intently reworked the parameters in the software. He almost missed the sound. A faint creak in the threshold of the doorway alerted him to a presence. Before he could turn in his chair, he was startled by an intense sensation at the crease of his armpit. It was as wet as his arm, but cold and clammy. The panic subsided. His dog Spencer had sniffed out another opportunity and earnestly licked the rivulets from Joey's shoulder blade.

Joey didn't need a bath after his shower—especially from a coarse tongue. He impatiently pushed Spencer's head aside. The dejected dog slinked to the corner and rotated two tight circles before slumping forlornly to the floor.

Joey held his breath and hit the enter key to test the result of his new insight. The cursor blinked several times before the screen rolled, continuously scrolling line after line of tightly packed data. He was gazing at unencrypted listings of genetic data. The contents of a GIG file. At last.

Joey's fingers trembled as he dialed his cell.

A sleepy response came from the other end. "Joey? Why are you calling me at this hour?"

"Dude! I'm sooo sorry. I've been slaving away for you—unpaid, I might add. But don't let that interrupt your beauty sleep. Call me after you get some rest, and I'll tell you all about your GIG files.

"What? You did it? Joey, you're a genius!"

"I thought you'd never notice. So, I guess you're awake now?"

"I'm sorry, man. I never dreamed you'd be working this late. Tell me what you found."

"I'm not sure I understand it all, but I think I'm seeing various client records. Each GIG file starts with an ID number and demographic data along with what looks like GPS coordinates. The rest of the monstrous file is filled with endless strings of the four letters that are near and dear to our hearts: *g*, *a*, *c*, and *t*—the letters that represent the four chemical bases of DNA. When I uncompressed the file, it was over three gigabytes."

"You've done it, Joey. The whole thing is clear now—and I think you've found a second meaning for GIG. The Genographic Project only authorizes twelve markers to be cataloged, which is a minimal amount of data. A file that size means Alomari is cataloging the complete genome for each of the subjects. No wonder he needed to compress the data." Eric sighed in satisfaction. It had taken a lot of energy to fully understand what Alomari was up to. "Now we can go to Larson with the proof we've been looking for. We finally have our smoking gun."

"Yeah. I wish I could be there to see Larson smoke Alomari."

Y

"Come in, Eric," Dr. Larson said, a grimace contorting his face. "Have a seat."

Eric didn't like the looks of this. He'd had a sense of foreboding since presenting his evidence to Dr. Larson this morning. He'd made his case thoroughly, starting with the DVDs that contained the raw GIG files, the printout from Muhammed that included some of the data, and, finally, the fruit of Joey's labor. He'd sat back triumphantly and expected Dr. Larson to express amazement at his tenacity and technical prowess. Instead, Dr. Larson had been edgy and distracted. He ended the meeting and told Eric they would reconvene after he conferred with his board.

Eric had been puzzled by Dr. Larson's initial reaction. As the day wore on, his emotions intensified and transformed from impatience to frustration to anger.

"Eric, I don't know how to tell you this..." Dr. Larson began.

Liam Roberts

227

This was going to be worse than expected. "Dr. Larson, don't tell me you're going to cave on this."

"Eric, my hands are tied. I talked to Prince Saud himself. He flatly warned me that Dr. Alomari is untouchable. The prince will withdraw all funding from our project if I don't back off. I don't like this any better than you do, but we simply cannot survive without his funding."

"I don't believe it."

"Believe it, Eric. You don't have to like it, but you have to accept it. I know this is a bitter pill, especially for someone so young and idealistic. Someday you'll appreciate that you have to carefully choose which hills to fight from."

"But, sir, these jerks are terrorists! You can't just roll over."

"That will be all, Eric," Dr. Larson said dismissively.

Eric stormed from the office and skipped the elevator, taking the stairs two at a time. He was on the ground floor long before the elevator would have arrived on the eighth. He violently shoved the panic bar, charged through the opening, and marched to the outdoor picnic area provided for society employees. The many cigarette butts littering the area attested to its preferred use. Eric perched on the picnic table with his feet resting on the bench. He flipped his cell open and punched up Joey's number.

"Hey, dude! I've been waiting for your call. How'd it go?"

Eric's hesitation said it all.

"Eric, the silence is deafening."

Eric couldn't remember the last time Joey had called him anything but "dude."

"Joey, I'm so ticked off I don't know what to say. But I have an idea. Contact our team, and tell them first of all how proud of them I am and that I'm very thankful for their faithfulness. Then ask them for one more favor."

Karāchi, Pakistan

Alana enjoyed the creature comforts that she would soon miss. The shower would be her last for a week. It felt wonderful. She packed her toiletry kit, which seemed so empty without makeup. She'd stowed makeup in a zipper compartment in her luggage. If she'd left it in her kit, she would certainly forget herself and absentmindedly apply it. She could not afford to offend the religion police by brazenly displaying eyeliner and lipstick. No sense in aggravating the hosts. At least they didn't force her to wear a burka.

Alana checked her e-mail. There was a message from Eric! She read the subject and opened it.

From: Eric Colburn
Sent: Mon 10/24/2005 5:04 PM
To: Alana McKinsey
Cc:
Subject: I'm frustrated
Alana:
You won't believe it. We finally cracked those files from the DVDs you gave me in Tokyo. I took everything to Larson. He was smacked down by the Saudis, so nothing will come of it. I'm so mad, I can't see straight. You can read more about it on Joey's blog. I don't want to reveal too much here.
I love you and can't wait to see your sweet face again!
Eric

Alana couldn't believe it. Larson's response was inconceivable. What was he thinking? She was ashamed of him for not standing up to the Saudis.

She opened her browser, navigated to Joey's MySpace site, logged into the blog, and scanned all the correspondence between Eric and his team. An impressive log of detective work. Today's entries included a summary from Eric of what had happened in his confrontation with Dr. Larson. This was followed by an appeal to the group from Joey:

WallCrawler: Team: We finally solved it! You are awesome. Thank you for your persistence. You made a positive contribution against these terrorists.
Eric has one more favor to ask. Can any of you help us develop a Magic Bullet? We need it to target unauthorized hackers. Here's Eric's idea: He wants to plant the bullet in a "trigger" directory on his computer. If a hacker clicks on the directory to check the contents, the Magic Bullet jumps the Internet and destroys their hard drive. The MB needs to be designed so it's inert unless accessed inside a directory named GIG. This should be a tempting directory if any of these jerks are snooping where they ought not to be. ☺

Alana chuckled to herself. It was a brilliant idea, but would anyone take the bait? The plan inspired an idea of her own. She and Razi were scheduled for a meeting at the lab after they concluded their safari. If she could get her hands on a Magic Bullet, maybe she could get into Alomari's computer and plant it.

As she watched the screen, another blog entry was posted.

> LizzyDaze: Eric and Joey: Kudos to the whole team. We're glad to help. I love your idea! Below this entry, I'm posting a Magic Bullet I designed for you that will work as specified. The file will be activated when it is renamed GIG.COM in a root directory named GIG. Be sure you don't click on the directory once the file has been renamed or you'll shoot yourself in the foot, so to speak.

Alana frowned at the pseudonym. LizzyDaze—that was the log-in name Liz Smith used in college. It must be her—the one who had edged her out in the valedictorian race. She'd been in Eric's study group. The sting of salutatorian would never bother Alana again.

Alana pulled a jump drive from her computer bag and inserted it in the USB port. Liz's Magic Bullet downloaded in less than a minute.

FORTY

Tuesday, November 1, 2005
29 Ramadān, 1426 AH
Karāchi, Pakistan

ALANA ROLLED OVER AND TURNED OFF THE ALARM FIVE minutes before it was scheduled. She hardly needed it with the *salat al-fajr* ritual down the street. It had so conditioned her that she'd probably awake at dawn for the rest of her life.

"Lord, open their eyes. Lift the veil that clouds their vision. I specifically pray for Razi, Lord. Give her the strength and courage to resist her family and challenge their beliefs. Use me as You see fit, and may You be glorified. Please give me the opportunity to do what must be done today. May I strike a decisive blow. Amen."

She rose from her bed and prepared for the day. It was nice being back in the hotel. The field conditions on the safari had been tolerable, but the cots were never comfortable. She cleaned up, gathered her things, and headed down to the lobby for a bite to eat.

As she waited for her food, she pulled out her laptop. She'd gotten in so late, she hadn't had the energy to check her e-mail. The wireless strength was satisfactory for downloading e-mail. Nothing from Eric. She checked Joey's blog and saw a notation that the MB had been planted, but there were no further developments.

She needed to let Eric know she'd returned from the safari safely. She also wanted to tell him about her plans.

> From: Alana McKinsey
> Sent: Tue 11/1/2005 8:09 AM
> To: Eric Colburn
> Cc:
> Subject: I'm back!
> Eric:
> The safari went very well. We accomplished much.

Razi and I have a meeting today at the Karāchi lab. I'm
anxious to see it. I hope I don't run into Alomari. I don't
know if I'd be able to disguise my contempt. Pray for me!

By the way, I read Joey's blog. You're a genius! And tell Liz
I'm proud of her.

I also want you to know that I downloaded a copy of the
MB and know how to install it!

I love you,

Alana

She clicked send as someone tapped her on the shoulder. She turned
and saw Razi with her elbows akimbo, leaning over the back of the booth.
"I'm surprised you did not hear me."

"I guess I was pretty focused on my computer. How long have you been
standing there?" she asked.

"Just a couple of minutes." Razi slid into the booth across from Alana.
"Was that your boyfriend you were e-mailing?"

"Yes. I miss him very much."

"Please forgive me, but I couldn't help but notice your comment about
Dr. Alomari. Why do you not like him?"

Alana was irritated at the intrusion on her privacy but stifled it. "I
don't even know him, so I can't say I dislike him. But I am aware of some
things he has done that I don't approve of. I'd rather not talk about it if you
don't mind."

Razi stiffened. She was subdued when the server approached. Razi
ordered tea. "I am sorry for looking at your e-mail," she said awkwardly. "I
did not mean to anger you."

Alana shrugged. "That's OK. Don't worry about it. I'm just a little
jumpy lately." She closed her computer and packed it away. "Our meeting
is at nine thirty. How far is the lab?"

"It is near the waterfront, but our meeting has been postponed until
tomorrow. You did not get the message?"

"No. Oh well. We aren't starting the next safari for a few days, so I
guess that will be fine. I suppose we can get caught up on the paperwork
we were going to put off until tomorrow."

Y

Eric parked in Joey's driveway, headed to the front door, and rang the doorbell. Spencer barked from inside as the front door opened to a smiling Mrs. Hampton. "Good morning, ma'am. How are you this morning?"

"I'm fine, Eric. Come in; come in. You're just in time for breakfast." She ushered him in and guided him toward the breakfast nook. "Would you like some coffee?"

"Yes, ma'am, that would be very nice. Just a pack of sweetener, no cream."

Eric pulled up a chair as Mrs. Hampton brought his coffee. "Do you like scrambled eggs with chives, Eric?"

"Yes, ma'am."

"Hey, dude!" Joey limped into the kitchen, leaning heavily on a cane, grinning broadly.

"Look at you! No more crutches," Eric marveled.

They enjoyed a hearty breakfast. Eric had to insist that he didn't want thirds and was certain Mrs. Hampton was going to pack him a to-go box.

On the way to the car, Eric remarked, "If I lived here I'd be three hundred pounds in a week."

Joey limped to the car a few paces behind him. "Mom feeds us well, that's for sure." Joey awkwardly dropped into the passenger seat, trying not to bend his knee. He rotated his hip and leaned in so his extended leg could clear the doorjamb. He strapped in, and they were on their way. "Dude, it feels good going back to work. I was getting stir-crazy the past few weeks."

"I can understand that."

They drove with the windows down and enjoyed the cool air. There was a slight fog that hugged the ground in the shallow recesses along their route. Wherever the road crested a hill, the fall colors sparkled through the drifting mist.

They arrived at work, and Eric pulled up as close to the main entrance as possible. "Why don't you get out here and I'll park the car?" he offered.

"Thanks." Joey clambered from the vehicle and shut the door. He limped to the entrance as the door opened. One of the guards had seen him approach and held the door.

"Hey, Joey! It's nice to see you back at work."

"Thanks, Barney," he winked. "It's nice to be back." The nickname Barney Fife had stuck since the altercation with Preedy.

Eric joined him, and they headed up to the seventh floor. The elevator doors parted, revealing a jubilant, noisy crowd. The cacophony of greetings, well-wishing, and high fives did not abate until Joey finally raised both arms and flexed his wrists and patted the air. The din subsided somewhat, but he had to shout to be heard. "Thank you so much. Your visits, cards, and gifts were greatly appreciated. I couldn't have gotten through it if I didn't know I had so many friends praying for me. I'm glad to be back."

Preedy stood at the back of the crowd with his hands clasped in front of him. The grimace on his face clearly telegraphed his disapproval.

Gradually, the throng dissipated as the staff noticed Preedy's expression. They didn't want to get on his infamous list. Preedy did not like to see productive time being squandered.

Steve Jones, one of the IT staff members, entered Joey's cubical as Eric was setting up a pillow on a box to elevate Joey's leg. Steve glanced furtively over his shoulder, and in a hushed voice asked, "Did you guys hear about Preedy's computer?"

Eric was still down on one knee and looked up. "What happened?"

"You know how he sometimes works with his office door closed? Well, he came in early—before any of the staff. A couple of us were at the coffeepot when we heard him yelling and throwing things in his office. He was loud enough that we could hear his cussing. He got pretty crude. A couple of the ladies were embarrassed and ran off to their cubicles.

"Then he opened his door and yelled for me to get my butt in there. He shoved his laptop at me and ordered me to rebuild or replace his hard drive and reinstall all his applications. I asked him what happened and he just glared at me. I got the message and got out of there quick."

"Wow. What do you think happened?" Joey asked.

"I tried to boot it before I did anything and got a 'No Media Available' message. I checked the BIOS, and it didn't have a hard drive listed. I had to FDISK it and re-create the primary partition. Whatever happened, it fried the thing pretty good."

"Amazing," Eric replied as he stood up. He turned toward Joey and caught a surreptitious wink. Steve turned and left the cubicle shaking his head.

Y

Eric knew Preedy would be on the alert. He now knew that somebody knew, and knew that they knew that he knew. Worse than that, Eric was surely the prime candidate for "knower."

　　　　　　　　　　　　　　　　　　　THE Y FACTOR

Because of this, he would have to be more circumspect at work. That included ignoring his Gmail account while still at the office, so he was anxious to wrap up his tasks and get away. Alana should be finished with the first safari by now. He was eager to see if she'd sent a message. Even more, he was anxious for her to get out of Pakistan and head home. She was in the eye of the storm, and the relative calm was misleading. Storm clouds threatened.

Eric took a late phone call from the West Coast. When he was finished, he buzzed Joey. "You ready to roll?" he asked.

"You bet," Joey replied. "I'm not used to putting in a full day. I'm exhausted."

"Since you're moving slow, why don't you head for the elevators now? I'll catch up with you in a few minutes. Hold the elevator for me."

Y

They parked in Joey's driveway just as a light rain started. Joey limped awkwardly to the protection of the porch. Eric trailed behind him, holding a file folder over Joey's head to shield him from the rain. "I'm OK, dude. A little rain never hurt anyone," Joey said.

"No problem. I wanted to come in for a few minutes. I thought we could contact the team and let them know the good news. I think they'll get a charge out of it."

Joey finished the blog entry and sent an IM prompt to LizzyDaze. He typed a quick note of thanks to her for her efforts.

Eric asked, "Hey—can I check my Gmail account real quick?"

"Sure."

Joey went to the bathroom while Eric sat down at the computer. A few minutes later, he emitted a groan. Joey came through the doorway and asked, "What's the matter?"

"I wish I'd checked my mail earlier," Eric said. "I just read an e-mail from Alana. I think she may be planning to plant the Magic Bullet in Alomari's computer in Karāchi! If so, she's in way over her head. Alomari is more dangerous than she realizes. Preedy would have surely put out the alert by now, and Alomari will be suspicious of anyone who gets near his computers."

"Can you send her a quick warning?"

"She's not on IM. It's nine at night here, and Pakistan is eleven hours ahead of us, so it's already eight o'clock tomorrow morning there. She's already at Alomari's lab, so I can't risk calling her. She's on her own, and I'm helpless to do anything."

FORTY-ONE

Wednesday, November 2, 2005
30 Ramadān, 1426 AH
Karāchi, Pakistan

Alana and Razi entered the lab—the lion's den. Alana bristled with anticipation and nervously fingered the jump drive in her pocket. She was anxious to plant the Magic Bullet and put some distance between herself and Alomari's lair. Eric would be so proud of her.

The first to arrive, they were escorted to the conference room. A delicious aroma of flavored coffees wafted from a sidebar at the far end of the room. They helped themselves and selected seats opposite the whiteboard. The other participants eventually filtered in, and the meeting began. It dragged on monotonously with haggling over meaningless details.

Alana was drowsy, so she sat forward in her seat. Soon, she was aware of a growing pressure in her bladder. She longed for a break. Her discomfort intensified. She began to wonder if breaks were only an American tradition. Finally, the host announced that they would break for lunch. Alana joined the queue in front of the bathroom. It appeared that there was only one bathroom for the whole facility, and she grimaced in distaste. By the time her turn arrived, she no longer cared.

Alana felt much better after she'd washed up. She exited the bathroom to an empty hallway. She walked past the vacant conference room and peeked around the corner. The lobby was empty as well. Where had everyone gone? She'd expected Razi to wait for her, but there was no sign of her.

She returned to the conference room and sat down. She noticed the computer mounted in the podium had been left on. The Windows logo moved aimlessly around the screen. Alana glanced at the door and got up from her chair. She walked over and pressed the enter key. The computer came to life. No log-in prompt. Alana looked toward the hallway. Still no signs of life. She launched an Explorer session and scanned the network until she found what appeared to be Alomari's computer. Did this computer have read/write permission? It was more than she could hope for.

Alana held her breath and clicked a series of commands: File, New,

Folder. An icon appeared with "New Folder" highlighted. She quickly typed GIG and pressed enter. The moment of truth: the folder name stuck, signifying full rights! She had passed the point of no return. Another glance at the hallway. As a precaution, she resized her Explorer window to a small, manageable size and moved it to the bottom of the screen. Next, she opened an Internet session and logged into the Dell Web site. If anyone challenged her, she was merely shopping, and she wouldn't be tempted to lie.

She fished in her pocket for the jump drive. With her fingertip, she flicked the lid off the drive and pulled it from her pocket. She leaned down to the floor-mounted PC and lifted a panel on the face of it. As she had anticipated, two USB ports greeted her. She inserted the jump drive and propped her purse to conceal it. She stood up and clicked on the icon that had appeared for the jump drive. It only took a moment to drag the "VIRUS.COM" file to the GIG directory. Another quick glance. She renamed the file "GIG.COM" and pressed the enter key.

"What are you doing?" A deeply accented and commanding male voice boomed from the doorway. "That computer is restricted."

As Alana turned, she closed the Explorer window, which the intruder couldn't have seen from the doorway. "I'm sorry. I was just checking on the cost of a memory upgrade," Alana said as she made eye contact with the intruder. He was quite tall. His swarthy completion and black beard were accentuated by his white turban. He strode into the room, a towering presence that exuded an expectation of intimidation.

Alana was not about to be intimidated. She nonchalantly reached for her purse. Her advance positioning paid off. She was able to simultaneously grasp her purse straps and the jump drive. As she slid the drive from the USB port, the computer emitted a soft ding. She froze momentarily, fearing the intruder may have been close enough to hear it. She held her breath.

He didn't react to the sound, and Alana shook off her momentary paralysis. She stood upright, surreptitiously dropping the jump drive into the open folds of her purse as the intruder approached. He craned his neck and scanned the screen to confirm that everything was in order.

"Who are you, and what are you doing in here?" he demanded.

"I'm here for a meeting with the lab staff. I'm from headquarters in Atlanta," she said sweetly. "My name is Alana McKinsey." Although she suspected who it was she was facing, she deferentially held out her hand. "And are you?"

He ignored the offer of her hand and smirked with distaste. "I am Dr. Ahmed Alomari. I am the director of this lab."

She indifferently dropped her hand. "Yes, I know the name," she said with a self-confidence that belied her anxiety.

"Then you know that all genographic activities here in Karāchi are under my absolute authority." He paused for effect. "And that includes your so-called safari team."

Alana bit her tongue. This jerk's ego would tolerate no equivocation of details. She would have to choose her battles carefully. She nodded but did not reply.

"Do you have a problem with that?" he demanded.

"No, I don't." She casually shook her head. He was scrapping for a fight, and a little taunting wasn't beneath her. He clearly expected her to appeal to her position as Dr. Larson's protégé so he could pull rank. She was glad Eric had told her of Larson's slap-down by Prince Khalid.

Alomari's confidence was predicated on his protected status. She wasn't about to engage in his competition when the outcome was predetermined. Besides, that was a guy thing.

Atlanta, Georgia

Eric was distraught with concern for Alana. "I never intended for her to take initiative like this. It's too dangerous," he said to no one. Eric sat on his bed and dropped his head in his hands. He hunched forward and rested his elbows on his knees. "Lord, I know I don't pray very well. I'm not sure how this should work, but I know I have no right to expect anything from You. Please forgive me for being so headstrong and ignoring You so much. If You will protect Alana, I promise to pray more and go to church more often."

Eric felt better. He hoped the Lord would answer his prayer and was sure that Alana's spirituality would make Him more likely to do so. Eric reflected on his conditional promises. At least he kept it vague. He had been on the verge of promising weekly attendance but knew he couldn't handle going every Sunday. He'd minimally meet his obligation of "more often" with attendance twice a year. Easter *and* Christmas. That wouldn't be too tough.

Y

Karāchi, Pakistan

Dr. Alomari summoned Satam and Murad to his private office adjacent to the lab. The side entrance opposite the lab assured they could come and go without being observed. Alomari ordered the others to sit while he stood.

"We have had an interesting development. Last night I received a warning from my sister who lives in the Great Satan. Although it seemed unlikely we would be affected, she warned me of a computer threat. Praise *Allāhu al-Khabir* for our discipline and thoroughness. The very threat surfaced this morning. It was found on my computer. I suspect the American bimbo planted the virus when she was unattended."

Murad spoke first. "I will snuff her out like a candle in the wind!"

Alomari loomed over him. "You will do nothing without my explicit command!" he seethed. "The Tall One has given his blessings to my project and has ordered you to follow my directives. You are not to take initiative in these matters. I am playing our enemies like a chess master. I alone have the ability to anticipate and counter their moves. Understood?"

"Yes, Doctor."

"It has been said, 'Only two things are infinite: the universe and human stupidity, and I am not sure about the former.'" Sarcasm was an effective tool to humiliate underlings. His efforts were lost on Murad, but Satam appeared to be subdued by the rebuke. He smiled inwardly at the irony. His men would be shocked if they knew he had just quoted Einstein, a filthy Jew.

"We will commit to fasting and prayer until the end of Ramadān in two days. By then, the American bimbo will conclude that her espionage was successful and will report back to her accomplices. Bring her to me on the first day of Shawwāl. We will celebrate the Eid al-Fitr feast and be purified. Then we will deal with the bimbo."

Y

Alana was so excited, and she had not been attentive during the afternoon. She'd done it! She begged off dinner with Razi and couldn't wait to get back to her room to e-mail Eric. She rode in silence, gazing at the city as they neared the hotel.

"What are you thinking about?" Razi asked. "You seem to be far away."

"I was. I was thinking of how nice it will be to go home after all these months. One more safari, and I'll pack for the last time."

"The safari departs on Saturday morning, yes?"

"Yes. I think we should start in the outlying areas and will work our way back to Karāchi on Monday evening. If all goes according to plan, I should be able to fly out next Wednesday, or Thursday at the latest." Alana realized that she'd not been very affirming and added, "I am confident that you will be able to carry on without me. You have learned very fast and are a diligent worker. I am going to miss you, Razi. I've grown very fond of you."

Razi seemed uncomfortable with the compliment. Her eyes flitted between Alana and the road. She stammered, "I have enjoyed working with you as well, Alana."

They pulled up to Alana's hotel. She collected her laptop and purse and opened the door. She rotated in the seat and bumped her purse against the dashboard.

She closed the door and turned to say good-bye to Razi. "Thank you for the offer of dinner, Razi. I'm just too tired tonight."

"That is fine," she said. "Another time, perhaps."

Alana turned toward the hotel entrance. Razi followed her progress. When Alana disappeared into the lobby, Razi leaned over and rummaged between the passenger seat and door. She had seen something fall from Alana's purse and was curious. Her hand brushed against something solid. She grasped it and held her hand up, rotating it slightly. The uncapped USB jack of the jump drive gleamed in the light from the hotel lobby. "What do we have here?"

Y

Alana went directly to her room and sent Eric an update. She reported on the encounter with Alomari and was proud to recount how confident she had felt in his presence. She attributed her boldness to the Lord, who gave her strength. Hopefully, Eric would read her e-mail and reply soon. She hoped he would pop up on IM so she could chat with him. Then she called room service and ordered a salad.

Alana pulled the various contents from her pockets. She noticed the cap to her jump drive and recalled that she hadn't taken the time to snap it back on when Alomari had interrupted her. She fished through her purse but could not find the drive. Trying to think of where she had last seen it, she realized it could have been dropped anywhere. Well, there was nothing on it to link back to me, she thought, hoping for the best.

Y

Atlanta, Georgia

Eric received Alana's e-mail and shook his head in amazement. She had pulled it off. However, he was angry with her. He did not like her being in harm's way, especially when he had been an unwitting contributor to her rash behavior. If anything happened to her, he would never forgive himself.

He launched IM and noticed that Alana was online.

> BizTekGuy: Alana! How r u?...

Half a planet away, Alana spotted Eric's chat milliseconds later. She smiled.

> GirlGenes: Eric! I'm fine. Did you get my e-mail? ☺
> BizTekGuy: Yes, I did. I'm so relieved you're OK. But you scared me to death. BTW: be careful what you type...
> GirlGenes: I understand. It was nothing, really.
> BizTekGuy: That was very brave but foolhardy. You're in the belly of the beast. Please be more cautious.
> GirlGenes: Yes, dear. ☺
> BizTekGuy: I love you, which makes it worse. I've never been more scared for anyone. I even prayed to God and asked Him to keep you safe.
> GirlGenes: Wow!
> BizTekGuy: Yeah, I know. Since He answered my prayer, I've got to go to church more.
> GirlGenes: LOL! That's great! I'll go with you.
> BizTekGuy: OK. It's a date.
> GirlGenes: Well, I'm pretty tired. I need to get some sleep. I'll dream about you.
> BizTekGuy: I love you and can't wait to see you!
> GirlGenes: I love you too. I'll write to you on Friday night. We're heading out on safari Saturday, and I won't be able to contact you again until we return to Karāchi on Monday. Bye for now!
> BizTekGuy: Bye!

FORTY-TWO

Friday, November 4, 2005
1 Shawwāl, 1426 AH
Karāchi, Pakistan

THE DAYS WERE GETTING SHORTER AND COOLER AS THE WINTER solstice approached. Razi had requested that they finish their work early in order to observe Muslim tradition that religious observances are to begin at sundown. She needed preparation time with the women of her household who were responsible for the feast.

Alana had her window open and was enjoying the cool evening breeze. The sun had set an hour ago. The sounds of celebration signaled the beginning of Eid al-Fitr. Intermingled was the ever-present call to *salat al-maghrib*. Pleasant aromas drifted in through the open window and reminded Alana she should visit the hotel restaurant soon.

Alana packed for tomorrow's safari. She was eager to begin the final phase of her extended trip. The collection efforts and training had been satisfactory, and the team would be self-sufficient under Razi's leadership once Alana left for the States.

There was a knock at her door, and she crossed the room. "Who is it?" she asked.

"Razi," came the reply.

Alana was struck with the sensation of déjà vu, so she pulled the security latch over the protruding peg and opened the door. She confirmed Razi's presence in the hallway and smiled. She partly shut the door to free the security latch and pulled the door wide. As she did so, she was startled to see two men.

They lunged for her. She retreated a step and swung the door as violently as she could. They were too strong; the door was thrust inward. She stumbled backward. They stormed into the room and threw her on the bed. This was déjà vu after all. Ominously, the men were not masked this time. And neither was Razi.

Alana suddenly realized why Razi had seemed familiar to her. It was her voice. The burka had muffled it that first night, but it had been her. As expected, the men forced a rag into her mouth. Her eyes bore into Razi's and communicated her horror at the treachery. Alana realized that the rag did not have the same chemical taste or foul odor as the first one. Something was different. She continued to stare at Razi.

"Alana, it did not have to be this way. I tried to warn you, but you would not listen. Now Dr. Alomari wishes to interrogate you, and we are to bring you to him.

"There are two ways this can be accomplished. We can drug you and roll you in a rug, or you can walk through the lobby and get in my car. The choice is yours. Be aware that our countrymen will not come to your aid should you do anything foolish. I am, however, concerned with Dr. Alomari's reaction should you arrive with your throat slit."

Alana struggled against her captors and tried to spit the rag from her mouth. She moaned with as much volume as she could muster. It was a pathetic sound and would never be heard above the din from the street below.

Razi merely shook her head. Her face was absent of compassion or remorse. "We will do this the difficult way. Drug her."

Y

Atlanta, Georgia

Eric was getting worked up all over again. It was the end of the workday and he hadn't received Alana's e-mail yet. It was almost 4:00 a.m. in Pakistan, so she wouldn't have left on the safari yet. He sent her a quick message and decided to wait a few hours to see if she responded. Then he thought better of it and wondered whether she would check her e-mail before leaving the hotel. He couldn't make up his mind.

Maybe he should call the hotel, but he'd wake her up needlessly and she might be irritated with his overprotectiveness. He could wait a few hours, but then he wasn't sure what time the safari would be leaving.

He suddenly remembered there was a way to confirm the departure time. With the complex worldwide activities of the National Geographic, it was important to maintain comprehensive schedules with the commensurate contact numbers for a variety of reasons, the least of which was the potential need to contact staff members in an emergency.

Eric checked the scheduling server to confirm the itinerary. They were scheduled to leave at seven. That was in three hours, so she'd be getting up in the next hour anyway. He made up his mind. He checked the itinerary for the hotel phone number, snatched the phone from the cradle, and dialed. A dual language greeting informed him to press one for English. He pressed zero instead. As expected, the hotel operator answered, "Karāchi Marriott, how may I help you?"

"Alana McKinsey's room, please."

"I'll connect you."

The phone rang a number of times. Finally, a recording came on that indicated the party was not available at this time. Eric didn't wait for the suggestion that he leave a message. He pressed zero again but was frustrated. There was no way to escape voice mail purgatory. Alana should have answered. It was too early for her to be in the shower; she should have still been in bed. She was a light sleeper, so there's no way she'd sleep through the ringing phone.

Eric pressed more buttons, all without effect. He slammed the phone down, snatched it back up, and pressed redial. He was eventually reconnected to the hotel operator. "Would you connect me to Alana McKinsey's room again—but wait," he shouted, "after you transfer me, can you stay on the line? If she doesn't answer, I need you to get the hotel manager on the line instead."

"Most certainly, sir. Connecting now. Please hold."

As with the first attempt, there was no answer. When the recording came on, the operator dropped the connection. "There was no answer, sir. I'll connect you with the manager at this time."

"Thank you," Eric said needlessly. She had already made the transfer. Eric heard ring tones.

"Hotel manager. My name is Mr. Habib. How may I help you?"

"Mr. Habib, my name is Eric Colburn. I am concerned for one of my employees who is staying at your hotel." Eric assumed he would get a better response by referring to her as an employee rather than his girlfriend. "I have called her room twice in the past few minutes but she does not answer. Would you mind sending your security person up to her room to confirm that she is OK? It is much too early for her to be out of her room, and I am concerned."

"Could you confirm the name of her company and her billing address? You understand that I must confirm that this call is legitimate."

"Of course. Ms. McKinsey works for the National Geographic Society, and the billing address is 538 W. Peachtree Street Northwest, Norcross, Georgia."

"Very good, sir. I will check on Miss McKinsey myself. Would you care to stay on the line? My phone is wireless, so we can continue speaking while I check."

"That would be very nice. Thanks." Eric could hear the sounds of the manager moving through the hotel. Within a few minutes he heard the characteristic ding that signified the arrival of the elevator.

Eric heard another ding in the background as Mr. Habib said, "I am on her floor now, Mr. Colburn. Please wait a moment." There was silence for a couple of minutes, then a knocking sound. After a pause, the knock was repeated. "There appears to be no one in the room, Mr. Colburn," the manager informed Eric.

"Do you have a key?" Eric asked.

"Most certainly."

"You have my permission to enter the room," Eric said tersely.

Eric heard a beep and the metallic click of the door opening. "Oh my," Mr. Habib said.

"What is it?" Eric shouted.

"Miss McKinsey is definitely not here. The bed linens are half removed. The dresser drawers are all pulled open, and her clothing is lying around the room. Her suitcases have been slashed open." He paused while he surveyed the scene. "Just a moment. I need to call security from the room phone, Mr. Colburn."

Eric heard him punching the digits on the phone. "This is Mr. Habib. Please call the police about a probable kidnapping. And send the security team immediately to room fifty-three twenty-four. Bring an inventory sheet for a standard queen room. We need to confirm all hotel property for the insurance firm. The rug is missing and probably more."

Y

Eric burst through the stairwell door, which swung through its arc and slammed loudly into the wall. He turned the corner and headed for Dr. Larson's office. He passed Stephanie on the run and didn't take the time to acknowledge her alarm.

Dr. Larson was just placing his phone on the cradle and looked up as Eric came to an abrupt stop at his desk. "Alana's been kidnapped!" he shouted.

"What?" Dr. Larson exclaimed. "Are you certain?"

"Yes. I talked to the hotel manager myself. I was on the phone with him when he entered her room. The police have been called. They suspect an abduction and will be mounting a search for her."

"What do they stand to gain by kidnapping Alana?" Dr. Larson asked. "This is an outrage!"

"I can give you an answer to that, but you wouldn't like it," Eric retorted. "Dr. Larson, I know we've had our differences lately, and I've put you in an uncomfortable position. In spite of all that, I need to ask one more favor. I'm going to Pakistan to see what I can do to help. I'd like your blessing, but you need to know—I'm going with or without it. Things would be much easier for me if you'd have Stephanie make the arrangements and have the society pay the fare."

Dr. Larson was ashen. "Eric, I am truly sorry for this. I have placed Alana in a dangerous situation. My first inkling is to give the police time to sort things out. But I have made too many wrong decisions in this affair. The next one could have tragic consequences." He leaned forward and rested his fists on the desk. "Eric, do what you can to find her."

Eric smiled. It would be his last smile for many days. "Thank you, Dr. Larson. I won't forget this." Eric turned and scurried from the office. As he went through the doorway, Dr. Larson called out to him.

"Eric! I want to say one last thing."

Eric turned around. "Yes, sir?"

"You have my solemn vow…if that precious young lady has been harmed, I will do everything in my power to ensure justice. And if Alomari is involved in this, the prince can keep his filthy money. We'll find a way to get along without it."

Y

Stephanie was able to book a flight from Atlanta International that would arrive late Sunday night and worked her magic to produce a visa. Eric had taken a cab and now had an hour wait. He checked his belongings to make sure he hadn't forgotten anything. He rummaged through his backpack and realized it was getting cluttered with all the evidence he'd accumulated, so a little organization was overdue. A Sharper Image store stood next to the security gates. He headed for it purposefully.

"May I help you?" a smiling clerk said, bearing down on him.

"Yes. Do you have any leather portfolios?"

"We have a few. Let me show you our choices. If you don't like the options we have in stock, there are many more online." She stressed the merits of the various brands, and Eric quickly narrowed the choices. The one he selected had a few storage pockets and would perfectly fit his purposes. He also liked the rough, football-like texture that felt good in his grip.

He paid for his purchase and headed to the international terminal.

FORTY-THREE

Saturday, November 5, 2005
3 Shawwāl, 1426 AH
Karāchi, Pakistan

Searing pain woke Alana from her drug-induced stupor. Her arms were on fire. She opened her eyes but could detect no difference. Opening and closing them repeatedly yielded no subtle shadows that would allow her to get her bearings. She was suspended by her wrists. If she twisted, she could brush the floor with her toes.

The tight bindings around her wrists had cut off all sensation in her fingers. Her arms felt as if they were being dislocated from bearing her full weight. Pain emanated from every joint. Her tongue was thick in her mouth, and her lips were cracked. She licked them to no effect. The stretching of her torso compressed her ribs. Breathing came with ragged, raspy effort.

Alana gasped her prayer again but with greater urgency: "Lord, my enemies are vigorous and strong, and many are those who hate me wrongfully. And those who repay evil for good, they oppose me because I follow what is good. Do not forsake me, O Lord; O my God, do not be far from me! Make haste to help me, O Lord, my salvation. Amen."

When would this end? Why were they doing this to her?

She trembled in terrifying isolation and cried out, "Lord, why have You forsaken me?" No point of reference. Nothing but heightened awareness of a searing, agonizing existence. Time was meaningless, its pace measured in pulsing, throbbing pain. The definition of hell.

Hours—maybe minutes—later, a serene peace washed over and shamed her. "Lord, forgive me for doubting You. Give me the strength I need for this trial."

A sound intruded on the inky void. A door scraping a threshold? No change in the light. Had someone entered this place of torment?

Something warm wafted against her neck. A foul breath. Someone was behind her. A tentative, exploring touch brushed her back. She recoiled in terror, squirming futilely. Hands were placed on her shoulders, and she screamed, "Who are you? What do you want?"

"Be still. Your struggles will accomplish nothing." His voice was deep, thick with accent. He was Punjabi. She had not heard this voice before.

"Please let me go. I've done nothing," she pleaded.

"Silence!" A violent blow struck the side of her head. Her ear filled with an echoing ring, her cheek burned. "You are not to speak unless I grant permission," he growled. "Ahmed will be here soon. First, I have plans for you." A guttural, grating laugh. Rough, calloused hands slid beneath her blouse at the waist. They drifted to her rib cage and cupped her. He squeezed crudely.

He embraced her tightly from behind, molding his body to hers. She couldn't breathe; a wave of nausea gagged her. Mercifully, the embrace suddenly ended. He pulled away from her, his hands tracing the panels of her bra. Realization shivered through her as his hands met at her spine. He fumbled clumsily with the clasp. The elastic recoiled sharply and dangled uselessly beneath her blouse. His hands began to reverse their course. He was about to embrace her again—without the obstruction of the bra.

His distance from her would be perfect now, a brief window of opportunity. She bit her lip and lashed backward with the heel of her right foot—the one strengthened from years of soccer.

The blow was perfectly placed, but the thrust propelled her like a pendulum. She swung to the apex and lurched her body. Rotating, she hoped she was facing her attacker. She could not see a shadow. Using the return arc for momentum, she arched her back, brought both legs together and locked her knees. She impaled him as he recovered from the first blow. The impact rocked her and threw her into a disorienting spin. A grunt betrayed her attacker as he fell noisily. She heard a series of gasps from somewhere beneath her. Her gyrations slowed as she arched her body to negate the pendulum effect.

The swinging disoriented her until she heard him struggling to his feet. Her foot brushed against something. With her bearings confirmed, she kicked again. A satisfying thud against his head rewarded her.

Another groan. "You infidel!" he grunted. "I will cut out your heart!"

In the distance, the scraping sounded again. Was it from the same direction? She was dizzy from the gyrations and couldn't be sure.

A single bulb flickered on. She rocked through diminishing arcs, staccato images flashing. Her attacker bent over, blood streaming from his nose. Alomari in a doorway. A bed. Filthy linens. A table and chairs. Grime-covered walls.

Alomari shouted, "Satam! What are you doing here?"

"Sir, I was preparing her for your interrogation."

"In the dark?" The question carried an ominous threat. "Leave us!" Satam scrabbled from the room, blotting his nose against his robe. Alomari slammed the door behind him.

Alana glanced at herself. Her clothing and body were filthy, as if she had been dragged through mud that had crusted in streaks. Her skin shone with a patina of sweat that had run in rivulets, leaving trails in the grime. Tendrils of damp hair clung to her neck. She wondered if he could tell that her bra hung askew beneath her blouse. He watched her with an amused expression as she twisted and rocked in a vain attempt to turn her back to him.

"Why am I here?" she shouted. "What do you want with me?" She could not mask the shrill whine in her voice, never having been so vulnerable in her life. She had to hold on.

Alomari laughed. "You don't sound as confident as you were yesterday."

"Please let me down," she pleaded.

"You will remain where you are until you have told me what I want to know."

"I have nothing to tell you."

"We will see." He dug into the recesses of his robe and lifted his hand. "Surely you recognize this?" he sneered. Her jump drive. "Perhaps you would like a closer look?" He moved purposefully toward her. He seemed to levitate; there was no rustling in his robes to betray the movement of feet. He glided toward her and stopped mere inches from her. "Do you recognize it now?" he asked, pressing the silver end of the drive sharply into her cheek.

She moaned in pain but did not speak. Tears rolled to the tip of her chin and dripped to the floor. "What if I do?" she finally said. She saw no purpose in lying. Then she wondered if the Lord would disapprove if she were forced to lie to this scum.

"Did you really think you could outsmart me?" Alomari laughed again. "Your pathetic attempt at sabotage was laughable. I want to know if it was Larson or Colburn who directed you."

"No, I was on my own. No one directed me. They don't know anything." Her confidence returned.

"How did you know of the GIG files? Who told you about them?"

She answered, "No one." There was no harm in blaming a dead man, so she hastily added, "Muhammed Haznawi was a lab technician in Tokyo. He left a journal and GIG files that I recovered while I was there."

This revelation seemed to enrage him. She flinched, expecting him to strike her, but realized his anger was focused elsewhere. "How did you develop this specific virus? You do not have the technical capability to do this."

"A college friend developed the virus. I did not know who was behind the GIG files, but I wanted them to pay for Muhammed's murder."

"Why would you avenge his death?" He was uncomfortably close and shouted in her face. "What could he possibly mean to you?"

Alana stubbornly refused to acknowledge the pain inflicted by Muhammed's death. She also feared for Si and what would happen if her involvement were to become known.

He altered his line of questioning. "Your attack was coordinated with someone in Atlanta. Who is it?"

Alana hesitated as she thought of Eric. What harm was there in confirming what Alomari already knew? They had already tried to kill Eric many times for what they assumed he knew. No, she couldn't take the risk. There is no way she would implicate her love. "I don't know anything about what happened in Atlanta. I've been in Asia for weeks."

"No matter. I am certain it was your impotent lover, Colburn," Alomari said contemptuously. He was fishing, and Alana remained impassively silent. "He has been a minor nuisance, but he is no match for me. Just as I lured you to Karāchi, I have laid a trap for him. He is on his way here as we speak." He had hit the responsive chord and smugly awaited the response.

"Eric? Eric is coming here?" Alana flushed with anger as she thought of Eric walking into a trap. "Leave him alone. Do what you will to me, but don't harm him." Alana sobbed with fear for him.

"That depends on your cooperation. I want to know what information Colburn has about my project."

"Why? What difference does it make?"

"In actuality? Not much. But I am a chess master; I am intrigued with how my adversary's mind works."

Alana hoped that a little information would not make any difference at this point. "All he knows is that you are driven by your hatred for Jews."

Alomari's façade broke. "How could he suspect this? What else does he know?" he screamed in her face. He pressed the tip of the jump drive against her skin at the edge of her bra.

She flinched, regretting her comment. "I don't know." She squirmed away from the pressure. Her shoulders protested from the renewed strain. They felt like they were dislocating. Her muscles and ligaments twitched with spasms. The agony was more than she could bear. "Only that you intend to enflame all Muslims in a jihad to drive Israel into the sea," she gasped. This was no secret; the Muslims had been vowing it for fifty years. "I've told you everything I know. Please let me down," she pleaded. "The pain is unbearable."

Alomari's smile returned. "That bit of information is insignificant, considering the magnitude of my plan." He slowly scraped the metal down her cheek. Then he spun her around, grabbed her from behind, and scraped the metal of the drive across her neck—tracing the path a knife would take if she resisted further. "He must have learned this from his Jew floozy, Barak."

Alana was filled with dread that a knife would be at her throat at any second, and it already hurt too much to resist. Too much was happening too fast—and he was unrelenting. She focused on his last comment. What did he mean? Her face telegraphed her vulnerability and confusion.

He smiled lasciviously. "So you knew nothing about his other lover?" he casually asked.

"You can't break me with your mind games," she spat defiantly. "Don't even bother."

She felt him reach into his robe and pull out another object. The knife. He slowly brought it around where she could see it. "So, he didn't tell you that he had been seduced by an Israeli spy? Men can be noble only to a point, you know," he said as he touched the flesh of her neck with the blade. "There are certain temptations that are greater than the strongest of us can endure," he murmured in her ear.

A fearful shiver of revulsion ran through her as he circled around and faced her directly. "You're lying." Her feeble denial lacked conviction, and she knew it.

He slowly withdrew something from the folds of his robes, staring intently in her eyes. He patiently rotated two small photos and smiled triumphantly, searching for a reaction. "What is the expression? I believe it is, 'Pictures do not lie,' yes?"

She stared at a photo of Eric seated next to a beautiful woman in a booth. She had jet-black hair and a dark complexion. The candle on the table illuminated her sensual face and reflected off the wineglasses in the foreground. She smiled as she gazed at Eric.

"That's obviously a doctored photograph," Alana replied. There was no confidence behind her statement.

"Ah, that is certainly a possibility," he said mockingly. "But a second one?" He slid the photo aside, revealing another.

This photo was a similar setting, complete with candles and wine. Alana couldn't suppress a sharp intake of breath as she recognized the shirt Eric was wearing. She had bought it for him as a graduation present. The shirt guaranteed the authenticity of the photo; her captors would not know its significance.

"She is beautiful, yes? Seductresses usually are, you know. It is a time-honored and effective tradition, so do not judge his weakness too harshly." His mocking was more devastating than physical torture. "First you were betrayed by Razi's perfidy, and now your lover's infidelity. Perhaps it is time to reevaluate your faith in human nature."

She hung her head in defeat. The tears flowed freely. She was nearly broken—but not quite.

"You have been somewhat cooperative. I will extend a small courtesy." He flipped a wall switch, and Alana heard the hum of a motor. She was lowered until her feet touched the bare concrete. Then he moved the switch to a middle position and the descent stopped, leaving her arms parallel to the floor.

She was able to loosen the bindings on her wrists. The explosion of blood through the constricted veins and arteries felt like a raging fire. She winced from the needles of pain. The pressure on her rib cage finally dissipated. She gulped the dank air greedily. Why had he done this? The small act of kindness was disorienting. Was this a technique of psychological torture?

"I regret that I must separate myself and confirm what you have told me," he said. "If you have lied, you will pay a bitter price when I return." He turned to the door and said, "Do not go anywhere," and laughed derisively. He turned the light off, and the door clicked behind him.

Y

Hours passed, and Alana lost all sensation of time. Her bladder had released quite some time ago. She was ashamed by the odors that enveloped her. The photo of Eric with the Israeli woman haunted her. He had never mentioned his Israeli connection was so alluring. What happened to honesty? How could Eric leave even a glimmer of doubt in her mind for this monster Alomari to use against her?

Eventually, there was a click and the door scraped open. The light came on, and she blinked at the abrupt change. Alomari entered. "I have confirmed what you told me yesterday. I will ask again and warn you to be truthful. What else does Colburn know?"

Alana was puzzled. "There is nothing else. Why? What else is there to know?"

"I find it curious that Colburn's passion could be so energized for the Jews, even with the persuasion of his lover. Surely he knows more. Has he learned of our plans to expose the Great Usurper?"

"The Great Usurper? What are you talking about?"

"Isaac. The Jewish patriarch."

Alana was completely disoriented. "This makes no sense. That's ancient history." Eric had not told her any of this—which was a blessing in disguise. Her incredulity was genuine.

"History would have been far less violent if he had never been born. His conniving mother Sarah would never have objected to Ishmael's rightful status. But then the usurper was born and everything changed. Ishmael's heritage was stolen."

"The Bible tells a different story."

"Of course it does! The self-serving Jewish swine twisted the truth."

Alana found renewed strength, even though argument was futile. "But the record was clear and consistently documented by multiple writers for centuries. Then two thousand years later, Muhammad dreamed up his revisionist account."

"Watch your tongue! Your throat is not too lovely to slit with my knife."

"Why are Muslims so afraid of the truth? By Muhammad's own testimony, he believed his epileptic visions were from demonic possession. You claim his visions and teaching were from God, then claim his prophetic authority is affirmed by the Quran. But the Quran is his own testimony. Can you not see the circular reasoning?"

"We do not need to quibble over the differences between our holy books. We now have scientific data that will set the record straight."

"What do you mean?"

"The genographic data, of course. We have cataloged the DNA of Ishmael's descendants and have conclusive proof that his mother was Mesopotamian, not Egyptian as the Jews claim. Therefore Ishmael was not a half-breed. He was the rightful heir to his father's blessings, not his sniveling half brother."

"But what could you possibly hope to gain with that?"

"Time. We will distract the world with this information. Our people hunger for what is due them. We have waited for thousands of years, and we will finally be vindicated. A worldwide jihad against the Jews and the decadent West will be launched, and we will take back what is rightfully ours."

"So, how will that gain you time? Time for what?"

"To complete my research." He chuckled derisively.

"But I thought you already determined Ishmael's lineage."

"Yes, that is true." He hesitated.

Alana sensed a reluctance to continue. What else was he planning? Based upon what he had already revealed, it would surely have disastrous consequences. She decided on a different tack. If she appealed to his vanity, his narcissism might just overwhelm his judgment. What would it hurt? She was a dead woman anyway.

"I can't imagine what else you might discover. It's amazing that you were able to deduce Ishmael's lineage from the genographic samples. I wish I could see your data."

"That would interest you?"

"Yes. I am not as educated as you, but I have extensively studied the human genome and am fascinated by what you have discovered."

"Perhaps."

The tipping point. In spite of her horrid condition, she smiled inwardly at the weakness of the male ego.

"Do you take me for a fool? Who is the chess master here? My research will continue unimpeded. Your Magic Bullet did not succeed; our data is safe. The theft of the GIG files is regrettable, but Muhammed has been suitably dealt with. The files are sufficiently encrypted; your people will not be able to discern our true objective. And your lover will be eliminated as soon as he arrives in Karāchi. All is well. I have no fear that your knowledge will see the light of day."

"So, you will kill me now?" Alana refused to give in to despair. There must be a way to save Eric.

"No." He walked to the table and pulled back a chair. "You are more useful to me alive. Pawns can be effective, if managed properly." He seated himself and adjusted his robes. "I will satisfy your curiosity. You will come to appreciate my genius before you die."

"I thought you were going to let me live."

He smiled and appraised her body from his improved angle of view. "We all die, do we not?"

"The Bible says, 'It is appointed for all men, once to die.'"

"Yes, and your appointment date is up to you. I will allow you to live as long as you are useful to me." He grinned suggestively. "Tell me, you don't find it curious that we were sampling complete genomes of all peoples, even non-Muslims?"

"Yes, I do. I don't understand why you took data from Japanese and other Asian peoples if your goal was to vindicate Ishmael. It seems you should have focused on Arabic descent only."

"You will soon answer that question for yourself. First, I will provide background information. You are aware that Islam agrees with the Jewish account of Creation?"

She had no idea where this was leading. "No, I never thought about it."

"We do." He had assumed a professorial, pompous air. "I believe that Adam was created perfect and would have enjoyed an eternal existence in paradise if sin had not entered the world. Logically, if he was designed for eternity in his physical body, then his DNA must have been perfect."

"That is an interesting idea. I've never heard it postulated before."

"His DNA would have remained perfect, but his sin brought corruption and death to the world. I believe the mechanism chosen by Allah to bring this about was through degradation in his DNA. This degradation continued to accelerate through the ensuing generations. What is the evidence for my theory? The measurable result was steadily decreasing life spans. This is documented in the patriarchal record. With few exceptions that are statistically insignificant, life spans from Adam to Noah decreased in a nearly linear fashion."

He paused as if she needed time to absorb the inescapable logic of his assumptions.

"I am a student of the Bible as well as of science," Alana said. "Your insight is fascinating, but I am not able to fully appreciate it in my condition. If you would release me from these bindings, there is nowhere for me to run. I will then be able to concentrate more fully on your scientific accomplishments."

He seemed to weigh the merits of her request, then stood and walked to the door. He flipped the switch, and the motor whined. Alana's heart jumped at the sound. She felt profound relief when the rope went slack. She dropped her hands in front of her, careful to keep her arms pinned at her sides. More slack played out.

"Sit on the bed," he ordered her. He moved to the end of the bed and cut her bindings before resuming his seat.

Alana glanced at the grimy blanket. It represented the only warmth available. With revulsion, she gingerly lifted it to her shoulders and huddled beneath it. Her hands ached, but enough feeling had returned that she was able to reengage the clasp. In spite of the filth and her bodily odors, she was grateful. "Thank you," she said humbly. "What you said about Adam makes sense. I've always wondered about the longevity of the patriarchs."

"I believe it is explained by the lingering efficacy of Adam's perfect DNA. Whether shortened life spans were due to cosmic radiation or some other mechanism, the DNA inevitably deteriorated over time. Through successive generations, DNA mutated. Further, chromosomes recombined endlessly throughout countless generations of the human race. To lesser scientists, it would appear to be a hopeless jumble of genetic data.

"The important thing is that each of us undoubtedly carries many original DNA fragments that have never mutated. This is why it was imperative that I collect samples from every genetic pool across the earth. By collecting DNA samples from hundreds of thousands of people from every tribe and nation, I have been able to statistically determine most of the markers that were present in Adam's original DNA."

The moment of truth. Alomari stood to emphasize the enormity of his success. "The most significant accomplishment in this research was to determine the construction of Adam's Y chromosome. It is *the* unique DNA component in the human family. It has not recombined through the generations. It was passed from Adam down to all living men intact. The only variation found within it is from random mutations, which are easily accounted for. It is the Y factor, and I have successfully reconstituted it!" He paused as his statement reverberated through the silent, stagnant prison.

"That was a crowning achievement in its own right. But it was only the first essential step in my research. Many great discoveries followed. The Y chromosome mutation patterns were analyzed as the standard by which I could compare all other chromosomes. Since the variation in those chromosomes was due to both mutation and recombination, the Y factor allowed me to hold constant the effects of the former. This was the key to unscrambling the omelet.

"As you are aware, the new science of gene therapy first identifies mutations in DNA. These mutations result in defective proteins that are causative agents in disease. The objective in gene therapy is to neutralize the effect of the errant protein by binding it with an inert molecule.

"I am taking a more aggressive approach. I am on the verge of creating a comprehensive collection of gene therapies that will obviate every single DNA mutation that has been identified."

Alomari was in a zone, completely obsessed with the revelation of his research. His voice grew louder and more passionate with each passing moment. "Before long, my test subjects will see their life spans increase dramatically as their susceptibility to diseases diminishes.

"As more mutations are cataloged, I will cross reference them with my genomic database and will be able to statistically determine the original DNA framework and add it to my gene therapy serum. Eventually I will succeed in turning back the aging process as well. I will be able to obviate every DNA mutation that has occurred since the original—and perfect—man.

"Do you appreciate the implications of this research?" he asked rhetorically. "I will possess the source of ultimate power, power that has been dreamed of in every generation since the dawn of time. Power that the cherubim have guarded with flaming swords since our expulsion from paradise. Power that was lusted after and was the impetus behind the launching of great armadas and global exploration."

He smiled triumphantly. "I will develop the genetic equivalent of the fruit of the tree of life. It will be within my power to dispense eternal life!"

FORTY-FOUR

Sunday, November 6, 2005
4 Shawwāl, 1426 AH
Karāchi, Pakistan

ERIC'S FLIGHT WAS DELAYED AND LANDED HOURS BEHIND SCHEDULE. Alana would not be waiting for him this time. He desperately hoped she could hold on and that he could come up with some way of finding her.

At the customs desk, an agent instructed him to empty his backpack. Eric did so. The agent took the backpack and dropped it into a box next to the wall. Eric was confused and tried to ask for an explanation. The language barrier made it impossible. "No allow. May be bomb!" was the most he could get out of him. Eric assumed that the backpack was contraband due to its potential use in concealing bombs. He had no choice but to carry his laptop and portfolio; there wasn't enough room in his small suitcase. He zipped the portfolio into the inner pocket of his jacket, stuffed his PDA in his pants and hoisted his computer.

He glanced hopefully at his backpack one last time. As he exited customs, a thought occurred to him: if Preedy had discovered his plan to fly to Karāchi, he would certainly alert Alomari. Eric fully expected to be intercepted by Alomari's henchmen—most likely as he exited the airport terminal.

He motioned to a female customs agent. "Excuse me, do you speak English?"

"A little amount," she replied.

"Could we talk in private?"

The agent nodded and led Eric to one of the processing rooms.

"I think there are Israeli agents waiting for me. My life is in danger. Is there another exit? I'm afraid for my life if I go to the main exit."

The young woman looked alarmed. "Jews?" she exclaimed. She turned and left the room. Eric saw her confer with another agent. They glanced at Eric through the plate-glass window. The other agent nodded her head. Eric's agent returned. "I get approval for you to leave through staff door." She motioned for him to follow her.

Eric was led down a series of hallways and ultimately through a door to the staff parking lot. He made his way to the highway and sought a cab.

Y

"You have certainly accomplished an incredible breakthrough." Alana couldn't believe what she had heard. The magnitude of the plot was enormous. It was far more extensive than what Eric had learned from the Israelis. No one would ever guess Alomari's true objective.

She had to get free, to sound the alarm. In the meantime, she had to keep him talking. "Why don't you go public with your research? You would certainly win the Nobel Prize and obtain unlimited funding for your research. You could benefit all of mankind and reduce untold human misery."

He smirked at her. "I do not wish to benefit mankind. My allegiance is to *Allāhu al-Khaliq* and his chosen people. We will live forever and rid the earth of all infidels. It will be paradise reborn."

"But eternal life is not a matter of biology. It's a matter of faith. Do you count yourself equal to God?"

Alomari laughed derisively. "What is it you Amrikans say? 'God helps those who help themselves'?"

"'That's not from Scripture," Alana rejoined. "But this is: 'God will not be mocked.'"

Y

Eric asked the driver to pull over to the curb when he spotted an American bank. He got out and went straight to the ATM. When he punched in his PIN, he received a response that indicated his transaction was invalid. "This can't be happening!" he muttered. He tried one of his other cards with the same result. Eric was furious. This didn't make any sense. There had to be an explanation. Preedy. He was sure of it.

Eric panicked. He could cover the amount on the taxi's meter with a little left over for some purchases he had in mind. He'd have to pay up now and continue on foot to conserve his cash. He'd have to leave his suitcase in the cab so he wouldn't be burdened with the extra load!

Y

Alomari laced his fingers together on the table and leaned forward on his elbows. "You are wrong," he said simply. "Allāhu has bestowed many blessings on my research and has given me victory at every step in my journey.

I do not need your affirmation to make it so. It is true regardless of your opinion.

"As I assured you, your life will be spared—for now. You will join the safari for its return to Karāchi. You are to be seen with the safari in order to dispel rumors that you have been abducted. I cannot afford to be harried by your State Department at this critical juncture. You will be kept on a short leash, and I warn you, do not attempt to escape. Razi has orders to slit your throat if you provoke her in any way."

Y

Eric fought the despair that threatened to overwhelm him. He had to clear his mind or all was lost. "Lord, give me wisdom. Show me what I should do," he implored.

His only connection to Alana was the safari team. If they were involved with her kidnapping, he might be able to follow them to where she was being held. But how could he find them? Where would he start? He pulled out his PDA and pressed the map icon with the stylus. It took a few moments for the GPS feature to plot his current location. He noted the genographic lab was not too far away.

Y

Alana was allowed to clean herself, and her clothes were taken and replaced with robes. She was ordered to don them along with a burka. Her meal was stale bread and murky water, which she consumed voraciously.

She was escorted to an ancient, battered Land Rover that had lost its shock absorbers in the distant past. After a long, dusty journey, they approached the safari camp. Alana could make out the tents in the glow of campfires. Her driver parked and approached a man who had a familiar look. They engaged in a heated discussion, and the man turned to a nearby tent. He shouted something, and the tent flap opened a few minutes later.

Razi exited and walked to where Alana sat. "Come with me." Her voice was harsh and was no longer reminiscent of Para's sweet, mellifluous accent. Alana complied and followed her to the tent. Razi held the tent flap open and silently motioned for her to enter. She pointed to a cot. Alana sat.

"You will sleep here. I will sleep there." She pointed to a cot with disheveled bedding. "I do not sleep heavily, and there is a guard posted outside. You do not want to know what we will do to you if you attempt escape. Your life hangs by a thread. Do not tempt us."

"Razi—I don't know why you have done this to me, but—" Alana's voice caught—"I want you to know that I forgive you."

"Shut up! I would rather slit your throat than listen to you. Do not think you can influence me with your Christian drivel."

Alana lay back on the cot. She whispered, "Thank You, Lord, for preserving me through this ordeal. I ask for Your protection over Eric. And forgive my enemies, for they are so confused."

Y

Eric pulled the portfolio from the zippered lining and consulted his notes. The lab had a server room with a long list of equipment, but he didn't see a notation for a wireless router. It was worth double-checking. He began to make his way toward its location, moving easily through the deserted streets.

Eric found the lab and took up an unobtrusive surveillance post. He could see lights through the front windows and occasionally noticed movement. No one came or went. He would not be able to get inside as long as there were technicians on site. Maybe they would leave before the next shift arrived in the morning. He held up his PDA but did not detect a wireless signal. Sometimes his computer had better success. Although the battery was low, it would only take a moment. He fired up the laptop. Still no signal. He shut the lid and tucked it under his arm with the portfolio. He might need to be closer to the lab to pick up a weak signal.

He scurried to the end of the block and approached the corner, hoping to get next to the back wall. As he rounded the corner and turned into an alley, a door opened in the building adjacent to the lab. The man exiting was backlit in the doorway, but his features were unmistakable. Satam. Eric's adversary looked up in surprise. Their eyes met.

"You!" He turned back into the doorway to shout a warning. Eric knew what he intended and momentarily debated the two adrenaline impulses: fight or flight. Maybe both. He rushed the door and hit it with his full weight. The door slammed into Satam, and his head bounced off the jamb. He slumped to the ground, blocking the opening.

Eric heard shouts of confusion from within and took advantage of the opportunity, escaping into the darkness. He ran a random route through a series of streets. When he was safe, he stopped to catch his breath and take stock. His laptop was fine, but he'd dropped his portfolio when he threw himself at the door. He shook his head and smiled silently as he slipped into the night.

Y

Alana remained awake for a long time. She evaluated her chances of survival, which weren't promising. She was under Alomari's protection, but only until she outlived her usefulness. Then all bets were off.

She prayed again for Eric, wondering if he'd arrived in the country yet. How could he find her? Was there any way she could get word to him? There seemed to be no options open to her, but she would be vigilant. "Lord, give me a sign."

Next page: The Peninsula. Enlarged, full-color map is available at www.y-factor.net.
Satellite image courtesy of GeoEye. Copyright 2009. All rights reserved.
Refer to the map on page 210 for the city of Karāchi, Pakistan.

GeoEye

Baba Channel

Eric & Alana's Hideout
24° 51' 02" N
66° 58' 33" E

SDV Landing

SDV Route

Fishing Harbor
West Wharf

FORTY-FIVE

Monday, November 7, 2005
5 Shawwāl, 1426 AH
Karāchi, Pakistan

Eric scurried to the end of the dirt alleyway, where it merged with the pitted asphalt of the main thoroughfare. The wind gusted between the rough-hewn tenement buildings and sent a shiver through him. He tugged the collar of his light jacket upright as a meager barrier to the chill.

He warily scanned the street vendors setting up their wares as the sun struggled to crest the distant horizon. A mournful chant could be heard in the distance as the faithful were summoned yet again for ritualistic prayers. Foul odors wafted from the gutter and mingled with, then were slowly replaced by, the savory aromas of the morning. His stomach gnawed at him, an urgent reminder of how long he'd gone without food. Eric ignored the temptation and shouldered his way into the growing throng. He clutched his laptop to his chest and hunched forward as if shielding it against the rain. It was a lifeline to Alana that must be guarded at all costs.

The street stalls began to thin. Backlighting the ramshackle buildings was the glow of neon lights and traffic signals in the distance. Eric's hopes were raised that he'd find what he needed in a civilized oasis of this sprawling wasteland of 15 million inhabitants.

He shuffled toward the light while he thought of how far he'd come in six months. Self-deprecation welled up again. How could he have been so naïve—so blinded by ambition? He bitterly chided himself for dragging Alana into this. She couldn't fathom the danger she was in. Today might be his last hope of saving her.

Two possibilities loomed in the next block. American commerce made its mark even in this godforsaken country. Starbucks and McDonald's stood in steel-and-chrome defiance against a backdrop of dilapidated brick and mud structures.

Eric turned and peered into the gloomy slums in his wake. The morning shadows were intense between the brilliant shafts of sunlight cutting between buildings. He couldn't be sure.

Uncertainty and hunger gave him pause. He made his choice. His stomach tightened as he plodded through the delicious aromas of the McDonald's and entered the Starbucks. He counted his remaining rupees and ordered the cheapest coffee. He relinquished the grimy coins and asked for the access code to the wireless network. The clerk stared contemptuously. "You buy coffee only!" he barked.

The sleepless night and anxiety for Alana had conspired in an assault on his temperament. The rebuke by the imperious Punjabi assured a hostile response from Eric. These people hated Americans and expected arrogance in return, so he responded in kind. "Look, you low-life, I'm a paying customer. Give me the code—*now*!"

The clerk glanced toward a doorway with a ragged curtain draped across the opening. He grunted a comment and was joined by another local who Eric assumed was the proprietor. They spoke furtively in Punjabi to prevent Eric from eavesdropping. A decision was made. The clerk thrust a slip of paper in Eric's face. He mumbled, "Only five minutes! That only is amount you acquire. Then you get out!"

Eric snatched the slip from his hand and found a table near the door. He tapped the mouse pad nervously while the laptop initialized. The urgent blinking of the low battery icon was ominous. It should last for his allotted five minutes.

He inserted his wireless modem and confirmed the signal strength. Not great, but enough bandwidth to let him accomplish his task. He glanced at the computer's clock and couldn't remember if he'd synchronized to the correct time zone but could not waste precious seconds confirming the correct zone. Would the server block his access because of a time zone mismatch? He couldn't remember the protocol. He wasn't confident of anything at this point.

Eric launched a software patch and established a VPN tunnel to the scheduling server in Atlanta. He was hopeful that the intrusion-detection system would not sense his presence.

He scanned the scheduling logs. Alana's collection team should be somewhere in the city later today. If he timed it exactly, he could intercept them when the caravan wound its way through the unpaved squalor of the Kharadar section. Traffic would be hopelessly slow as the throngs pressed them for handouts.

A gust of chilly air swept across him. He glanced up to see two men in turbans and sweat-stained robes enter through the delivery door from the back alley. He turned his attention back to his computer as the newcomers huddled with the manager.

His legs twitched reflexively as he scrolled frenetically through the log. There was the entry! The collection team was scheduled to stop at the Meetha Dar—"The Sweet Gate." It would be his best chance for a link to Alana.

But the time of day notation troubled him. It must be the time zone shift; his laptop incorrectly converted the time. What was the offset? He launched the appropriate utility. The splash screen appeared, but the cursor morphed to an hourglass and stubbornly froze. "What the—"

Eric glanced over his shoulder. The café manager smugly held a dangling electrical plug. He'd killed the router. Eric was out of time. The men rounded the counter and intently scanned the crowd. *Jerks*, Eric thought. They would be on him in a few moments. He slammed the lid on his laptop, tucked it to his chest, and raced into the street.

Y

The work was difficult and was made more so by the burka. Alana struggled for breath under the heavy fabric. The warmth and moisture from exhaling were trapped in the confined space, increasing her discomfort.

She was working with Razi, but their roles were reversed. Razi had assumed an authoritative demeanor and was commanding the collection efforts. They finally finished with the long queue that had formed early this morning.

Y

Eric made his way through the Kharadar district. He was within a mile of the Meetha Dar when he eventually spotted a vendor selling what he was looking for. He haggled with the merchant and settled on a price far below what he had expected to pay. He still had adequate cash for bribes.

Eric had worked out the probable time differences from his review of the scheduling computer and purposed to arrive at the Meetha Dar early. He would camp out as long as it took. The plan would provide a margin for error.

He arrived at his destination and methodically paced off the area. He made mental notes of spacial relationships and examined all vantage points. He did not know where the safari would take up station and needed to have contingencies in place. Time would be of the essence once the collection station was set up.

As he walked through the throng, he was continuously beseeched for handouts. He shouted at them, "Do any of you speak English?" They gazed at him with hungry perplexity, but no one responded. He continued to wend his way through the pressing rabble. He repeated his question frequently to no avail.

Eventually, he heard a voice from the crowd. "Yes. I speak English little bit."

He couldn't see the source of the voice but shouted, "Come here if you would like to earn money." He craned his neck, peering through the crowd. He finally detected the purposeful movement of his new assistant elbowing his way to the front. "What is your name?" Eric asked.

"Abdulaziz," was the response. He was diminutive, probably due to a lifetime of a meager diet. He appeared to be in his early twenties. Old enough to be reliable yet young enough to still dream of great wealth. Perfect for the task at hand.

"OK, Abdulaziz, do you know what these are and how to use them safely?" He held a bag out in front of Abdulaziz.

Abdulaziz peered into the bag and smiled, "Yes, sir, I know."

"Good. Here's what I need you to do. I will pay you five American dollars now."

Abdulaziz's eyes lit up at his newfound wealth. "Yes, yes!"

Eric knew it equaled a month's wages—provided one could find a job. "And I'll pay five more if you follow my instructions correctly."

Abdulaziz hopped on one foot, then the other in anticipation. "Tell me, tell me! I earn!"

"Do you see the meat vendor just on the other side of the Meetha Dar?" He pointed to a stall where wisps of smoke swirled.

"Yes, yes!"

I want you to go over there and wait. When you see a caravan of motor vehicles pull up to a stop, look for my signal. I will wave this red cloth. You are to light the M-eighty fuses and throw the bag beneath the bush next to the meat vendor. Be careful that no one notices. The M-eighties have long fuses, so they will not explode for three minutes. Then hurry around the square to where I will be waiting." Eric pointed to a spot in the shadow of the nearby buildings. "I will pay you the other five dollars when the first M-eighty explodes."

The supplies were packed up, and the caravan set out on the return route to Karāchi. Eventually, Alana saw the Meetha Dar in the distance. The crowds were quite heavy and seemed to be in a spirited mood. She assumed it was the residual celebration of the feast of Eid al-Fitr.

Razi moved to the seat beside her, probably to assure that Alana would not jump from the vehicle as it slowed and escape in the crowds. "It is important that you be seen at our next stop. I will tell you to remove your burka after we set up the collection station. You will leave it off until we pack up to leave. Understood?"

"Yes." Alana nodded, despondent of all hope.

Y

Eric donned a turban and robes that the fireworks vendor had thrown in at no charge. They would allow him to blend in with the crowd.

A dust cloud billowed its way down the main thoroughfare and blew into the marketplace. The safari had arrived. The caravan came to an abrupt halt. Eric saw no sign of Alana, and his heart sank. He wouldn't need Abdulaziz's distraction after all. He threw the signal rag down in disgust.

His backup plan was dicey. He would have to strike up a conversation with one of the women. Most of them should speak English passably well since they were on the genographic team. He would ask if any of them knew Alana and where she might be. If they resisted conversation, he would be able to discern whether it was due to cultural mores or complicity in Alana's disappearance.

If that failed, his last resort was to try to keep up with the caravan in the hope that it would lead him to Alana. That would be tough to do on foot. He hoped it would not come to that.

Eric watched as the collection team descended from their vehicles and off-loaded their supplies. He casually made his way toward them and looked for an opening to speak with one of the women.

Y

Razi instructed Alana to place the crate of test tubes on a makeshift table and scanned the crowd. "Now is the time. Remove your burka, and make sure you stay visible to the crowd."

Alana was only too happy to comply. Wearing the burka had been an awful experience.

She was facing the Meetha Dar when the crowd parted, and her attention was drawn to a tall young man in the crowd. His gait and mannerisms looked so familiar. The turban he was wearing partially obscured his features, but…

"What are you waiting for?" Razi shouted. "Did you not hear me?" She reached out, grasped the burka, and pulled firmly. "Stupid bimbo!" She grasped the cloth as well as a lock of Alana's hair. When she yanked, she jerked Alana off balance.

Alana shrieked in pain and slapped Razi's hand away. Infuriated, Razi backhanded Alana across the head and sent her sprawling, sending the test-tube crate crashing to the ground. Alana lurched across the makeshift table, her arms flailing to catch herself. The flap of the burka flew up in her face, obstructing her vision. Blinded, she tripped, rolled off the table, and fell heavily at Razi's feet. As she fell on her backside, the shock jostled her hair clip, which sprang open. Her long blonde hair tumbled into view beneath the fringe of the burka.

Y

Eric was intrigued by the catfight that had erupted in front of him. He started to laugh as one of the women scrambled to retain her balance and fell on her butt. Then he saw her blonde hair. That was too coincidental; the odds were long that he'd happen across a blonde woman in Karāchi, especially one traveling with the genographic team. Could it be—?

He dug in his pocket for the red cloth and recalled discarding it. He looked through the gate and made eye contact with his new assistant. Abdulaziz shrugged in confusion. He wasn't too far away, so Eric made his way over to him.

Abdulaziz stared at him in puzzlement. "What is happening?" he asked.

"Change of plans, Tonto. I lost my bandana. Light the fuses now, and come with me! By the way, here's the rest of your money." He handed over the other five and hoped it would persuade Abdulaziz to help him further. "I may need some more help. Can you show me the way to the train station by the Lyari River for another five?"

"Most certainly!"

"OK, light the fuses, and stay close."

Abdulaziz ran to where he'd concealed the M-80s. He lit them and ran after Eric, who had taken up a strategic spot a few yards from the safari vehicles.

Eric whispered, "Abdulaziz, we need to look like we're haggling over prices so we don't draw attention." Eric gestured emphatically, and Abdulaziz caught on quickly. As far as anyone would notice, they seemed to be arguing the same as everyone else in the square and were effectively invisible.

Y

Alana was humiliated. She tried to clamber to her feet but was hampered by the long robes. Her vision was still obstructed, and she found it awkward to maneuver. She got to her knees as gunfire erupted nearby, followed by a flurry of activity as the men of the safari responded to the threat. Alana heard orders being shouted but couldn't understand them. The best way to avoid stray bullets was to stay low. She hunched down.

Suddenly, she heard a voice at her side: "Alana?"

She whipped her head toward the voice that was so dear to her. She tipped her head to see through the burka. It was him! "Eric!"

"*Shhhh.* Come with me." He grabbed her arm and pulled her to her feet. They scurried away as quickly as her robes allowed.

Alana righted the burka and glanced over her shoulder. Razi had seen the movement and turned. Their eyes met. Razi screamed a warning, but the men were too far for her voice to carry. She ran after the fugitives.

Alana stepped on her robe and stumbled. Eric leaned over to help her. As he stooped, Alana saw Razi come up behind him. A knife was drawn from the folds of Razi's robe. "Eric—look out!" Alana screamed.

He turned as the knife rose, glistening in the afternoon sun. Without hesitating, he lashed out and planted his fist in the middle of the burka. Razi's nose was crushed under the blow, and she collapsed in a heap. Eric turned back to Alana and urged her forward. They fled the marketplace with Abdulaziz in the lead.

"Follow me," Abdulaziz said over his shoulder. They wove their way through the throng toward sanctuary.

After many blocks, Eric gazed back though the path they had taken and saw no sign of pursuit. He called out, "Abdulaziz, no one is following. If we go slower, we will be less obvious."

A few blocks later, Abdulaziz stopped. "You safe now. No one follow. I leave and you go that way." He pointed toward a hazy horizon. They could make out where the river joined the Arabian Sea. The Mauripur train station was located at the mouth of the river. "Thank you, Abdulaziz. Here's the money I promised." He handed Abdulaziz another five.

Abdulaziz bowed and backed away from them. He turned and retraced the route they had taken. Eric watched him depart. When he turned back to Alana, she had taken the burka off, and she threw herself in his arms. She took his head in her hands and kissed him repeatedly.

"Hey—I love you too, but we need to be careful. They frown on PDA here."

"You're right," she whispered between kisses.

"We have to keep moving. If they come after us with the Land Rovers, they'll gain on us rapidly."

"OK. What's your plan?"

Eric hesitated. "Well, I had a plan, but I was blocked from making an ATM withdrawal. I don't have enough for a taxi—or plane tickets."

"I can't help. I don't even have my own clothes anymore. I'm in my underwear beneath these robes. I guess my hotel room is off limits."

"Absolutely. I'm afraid to try the consulate either. They'll be watching both locations. I think our best bet is to find a place to hide and wait a few days. By then, they'll assume we're out of the country."

"I hope you're right. Alomari told me too much to let me live. Let's find a hiding place, and I'll tell you everything."

The sound of approaching vehicles startled them before Eric could reply. He pushed Alana into a narrow space between two buildings and shielded her with his body. Two Land Rovers sped by. As they crossed his narrow field of vision, Eric saw a number of men with automatic weapons standing in the back of each vehicle. In the front passenger seat of the lead vehicle, he noticed something else. Abdulaziz was propped against the windowsill with a bloodied rag against the side of his face.

"We have to move quickly!" he said tersely. "Put your burka on, and follow me."

Eric led the way through a number of blocks south of the river. He then turned southwest, angling away from the river. "We have to assume they're forming a cordon around this area. The river hems us in on the north, so they'll concentrate on the other three sides. We have to slip through the net before it collapses on us."

They crossed several blocks of run-down tenement houses and shacks that would not meet minimum building codes in the Appalachians.

Eric had to assume that Abdulaziz would reveal he knew they were headed for the waterfront. He decided to cut through the old city district and head west to the fishing harbor. He'd seen something intriguing in that area as his plane had descended to the airport. It might be their best hope for now.

They intersected the railroad tracks about a half mile southeast of their original destination, the Mauripur train depot. Eric wanted to follow the train tracks away from the station. He could have chosen the highway parallel to the tracks, but they would be more exposed there, and he didn't trust their safety to the erratic drivers along the Mauripur Road.

They would stay on the tracks until the Wazir Mansion train station, about a mile away. The terrain was passable, but they needed to be cautious of losing their footing on the rocks along the embankment.

A train whistle wailed in the distance and reminded them of a call to prayer. The whistle sounded again. The pitch was higher, signaling it was approaching as it gathered speed out of the Mauripur station. They moved farther from the tracks as the signalman blew the whistle for the approach to the next station. When it passed, the pitch dropped as the sound waves were stretched by the acceleration away from them. It now sounded like a foghorn.

As the caboose came into view, something sparked on a rock near Eric. He looked toward the caboose as a robed figure jumped from the platform, gun in hand. He landed heavily and cried out in pain as his foot rolled off a rock. His momentum threw him forward, and he dropped both his gun and a book he'd been carrying. He lurched forward, favoring the injured ankle. He rose on his hands and knees and began scrambling for his weapon.

Eric crested the embankment on the run and was face-to-face with Satam once again.

"I should have slit your throat in Cairo." Satam seethed.

Eric dove on him just as Satam wrapped his fist around the handle of the gun. The impact knocked the wind out of Satam, and he lost the weapon again. It clattered over the rocks and came to rest a few feet away.

Satam punched Eric and drew the knife with his free hand. He slashed at Eric's throat. Eric saw the blade and dove away from him. The blade missed his throat but grazed his shoulder. Without Eric's weight restraining him, Satam rolled to his knees and shrieked, "You are mine, infidel!"

He crouched low, holding the knife horizontally like a spatula. The fluid, oscillating sweep of the knife meant he was an experienced knife fighter. Eric backed away.

Satam lunged. In spite of Satam's bad ankle, Eric was at a disadvantage as he backpedaled. He lost his footing, and Satam exploited the opportunity. As he lashed out, Eric was able to roll into his fall, and the knife glanced off of the rocks. Satam recovered and closed the gap. Eric continued rolling, ignoring the bruising of the rocks and his previous wounds. If he could put some distance between them, Satam would not be able to keep pace.

But Eric had to retrieve the gun. Satam moved swiftly and overtook Eric as he struggled to his feet. Eric grasped his wrist as the killer lunged a second time. They fell once again, and Satam gained the upper position. He was stronger and had the advantage of weight behind his thrust. Eric was gasping heavily, and his arms burned; the exertion was taking its toll. Inexorably, the blade descended toward his neck.

Satam grunted, and his arms inexplicably went flaccid. The pent-up tension in Eric's arms pushed the knife toward Satam's face. He lurched to the side and the blade slipped by. Almost. It barely flicked his exposed neck. Anywhere else, it would be a minor flesh wound. But the jugular is vulnerable, and this was a fatal cut; he would bleed out in a matter of minutes.

Satam fell away and rolled on his back. As he dropped, Eric saw the reason why he'd shouted. Alana stood with her arms hanging. A large rock was cradled in her hands.

Eric struggled to his feet and walked to where the weapon lay. He noticed the other item that Satam had dropped. It wasn't a book; it was Eric's portfolio. Eric retrieved it and returned to where Satam lay dying. Alana was crouching over him.

"Get away from me! I prepare myself for *al-jannah* and do not want your gloating face as my last sight."

Alana would not be rebuffed. "Move your hand away. I need to apply pressure to the wound."

Eric was astonished at her compassion. This scum had tried to kill them a number of times, and here she was offering aid and comfort at the end.

"I may be able to give you a few more minutes of life. That is time enough for me to say something important."

His face was a mask of hatred.

"You know you are dying. What you don't know is your fate on the other side of the grave." Alana persisted.

He laughed contemptuously. "I have given my life in holy jihad! *Allāhu al-Afuw* will reward me handsomely."

She shook her head sadly. "You have never known the Lord, but He will still forgive your sins. Even now Jesus extends His offer of salvation. There isn't time to convince you of His wonderful grace. I implore you to confess your sins and accept His forgiveness before it is too late."

Satam sneered. "Your forgiveness is your weakness! I have not succeeded in taking your life today, but my brethren surely will. Your Jesus and His Holy Ghost can rot in hell! *Allāhu al-Wahed* is one and does not share his glory with anyone!"

Alana looked upon Satam in horror. He had no idea of the enormous consequences of that statement. Tears sprang to her eyes as she contemplated the torment he would soon endure—and would suffer for eternity.

Eric was not as forgiving as Alana but was struggling with the idea of loving his enemy. He stood over Satam and gazed down on his opponent. "Satam, I've got something to say too." He held up his portfolio and could tell Satam recognized it. "You didn't realize what this is made of, did you? I need to tell you that it's made of pigskin."

Satam's hate abruptly morphed into horror.

"If I remember your theology correctly, Allāhu will never forgive you for defiling yourself. If your concept of heaven is beyond reach, it is not too late to consider what Jesus is extending to you."

"No!" Satam screamed as he began to lose consciousness. The last thing he saw in this world was Alana's lovely face. Her expression was far from gloating; it was filled with compassion.

Then the gates of hell beckoned.

Y

They had no choice but to leave the body. They dragged it from the side of the tracks to a spot that wouldn't be too obvious by the tree line. If they tried to conceal it, it would only delay their escape, and Satam's body would certainly be found by his henchmen when they came looking for him.

They continued along the tracks for a quarter of a mile, then skirted the Wazir Mansion train station and turned right, toward the West Wharf. There were no additional signs of pursuit, but that would change when Satam's body was discovered.

At the north end of the West Wharf, there was a peninsula with a left dogleg that enclosed the fishing harbor. As they approached, Eric confirmed what he had seen from the air: The whole peninsula was covered in orange soil. He also confirmed what he suspected was the cause: the peninsula was covered with the countless hulks of ancient, deteriorated ships. The color of the soil was due to runoff from the oxidized nautical graveyard. Decades of rainwater had washed the rust into the Arabian Sea. This was the perfect place to hide from their pursuers.

They scurried from boat to boat through the mouth of the peninsula, an area as wide as two football fields and three times as long. They turned left into the dogleg. The rusted ships stretched for a half mile in front of them. The patina of rust had formed a light crust over the ground like a mild thaw that freezes over a snowy field. It crunched when walked on and would serve as an early warning system if anyone approached.

Eric wasn't concerned with being trapped on the peninsula; a number of piers jutted into the harbor on one side and the Baba Channel on the other. Hundreds of small boats competed for dock space on these piers. In an emergency, Eric planned to commandeer one of these boats.

He checked a number of the dilapidated ships to find one that would provide suitable shelter from the elements. He selected one that had three holes in the hull, each large enough for a hasty exit, should the need materialize. The boat sat perpendicular to the peninsula's length and was clear of debris for one hundred fifty feet on all sides, which would make it impossible to approach unobserved. A bridge thirty feet above provided an unobstructed view of the peninsula, harbor, and wharf. It would be an excellent observation point.

They settled into their spider hole, and Eric pulled out Satam's gun for inspection.

Alana asked, "Do you know how to use that thing?"

"Not really. I've never fired one before."

"I didn't think so. Be careful—the safety's off. Do you mind if I look at it?" She extended her hand, and he passed it to her.

She deftly ejected a shell from the chamber, cocked her hand forward, and pressed something on the handle. A cartridge flew from the base, which she deftly caught with her free hand. She counted the rounds, inserted the ejected shell into the cartridge, and reinserted the cartridge into the handle, snapping it into the base with a sharp blow on the heel of her hand. She pulled the slide back, seating the first shell in the chamber. Finally, she engaged the safety. Her motions were fluid and confident.

"Eleven rounds left," she noted as she extended her arms in a two-fisted pose and squinted down the gun sights.

"My guess is you've done that at least once before." Eric was wide-eyed at her poise with the deadly weapon.

"My brother taught me. He's taken me to gun ranges for years. I guess I'd be an expert marksman if I were in the military. I've never shot anything but paper targets, but I can place a nice, tight pattern at two hundred feet," she said with not-so-subtle pride.

"Let's hope we don't need to call on those skills," he commented. "It looks like we'll be here for a while. Why don't you fill me in on everything that's happened? First of all, who was that woman who pulled the knife on you in the marketplace?"

"That was Razi. She was my assistant and the one who was supposed to take over after I left. I thought she was a friend, but she betrayed me. I imagined myself a good judge of character, but she had me completely fooled." A shadow fell across her face. "There's something that I have to ask you. I haven't been able to get it out of my mind, and I need a straight answer."

Eric was caught completely off guard. He couldn't imagine what was coming next.

"I was interrogated—practically tortured—over the past two days. In my darkest moment, I was shown pictures of you having candlelit dinners with a beautiful woman. Do you care to explain that?" Accusatory tears filled her eyes. "I thought you promised no more secrets."

"I can think of only one person it might have been," Eric said. "If she had dark hair and a dark complexion, then is was Shoshana, the Israeli I told you about."

"You told me about the Israeli, but you never mentioned she was a woman—a lovely, sensual woman at that. Need I remind you of a certain conversation we had in Tokyo?"

"No. I remember."

"Alomari said she seduced you…"

"Alana—how can you think that?" He was in anguish and at a loss for how to respond. Her withering glare disarmed him. No matter what he said, it would be insufficient. He searched her eyes and simply said, "No. I did not sleep with her." It was vital that he maintain eye contact with her. It was the only defense he could offer.

"Alana…I'm…" *Sorry* would be insufficient.

She held up her hand, fingers splayed. She turned her head away. "You should have told me about her in Tokyo."

"I know. I'm sorry."

"I need to be alone for a while."

With a wrenching ache in his chest, Eric stood and said, "I'll be up on the bridge. I should see if we've been followed."

Eric sat alone on the bridge. He surveyed the peninsula but couldn't get his mind off how he had hurt Alana. Why hadn't he mentioned Shoshana to Alana?

There was no question that he had hurt Alana—again—on top of everything else she'd been through. The problem was how to fix it this time.

His problems with Alana were not the primary issue; they were symptomatic. At this moment of introspection, Eric was face-to-face with the fact that he hadn't learned to trust anyone, not even Alana.

Noise and movement on the wharf shook him from his reverie. A forklift was lifting a boat from the water, and the tether had snapped. A crowd had formed, and the obvious boat owner was gesticulating wildly. Eric scanned the area but did not detect any furtive movements that might signal a threat.

Y

Alana was indulging in self-analysis of a different sort. The past two days had been more harrowing than her wildest nightmares. She had gotten through them only by the grace of God. He had given her strength to endure things that she otherwise was incapable of surviving. She was so thankful for His faithfulness.

"Lord, You have protected me from my enemies and preserved me. I thank You for Your care and protection. May I prove myself worthy." Alana knew what she needed to pray for next but was afraid to give voice to her fears. "I ask that You give me wisdom in this relationship. I have wanted it for so long and with such intensity. I confess that I have not been still enough to hear Your voice. Please honor my plea and bless this relationship. But if this is not of You, I ask that You make it clear, and I will accept Your will. Amen."

In the tepid silence of the ship's hold, Alana could hear a distant voice echoing from the gangway. She edged closer to the source. Additional sounds drowned out the distant shouts, sounds that signaled Eric's return. She sat silently as each step on the ladder reverberated through the hull. Now he was moving through the gangway, and the echoes became louder. Moments later, she saw his head poke through the hatch that opened to the compartment she was in. "Can I come in?" he asked tentatively.

"I suppose so."

"Look, Alana, I know I screwed up again. As much as I need to prove to you how sorry I am and that I am able to change, I'm still shaken up about killing Satam, and I know you went through an awful ordeal too. I don't know if we're emotionally able to deal with our personal issues right now. How about we call a truce until we get out of this, and we can focus on our relationship later?"

Alana wanted to yell at him and tell him how much he'd hurt her, but she admitted to herself that her emotional state was too fragile to communicate coherently. "All right. I can be civil, but don't mistake that for acquiescence."

"I won't. Look, I have to keep watch at least until sundown. I'm going back to the bridge, and I'll return after dusk. If I don't see any signs of pursuit by then, we're probably safe at least until morning. I'll be back."

Y

Murad stood in the back of the Land Rover and stabbed the keypad on his cell phone in frustration. He glanced at the waterfall below the railroad trestle spanning the mouth of the Lyari River, but he was in no mood to appreciate the scenery. Satam had not returned to the Mauripur station, and Murad's scout team was now long overdue. His last five calls had been unsuccessful. He would have to petition Alomari for the satellite phones that had proven so effective in Afghanistan; the domestic cell service here was pathetic.

The phone popped and hissed, but he finally heard a voice. "Where are you?" he demanded.

"We did not f…Satam…the Wazi…tion. We…retur…ing…foot. Some…s are on…Mauripur Ro…and…the…are chec…he tracks. We…ne kilom…away from…Maur… statio…"

Murad hung up in frustration. He ordered his driver to climb the embankment to the highway bridge. The cell signal was a bit stronger at the top, but the vehicle was now more vulnerable to the hazardous highway. He pressed redial. "Where are you?" he shouted again.

"Did…ou no…under…nd me? We are…the…uripur Roa…an…tra…trac…s."

"Why are you on the tracks? I ordered you to find Satam at the Wazir station and come back on the return train!" The cell phone died again. He threw it down in frustration. "Drive!" he barked at his driver and pointed southeast, down the Mauripur Road. "You watch the road, and I will observe the tracks." He stood higher in the back and clutched the roll bar for support.

They had traveled less than a kilometer when Murad shouted, "Stop! Get me closer to the tracks." He jumped down from the vehicle and crossed the tracks to where he had seen a huddle of men at the tree line. He sprinted toward them.

One of the men looked up from the huddle and waved frantically at Murad. As he approached, the men backed away, clearing a path for him. He slowed his pace as the scene took shape. He cursed violently when he realized he was looking at Satam's lifeless body.

One of them spoke for the group. "We spotted blood on the rocks up there by the tracks," he said, gesturing toward the top of the embankment. "There was a trail that led down here to the trees. We found him here. His throat has been slit."

Murad clutched his fists around his Kalashnikov and glared at them.

"We did not find his gun or his knife."

"He was carrying the infidel's notebook," Murad observed. He looked around the area but did not see it. "It was meaningless to anyone else. They did this. Now they will be foolhardy with his gun." He smiled wickedly. "I have slain Soviet and American Special Forces and never received a wound. These two will be no match."

He stood and surveyed the scene, then pointed to the bend in the highway that followed the railroad tracks. "They must have gone south. They would not be foolish enough to go to the Wazir station. They knew we would watch the trains. Position our best marksmen around the Great Satan's consulate. That will cut them off from their best route of escape. We will fan out from here to the hotel district and seal off any path to the north. Then we will work our way west from the hotel district and drive them south, toward the docks. We will hunt them down like wharf rats. Now go!"

Eric cautiously peered above the gunwale of the boat and keenly observed the entrance to the peninsula. This was a perfect location. Anyone coming into the peninsula would be focused straight ahead, looking for their prey among the lined-up boats. They wouldn't turn their sights down the dogleg until they had made the bend. Eric's position gave him a perfect oblique angle for observation and reduced the chances that predators would be staring right back at him.

A number of lights on the West Wharf blinked on, revealing the outline of the warehouses. There had been no activity for some time. Eric could see the last of the fishermen crowding their boats into any available space in the fishing harbor. Other than occasional vehement shouts as they jostled into position and roped off their vessels, it seemed to be a peaceful evening.

He rose stiffly into a crouch and stretched his cramped leg muscles. He scanned the area one last time and climbed down the ladder into the lower decks where he found Alana sitting quietly in the shadows. Light refracted through the breach in the hull, dimly illuminating the interior. As his eyes adjusted to the gloom, he could make out her silhouette. "Hi," he said simply. "Are you OK?"

"I was much worse at this time yesterday. I'm thankful to be safe. And I want to thank you for rescuing me. I realize how much danger you put yourself in for me, and it means more than I can ever express."

"I had to come for you. I knew you were in danger, and I was so frustrated sitting in Atlanta. I still can't believe I found you in this huge city. The Lord must have directed me to you." Eric reflected on the coincidences that had led him to the Meetha Dar and how effectively his plans had worked out. It was amazing. "Do you feel like talking about what happened to you? We have a lot of time, and if it would help, I would like to listen."

"I need to talk about it." She told Eric about all that had happened since she'd arrived. She filled in many details that she had not been able to write into her e-mails for fear of discovery. "I thought I was pretty clever planting your Magic Bullet. I shouldn't have been so foolish."

"I was so scared for you when I realized what you were about to do. By the time I read your e-mail, it was too late to stop you. I had already planted the bullet in Atlanta, and it nailed Preedy's computer. He must have alerted Alomari by the time you got to the lab."

"I thought I had gotten away with it because nothing happened right away. Then Razi and those animals drugged and kidnapped me from my room. When I came to, I was suspended like a side of beef. It was humiliating to be that vulnerable and helpless. I think Satam would have raped me if he hadn't been interrupted by Alomari." She faltered and couldn't go on for a few minutes.

Eric reached out and took her hand in his. She didn't resist.

"Then I thought Alomari might rape me too. I was so scared. Then he backed off when he realized that you only knew part of his plan."

"The worldwide jihad? That isn't the plan?"

"Yes, it is, but it's only a front to his real objective. He says he's developed a serum that combines all known gene therapies—and many more that he's developed. Eric—his serum will counteract DNA degradation and reverse the aging process. He thinks he has the secret to immortality."

"Is that possible?"

"In a twisted sort of way, yes. Even if his serum is incomplete, imagine the consequences if Muslim terrorists didn't age—and retained their vitality until a hundred years old or longer. He claims to have accomplished even more, and the ramifications are terrifying. He vows that they will rule the world."

"Why would he tell you all that?"

"It wasn't very cautious of him. I think his ego got the best of him. He expected me to be swept away by his brilliance and was preening like a teenager. In his own warped way, I think he was trying to weaken my resistance and seduce me—at least intellectually."

"Many guys are like that when it comes to beautiful women. We strut our stuff and usually make fools of ourselves."

"Tell me about it. It's really irritating on the receiving end." She shook off the memories of her captivity. "I think it was about this time yesterday, but I was in a cell and couldn't tell the time of day. They gave me a little to eat, and then drove me out to the collection team's campsite where they kept me under close watch. They wanted me to be seen at the Meetha Dar because they were catching heat from our State Department. And that's when you found me. Thank you again." She squeezed his hand.

"Don't be too quick to thank me. I really didn't plan this out very well. I don't have much money left. I tried to make an ATM withdrawal but was blocked. If Preedy was behind it, he was probably alerted that I attempted a withdrawal. All I accomplished was to telegraph that I'm low on cash. They know we were headed for the train station. The only reason we'd be doing that is because it's cheap. So they don't need to waste any resources watching the airport." Eric swore under his breath. "I feel like I'm walking into a checkmate."

Alana recalled Alomari's comment about being a chess master but decided it would only demoralize Eric to mention it. "Eric, I'm exhausted. I was in so much pain during the abduction I hardly slept. I need to get some sleep to get me through what's coming next."

"OK. I'm going to think about our situation. We'll come up with a plan when you're rested."

She rolled on her side and tried to get into a comfortable position. Eric pulled out his PDA. His laptop battery was about shot, but he could accomplish what he needed using the PDA. He checked for a wireless signal and found only two. The strongest of them registered a single bar. Even if the signal was stronger, he couldn't risk hacking into an unknown host network. The Hyatt and Marriott hotels would certainly have wireless access, but they were three miles due east. He would have to get closer to send a message.

But who would he send it to? He mentally ticked off the options. He couldn't get a message through to Larson; Preedy would certainly intercept it. Joey was a possibility, but would anyone take Joey seriously? Even if they did, he'd heard horror stories about the slow wheels of bureaucratic processes. Alana and he couldn't afford to wait for a diplomatic solution. He was stymied.

If he could figure out a solution, the first thing he would need to communicate was their location. He clicked the GPS function that displayed the coordinates: 24°51' 02.87" N, 66°58' 33.34" E. Eric mentally debated his dilemma. He knew he'd have to encrypt the coordinates in any outgoing message because of the risk of it being intercepted. But how would the intended recipient decrypt it?

FORTY-SIX

Tuesday, November 8, 2005
6 Shawwāl, 1426 AH
Karāchi, Pakistan

ALANA AWOKE SUDDENLY. SHE URGENTLY WHISPERED, "ERIC? Are you here?"

"Huh? What?" It took Eric a moment to get his bearings. "Alana, are you OK?"

"Yes. Where are you?"

He moved closer to her voice, patting the floor blindly in front of him. His hand brushed her calf, and she reached out, clasping it firmly. He scooted toward her as she reached out with both hands to take hold of him.

"Can you stay close to me?" she asked. "It was so dark, it took me back to my prison cell, and I panicked."

He smiled in the darkness and wrapped his arms around her, snuggling against her back. He rested his chin on her shoulder. "Is that better?"

"Yes." She wiggled her shoulders and molded herself into him, then pressed her head into the crook of his neck and rolled it slowly back and forth. "You feel so good. I feel safe in your arms."

He wrapped his arms tightly across hers and squeezed. "Have you come up with any ideas?" she murmured.

"No. I checked for hot spots, but I didn't get enough signal strength. The hotel district is three miles from here. If I can get closer, I should be able to get enough signal strength to get a message out. But the bigger problem is—who do we send a message to?"

"I don't know," she said. "Can I ask you something? You dismissed the consulate as an option. Why? Is it too far?"

"No. Actually, it's fairly close—about three and a half miles, just south of the hotel district. The problem is, the compound sits in a triangle surrounded by wide highways. Alomari would have snipers at the three major intersections with clear sight lines. We'd be sitting ducks trying to get in there."

"That's it!" Alana sat up suddenly and head-butted Eric in the dark. "I'm sorry. Did I hurt you?"

"Not too bad," he replied, dabbing his nose to see if blood was flowing. "What do you mean?"

"You mentioned snipers and gave me an idea. My brother! He went to sniper school as part of his training."

"Remind me to never make him mad."

"What I meant was—maybe we could get a message to my brother. The SEALs are experts at hostage rescue and extraction. And Special Forces won't drag their feet like the State Department. What do you think?"

"I don't know. From what I've heard, those guys have more important missions than rescuing family members who aggravate mad scientists. How would he sell that mission to the upper brass?"

"I don't know, but it's worth a try, isn't it?" she asked.

"I suppose. There are a few logistical issues in getting any message out. But the alternative is to sit here and wait for the inevitable. I'd feel better trying anything that could improve our odds.

"The challenge is that I'll have to venture out to upload the message. I may have to travel as far as two miles. The guys hunting us are resourceful and will be monitoring the wireless traffic in the area. If they see a distress message going out, they may be able to triangulate my position, and that will be the end of Mrs. Colburn's favorite son."

"You're her only son."

"Exactly." Another thought occurred to him. "Before I can send a message, we need to encrypt it so we don't lead the terrorists right to us. But if we encrypt it, your brother wouldn't know how to decrypt it. We can't include the solution key, obviously. So that's a big problem. Even if we can come up with a solution to those problems, do you know his military e-mail address?"

"No, I don't remember it, but let me think for a minute," she said. "There may be a way. Here's an idea: my brother's college roommate, Kyle, is stationed in Japan. I know his wife's e-mail address, so we can e-mail her. I can type the message to her in plain English, but will be vague, and I'll ask her to send it to her husband. He's on deployment, but I'm sure he can find out where my brother is and forward the e-mail through military channels. If everyone reads and forwards their e-mails, we may be able to get through to him in a matter of hours."

"We still have the encryption issue to deal with."

"I have an answer to that too. My brother taught me a code that he and Kyle developed in college. I'll write the second part of my e-mail in that code. Kyle can decode the message. When he realizes the danger we're in, I'm sure he'll get it to my brother as quickly as possible. Even if the terrorists have the resources to crack my code, it will take them too long. I'll make the e-mail short, which makes it virtually impossible to find patterns in the message, which is the essential step in code breaking."

"So, how will we know whether the cavalry is on the way?"

"I'll ask for an acknowledgment, which he would encode. We'll venture out once a day to check. If they can't—or won't—mount a rescue operation in a couple of days, we'll have to figure out some other way of getting out of Pakistan on our own."

"Well, it may be a slim chance, but that's better than none at all." Eric pulled out his PDA and pressed the stylus against the screen. The backlight flared and surprisingly illuminated their spider hole. He selected his e-mail software and pasted the GPS coordinates into a new message. "Here you go. I put our coordinates in the e-mail for you. Be sure to code that too."

"Got it," she said with just a little irritation.

"I'm sorry. I'm just a little paranoid." She merely frowned at him. "Do you have Excel on this PDA?" she asked.

"Sure, why?"

"I need it to encode my message." She found the icon and opened a new spreadsheet. She typed her message, one character per row, with no spaces, down column A. The message finished on row 185. She then typed out a formula in the first cell of column B:

```
=TEXT(IF(LEN(CODE(A1))=2,"0"&CODE(A1),CODE(A1))+1,"000")
```

She then copied the formula through the length of the column.

Eric was impressed. "I thought I was the programmer. What is all that?"

"I'm converting every character in my message to a three-digit code using standard ASCII nomenclature. Since that would be pretty simple to decode, I'm adding an offset of one to each number. Pretty basic technique and nearly impossible to translate, especially since I'm including punctuation and no spaces. Like I said, code breakers need to find patterns, like short words that are used frequently. There's no way they can discern where the various words begin or end in my message, which makes it virtually impossible to crack.

"I need to double-check my formula before I copy and paste the coded message. I have one hundred eighty-five rows. Since each letter or punctuation mark has three digits in its associated code, I should end up with five hundred fifty-five numbers in the coded portion of the message."

She created a formula to calculate the number of characters and confirmed that it cross-balanced. Finally, she copied the code and pasted the results into her e-mail. "The first part will need to be in plain English because his wife doesn't know the code. I'll make it seem like a girly gossip. Hopefully that will distract anyone who may intercept it."

From: GirlGenes
Sent: Thu 11/08/2005 1:12 AM
To: LadyGhengis
Cc:
Subject: Greetings from Pakistan
Susan:

Read between the lines... You won't believe what happened! My boyfriend is here visiting unexpectedly. If things weren't so tense, we'd be able to enjoy one another much more.

Remember the guy with injured foot? He arrived here and was anxious to get together with me. He was persistent and brought all his friends to the party. You remember how much fun we had with them? This was way more exciting.

The info below will make sense to Ghengis. Please forward it to him immediately. He'll know what to do with it.

Best regards,

GirlGenes

10812210910205908110910209811610210410211711710510611
61101021161160981041021171120851121111220851121111122059
08810209811510209910611110410010509811610210109912211
710211511511211510611611711604708011110211210311710510 21
10106116108111112120111099122117105102079098119122059 0
78118115098101079098116105106115106047080118115072081
08410011211211510110611109811710211609811510209910210 9
11212008110910209811610211610211110109811510211610011 81
021171020981100470881021151021151181111111106111104112 11
811711210311710611010204708410611611304711604708410211
1101066100108
05105317705405004004905104705705603507905505517705
40570400520520470520530350 70

Eric read the header. "Ghengis and LadyGhengis?"

"Kyle's a fighter pilot. His call sign is Ghengis, so his wife picked Lady-Ghengis for her e-mail."

"What's the bottom set of numbers below the blank row?"

"It's the encrypted coordinates."

"Pretty clever. Your intro is pretty straightforward but not too revealing. If their computers are scanning text messages, there're no words that would raise a warning. And this is a better idea than sending a computer-encrypted message, which would send up a red flag."

"Thanks."

"The next step is to send the message. I'll wait until five o'clock to venture out. Street vendors start setting up their booths by then. Maybe I can bring back some food."

"That sounds so good. I'm very hungry."

"Why don't we get some more sleep until then? We're going to need it." He turned off the PDA, and darkness swept in to fill the void. They cuddled again, this time for warmth.

Alana's mood seemed to have improved markedly. Eric had hoped that bantering with her would raise her spirits. It was a vital connection to normalcy, even while running for their lives.

FORTY-SEVEN

Tuesday, November 8, 2005
6 Shawwāl, 1426 AH
Karāchi, Pakistan

FOR THE SECOND DAY IN A ROW, ERIC FOUND HIMSELF WANDERING the streets of Karāchi at dawn. He had traversed two and a half miles along the railroad tracks, which led directly into the hotel district, before they veered to the southeast.

As he had anticipated, street vendors had begun setting up their stalls. He found one with food and bought enough to sustain them. He had enough cash for one more food purchase.

Eric watched the signal strength of various hot spots steadily climb as he continued moving toward the sunrise. New hot spots appeared as well. He intended to pick one least likely to be monitored. The HyattReg signal was the strongest, so he selected it and hacked in. The stylus quivered above the send button. He pressed it and glanced around, expecting crazed bedouins to rush him from the shadows, which would not surprise him at this point.

He moved swiftly along the route he had come. If his adversaries picked up the signal and suspected its source, they would descend on this location in a fury.

He arrived back in the fishing harbor long after the fishing boats had gone to sea and was unobserved as he made his way back to the spider hole. He called out to Alana when he was close. She responded as they had agreed, and he proceeded into the wreck that had ironically become their first habitation together. He unpacked the food he had procured. They sat together, held hands, asked a blessing for the food, then devoured it greedily.

Tokyo, Japan

Susan was puzzled by the e-mail from Alana. She immediately understood the importance and didn't hesitate to forward it to Kyle. For his benefit, she included Murad Nashiri's name and reminded him that Nashiri was the one who had accosted her. She also relayed the information provided by the DOD investigator.

She couldn't wait to learn the nature of the unusual message from Alana. Susan realized Si would want to know about the message from their friend. She picked up the phone and dialed.

Over the Sea of Okhotsk

Kyle checked his heads-up display, which showed his two-jet fighter formation two miles from the BGB—"big gray boat." Bingo fuel dictated he had to land on the carrier; the mainland was over two hundred miles to the west—and was unfriendly territory.

He dropped his landing gear and lined up his F/A-18E/F Super Hornet for final approach. The heaving deck was cleared for his landing, which would be dicey in the driving rain. His navigator gave him the final approval, and he feathered the stick forward. He needed to hit the deck as it fell away, minimizing the chance of bouncing the tail hook over the arresting cable. It would also be less bone-jarring than hitting the deck as it rose on the ocean swells.

He fought the crosswind, the wings vibrating from the strain. The deck crested and began to fall away. He throttled back and felt the wheels and tail hook kiss the deck. The arresting cable snagged the plane, throwing him forward against his restraints. He shoved the throttle forward, and the engines roared in protest. The moment of truth arrived: if the cable broke, he must have enough thrust to get airborne again. The alternative was to skid impotently off the forward end of the deck. The cable vibrated and shrieked but held. He looked toward the deck chief and was rewarded with a grinning thumbs-up. Kyle killed the thrusters, sat back, and inserted the safety pins in his ejection seat.

His navigator leaned forward and slapped him on the helmet. "Nice work, Ghengis."

"Thanks." He pressed the release to lift the canopy and unclipped his chinstrap. The deck crew rolled the ladder to the cockpit, and he descended, ducking his head from the rain.

In the briefing room, Kyle conferred with his squadron commander about the results of the touch-and-go drills. The training had been grueling but rewarding. He finished the debriefing, stood, and saluted. On his way to his bunk, he stopped by the officer's dining room, where two PCs were set up for personal use. He logged into his account and was happy to see an e-mail from Susan. Alana's intro was a bit confusing. Then Susan's explanation alarmed him. He noticed the code Alana had inserted and frantically scrounged the desk drawer for a pencil and paper.

Y

Karbala, Iraq

LCDR Tony McKinsey was the quintessential SEAL. He had earned the coveted special warfare billet upon graduation from the U.S. Naval Academy. Competition was stiff; there were only ten spec war slots allocated in a graduating class of over one thousand.

Tony had gone from one success to another in his early training. Basic underwater demolition/SEAL training—BUD/s—was the most arduous training in the military—any military for that matter. Out of the 134 who entered the indoctrination phase, only 12 graduated months later. Tony was one of 4 officers who hadn't dropped on request (DOR). The detailers relished the only opportunity in the U.S. military where enlisted can rag on officers. Well over a hundred green helmets had been lined up beneath the infamous ship's bell on graduation day, but not his.

Within months, Tony had earned the fearsome Trident, the largest insignia on any American military uniform, affectionately referred to as a Budweiser in the SEAL community. Currently, Tony was stationed in Iraq. He was contemplating a career in the navy and had re-upped the year before. The prospect of being a desk jockey for the rest of his naval service loomed before him, which is a difficult transition for a SEAL. Years of grueling sacrifice and physical regimen hone the prowess of the most revered warriors on the planet. Not something that can easily be switched off.

Tony opened the door to the operations center. His chief petty officer spotted him and saluted. "Sir, a classified signal just came in for you. Kind of strange—it didn't come through normal channels."

"Thank you. Please print it for me."

"Yes, sir."

The chief returned a few minutes later with the signal. It was from Ghengis. "Well, that *is* strange," he muttered. Kyle had used the code from their academy days. Tony hadn't seen that in years. He went to his office, where the computer was already on, and clicked the Excel icon and proceeded to decipher the message.

He seethed with rage and concern for his sister. He hit the intercom button. "Chief, come in here. I need you to research something." The chief entered his office and stood stiffly in front of the desk. Tony scribbled a name on a memo pad. "See what you can find out about this guy. He's a terrorist that has some connection to the navy." He tore the sheet from the pad and thrust it at the chief, who immediately turned away. "And, Chief," he called out, "I need it yesterday."

"Yes, sir!" The chief picked up the pace.

Y

Tony stood before Commander Thompson's desk. Charlie Thompson was intelligent but reserved. He did not rush to judgment and liked to talk through scenarios a couple of times before rendering decisions. Tony hoped this would not be one of those occasions. He had worked up a mission profile and patiently waited at attention while it was reviewed.

Commander Thompson finished and threw the profile on his desk. He leaned back in his chair, propped his arms on the padded rests, and steepled his fingers in front of his mouth. "McKinsey, you're killin' me here. This mission appears to be hastily formulated. You know poorly designed missions result in dead SEALs. Then the unlucky jerk who signed off on the poorly designed mission is the sacrificial lamb. You like lamb, McKinsey?"

"Not any more than you do, sir!"

"Didn't think so, McKinsey. There's something I don't understand in your mission profile."

"Sir?"

"I thought you SDV jockeys relied on Super Stallions to deliver your subs. You're calling for a fully loaded Trident to ferry you in. Do you know what the per-hour operational cost of an Ohio-class sub is?"

"No, sir, but the helo wouldn't be practical for this mission. The cruising range of the CH-fifty-three E is five hundred forty nautical miles. That would be a minimum of two in-flight refuelings for the round-trip since we can't land in Iran for gas. As you know, in-flight refueling is pretty dicey for a helo—especially when it's hauling an SDV. In addition, the helicopter could not stay on station during an extended extraction, so two round-trips would be required. This is further complicated by the need for stealth *and* plausible deniability. If the mission goes wrong, it would be far easier for our enemies to attribute blame to the U.S. if we relied on a high-profile helicopter insertion and extraction. With all due respect, sir, the Trident is our best option."

Tony continued before he could be interrupted. "Sir, there's also a strategic advantage that I didn't spell out in the profile. The team I want to take in is my former SDV platoon. We're very familiar with each other, which is critical to mission success. In addition, the timing couldn't be better. They just finished exercises in the United Arab Emirates. Their SDV is housed and ready for transport on the deck of the USS *Louisiana*, which can set sail at a moment's notice. It's about eight hundred thirty nautical miles to Karāchi from Dubai. At their cruising speed of twenty-five knots, they can be off-station thirty hours later. The timing is very fortuitous and supports a rapid response. The likelihood of a successful mission is high."

"That may be, son, but we have to also evaluate the cost and benefits when we're considering a civilian extraction."

"Permission to speak freely, sir?"

"Proceed."

"Sir, the mission is laid out with the primary objective of extracting civilians from a volatile environment before they are overrun by hostiles. However, there is a secondary objective I would like to present. Here is another report that is not part of the official mission profile." He handed an EYES ONLY folder to the commander. He scanned the contents intently.

"Sir, you are looking at a photo of Murad Nashiri, a known al Qaeda operative. He is the brother of Abd Rahim Nashiri, the mastermind behind the USS *Cole* bombing. Both of them were implicated in a similar plot on a navy ship that failed. Recently, this guy was spotted in Tokyo, scoping out our carrier base. We both know what his objective was. Our boy is a real player in al Qaeda and allegedly reports to OBL himself.

"Sir, we have confirmation that Nashiri and his al Qaeda cell are in Karāchi right now. With your permission, sir, I would like to unofficially expand the mission objective to take out this cell. Our navy will be more secure if we can take this guy out before he strikes again."

Tony had hit the responsive chord. He could read Thompson like a book and knew he was savoring the kudos he'd enjoy with that outcome. But Tony knew he couldn't appear to give in too easily. "McKinsey, I've still got some reservations about this mission. I'm thinking we should have a meeting with my staff and discuss the merits."

"With all due respect, sir, time is of the essence. We know where these terrorists are now, but we know how fluid these situations can be. It would be embarrassing to get all dressed up for the party and then find nobody home."

That worked. The commander slapped the folder on his desk. "McKinsey, don't fail me."

"Yes, sir! That is…no sir!" He saluted smartly and left the office before the commander second-guessed himself again.

"McKinsey!" the commander shouted.

"Oh no," he muttered under his breath in mid-stride. He cringed at what might come next. He turned and faced the commander. "Was there something else, sir?"

"I noticed the civilian's last name in your mission profile. Same as yours. What is she, your mama?"

"No, sir. She's my sister."

"Figured as much," he grinned. "Dismissed."

"Thank you, sir." Tony grinned triumphantly.

Karāchi, Pakistan

"Enter!" Alomari was at his desk. Murad entered the room and immediately detected the hostility in the air. "Have you found him yet?"

"I have unfortunate news. We found Satam's body last night."

"His body? Satam is dead? How did this happen?" Alomari raged. "Why am I just now hearing this?"

"I am sorry. Our communication devices failed again." Murad needed to redirect the conversation. "Satam's throat was slit."

"That is impossible. He was highly trained. These soft Amrikans do not have the stomach for hand-to-hand combat or the skill to overwhelm a man of his experience. There is more than meets the eye here."

"The last my men saw him was when he boarded the train at the Mauripur station. He was to check the train to make sure the Americans had not boarded. When he didn't return, we checked along the tracks and found him midway between stations."

"I want these Amrikans to suffer. Are the still in the city?"

"I believe so. We picked up a wireless transmission before dawn and believe it is from the blonde woman. It was relayed from a hot spot at the Hyatt, which has the best signal strength in the area. We know they were not in the hotel or we would have seen them. They must have traveled close enough to send the signal from outside the hotel. The gulf is to the south, so they must have traveled from one of the other directions to get within range. There are other hot spots to the north and southeast of this hotel, which would have been as suitable if they had come from either of those directions. Therefore, they must be somewhere to the west of it. We found Satam's body four kilometers to the northwest, which provides the outer perimeter for their location.

"We are now concentrating our efforts. My men have formed a cordon around the area. The Arabian Sea blocks their escape to the south. We will now tighten the noose."

"That is an excellent analysis and plan. Make it so, and quickly."

Murad bowed. "*Allāhu akbar!*"

Y

Al Jahra, Kuwait

LCDR McKinsey muttered in frustration. He had hitched a ride on the first flight out of Iraq, a C-130H Hercules headed for Kuwait. His plan called for a transfer to a supply flight to Dubai, where he would join the SDV team before the *Louisiana* sailed. The plan was scrapped when his connecting plane was grounded by a hydraulic leak.

The problem was timing. The *Louisiana* had a narrow window for departure. They couldn't leave until after sundown, which was at 1845. Sailing time was thirty hours—if they didn't hit a traffic jam in the Strait of Hormuz—which meant they couldn't be off the coast of Karāchi until 0100 the day after tomorrow.

Tony had overlooked a time zone change and had to adjust his calculation. Now, 0200 was cutting it close. That left four hours for the SDV team to get ashore, load up, and be through the channel before dawn.

So—the *Louisiana* would not be able to wait on him. They had to get underway as scheduled.

Now he faced a difficult choice. He eliminated the option of sending the SDV team on the mission without him. There's no way that was going to happen. The next option would be to rendezvous in the Arabian Sea. The logistics were bad enough, but the inevitable mission delay scratched that option.

The best option was a night jump into Karāchi while the *Louisiana* was still en route. A high altitude low opening (HALO) jump would be preferred, but violation of Pakistani airspace was out of the question. No, it would have to be a high altitude high opening (HAHO) jump from beyond the territorial waters, which would assure enough height to glide into the coastline.

A lone ranger confrontation with al Qaeda warriors was risky, but he hoped to secure the site and scope out the danger to the SDV team. He could wave them off if needed.

Now he had to obtain approval for the jump off of Karāchi, which meant a flyby of Pakistan's sovereign territory. There was no way he could coordinate the jump before dawn tomorrow. He'd waste another day.

Karāchi, Pakistan

The day wore on without incident. Eric had stayed on the bridge for much of it. There had been no suspicious activity on the peninsula.

He checked the West Wharf one last time and returned to the lower deck where Alana was waiting. "If they had intercepted my transmission, I think I would have run into them on my way back this morning."

"Maybe," Alana said, "or maybe they picked it up and didn't translate it until later. That's what happens with the NSA. They get a lot of terrorist traffic, but they don't have enough translators to keep up with the volume. By the time they get a positive lead, it's weeks old. Those real-time interceptions only happen for Jack Bauer."

Eric chuckled as he realized something. "Hey—if we get out of here in the next month, we'll be home in time for the next uninterrupted season of 24!"

"That might have sounded inviting a few months ago, but I'm fed up with intrigue and hatred. It's so much worse in real life."

"I'm sorry I dragged you into all this, Alana."

"Nonsense. I made my decision with my eyes wide open. You couldn't have anticipated all this; no one could have."

"Well, I only want to get you out of this nightmare and back where you'll be safe."

Alomari was enraged. Another day had passed, and he began to worry that the infidels had escaped.

He snatched the phone and dialed. When it was answered, he barked, "Murad! Have you found them yet? I am at the end of my patience!"

"I am sorry, Your Eminence, but we have seen no further activity. We are searching house-to-house and are tightening the cordon. But this is a large area, and progress is slow."

"I do not want excuses, Murad," he warned ominously. "If I must report failure to the Tall One, you know who will be found at fault."

"Give me one more day. I assure you we will find them. We have confirmed that the message we intercepted was from the infidels. We also know who it was sent to. It was sent to the wife of the navy pilot—the same one I had approached in Tokyo."

"Why would they contact her?"

"We do not know, Your Eminence."

"Tell me what the message contained."

"The message started in English and did not include much information. There was a reference to Ghengis Khan, which we do not understand. At the end of the message there are many numbers, but they make no sense. We are trying to determine whether they were appended by the e-mail server or whether they were part of the original message."

"It must be a code! Contact Karāchi University and find out if they have a code specialist among their faculty. We must find the meaning of their message."

"It is late. I will contact them in the morning."

"Do it now!" he shouted. "The morning will be too late."

Y

Abu Dhabi, United Arab Emirates

The USS *Louisiana* slipped silently from her berth as the last rays of the setting sun were extinguished in the Persian Gulf. They had waited for the cover of darkness to depart, which was the closest a U.S. nuclear submarine could get to being stealthy.

"We should arrive at the headland of the Musandam Peninsula in an hour and a half." The captain pointed to the chart. "It will be high tide when we make the hairpin turn into the Strait of Hormuz, so we'll have about one hundred twenty feet of depth to work with. Keep a sharp eye out for LPG tankers on our way in. We'll have to time our run carefully and feather our way in between them."

"Yes, sir."

FORTY-EIGHT

Wednesday, November 9, 2005
7 Shawwāl, 1426 AH
Karāchi, Pakistan

Eric woke up and checked the time on his PDA: 4:43. He should head into the city now. He didn't want to be roaming the streets after the sun rose.

Alana was sleeping peacefully beside him. She would freak out if she woke up and he wasn't there. He pressed the backlight on his PDA, then leaned over and gently kissed her. If he startled her, she would at least be able to see him in the dim light. "Alana," he whispered.

She stirred and moaned softly.

"I need to go into the city. I'll bring back some food."

She smiled dreamily and opened her eyes. "Sounds good—and maybe some coffee?"

"As long as you don't get too used to it."

"Hey—my dad brings my mom coffee in bed every morning, and I'll expect my man to do the same. Besides, the Bible mandates it."

"Yeah right."

"Really. There's a whole book on the topic. It's called He-brews."

"Ha." It was too early for tacky humor. "I have to leave now." He donned his robe and turban and threaded his way to the nearest breach in the hull. "See you soon."

Eric followed the same route as yesterday morning and was able to find the food vendor from yesterday. Being a repeat customer allowed him to negotiate an even better deal.

He continued east toward the Hyatt until the signal strength was sufficient. He hacked in again and pressed "Send/Receive." There was an inbound message! He indulged in hope for the first time in days. He couldn't wait to get back to the boat and show it to Alana.

Y

"There it is!" The young recruit gazed at Murad with unabashed admiration. "You were wise to watch for the Amrikans at the same hour!"

Murad smiled with smug satisfaction. "Yes, and like all infidels, they are very stupid," he grunted. He flipped open his cell and pressed redial. "They are here! Surround the hotel. Watch all exits and check the parking area immediately. If they are not in the hotel, they will be nearby."

Y

Eric cut diagonally through the parking area and noticed a young couple trudging to their car, loaded down with suitcases. He moved into the shadows at the edge of the property.

"You there! Stop or we will shoot!" The shout came from behind him. He raised his hands and turned slowly, scanning the area for a promising route of escape.

A woman screamed. A gun was fired, and Eric reflexively ducked. He looked through the trees and saw the young woman being knocked to the ground by a gang of thugs. Her partner was lying in the midst of the suitcases, his arms and legs bent in unnatural positions. The thugs hovered over the couple and shouted threats. They kicked them until they rolled on their backs.

One of the attackers shouted an exclamation, and the rest of them turned abruptly, no longer interested in the stricken couple. They scanned the area in earnest and fanned out in all directions. One of them headed directly toward Eric.

Eric silently scurried along the bushes at the property line, keeping clear of lighted areas. When he was out of range, he began to run, taking a circuitous route back to the boat in case they overtook him. The last thing he would do is point them in Alana's direction.

Y

"Your Excellence, we intercepted another message. This time it was an inbound message to the infidels." Murad frowned as he anticipated the inevitable question.

"Did you catch them this time?" Alomari asked.

"No. We did not know his exact location, and it was dark."

"I grow weary of your excuses, Murad."

"We can now cut our search area in half. Surely they must be coming from some distance to transmit their messages. They would not risk drawing us to their hiding place."

"Perhaps. But the longer they stay free, the greater the chance that they will escape."

"I told you I would find them. I am confident that this will be the day that Allāhu al-Muqaddim will deliver them into my hands."

Y

Eric called out the signal to Alana. He remembered her skill with the pistol and didn't want her to shoot first and ask questions later.

She responded appropriately. He was cleared to reenter the boat. "Permission to come aboard?" he asked when she peered through the breach in the hull.

"Permission granted."

"We received a message!"

"Let's see." He held out the PDA before clambering through the opening.

She opened his e-mail and clicked the message. "It's from Tony!" She said. "It will take me a few minutes to decode it."

"I'll get breakfast ready as soon as you finish that. I'm sorry, they were fresh out of coffee."

Alana appeared to ignore his comment. She sat down and he stood behind her, peering over her shoulder. She copied the series of numbers that made up the e-mail:

```
0841061160590741041121171221121181151101021161160 98
1041021020340741031131309098111116120112115108045 1
0212111310210011708409811111709812003911510210611 1
1011021021151171051061161130471100470841170981220 9
811712211211811507208108410911211910204506711511 2
```

She selected the Excel icon and pasted the numbers into cell A1.

She then moved to cell A2 and typed "1." In cell A3, she typed a formula: =A2+3. Next, she positioned her cursor in B2, next to the number 1 she had typed earlier. In this cell, she typed a formula: =MID(A$1,A2,3). Finally, she moved the cursor one cell to the right, C2. In this cell, she typed another formula: =CHAR(B2). To test the results of her formulas, she copied them down a few rows to see if the beginning of the message made sense:

1	084	T
4	106	j
7	116	t
10	059	;
13	074	J
16	104	h
19	112	p
22	117	u
25	122	z
28	112	p
31	118	v
34	115	s

Eric frowned at the results. It was gibberish. He watched as she retraced her steps through each formula. "What's wrong?" he asked.

"I must have typed a formula wrong here. Give me a minute."

"Why don't you think out loud? When I get stumped with programming, it helps to talk through my steps. I can often catch the oversight as I explain the logic."

"OK. I pasted Tony's message in the top left cell. In the cells below it, I inserted a simple formula to sequence each entry by three. There's a couple ways to do this, but copying the formula is pretty quick. The results are right because the numbers are ascending by three: one, four, seven, ten, etcetera.

"In column B, I have a formula that parses the data into three-digit sets, starting with a position dictated by the number to the left. So the formula in the first row will pick up the three digits starting with position number one. The second row picks up three digits starting with position number four, and so on. This will automatically parse the digits into their ASCII code numbers. The third column is a formula to assign the proper letter or punctuation mark for the ASCII code found in column B. I copied the first several rows to test my formulas. Everything looks right, but the resulting text is gibberish. The first part reads, 'Tjt;Jhpuzpvs.'"

She stared at the screen for a moment. "Oh—I can't believe I overlooked the last step!"

"What?"

"Remember, I said we add an offset of one to each number? Well, I forgot to subtract the number one when I wrote the formulas." She typed the correction and the formula now read: =CHAR(B2-1). She copied them down a few rows to test the results of the revised formula.

"I think I have it." She quickly copied the formulas down one hundred rows, then sat back and read the results:

Sis: Igotyourmessage!Ifplanswork,expectSantaw/
reindeerthisp.m.StayatyourGPSIoveBro

"Tony is coming for us!" she screamed. She jumped up and threw herself at Eric, wrapping her arms around his neck. "You did it! We're going home!" She kissed him enthusiastically as he lifted her off the ground.

"When's he coming?"

"Tonight!"

"Let's see." She handed him the PDA, and he scanned the message. "Santa with reindeer? I guess that means his SEAL team."

"I suppose so."

"We're supposed to stay put. Well, I guess I should serve breakfast. It may be awhile before we eat again."

Y

LCDR McKinsey walked down the transport's ramp and squinted in the brilliant Abu Dhabi sunlight. He saw a hand wave from behind the windshield of a Humvee parked on the tarmac. He approached the vehicle. Gunny jumped down and met him halfway. He stopped short and saluted. Tony returned the salute as Gunny grabbed his duffle bag. "How we lookin', Gunny?"

"I've made all the arrangements, sir."

"Talk to me."

"There's a chair force C-five Galaxy transport to Diego Garcia that's scheduled to leave at eighteen hundred. They'll fabricate a couple of reasons to delay the departure until twenty hundred for us. Their normal flight plan flies southeasterly, then south along the island chain that stretches all the way to Diego Garcia. The closest they normally get to Pakistan is two hundred miles off the coast, but they're going to report turbulence and get clearance to fly around it. They can get us as close as twenty miles off the coast. That's well outside the Pakistani air space, so we won't draw any undue attention. We'll make the jump from thirty thousand feet, which gives us enough clearance to traverse the twenty miles to the coast."

"What about the winds? That's cutting it a little close if we have to fight a headwind."

"Yes, sir. That was my next point."

"Sorry to interrupt, Gunny. Of course you thought of that. Continue."

"No problem, sir. I've been studying the meteorological data while you were en route. The winds will be from offshore, so they'll be at our backs. It's going to be pretty cold up there. I'm anticipating forty degrees below. With the wind stream, it'll be about one hundred twenty degrees below."

"I get the picture, Gunny. Good work." Tony checked his watch. "We have a few hours before we need to load our equipment. Let's grab some chow."

"Sounds great, sir. There's a great restaurant nearby that ships in genuine USDA prime, Iowa corn-fed beef."

"You convinced me."

Karāchi, Pakistan

Eric continued to check the area for suspicious activity every half hour. Everything remained clear on the peninsula. He was about to duck below again when something caught his eye on the far side of the harbor.

On the West Wharf there were a number of men walking purposefully toward the south end. Eric shielded his eyes and squinted. It was hard to be sure at this distance, but it looked like they were carrying weapons. They were heading away from the entrance to the peninsula, so they weren't an immediate threat.

Eric joined Alana below.

"See anything?" she asked.

"No, it's all clear. I did see some men over on the wharf. I think they may have been carrying guns, but I'm not sure."

Alana glanced out the hull opening in alarm. "Mind if I take a look?"

"No, come on. I'll show you." He led her up the passageway to a ladder. "I'll go up first and move out on the bridge. Be careful to stoop when you get to the top of the ladder. Your blonde hair would be easy to spot up there."

Eric waited at the top of the ladder. He held his hand out and guided her as she crested the top. She followed his instructions and kept low. They were on a gangway that went the length of the boat. There were moldy windscreens laced below the handrail that provided excellent cover. They scooted along the walkway to the first vertical support post. There was a four-inch gap on either side of the post where the lacing stretched to the tarps on each side. "This is a perfect observation point. The opening is narrow, which gives you a secure vantage point. See the entrance to the peninsula?" Eric asked.

"Yes."

"OK, look to the right. See the boats crowded around the piers in the harbor?" She nodded. "The far shore of the harbor is the West Wharf. Look a little farther to the right and you'll see rows of warehouses stretching to the south."

"I see them."

"Keep watching the gaps between the buildings. You should see them as they move down the wharf."

Alana stared for a long time. "I'm not sure I'm looking in the right...Wait a minute. I see them! I think you're right. I think they're carrying weapons."

"You can see they're moving away from us, so it may be nothing."

"Maybe. But isn't the wharf a peninsula too?"

"Yes. Why?"

"How long is it?" Alana asked.

"It's about two miles to the south of us. Then there's a channel on the far side of it. On the other side of that is the East Wharf."

"What if those guys are looking for us? It won't take them long to finish searching the wharf. What if they decide to check out our peninsula on their way back?"

"That's a possibility, I guess. I tell you what. Why don't we stay up here on the bridge? We can keep a constant watch. It will be dark soon, so maybe they'll knock off at sundown. If not, they'll have to move more cautiously after dark, and they'll have to use flashlights. We can keep an eye out for them while we wait for your brother's team."

"OK. But this makes me nervous."

Abu Dhabi, United Arab Emirates

LCDR McKinsey and Gunny strapped into their seats in preparation for takeoff.

They didn't have the luxury of sitting with the crew due to space limitations. As guests of the air force, they were relegated to the cavernous cargo hold. They were in for a noisy, bumpy, chilly ride.

Shortly after takeoff, a crew member came back with a checklist in his hand. He saluted. Tony returned it. The crewman nervously glanced back and forth between them but addressed Tony. "Sir, regulations call for me to review safety procedures with all non–air force personnel. Then you need to sign off on them."

"You're kidding me." Tony was incredulous. "You do know we're SEALs, right?" Although Tony preferred not to play the SEAL card, he made exceptions when it came to mind-numbing bureaucracy.

"Sir, yes, sir! Please bear with me, sir; it's my job. I'm the newest grunt on the crew, and they're up there laughing about throwing me to the wolves. They figured you guys'd eat me alive."

Tony felt sympathy for the youngster. "Go ahead, crewman."

He held up the clipboard and consulted the instructions, informing Tony of the signs of hypoxia and decompression sickness.

He handed them some oxygen masks and pointed to a connection point for the hoses. "You'll be breathing one hundred percent aviators' breathing oxygen as we climb to jump altitude. Continue on ABO until we are over the jump zone.

"Sir, if you understand all this, please sign at the bottom of this form as the officer in charge of your jump team."

Tony rolled his eyes at Gunny and signed. "Here you go, crewman. My team of one understands as well."

Y

Karāchi, Pakistan

"Alana! Take a look at this!" Alana joined Eric at their observation point. They peered through the lacing on either side of the support post. "Look to the right—at the fishing harbor." He instructed. "See the moving lights?"

"Yes, I do. They don't look random, do they?"

"No. It's definitely a methodical search."

From their vantage point, they could see three piers jutting into the middle of the harbor, two from the main part of the peninsula and one more from the dogleg. Dozens of small fishing craft clustered around each pier. There were so many that only a fraction was tethered to the docks. Dozens more were rafted off of each other in a helter-skelter fashion. Men were methodically checking each boat, stepping from boat to boat and shining lights into the interiors.

"Stay here," Eric said. "I'm going around to the other side of the bridge to check the other end of the harbor. See if you can count the number of flashlights. It will give us an idea of the numbers we're up against." He returned a few minutes later. "There's one pier directly astern of our location and five more stretched down the length of the harbor. There are no more searchers down that way."

"I counted thirteen searchers on those two piers." Alana pointed toward the first two. "They'll probably work their way around the bend, then down the length of the harbor. At the rate they're going, it will only take them a half an hour for each pier."

"That's what I'm afraid of. Once they get to the mouth of the harbor, their return route is back up the peninsula. They'll certainly be checking our nautical graveyard on their way back. We can hope they'll check all the seaworthy boats first."

"Tony had better get here soon. We only have a handgun to hold them off. And I don't know if I could shoot a man when it comes right down to it."

Over the Arabian Sea

The red light came on by the cargo ramp, signaling five minutes until the jump. Tony and Gunny thoroughly checked each other's MT-5 high altitude precision parachute systems (HAPPS), which consisted of a backpack-like rig. They donned their helmets and confirmed the oxygen lines were free of kinks or obstructions. The GPS/altimeter units were activated and plugged into the comm systems. Everything requiring digital dexterity was finalized. Then they pulled on thick thermal gloves that would protect against frost-bite. Their M16s were strapped diagonally across their chests. Large duffle bags filled with ordnance were attached by tethers to their HAPPS.

A crewman in arctic gear stood at the side of the cargo ramp. He tugged on a red lever. A warning Klaxon sounded, matched by a pulsing red strobe. The cargo ramp dropped away, inviting a bitter wind that whipped through the hold.

The two skydivers edged into position.

"Comm check, Gunny. Do you read?"

"Loud and clear, sir! The GPS units are active and tracking."

"Roger that."

The red light next to the crewman turned green, and he thrust two thumbs in the air.

The SEALs trotted to the opening and launched themselves into the frigid blackness.

Karāchi, Pakistan

Eric kept watch on the starboard side of the ship, but Alana had moved to the port side, where she monitored the progress of the searchers.

The search had gone more quickly than estimated. The searchers were down at the far end of the peninsula, about a half mile away. They had finished searching all the boats in the fishing harbor and were now working their way through the derelicts littering the peninsula.

There seemed to be less discipline in their search patterns. Undoubtedly, some of the searchers were getting sloppy. They took shortcuts, either from boredom or fatigue, or both. The line of advance was irregular. The lead elements would be within range in minutes.

"Alana!" Eric whispered urgently. He had rejoined her and quickly took stock of their situation. "We have a tough choice. I haven't seen any signs of activity at the mouth of the peninsula, but that doesn't mean they aren't lying in wait and using these guys to flush out their quarry. So I think we should stay put. Besides, if we abandon our position, your brother would never find us. If we have to defend our position, we have the high ground and a clear field of fire around the boat. But if they rush us from multiple sides, they'll overwhelm our position quickly."

"We could try another tactic," Alana suggested. "We could wait and see how many of them enter the boat to search it. I've been watching them, and sometimes they send in only one man. Maybe the guy that's assigned to us would be one of the sloppy ones."

"I've been watching too. Even though they send in only one, they trade off. A partner watches until the first one exits his boat; then the first one watches while the second guy checks the next. Even if we could overpower our guy, the alarm would go up pretty quickly. Some would be too close to our boat to set up a field of fire. They'd be inside the ship and attacking us while the others converge. I think our best option is to pick off as many of them as we can when they get within range. The others will hold back, at least for a while. They won't be too anxious to charge until they assess our strengths. The more effective we are, the longer they'll delay." He hesitated to state the obvious. "I hate to pressure you, but *you* are the experienced marksman. Can you do it?"

Alana shuddered. "Eric, I don't know. On the one hand, the Lord tells us to love our enemies. On the other, He commanded His people to rid the land of the wicked, as a deterrent."

"Alana, they don't come any more wicked than these guys."

"I know that. I'm torn up. What should I do?"

"Let me pray for you." He put his hand on her shoulder and bowed his head. "Lord, our enemies surround us. They are like a pack of jackals who seek to devour us. Give us courage, Lord. And I pray for Alana. May this cup pass from her. But if it cannot, I pray that You give her a peace about what she must do."

They said, "Amen," in unison.

They could hear sharp commands and responses from the men as they inexorably closed the distance. It wouldn't be long now.

Alana raised up on one knee and rested the muzzle of the gun on the handrail. Eric heard the soft click of the safety. She took a deep breath and held it, sighting down the barrel.

A terrorist exited a boat one hundred fifty feet away. His turban was a bright spot in the moonlit wasteland and made an excellent focal point. She eased her finger through the trigger guard and rested it on the cold, thin strip of metal. She firmly applied pressure. "Lord, forgive me."

Over the Arabian Sea

"Gunny, do you read me?"

"Loud and clear, Preacher." Preacher was Tony's unofficial moniker. It came from his refusal to swear like the other SEALs. Some guys assumed he was a bit of a Holy Roller, but his men fiercely stood up for him, sometimes earning a bruise or two. He was one of their own, and they'd follow him anywhere because he didn't command from the rear; he led from the front. They were never asked to do something that he wouldn't do himself, which couldn't be said about any other officer they'd ever known.

"Form up on my six. I want to start on the high side of the glide slope. As we descend, we won't have as many options to adjust our height, but we can tuck into a spiral if we overcompensate. Once we're over dry land, we'll have more room to maneuver."

"Roger that, sir."

Y

Karāchi, Pakistan

The muzzle flash blinded her in the eye she had sighted with. She opened the other eye and pivoted the barrel to the next terrorist. He was stooped over his partner, who had dropped heavily. Alana squeezed off another shot, and he dropped his rifle, staggered, and fell heavily atop his partner.

Shouts of alarm were raised. The searchers abandoned their assignments and moved stealthily toward Alana and Eric's ship. A couple of them were in range. They lifted their rifles.

Eric saw the danger first. "Get behind the bulkhead, Alana!"

The next two terrorists reacted quickly. They engaged their enemy, providing cover for their teammates to advance. Then two more returned fire, which allowed the first two to advance. It was a disciplined approach that made Eric think the earlier sloppiness in their search patterns was a ruse designed to put them off guard. More terrorists were moving into strategic positions.

Eric feared that others could be converging on the starboard side of their ship. "Alana, can you move to the other side? These guys are going to keep up the suppressive fire, so you won't be able to get a shot off anyway. There may be more of them on the starboard side."

"OK." She ducked down and scurried around the bridge.

Beneath the Arabian Sea

Captain Lloyd called out to his first officer. "All engines stop. Make your depth thirty feet." The command was repeated to the helmsman. "Notify Lieutenant Evans that we have arrived at the designated coordinates. He may proceed with the extraction."

Karāchi, Pakistan

"Did you see that, sir? Muzzle flashes at twelve o'clock. Kalashnikovs."

"Roger, Gunny. Lock and load."

"My thoughts exactly, Preacher. Let's crash this party."

With years of combat training, both men assessed the battlefield conditions and determined the best method of dispatching the enemy. In contrast

---

to a Hollywood script, there was little advantage in firing during their descent. The rapidly shifting perspective made it impossible to hit a target, and muzzle flashes provided a bull's-eye for the enemy.

"Gunny, you can see the ship they are directing their fire at. That's our objective. Let's drop in behind these guys and deliver our RSVP. Let's take the first few down quietly."

"Understood."

Both men pulled down firmly on their chute's directional handles, which flared the canopies in the last seconds of descent. They landed soundlessly with less force than if they'd stepped off a curb. They were careful to avoid the rucksacks of equipment that had dangled five feet beneath them.

They wrestled momentarily with their chutes, collapsing them into a heap. In one swift motion, they unclipped and stepped out of the HAPPS rigs. They pulled their combat knives from their sheaths and approached the first two terrorists from the rear. They dropped them soundlessly, carefully retrieving the AK-47s before they clattered to the ground.

The SEALs were not concerned with being seen; their adversaries did not expect an attack from the rear. The SEALs confidently advanced on the next two and dispatched them effortlessly. The time for stealth had passed. The remaining terrorists were expecting a burst of suppressive fire from their now-dead comrades and would be shouting questions soon. With a nod, both M16s came up to firing position. The strategic shots were methodical and sparse.

Within a few minutes, there were no remaining targets of opportunity on the port side of the ship. Shots came from the other side, however. Before they regrouped, they scanned the ship with their night-vision goggles.

They saw a man on the bridge, hunched down behind a bulkhead. Suddenly, a woman came around from the starboard side of the bridge with a pistol held vertically next to her ear. She dropped to one knee and raised the pistol.

Tony and Gunny reacted simultaneously as a shot rang out. They dove and rolled from the killing zone. The bullet hit the dirt right where Gunny had been standing. "Was that your sister?" Gunny whispered urgently.

Tony smiled proudly. "Yeah, I taught her everything she knows." Without lifting his head, he shouted, "Hey, Munchkin! It's me!"

They heard a shout from the bridge. "Tony! Oh, thank God!"

A male voice shouted a warning from the bridge. "They're advancing on the other side!"

Tony and Gunny were already on their feet. "You take the stern; I'll take the bow," Tony ordered. As he rounded the bow, he glanced up momentarily. His sister was leaning over the railing, looking for him in the shadows. He smiled up at her. "Take a break, sis. I'll be there shortly."

Y

Lieutenant Evans, going by the moniker of Deacon, assessed the strengths and weaknesses of his team as they conferred one last time. "There's only going to be the four of us on this mission. We have to leave room for Gunny, Preacher, and Preacher's sister. And we need to anticipate one or two more—we're not certain. Even two will be crowded."

He looked from man to man. "Chief—you're the pilot. I'll navigate. We've got two combat swimmers who are certified SR snipers. I hope we won't have to plant any mines, but we have a lot of unknowns and need to be ready for all contingencies. OK, gentlemen. We're on deck. Let's move out."

The men were already outfitted in their wet suits and Dräger rebreathers. Deacon led the ascent up the ladder and opened the hatch to the transfer trunk—the passageway into the dry deck shelter (DDS), the cigar-shaped enclosure that houses the SEAL delivery vehicle, a flooded transport vehicle that transports combat swimmers and surveillance/reconnaissance scuba divers to strategic locations. This craft would eliminate the transfer through an air hatch. The SEALs could slide the exterior hatch door open and swim to their target. At mission completion, the same efficiency would be vital to a hasty retreat from the scene of mayhem.

They edged around the bulky vehicle as the hatch was closed below them. Within moments the chamber began to flood. The SEALs tightened the straps of their full-face masks and adjusted the valves on their Drägers. The rebreathers would capture their exhaled gasses in a scrubber compartment, where the carbon molecules would be chemically detached from the oxygen. The scrubbed oxygen was then recycled to the diver. It was extremely efficient and allowed a diver to stay submerged for up to twelve hours instead of the thirty minutes allowed by conventional tanks. The critical advantage for combat swimmers was the complete absence of telltale bubbles. This allowed them to stealthily approach a target with minimal risk of being detected.

Deacon swam to the edge of the DDS hatch and pressed the winch button. The shrill whine of the motor broke the silence. The bulbous nose of the SDV crept silently from the shadows.

The team swam aboard while the chief checked the navigation computer and sonar system. He plugged into the comm system again. "OK, everyone, sound off."

Each of the divers responded clearly. All systems were go.

"Chief, how about I take a quick sneak peek?" Deacon asked.

"Aye, aye, Skipper," he replied. He silently directed the sub to the surface and leveled off.

Deacon slid the navigator hatch and hoisted himself up in the seat until his head was above the water level. Their forward progress was four knots, which churned up a bow wave at his neck. He scanned the dark surface of the water for any activity. There was none. He dropped back into the SDV and slid the hatch back into position. "Make your bearing one hundred fifty-four degrees for twenty-four thousand feet. And put the pedal to the medal."

Y

A cacophony of shots were fired in the darkness. Explosions lit up the night. Eventually, the firing diminished and silence returned.

Alana and Eric had moved to the starboard side of the bridge for an excellent vantage point. They were amazed to watch the devastating efficiency of the SEAL team. The remaining terrorists retreated to the mouth of the peninsula and were lost to view behind warehouse buildings on the West Wharf.

The SEALs retreated to the ship and entered through the breach. They made their way to the bridge.

As Tony removed his goggles, Alana ran to him and threw herself around his neck. "Tony, I was so scared! I can't believe it's really you! Thank you for coming for us."

Tony smiled fondly at his little sister. "No problem. I didn't have anywhere else to go tonight." He glanced at Eric. "Who's this guy?"

Alana grabbed Eric's hand and pulled him forward. "This is my boyfriend, Eric. Eric, this is Tony. And—you look familiar, but I'm sorry, I forgot your name…" She gestured toward Gunny.

"Senior Chief Witherspoon, at your service. You can call me Gunny. That's a reference to my former job. I was a gunnery sergeant with the marines before I transferred."

"OK. We can socialize later." Tony was all business again. "We need to set up a watch. Those guys will be calling up support elements. They won't roll over and play dead. Our SDV team won't be here for at least a couple of hours. We can't let our guard down until we're out of this stinking country." He turned to Gunny. "I'll take the first watch. Why don't you take the digital camera and get photos and swabs from our hosts? I'll make sure no one interrupts you."

"Sure enough, Preacher."

Alana questioned, "Photos and swabs?"

"Yeah, we need to ID the guys we took out—both photo and DNA confirmation. They may be on the terrorist watch list. The DOD positively IDs all bandits and updates the list."

Tony surveyed the bridge, the surrounding area, and the approach from the mainland. He nodded silently to himself and turned to Alana and Eric, who were watching him carefully. "Who picked this location?"

Eric stammered, "Uh...I did."

"This is a good defensive position. It has a commanding vantage point, no blind spots, and is a tough fortification. The enemy cannot easily storm the gates. Three points of egress for emergencies. Well done."

Eric self-consciously replied, "Thanks."

Alana smiled proudly. "I can't wait for the two of you to get to know each other."

Tony quickly replied, "There'll be time for that later. Meanwhile, we're not out of the woods." He put his hands on his sister's shoulders and gazed intently in her eyes. "Alana, I saw a couple of bodies on the ground as we began our assault. Was that you?"

Alana's eyes clouded. "Yes."

"I'm proud of you. What you did was not easy but was necessary. Your lives were in jeopardy, and you were given no choice. The Lord understands and is gracious to forgive."

She hung her head and nodded feebly.

"Now...you've done more than enough for one night. You're going to struggle with nightmares as it is. Why don't you go below now? Gunny, Eric, and I can handle things here."

Eric was unbelievably flattered to be counted as part of the team.

"Sure. Thanks, Tony." She kissed him on the cheek. "Thank you again for coming for us." She turned to Eric. "I'll see you in a little while." She gave his hand one last squeeze and descended the ladder.

Y

"OK, Chief, time for another peek." Deacon cautiously raised his head above the water and looked to his right. They were passing the mouth of the harbor between the East and West Wharfs. The southern tip of the West Wharf peninsula loomed. There was no activity on the water. "Prepare for a heading change to thirty degrees on my mark. A few minutes later, he announced, "Mark. We're in the Baba Channel and will proceed parallel to the peninsula for eighty-three hundred feet. Make your depth three feet, and raise the antennae. It's time to call Preacher."

Y

Tony watched Alana descend the ladder. When she was out of earshot, he turned to Eric and abruptly asked, "Do you love her?"

Eric's insecurity ratcheted up a few notches. "Yes, I do."

"How much?"

"If we get out of this alive, I want to marry her."

"Then we need to talk. Follow me." He led Eric to the stern, the best position from which to observe an approach by hostiles. They sat behind the tarped handrail. It was more weathered there, the sunward side of bridge. It was torn and hung limply in places. Nevertheless, it provided ample cover for them. "Hold on a minute." Tony pressed his hand to his headset. "Gunny, how's it going?"

"I'm just about finished."

"Good. I'm on the stern and have a good view of the approaches. When you're finished, take up a position off the bow. Sound the alarm if you see any movement."

"Roger."

Tony turned his attention back to Eric. "OK. We have a few minutes. Listen up." He set his jaw, and Eric withered under the penetrating stare. In clipped, even tones, Tony asked, "First of all, are you treating my sister honorably?"

The frontal assault unnerved Eric. "I guess SEALs don't mince words, huh? Well, the answer is yes. There was a time when I thought she was a little prudish, but now I respect her beliefs and abide by them."

"Good. Make sure you keep it that way. If you haven't noticed, I'm protective about my little sister. I've run off more than one boyfriend that I didn't think was worthy of her. We're very close, and there isn't anything I wouldn't do for her. You catch my drift?"

"Yes, sir."

"There's something else I need to say to you. Alana and I were raised in a Christian home. Because of her beliefs, Alana wants more than anything to have a strong Christian husband who will be the spiritual leader of the household. Has she mentioned this?"

"Not in so many words…" Eric was uneasy about where this was going.

"Well, believe it. She's prayed since we were kids for the Lord to bring a godly husband to her. Do you think you're the man to fill that role?"

Tony seemed to grow larger by the minute, and Eric proportionately shrank. In spite of this, Eric had done enough soul-searching lately that he no longer doubted himself. "No, I don't think I'm that man today, but lately I've come to grips with my tendency to be too self-reliant and independent. I realize that Alana takes her faith much more seriously than I do, but I want to change. I want to be the man she deserves. If she'll have me, I want to live up to her dreams and prayers."

"Well, I suspect she's nuts about you. If you had answered any differently, I wouldn't have given your relationship a snowball's chance. That's why I needed to set the record straight right now. If she was going to be heartbroken, better sooner than later. I guess I owe it to her to save your butt now." Tony smiled, but it seemed slightly forced. He stuck out his hand. "Nice meeting you, Eric."

Eric's hand was crushed in Tony's iron fist. Point taken. "My pleasure," he managed. He was relieved to have this talk over with. He'd never had a conversation quite like it.

Tony's radio squawked in his ear, and he held up his hand to silence Eric.

"Deacon to Preacher! Deacon to Preacher! Do you read?"

"Affirmative, Deacon. Preacher here. What's your twenty?"

"Altar call scheduled for zero two hundred. I repeat, altar call scheduled for zero two hundred. Copy?"

"Affirmative. Prayer partners should expect two new converts. Amen?"

"Amen, Preacher! I make that two converts."

Tony smiled at Eric. "A bit unorthodox, but effective." He checked his watch. "Our ride will be here in fifteen minutes. Go below, and look for a rucksack I left next to the hole in the hull. You'll find several wet suits. There's one sized for Alana, and we brought a few others for contingency. Find one that fits, and get it on. Tell Alana to do the same and be ready to move out. Then come back up here."

Y

Murad had rallied the remnants of his team behind the first row of warehouses on the West Wharf. He was bitterly confused at the mysterious developments on the peninsula.

There had been no contact for the past hour with the advance team that had searched the harbor. He had heard the distinctive sound of their AK-47s and responding gunfire from an unknown source. None of them had checked in, nor had they responded to his calls. He assumed they were dead. But how? This could not be the work of the two Amrikans. Satam's handgun could not be that effective in their inexperienced hands. No, this was something more. The survivors from the north end of the peninsula swore they heard M16s. They had enough experience to know the sound. The unexplained explosions had unnerved his men. They had drawn their own conclusions and had beseeched him to call off the attack.

Dread shivered up his spine. He had seen tactics like these in Afghanistan. Special Forces. It had to be. But where had they come from? How had they arrived on the peninsula? What was their strength?

His mind went back to an incident in the Afghan mountains the previous year. Tribal shepherds had reported a band of four Amrikan soldiers making their way across a mountain pass. His cousin had led his forces in an ambush. They had overwhelming numbers, the high ground, and element of surprise. In spite of the tactical advantages, the Amrikan warriors fought valiantly and decimated the Taliban fighters with their superior training and weaponry. It was only the superior numbers that eventually overcame the enemy. The Amrikans had been slaughtered.

A helicopter had been dispatched for a rescue mission but struggled with maneuverability in the thin air of the high mountains. It was an easy target for a surface-to-air missile, provided by the CIA during the Soviet occupation. It had been a glorious day for his cause; they had killed more SEALs in one battle than had ever died in any military action.

Was he now facing a similar threat, or was he being spooked by his superstitious men? He would err on the side of caution.

Y

Eric returned to the bridge. Tony handed him night-vision goggles. "Put these on and I'll adjust them for you." He stood behind Eric and adjusted the straps. "OK—I want you to keep watch on the port side. I expect the attack to come from starboard, but we need to be sure they don't get the drop on us from our rear." Tony handed him a pistol. "Do you know how to use this?"

"No, but Alana showed me how to turn the safety on and off."

"That's all you need to know for now. If you see anyone, fire a few bullets in their direction. That will pin them down long enough for Gunny or me to hear you. We'll provide all the backup you'll need. Just be careful to move after you fire the shots. They'll send a few rounds at your muzzle flash."

"Yes, I saw them try that with Alana."

Y

Gunny had maintained his vigil down below. He noticed increased activity near the warehouses on the wharf. He pressed the zoom on his night-vision goggles and stared at the narrow opening between the warehouse buildings. The world was bright green when viewed through the goggles, and slightly fuzzy. Rapid movements streaked any bright spots in the viewer. It was enough to give him a splitting headache after a couple of hours. He'd be ready to lose the goggles when they boarded the SDV.

There was another movement near the warehouses. "Preacher—I detect movement on the wharf. Please confirm."

"Roger, Gunny. Hold on. Affirmative. It appears their cavalry has arrived. I count forty unfriendlies. I repeat four-zero hostiles moving onto the peninsula. *Where is the SDV?* Deacon, did you copy that?"

"Affirmative, Preacher. We're five minutes out. Alter the altar call?"

"That's an affirmative, Deacon. Proceed to the northwestern point on the peninsula, and establish firing positions. Our location is in the middle of the dogleg. The hostiles will be coming right at you and will turn to your right to engage us. Hold your fire until they've made the turn. We'll open fire simultaneously and pin them in the cross fire."

"Nothing like a little hellfire and brimstone for the pagans, right, Preacher?"

"Roger that."

FORTY-NINE

Thursday, November 10, 2005
8 Shawwāl, 1426 AH
Karāchi, Pakistan

ERIC WAS MORE UNSETTLED THAN HE'D EVER BEEN. THE SURREAL experiences of the past few days had taken him to every emotional extreme. When the terrorists were closing in on them, he was gripped in profound despair. Then hope was tantalizingly dangled with the arrival of Alana's brother. Now they may have to fight for their lives again with their rescue only minutes away.

The will to live was an emotion he'd never thought about before, but now it burned within him. Will. That was a strange thing to focus on at a time like this. A phrase came from nowhere: "Not my will but Yours be done." Where had he heard that? It was what Jesus had prayed. Right before He was arrested. Just as He faced the greatest challenge of His life—something Eric could finally relate to.

Eric was moved to pray. "Lord, I am confused and afraid. I've made such a mess of things. I realize that I don't seek Your will. I am stubborn and proud. But I am at the end of my ability. I need You to lead me. We're being hunted, and I'm scared for our lives. Please protect us.

"Lord, if we live through all this, I ask that You make me the kind of man Alana has prayed for. I admit that I have wanted her to meet my needs, but now I realize my needs are greater than she can fill. I need to seek You and trust that You will give me whatever I need. Please forgive my sin. Help me to learn from my mistakes and not repeat them. Amen."

For the first time in his life, Eric felt his prayer was sincere. He wasn't worried about what anyone else would think or whether he followed the right formula. He had finally connected with God.

Y

Murad led his al Qaeda fighters to the mouth of the peninsula. Their fear was barely beneath the surface and required that he maintain tight discipline to keep it in check.

He estimated the last position of the infidels and calculated the most effective angle of attack. The strength of his adversaries had to be ascertained before committing to a frontal assault. Revenge for the humiliating loss of his men would be sweet. If these were Special Forces he was facing, it would be all the sweeter. A glorious victory would redeem his reputation with the Tall One.

Y

The chief eased the SDV to a stop and let it settle gently in the silty bed of the channel. The four SEALs slid their respective hatches and swam silently to the shoreline.

Y

The al Qaeda fighters moved cautiously in alternating waves. From boat to boat and building to building, they drew closer to their adversaries. They thoroughly checked each potential sniper position. Their battle-hardened experiences from the Afghan mountains dictated a thoroughness much greater than their fallen comrades had exercised. A bank of warehouse buildings loomed one hundred meters ahead. They were on a forty-five-degree angle to the dogleg and represented an excellent vantage point for enemy snipers. Murad sent a small team to eliminate that possibility. He would not risk exposing their backs once they turned into the dogleg.

Y

The murky water of the Baba Channel betrayed no movement. Mist blanketed the surface, punctuated by thin reeds along the shoreline. There was a slight disturbance. Gentle ripples rolled outward. It could have been a fish snatching a bug from the surface. A second disturbance erupted, then simultaneously, two more.

They took form slowly as they rose in the gloaming, like specters from the deep. The SEALs cobbled onto the rust-laden mud of the north shore. The snipers unpacked their rifles from waterproof containers and took up their positions, lying prone on the embankment. Deacon and Chief unpacked their M16s and grenade launchers. They fanned out to the right, prepared to lay down a suppressive fire. A bank of buildings angled away to their left. From their position, the mouth of the peninsula was at eleven o'clock, and Preacher was at three.

"Preacher, this is Deacon. We are in the pews and ready for your sermon."

Y

Murad's team was at the fateful turn. The buildings had been secured. There would be no treacherous fire from the rear. They moved steadily forward, checking each of the derelict boats lined up like goats at a feed trough. Still no sign of the enemy.

Y

A SEAL called Sniper breathed calmly and gripped his rifle. He panned slowly, seeking a target.

"Deacon, I have acquired a target," he whispered as he steadied the cross-hairs. The man stopped and gazed intently into the shadows before him. In the scope, he faced to the right, the crosshairs centered on his ear.

Y

Murad led his team to the head of the peninsula and turned to his left. Everyone froze, awaiting his command. He squinted between the shadowy hulks of ancient ships that stretched for a full kilometer.

It was time. His hand raised slowly, his men poised like runners in their blocks. His hand chopped through the air. "*Allāhu ak...*"

Y

Sniper sighted through his high-powered scope, estimating five hundred feet to his target. His headset crackled. "Deacon to prayer team: fire at will."

The fifty-caliber match-grade sniper shell exited the muzzle at 2,750 feet per second. He had not factored a slight breeze from offshore. In the 459 feet to its target, the downdraft deflected the trajectory. The shell dropped 1.1 inches and impacted below the jawline with over 14,000 joules of energy.

Y

Murad's life ended in fitting irony. As he had beheaded countless victims, his head was separated from his body. It was more merciful, however; he was spared the sawing of a blade across his throat.

His allotment of mercy expired with his death. He would soon recognize the eternal consequences of his savage life, even as his lifeless body slumped to the earth.

Y

Absolute silence ensued in the wake of the explosive gunshot. The echo reverberated off the hulking derelicts, its source seeming to emanate from every direction. Without their fallen leader, the fighters were paralyzed. Demoralized, most of them turned and fled. A few raised their weapons to retaliate.

The SEAL team mowed them down in a blistering cross fire of heavy weaponry.

Y

"Preacher, this is Deacon. Do you read?"

"Loud and clear."

"Baptism is scheduled in ten. The baptismal vessel will be at the designated location."

"Roger."

One of the frogmen handed out dive masks tethered to the bulkhead. "These are full-face masks with built-in regulators," he said as he donned his. "You can breathe and talk normally. You'll be connected to the comm system and will be able to hear us." His voice was muted but understandable.

Gunny backed up to the sub, scanning the perimeter, his M16 ready for any threat. He clambered aboard and stood guard in the opening as the sub began to descend. The sub came about, and Gunny squeezed into the seat next to Tony. The water rose to the top of the hatches, and Alana stole a final glimpse of the ship that had served them so well.

Y

"I think we have a problem," Deacon announced.

"What's the sitrep, Deacon?" Preacher asked.

"There's an LPG tanker tethered to two tugs that just pulled away from the docks. Two shore-patrol cruisers are interdicting them. The whole channel is blocked."

"Do we have enough depth beneath them?" Preacher asked.

"It's too close for comfort. The docks are to port and the shoals to starboard." Deacon pointed to the screen. "The tanker is loaded and sitting low in the water. We could try to thread our way between the gunboats, but the tide's coming in. The water will be running fast through the middle of the channel. Too difficult to maneuver if we have to."

"How long to the rendezvous with the *Louisiana?*"

Deacon checked his dive watch. "Fifty-six minutes. We can't putt around here too much longer. If we miss the first rendezvous, we'll have a problem fighting the tide to the next set of coordinates an hour later. What do you recommend?"

"I'm thinking of running us close to this tugboat." He pointed out the bright spot on the screen. "We clamp a mine on the bow, above the waterline so she doesn't sink. When she blows, the gunboats will move in to investigate, which will clear a path on the southwest side of the channel. We'll slip through and be on our way."

A layer of mist rolled in from the sea and swirled between the shadowy silhouettes of the gunboats. Searchlights swept randomly across the channel. Deacon raised his head above the murky surface and affixed an explosive to the hull. As he prepared to submerge, he heard a distant cry echo across the water. One of the searchlights doubled back on its track and swept across him. The searchlight of the other cruiser followed suit as the inboard engines from the first gunboat rumbled to life. Deacon dropped into his seat. "Chief, we have company. Get us out of here!"

The first gunboat to respond was already off the port bow of the lead tugboat. A sailor on the bridge wing directed his searchlight at the waterline and pointed with urgency. The captain recognized the danger and ordered full reverse. When the mine blew, he intended to be well clear of the shrapnel.

The captains of the gunboats had barely conferred by radio when the explosion rocked the waterfront, sending a shock wave across the channel.

A gunner on the first cruiser had his deck gun directed at the bow of the tug when the explosion knocked him back against the bulkhead, causing him to lose his footing. As his feet slid out beneath him, he reflexively pulled on the gun handles to right himself. The effort failed, and he dropped to the deck, jerking the muzzle of the gun upward. The jarring impact caused him to fire three shells, which traced a pattern across the bow of the LPG tanker. The red-hot shells penetrated the forward cargo tank on the starboard side.

At first, there was no reaction. Then the tank erupted in a mighty fireball, sending a mushroom cloud into the night sky. Moments later, the port-side tank blew with similar effect.

Deacon observed the mayhem and felt the intense heat of the explosions through his face mask. The captain of the surviving gunboat ordered full speed to the mouth of the channel. Whoever was responsible for this atrocity must be cut off from escaping to the Arabian Sea. He ordered his crew to crisscross the channel and throw hand grenades into their wake. It wasn't as good as depth charges, but the concussive underwater blast from grenades could easily kill a diver.

"These guys don't give up!" Deacon slipped back into his seat. "Move out, Chief—full speed."

"What now?" Preacher asked.

"A gunboat is headed our way. They're covering the channel with explosives. Chief, keep close to the shore. We're past the shoals, and the water is deep enough. The gunboat won't run us over, but they can lob explosives close enough to do damage."

A nearby explosion shook the SDV, and the sensitive instruments blinked.

"The Doppler unit just died," Deacon announced. "The last reading I got showed an eight-foot depth under our keel. We're heading to deeper water, so we can get by without it—just maintain this depth, Chief. We can't take another shell as close as that last one. If we lose our sonar or GPS, we could have a real problem."

"I have an idea, Deacon," Preacher said. That gunboat sounds like he's working a grid, hoping to nail us with the random explosives. When he turns away from us, his engine housing is exposed. If we wait till he makes his next turn, our snipers can put a couple of shells in his engines."

"Sounds good," Deacon confirmed. "OK, get your rifles ready, guys. We'll wait for their next pass. You'll have to work quickly before they get too far downrange."

The deep rumbling of the twin inboard engines grew louder, punctuated by explosions that reverberated through the hull. They waited for the shift in timbre that would signal a course change.

Suddenly, it was time.

The SDV bobbed to the surface as the rear hatches slid forward. The snipers pulled their dive masks from their faces and lifted their rifles in synchronized movements. They wrapped the straps around their forearms and rested their elbows on the hull. The wake from the gunboat had passed and was replaced by a gentle swell.

Sniper broke the silence: "I'll take the starboard engine; you take port. The bow is bobbing through the chop, but the stern is pretty steady. Adjust your scope by six clicks."

"Roger."

As the shots rang out, the deep rumble of the gunboat engines turned into a cacophony of rending metal. The bow dropped abruptly. Men scurried around on the deck, one of them pointing directly at the SDV.

Sniper scanned the deck through his scope and brought it to rest on the deck gunner as he swiveled toward his stern. "Uh-oh." He took a deep breath and squeezed off a second shot. The rifle bucked. When he reacquired his target, the deck gunner was clutching his right arm. They would be long gone before a replacement gunner could get in position.

Preacher spoke for all of them: "Nice work, guys. Let's go home."

The SEALs swam out of the SDV and strapped it to the track. As the winch drew it into position for the trip home, Alana and Eric sat beside each other in the gloomy interior. Eric could see Alana's features from the illumination of the navigation panel. "Can you hear me?"

"Yes."

Her voice had a tinny edge through the comm. "It looks like we have just a few minutes while they get the minisub loaded up. I don't know when we'll have another chance to be alone for a while. I want to tell you about something that happened to me back on the boat."

Alana sat silently, watching him through their masks.

He struggled with what he needed to say. "I was on the bridge right before the final assault, and my mind was racing. I didn't know if we were going to live or die. More than anything else, I wanted one last chance to tell you how much I love you. But I had to stay where I was. Your brother was depending on me to keep watch.

"For the first time in my life, I felt completely beyond my abilities. I was holding a gun that I didn't know how to shoot, and afraid I'd get killed if I tried. The only thing I could do was pray.

"Alana, I felt closer to God during that prayer than I ever have. I acknowledged to Him that I was beyond my resources and if anything was to be done, it would have to be Him that did it. I realized that I've always pushed God aside and took control of my circumstances. I admitted that I had screwed up with you again and that I didn't deserve you.

"I want you to know that I'm not saying this to win your approval in any way. I just want to share with you what I prayed about and leave it at that. I didn't try to bargain with God because I realized that my problem is much bigger than how I hurt you. I have a strong ego and have been unwilling to submit to the Lord. So I promised Him that I will be different from this point on." Eric stopped talking. He had said everything he needed to say.

"Eric, I—"

There was a loud clang from outside the SDV, followed by a rush of bubbles and gurgling water. Alana raised her voice so she could be heard above the racket. "Eric, I have already forgiven you. I love you, and that means being patient while God continues to mold you. I was praying that He would use our circumstances to get your attention. It sounds like He answered my prayer."

Eric could see her smile, though it was distorted by a riot of bubbles as the water level began to drop. "I guess we can take these masks off now," he observed.

"It would make it easier to kiss me." She smiled sweetly.

He removed his mask and laid it aside, then gently pulled her mask from her face. He kissed her tenderly and would have lingered for quite a while but was interrupted by a very intimidating team of SEALs staring at them through the open hatches.

Y

The hatch to the transfer trunk was spun open and dropped with a shower of water into the recesses of the *Louisiana*. LCDR Tony McKinsey was the first to exit. He dropped to the deck and turned to face Captain Lloyd. He snapped a salute, which was returned smartly. "Permission to come aboard, sir?"

"Granted. Let's get you and your team into some dry clothes, shall we?"

"Yes, sir. We have a couple of visitors I'd like to introduce first."

While the interchange had been taking place, Eric had descended and helped Alana off the last couple of steps. She turned to face the captain.

Tony smiled proudly at his sister and said, "Captain, I would like to introduce Alana McKinsey, my sister."

The captain smiled warmly. "Ms. McKinsey, I am honored to welcome you aboard." He looked around at the crewmen crowded into every available nook, then turned back to her. "I also would like to acknowledge we are a part of history in the making. This lovely young lady is the first woman ever to board a U.S. nuclear submarine in a combat zone."

Loud cheers and earthy comments gave tribute to her accomplishment. Alana blushed at the attention and nervously tucked her wet hair behind her ear.

Captain Lloyd turned to Alana. "In honor of this auspicious occasion,

I would like to present you with this T-shirt with the logo of the USS *Louisiana*. It has been dated with today's date and signed by each of our crew members."

Someone yelled from the back of the gangway, "It's supposed to be a *wet* T-shirt, Captain!"

This was followed by lascivious grins and guttural laughter. Alana's blush deepened.

"Settle down!" the captain ordered. He put a protective hand on Alana's shoulder. "Let me apologize on behalf of our whole crew. These men are at sea for months at a time, and they sometimes forget their manners."

"I understand." She smiled at the crew. "I want to thank you for coming to our rescue. I will never be able to repay you for your bravery and sacrifice. I am honored to receive this gift and will wear it proudly—and it won't be wet!" She grinned.

"Hoo-yah!" They laughed and cheered at her poise in the midst of a very intimidating environment.

Tony continued, "We have another guest, Captain. This is Eric Colburn." He glanced at the crewmen meaningfully. "He's Alana's boyfriend."

A collective groan erupted from the troops.

Y

The sun crested the hills on the eastern side of Karāchi and revealed a shattered waterfront district. Flames rose through the mist and greeted the first rays of the sun. Pulsing lights marked the emergency vehicles that roamed aimlessly, their sirens mournful. The mystery of what had happened would never be solved. Only one thing was certain: al Qaeda had been dealt a severe blow.

Miles offshore, a United States nuclear submarine slipped silently into the depths of the Arabian Sea.

EPILOGUE

Monday, November 21, 2005
19 Shawwāl, 1426 AH
Atlanta, Georgia

D R. LARSON WALKED TO THE BANK OF MICROPHONES AT THE PODIUM. His diminutive stature was made more so by the expansive stage of the auditorium. He was bracketed on the left by the distinguished directors of the Genographic Project, and by his team of executives on the right.

He shielded his eyes against the flashing of cameras and tapped the microphone. Satisfied with the volume, he began. "Ladies and gentlemen, thank you for coming here for this auspicious occasion. I am pleased to announce the conclusion of the first phase of our Genographic Project. The incredible results are outlined in the media kit you have just been handed. Section two outlines the objectives for the next phase of the project. We expect to once again rewrite the anthropology textbooks with our research." He continued with a number of forgettable details, all of them captured faithfully by the cameras.

Eric leaned over and whispered to Alana, "Video at eleven."

Dr. Larson glanced over his shoulder at Eric. For a moment, he thought he'd been overheard.

"Ladies and gentlemen, I have another announcement that is not in the press release. Our board of directors—" he turned and swept his hand deferentially toward the dignitaries seated behind him—"has just approved my recommendation for changes in our structure. First, I would like to announce the addition of Dr. Harold Foster to our board of directors, replacing the esteemed Prince Khalid Saud, who has stepped down."

Dr. Foster raised his hand and waved for the cameras.

"I would also like to announce the new director of computer operations for the Genographic Project, Mr. Eric Colburn."

Eric stood and raised his hand self-consciously, then returned to his seat.

Alana beamed lovingly at him. She leaned closer and whispered, "I'm so proud of you! Congratulations."

Dr. Larson continued, "Mr. Colburn will have many challenges in his new position, the first being to restore our Internet connection which has been down all morning."

There were a few chuckles from the crowd, and Eric grinned sheepishly.

Dr. Larson entertained a few questions, and the press conference concluded. He was immediately beset by a dozen reporters.

Alana slipped her hand inside Eric's arm and hugged it with the other as they walked to the elevators. Eric made sure his ID was in place as they approached. He pressed the button for the eighth floor.

As they exited the elevator, Preedy walked briskly past them without acknowledging their presence. He had not been invited to the press conference and had just been summoned to Ms. Knowles's office. The door closed firmly behind him.

Eric smiled at Alana conspiratorially. "Follow me." He walked briskly to Preedy's office where the magnetic lock clicked softly. He entered without slowing his pace. "Have a seat; I'll just be a minute."

He sat in Preedy's chair and opened the cabinet door opposite the desk. The server blinked in all its glory. Eric rotated to the desk and picked up the phone. He punched three digits. "Joey? It's me. OK, you can bring it up now. Oh—and Joey, you'll be happy to know the server is still here...Yes, I'm taking care of it right now."

Eric plugged a jump drive into the USB port, picked up Preedy's remote control, and pressed the select button a couple of times. The monitor toggled between two screens until he confirmed he was looking at the server. After a couple of minutes' search, he found an encrypted e-mail system.

Preedy had not logged off. Eric was able to scan the contents. He checked a number of messages in the sent box and in-box. He found an appropriate message and clicked "Reply to All." He typed a few words in the body of the e-mail, then selected the paper clip icon. He navigated to the jump drive and selected a file.

Eric was about to send the message when the door to the office opened and Preedy entered, flanked by two security guards. Eric leaned back in the chair and propped his feet on the desk. Preedy glanced at him and was speechless. He fumed but was powerless to say anything.

Eric feigned a look of innocence and said simply, "You've got mail!"

"What do you mean?" Preedy spat back. "The Internet is down."

"It was, but that was intentional. I couldn't risk having you get wind of the shake-up and alerting your buddies. I had Joey bring the Internet back up a few minutes ago when you were called to Ms. Knowles's office. While you were busy getting your butt fired, I took the liberty of reading an urgent e-mail that just arrived from your brother-in-law. I just about finished a quick response on your behalf. I'll finish while you pack up your things."

Preedy gruffly threw his personal effects into a mailroom carton and nervously eyed Eric, who typed with a flourish.

"Oh, I almost forgot—" Eric looked up from his typing—"you had a phone call a few minutes ago from the guard at the front desk. I think you know him as Barney Fife. He wanted to personally let you about the Homeland Security guys who are waiting for you downstairs. I guess you didn't know about my meeting with them yesterday, did you? They came back this morning with a search warrant and want to give you a lift home.

"Well, enough of this small talk. I have a busy day ahead of me." Eric rolled the cursor and clicked send. He looked at the security guards. "Would you please escort Mr. Preedy to the guard desk?"

The guards guided Preedy to the elevator.

Eric stood and reached for Alana's hand. As they exited the office, Preedy entered the elevator. He turned and glared contemptuously at them.

Eric had a final comment. "Your brother-in-law is in for a big surprise when he opens your e-mail." He winked at Alana.

"What have you done?" Preedy sneered.

"Not much." Eric shrugged. "I included a special attachment. You know what a Magic Bullet is."